The Purified

A Montana Wylde Mystery

Melinda Tyler

NVP

Nothing Ventured Press, LLC
Woodville, Massachusetts

NVP and colophon are trademarks of Nothing Ventured Press, LLC

Nothing Ventured Press, LLC
P.O. Box 166
Woodville, MA 01784-0166 USA
www.nothingventuredpress.com

This is a work of fiction. Names, characters, places, and incidents are a
product of the author's imagination, or, if real, are used fictitiously and
are not intended to describe their actual conduct. Locales and public
names are sometimes used for atmospheric purposes. Any resemblance
to actual people, living or dead, or to businesses, companies, events, insti-
tutions, or locales is completely coincidental.

Book Layout & Design ©2017 - BookDesignTemplates.com.
Portions ©2017 Nothing Ventured Press, LLC

Quantity sales: Special discounts are available on quantity purchases by
corporations, associations, and others. For details, contact the "Special
Sales Department" at the address above.

The Purified / Melinda Tyler. -- 1st ed.
ISBN 978-0-9984341-1-7

For my beloved husband, who calms every storm in Melindaville. With you, all things are possible. I love you.

Purify: Pu·ri·fy
verb \ˈpyu ̇r-ə-ˌfī\
transitive verb

1: to separate impurities from, as through distillation; "purify the water"

2: to remove sin or guilt; "his confession purified his soul"

The Purified

Prologue

SHE STAMPED HER FEET against the rain soaked pavement—more from frustration than to fight off the spring's early morning chill.

Desperation was kicking in. She'd worked the stroll for hours but had nothing to show for it. Usually the street buzzed with activity, but tonight, stinging pellets of rain chased customers away.

Worse, what little money she had made was long gone—spent on crack. With her high wearing off, familiar clouds of depression settled in. If business didn't pick up, her pimp would beat the crap out of her—even though he knew it hurt her earning potential. Only twisted tricks were interested in damaged goods but that didn't stop her pimp from dotting her eye when she didn't meet quota.

It didn't look as though business would start booming tonight, either. Dawn would soon break and the street would again reveal its drab colors of the poor, working class neighborhood it was. The last decade of economic meltdowns and devastation of recent super-storms had forced most businesses to close. When the remaining merchants returned in the morning, the streetwalkers would have to clear out fast. If they didn't, vice was more than happy to chase them away.

Just as she was ready to give it up and return to her pay-by-night hotel, she noticed the sleek town car had now circled her corner for a second time. The car was promising: expensive with tinted windows, the kind celebrities drive. When the vehicle rounded for a third look, she pulled her sweater down low enough to let a nipple pop free.

That brought the car to a screeching stop.

Finally, she thought, finally luck was on her side. Now, they began the seductive dance of the world's oldest profession. She shimmied up to the car, doing her utmost to convey the come-hither look that Julia Roberts was so successful in using on Richard Gere in Pretty Woman. It was her favorite movie.

The driver unrolled the passenger window, causing the interior to become wet with the light splatter still coming down.

"Hey," she breathed in a husky whisper.

He stared ahead, unsmiling. "Hey yourself."

"You want a good time?" She gave him a seductive smile but something was off. His stern expression stared straight ahead, despite the exposure of her nipple now erect from the cold night air. She knew she should cut him loose but she was desperate for cash.

Just as she was ready to back off—broke or not—he turned an impassive face to her. His eyes flicked from her face to her chest and back. "Let's cut to the chase. How much for half and half?"

She smiled in relief. She knew he wasn't a cop because he solicited her. Vice cops never did that because of entrapment laws. Not that she'd been that worried. Like most working girls, the street had honed her radar to distinguish cops from customers. Tricks' expressions read, 'I want to fuck you' whereas cops' faces said, 'I want to bust you.' She was street-seasoned enough to know the difference.

"A hundred dollars, sweetie," she replied. He wouldn't likely agree to such a hefty price. They rarely did, but her pimp taught her to start high. While she could always go down, she had only one chance to aim high.

"Okay." Staring ahead again.

Her eyes narrowed in suspicion. Tricks rarely agreed to the first price. Now her radar buzzed. Something was off.

She licked her lips. "Honey, I just need to see the color of your cash before I get in."

Pulling bills from his inner jacket pocket, the five twenties got her immediate attention. He fanned them out. "These are yours once you get your bottom in the car."

"All right then." She got in, cursing herself for negotiating too low.

Before she had a chance to put the bills in her pocketbook, the car jerked forward, its furious wheels spinning against the rain-soaked pavement.

"You sure are in a hurry." She glanced at him with a nervous smile. "Where are we going, sweetie?"

"Shut the fuck up."

The sudden menace in his voice made her heart drop. Why hadn't she listened to her instincts? She'd known he was trouble. She would rather face her pimp's ire than deal with an unpredictable man who was transforming before her eyes.

Her bowels churned. "H-honey," she stammered. "I d-don't want any t-trouble. I j-just remembered I'm supposed to meet my b-boyfriend right now. I g-gotta go."

He stared ahead, the car gaining speed. She gauged her chances of a successful escape—she had jumped out of a few cars in her career. All she needed was a break—a red light—but luck was against her. Every light turned green as the car approached.

Finally, she saw her chance as an upcoming yellow light turned red. He wouldn't be able to plow through it because the car directly ahead of them was slowing to a stop. As the car finally braked, her survival instincts kicked in. She was going to make a run for it. Relief flooded her as she groped for the door's handle.

But something was wrong. Her hand fumbled around the inner car door. She could feel nothing but the side of the door. She glanced down and her heart stopped.

He had removed it...and then she knew.

The light turned green.

"Please," she whispered, her eyes wet with tears.

The last thing she saw before the syringe plunged into her neck was a glint of the tiny needle. Just before she lost consciousness, she saw his face had twisted into a cruel grin.

He'd smiled after all.

Part I
The Missing

1

MONTANA WYLDE usually took care of business before pleasure but Harvey the Pie Man was an exception. She had known him for years—it was just a
thing he had. He didn't like paying before his session because it interfered with the fantasy. Few clients earned this
privilege and in the beginning, Harvey had to shell out up
front just like everyone else. It took several months of regular visits but he finally earned the favor of paying just before leaving. That type of special treatment kept clients loyal
to her. Loyal and generous.

He finished toweling. Their business required all clients
to shower before a session but some did after as well. In
Harvey's case, it was necessary. She watched in silence—per
his request—as he completed his routine. She pondered
what led him to his particular fetish. But then—what drives
any obsession?

Years in the sex industry had taught Montana how little
eroticism has to do with the body and how much it relies
on imagination. Forget rattlesnake blood; the brain is the
most potent aphrodisiac where secret desires—both whole-
some and depraved—roam free.

Montana wore many hats: psychologist, confidante,
teacher—and more. Her primary role was an illusionist, be-

coming whatever her clients desired. As she had learned in her first economics course, it came down to supply and demand. She supplied whatever fantasies her customers demanded. And no matter what the economy, business was never slow.

Along with her best friend and business partner Suzette Peterson, Montana owned half the Coop, which rhymed with loop. They derived the name from co-operative, which was what it was. They leased the midtown Manhattan apartment and split expenses. Each pocketed her own profits, giving none to madams or pimps. They both had loftier ambitions; they did not intend to make their current business a life's vocation.

Harvey was almost finished with his routine. He pulled a battery-operated shaver out of his gym bag and rubbed it over his face, erasing the afternoon stubble. Next, he splashed expensive cologne on his face and neck.

After ten years, she knew his routine by heart. Harvey slipped into the shower to wash away the pie, after which he shaved and splashed on cologne. Today he was dressed in an impeccable Armani suit. Montana eyed it, wondering what his clients might think if they knew how their well-paid attorney got his jollies. Not that she'd breathe a word. Confidentiality was as crucial to her business as it was to any attorney, doctor, or other elite professional.

Harvey broke into her musings when he pulled a gold monogrammed money clip from his pocket. He peeled off many bills and handed them to her without a word. She didn't count—no need to after so many years. The two grand would be there, as it always was. He gave a near imperceptible nod toward the door.

She scanned the hallway through the peephole, ensuring Harvey wouldn't run into anyone.

"Coast is clear, Harvey."

"Did you check to see if the elevator was on its way up or down?"

They replayed this same scene each time. "The elevator is clear—it's on the lobby now so I doubt anyone will be using it, so you are good to go."

"Thank you. See you in a month." He hung his head in shame.

After he left, she shut and double-locked the door. What an odd duck he was—but then, aren't we all?

With Harvey as the last customer of the day, Montana relaxed. She had a couple of hours to kill. Suzette was gone for the day, out with a VIP. When they had talked earlier in the day, they had agreed to meet for dinner and drinks at the Lazy Turtle at six o'clock.

Montana began cleaning up the remnants of Harvey's session. The Coop had nightly cleaners but Harvey's mess wasn't part of their job description. Huge black trash bags, the kind used to haul massive amounts of debris covered the floor. Demolished cream pies covered the bags.

The first time Harvey called, his request sounded so strange she had almost turned him away. But, because the business was still new, she took a chance. Montana and Suzette hoped to establish a stable of elite clientele. It seemed a man with such a strange kink might well become a regular, and it turned out she was right. She reasoned that safety would not be a concern because only two weeks before they had hired a bodyguard named Hanky.

Suzette met Hanky when they both won roles in an Off-Broadway musical, a stomping good time called *Bring on the Cheers*. Soon, they were best friends and confidantes. Less than a handful of Suzette's theater pals knew of the Coop but Hanky was one. When Suzette and Montana decided they needed security, Hanky was their first choice. They trusted him without hesitation. He was perfect at 6'2" and two hundred and twenty pounds of well-honed muscle. His real name was Howard but he preferred Hank. When Suzette met him, she'd found him so hunky that she'd started calling him 'Hanky' and the name had stuck. Since he was gay, no sexual tension existed between any of them. His training in the martial arts and experience with security made him the perfect solution.

The first thing Hanky did was install an extensive security system. Under his watchful eye from a third bedroom, he monitored several screens linked to hidden cameras covering various parts of the apartment. He'd installed one outside the front door, one in the front parlor, and one in each bedroom. Hanky could handle any customer who came close to being out of line. With so many regulars making up their client list, Hanky now only worked when the women saw new men.

Reassured by Hanky's presence, Montana took a chance with Harvey. Part was intrigue. Always inquisitive, his request was so unusual it piqued her curiosity. She recalled his first phone call.

"Um, hello, is this, um, Tana?" The timid voice on the other line was typical of almost all their new clients—ridden with guilt and pitched just above a whisper.

Tana was Montana's business name, while Suzette chose Suzy. Both adopted Coop names that were similar to their own just in case a client saw one of them in a public venue. Each had her own reasons for keeping their business private and they did everything possible to guard against messy conversations with those not privy.

"This is Tana. Have we had the pleasure of meeting?" Her repartee was more than small talk; it was a screening method. After a client's first visit, the women usually gave them the Coop's private number. If a client claimed to be a regular on the new client line, he could have lost the private number but chances were greater that he was a cop.

Cops rarely went after discreet high-end houses. When they did, it was usually an election year. They tried coaxing the women into soliciting them on the phone. If anyone was stupid enough to do that, the NYPD could issue a warrant but even then, convictions were rare. New York's busy district attorneys weren't going to overload the courts with what most considered victimless crimes. In the rare case where a vice cop arrested a prostitute, the charges were usually dropped.

"Uh, no," the hushed voice continued. "I, uh, saw your ad and you, uh, mentioned fantasies." Montana strained to hear him. "It's, uh, nothing that will harm you in any, uh, way, uh, please believe me. In fact, uh, I don't even want you, uh, to perform, um, sex."

Although new to the business, Montana had already heard enough wild fantasies to be on guard. Many men got their rocks off by detailing their fantasies on the phone with no intention of making appointments. They didn't want to pay for their jollies. They would begin describing their turn-ons. Soon the women heard their breath quicken, culminating with the unmistakable scream of an orgasm. Then the sudden click of the phone indicated the wankers had gotten the freebie they wanted. It pissed both women off to no end. When Harvey's call began, Montana suspected he would be yet another wanker. But he surprised her.

"What does your fantasy involve?"

"Pies," he whispered in a furtive tone.

"Pies?" Huh—this was a new one. Intrigued, she had to ask, "What do you want with pies?"

"I would prefer not to discuss it further. I promise I'll pay you well and we won't touch."

Montana agreed. He seemed too meek to be harmful. Besides, she loved pie and try as she might, she couldn't think of a single evil that could involve them. She told Suzette about him.

"Pies?" Suzette's nose crinkled. "What in the world does he want with pies?"

"I have no idea, but he sounded like a guilty little boy afraid of a spanking—or his wife. He didn't register a blip on my danger radar though."

Suzette snapped her fingers. "I know. Banana cream pie. He wants you to put pie on his banana and lick it off."

Montana laughed and shook her head. "He said we wouldn't touch."

"Maybe he wants to *watch* you rub pie all over yourself?"

"I'd rather eat it. We'll find out soon enough."

"Well, maybe he wants to watch you eat it?"

"Wouldn't that be awesome?"

As it turned out, Harvey had no interest in either of them consuming pies. He showed up with two huge pastry boxes, each containing five cream pies. She led him to one of the fantasy rooms where she asked what his fetish involved.

"Um, what I want you to do, um, is to, well um, take each pie, um, one by one, and throw them at me." His head hung in humiliation.

"You want me to throw the pies at you?"

"Um, yes—but that's not all. When you throw the pies, um, laugh at me. Laugh as much as you can. Oh and um, I-I also want you to, um, insult me—um, you can yell—um, I want you to. You, can't, um, insult me enough."

"This is quite an unusual fantasy....and the more unusual the fantasy, the higher the..."

He cut her off. "I'm prepared to pay you two thousand dollars for you to throw the pies while insulting and laughing at me."

"Do you want me to undress?"

"I like lingerie." His voice was so hushed she could barely hear him.

Montana was quick to oblige. Two thousand dollars was far more than she had imagined for such a fantasy. "That sounds like a fair price. I'll be right back. Why don't you make yourself comfortable and prepare for the...pies."

She felt an instant high. It was the most any client had offered her for a single hour session. She went into the apartment's dressing room and chose a pale pink and black lacy bra, with a matching garter and G-string.

When she slipped back into Harvey's room, he had placed all the pies on the two matching dressers of the bedroom. He gave her a quick glance and nodded his approval at her lingerie. Then he pulled a carton of trash bags from his duffel. Montana watched in fascination as he covered the floor, bed, and overstuffed chair with them. Then he stripped naked, mumbling his directions in the same guilt-ridden voice she'd heard on the phone.

He was aroused to the hilt as she decorated his naked body in creamy goodness, while screaming insults.

"Bark," she shouted. "Bark like a dog, you insignificant bastard! Bark!"

To her surprise, she enjoyed his fantasy. It wasn't hard to laugh at him and there was no touching at all, as he had promised. It even helped blow off steam, but that wasn't the best part. Overriding everything was the thick wad of cash at the end of each session.

After Harvey left, Montana was in a great mood. It had been a lucrative week, with Harvey's session making it all the more profitable. When the Coop first opened, Suzette and she had always worked at least one weekend day. Ten years later, they still saw an occasional VIP on a Saturday or Sunday but they no longer had to. These days, they liked having their weekends free.

Enjoying her solitude, she walked to the control panel, one of her favorite luxuries of the apartment. She pushed a button and a moment later, the musical genius of Madame Butterfly filled the room.

She lit some candles and relaxed in the Jacuzzi, watching the soft lights flicker on the water as the jets massaged the tension from her muscles. Her life was on track. She had recently graduated from Columbia University's prestigious School of Law. It was the final step of a daunting journey. Twelve years earlier, she had begun her academic trek without even a high school diploma. Relentless in her determination to propel herself forward, her academic advisor said she'd never seen anyone more motivated than Montana. It had taken only six months to complete her GED. Once finished, she began classes at a low cost community college. No one was more surprised than she was when she graduated top of her class with her Associates degree. It was the proudest day of her life. It was the first time she had ever accomplished anything that required delayed gratification.

Away from her dysfunctional childhood home, school opened a world she had never known existed and she discovered she loved it. Her professors encouraged her to continue with her Bachelor's Degree. It paid off. NYU accepted her into their criminal justice program where she completed the last two years of her BA with a 3.94 GPA.

Always fantasizing about attending Columbia University's law school, she hadn't had the confidence to pursue that dream until a favorite undergrad professor pushed her.

"Nothing ventured, nothing gained," he'd said.

When she tore open the fat manila envelopment containing the University's enrollment materials, she raced back to the professor. "Nothing ventured, nothing gained," she said, beaming as she handed him the acceptance letter. To this day, it was a favorite mantra.

The only thing keeping her from practicing law was passing the bar exam. She had put it off for several months but she knew it was fear holding her back. She wasn't worried about passing the bar; her concern was whether she could succeed as an attorney. At the legal conferences she'd attended, she had felt like an imposter—as though she'd been playing a role in an alternate universe. Then there was always the concern that someone somewhere would recognize her from the Coop. That trepidation prevented her from developing close relationships with her classmates. Now, ready to cross the finish line, she realized that while working toward a goal can be comfortable, taking that final step was daunting.

Stepping out of the Jacuzzi, the remnants of Tana swirled down the drain. She dried off with a thick Turkish towel and then rubbed a pampering thick cream onto her skin, making it glow. Blowing her hair dry upside down, she scrunched it with her fingers to give it volume and the natural waves of a woman fresh off the beach.

When Madame Butterfly ended, she returned to the living room and turned on the five o'clock news. She watched half-heartedly as she did her evening makeup. The Church Murderer, whom the media now referred to as the 'CM,' was the night's big story again. His killings and the subsequent media coverage had rolled the story into a huge snowball of blame for an inept police department that hadn't picked the ball up quickly enough for a forgotten and vulnerable class of women. Regardless of blame, the CM was a maniac who thrived on picking up, torturing, and killing street prostitutes. He took depravity to a gruesome new level. After killing the women, he dressed them in vintage wedding dresses and left them propped up in the city's various houses of worship, for unsuspecting parishioners to find.

Like the CM's previous victims, the latest was a streetwalker. They were easy prey for any killer because of their transient lives. Almost invisible, they moved from whore stroll to whore stroll, city to city—tethered only to their abusive pimps. The pimps kept their women submissive and dependent through drug addiction and indoctrinating them into believing they deserved their frequent beatings. Most often, the girls were young runaways who had escaped abusive pasts. Because of their disorganized lives, they were unable to build up a cache of regular clients as more savvy working girls did. Their clients were usually 'one and done.' They didn't worry about having a client list of regulars like the girls who worked hotels and relied on using websites and cellphones to promote their business. Streetwalkers were of a different ilk; they knew another faceless man would pull up to whatever corner they happened to be on the next day.

The latest victim's face appeared worn beyond her years. Despite her sympathy, Montana couldn't relate. Their two worlds couldn't be more different. Unlike the hazards of life on the street, the Coop cradled Suzette and Montana in plush luxury, with door attendants and a bodyguard to protect them.

The rage and regularity of the CM killings had become more frenzied in the past few months. The first murder had occurred the previous June. Three months later, a parishioner found the second victim at different church. The NYPD was initially slow to label the perpetrator a serial killer but they did so after the third murder. The latest was his fifth victim and he seemed intent to continue his psychopathic run.

A certain type attracted him. He liked women who were shorter than 5'2" with slight, boyish figures. Each had dark hair and eyes. Montana stared at the sad collage on screen. The photos, mostly mug shots, revealed their hard and wasted lives.

The newscast cut to a reporter holding a microphone to the face of the most recent victim's 'friend' whom Montana knew had to be her pimp. He said someone saw his girl get into an expensive town car after which she had vanished. Montana viewed the pimp with disgust. He had failed to protect his girl when she needed him most. For the life of her, Montana could never understand why any woman would give her hard-earned money to a lazy, abusive pimp.

As the news turned to a story about a murder-suicide, she clicked off the television. She didn't want depressing news to cloud her otherwise perfect day.

She glanced at her watch. It was almost time to meet Suzette. She put the final touches on her makeup and unclipped her hair, allowing her dark locks to fall into waves about her shoulders. She gave the Coop a final once-over, ensuring that everything was ready for their nightly cleaners. As she checked the front kitchen—used only for making clients' drinks—she noticed a fancy gift box on the counter. She peeked inside and saw nothing but several layers of tissue remaining. She threw the tissue away and folded the box for recycling. After a quick approving glance in the parlor's full-length mirror, she struck a pose and in her best Elvis voice drawled, "Tana has left the building."

2

GROGGY and as she began emerging from uncon-sciousness, questions began rising to the surface. Her world was pitch black. As she awakened, the initial discomfort began turning to pain. Had she been in an acci-dent? Where was she? Fractured memories began return-ing...the rainy night...the crack house...returning to her corner hoping business would pick up. It hadn't—until the expensive town car had stopped in front of her.

She'd had a bad vibe from the start but brushed it off when the man flashed the five twenties and told her to get in the car. Then the nightmare began. She recalled her mounting terror when he got onto the main road heading toward the freeway. Every light turned green as he sped down the middle lane. When a red light forced him to stop, she had been going to make a run for it. Then hope died when she realized he had removed the door's inner handle.

The last thing was his hideous grin, seeing the metallic glint before the sharp pain of the needle dug into her neck.

Where *was* she? She strained to open her eyes but he had secured them somehow, perhaps with tape. She was thirsty and needed water. She opened her mouth to speak but could not. The unsmiling man had bound her mouth shut as well

She strained to lift her arms and legs but they were too heavy. Something—either ropes or wire—was securing her down to a table or metal rack of some sort. How long had she been unconscious?

She lay in the dark stillness for an indeterminable time. Finally, she heard footsteps. They grew close until she sensed the person had stopped next to her. Dreadful silence hung for several agonizing moments until she felt searing pain and heard the loud rip of a bandage torn from her eyes. She blinked, adjusting her eyes to the dim light.

She recognized him right away. The man with the expensive car and the five twenty dollar bills.

In his hand was a small penknife. He lowered it over her and she felt its sharp tip carve into her tender right breast. It hurt more than any of the three tattoos a jailhouse artist had given her but the pain wasn't yet unbearable. When he finished with her right breast, he carved her left one and then traced the tip down to her belly where he cut into her again. *Now* it hurt. In fact, it hurt like hell. What the fuck was this man doing to her?

Finished with the knife, he began fiddling with a bottle of fluid. That was when she noticed he'd placed a needle into her vein leading out to a tube hooked into to an IV. Why had he put her on an IV? This was no hospital, and this man was no doctor. A scream died in her throat as she felt the warm release of her bladder. Helpless tears slid down her cheeks. She hadn't wet her pants since she was five. He replaced one IV drip with another filled with cloudy liquid. Terror filled her as she watched the IV with the malicious looking fluid run down its tubing to reach the vein on her inner arm. A millisecond later indescribable agony streaked down her arm and into her body. The IV had lit a fuse to her vein, burning her body from the inside out—scorching, horrific pain. The torture of nightmares.

As searing agony overpowered her, she saw a bible in one hand and a vial of clear liquid in the other. He flicked droplets onto her face and body as he read:

"*Then one of the seven angels who had the seven bowls came and spoke with me, saying, 'Come here, I will show you the judgment of the great harlot who sits on many waters, with whom the kings of the earth committed acts of immorality, and those who dwell on the earth were made drunk with the wine of her immorality.' And he carried me away in the Spirit into a wilderness; and I saw a woman sitting on a scarlet beast, full of blasphemous names, having seven heads and ten horns.*"

Then it was mercifully over.

3

A SLEEK TOWN CAR pulled up to an elegant townhouse on Manhattan's illustrious Upper East Side. Moneyed New Yorkers vied to own homes on this particular street although they rarely came up for sale. When they did, competition was fierce.

A moment after the car pulled up, an obsequious door attendant rushed to the well-dressed man who emerged from the building. The immaculate tailoring of his Armani suit and polished Gucci loafers denoted his prosperity but without the flash of new money. His was the confidence of old money; he walked with a purpose. As he approached the car, the driver jumped to his attention as well.

The town car then wound its way through Manhattan's sea of yellow taxis until it finally arrived at a posh Murray Hill building. The car pulled up to the front. Upstairs a stunning woman checked a full-length mirror for final approval. She looked magnificent, as the man in the car would expect. He had a penchant for women who wore fine silk lingerie. This morning, as occurred on each of their dates, she received a special delivery of delicate undergarments.

Today, a sleek white box from La Perla arrived, tied with a glossy red ribbon. Tucked between layers of black and white tissue was an exquisite silk bra and panty set. Her mouth curled into a smile as she remembered the story behind the lingerie. During the turn of the twentieth century, Flo Ziegfeld, a theatrical producer, created extravagant theater revues. Legend had it that all his showgirls wore silk undergarments because Flo felt they would move with more elegance if they did. The man awaiting in the car downstairs presented his woman with her own delicate lingerie before each of their encounters. He wished her to feel as extraordinary as one of Ziegfeld's follies.

Over the whisper of silk, she wore a stunning Chanel suit. The famous fashion house had hemmed its skirt with tiny gold chains, allowing the cashmere to swing as she moved. She topped off her outfit with pale pink Manolo pumps. She slipped a cellphone, slim wallet, and compact into a matching clutch purse. Giving herself a final nod, she headed out to meet her date. She looked every bit as sunny as the cloudless New York sky waiting to greet her.

She moved with the polish of a socialite or up-and-coming model. As she crossed the lobby, the building's attendant rushed to open the door for her. As soon as she emerged, the driver of the town car hopped out. He showed her the same deference he had to the man as he opened the back, curbside door. She paid no mind to the men gaping at her in longing or the women glowering in envy. She was unaware of the impact she made, which was only one of her many charms.

"Where are we going?" she asked, snuggling closer to her companion.

"It's a surprise." He wrapped a protective arm around her.

"I need to be back before 6:00 tonight."

He glanced at his watch. "That's no problem. We have the rest of the morning and a long afternoon." He smiled at her lovely face. "It took some doing to get that much time away with you but we have enough for a wonderful day."

"I'd love to wake up with you someday."

He placed his hand on her chin, turning her face toward him. "I wish we could. For now, we must enjoy what we have." He tightened his arm around her.

Resting in a large bucket of sparkling ice was a bottle of Bollinger Les Vieilles Vignes Françaises. The man opened a fine wooden box lined in velvet and took out two crystal champagne flutes. He filled one, handed it to her, and poured another for himself. He lifted his glass in salute.

"Here's to my angel." Their glasses clinked.

She relaxed, sipped her champagne, and enjoyed the ride. It looked like they were heading to the Hamptons. They were going in that direction, anyway.

It was shaping up to be a perfect day.

4

WALKING TO MEET SUZETTE, Montana reminisced on her early days in the city. She had grown up in a dysfunctional home in the poorer east side of Buffalo, New York. Aside from an early bliss-filled two years when she stayed with her grandmother, she had grown up with an alcoholic mother and abusive stepfather. When her stepfather's inappropriate touching became forced oral sex, Montana told her ambivalent mother what was happening. Her mother had drunkenly waved her daughter off, dismissing the claims by telling her that she must have been dreaming. Montana never tried approaching her mother about the abuse again. Why bother?

Two days before her seventeenth birthday, her stepfather raped her while her mother lay passed out in the living room. She had lain in bed until dawn—too numb and hopeless to cry. As soon as she heard her stepfather leave for work, she ventured out from her bedroom. Her mother was snoring on the couch with two empty bottles and an overflowing ashtray on the coffee table beside her.

Montana packed most of her belongings into two small bags. Using the babysitting money she had hidden from her parents' prying hands, she left Buffalo for good. She was going to New York City. She would never look back.

She arrived at The Port Authority Terminal with a little over five hundred dollars, a pitiful amount by New York standards, but to Montana, it was a fortune. She hid the money in her sock tucked between her foot and the sole of her boot. The five hundred along with her best thrift shop clothes, a few toiletries, and her prized secondhand laptop were all she had.

She had researched her plan long before acting on it. Moving to Manhattan had been a lifelong dream. In childhood, Montana had spent many comforting hours in the public library, devouring Kay Thompson's books about Eloise, who lived a life of luxury at the Plaza Hotel. Eloise's adventures had planted their seeds in Montana's young imagination. She dreamed that she too would one day live an illustrious life high in the sky, with New York's magical lights twinkling around her.

With her computer and the bus terminal's free Wi-Fi, Montana did her best to prepare for her arrival in the city. She found The Smithson, a small residential hotel on the Upper East Side that catered only to females. Far from opulent, the rooms were clean and the rate included breakfast and dinner. Their rules were strict but Montana didn't mind. She could stay only a few days at the Smithson because even with their low rates—by Manhattan's standards—it was more than she could afford on a permanent basis. She took the minimum stay allowed—three days—and even that devoured a third of her money. She rationalized that it would be an ideal refuge while she looked for work and a less expensive place to stay.

Kay Thompson's books could have never prepared her for the harsh shock of living in the city on a meager budget. She spent most of the first two days looking for work, but by the end of the second day, her sole focus was on finding a less expensive place to stay. By the third morning, she was frantic at the thought of peeling off another hundred and sixty-five dollars for another three days at the Smithson, which would leave her almost penniless.

Nearing the end of the third day, she spotted a sign outside the Shirley Hotel. It was located on 11th Avenue—smack in the middle of Hell's Kitchen. The residential hotel had seen better days but its rates were less than half than that of the Smithson. She shrugged and thought it wouldn't hurt to look.

The middle-aged clerk perked up when he saw her enter. "Can I *helllp* you?" he asked, in an accent she couldn't quite place. His eyes, under dark bushy eyebrows, never left her breasts. She hated the place on sight but exhaustion and desperation propelled her forward. If she'd had any more time, she would have walked right back out. Unfortunately, she didn't have that luxury.

Montana lowered and then tilted her head to force the manager's eyes away from her breasts and on to her face. He got the message and as he straightened up, she mused that perhaps he wasn't as dim as his initial impression suggested.

"I saw your sign." She forced a smile. "What are your rates?"

"You wanna week or a month?" With his heavy accent, 'month' came out 'munt.'

"How much is a month?"

"Six hunnert dollars for the munt and we don't take no checks. Credit cards or cash."

The price punched her in the gut. "How much for a week?"

"A hunnert and seventy five—you see youse gets a better price if youse pays for the munt."

"May I see the room?"

He eyed her again, with another long intermission at her breasts. "Sure, honey," he grunted, "no problem." He grabbed a key from a hook on a corkboard behind the desk.

As he led her to the room, a myriad of foreign languages and exotic cooking smells assaulted her. Underneath was the pungent scent of disinfectant. Halfway down the hall, a lone lazy cockroach sauntered by as though it had all the time in the world. That was a bad sign. If you saw one cockroach, hundreds more would follow. She shuddered at the prospect of meeting its friends and family.

The room was depressing. It contained a bed, a worn easy chair, a lopsided desk that doubled as a table, and one hard straight-backed chair. The 'kitchen' consisted of a stained counter holding an electric hotplate and an outdated microwave, plus a tiny refrigerator. There was no purpose to the one grimy window: it looked smack onto another brick wall of the building next door. Thankfully, she would have her own bathroom, although there would be no baths. Crammed into the tiny space was a cracked toilet, rusted sink, and shower designed for thin people.

"Oh, one more ting. We don't do no housecleanings," the clerk said. "That's up to you—but we gives you fresh sheets and towels every Sataday."

She eyed the threadbare towels and face cloth folded at the bottom of the bed. "I'll take it," she said with a heavy sigh.

At the front desk, she paid one week in advance.

After moving her meager belongings to her new residence, she stopped at a nearby market and bought a jar of peanut butter, a box of crackers, ten bags of ramen noodles, and a can of bug spray. She had less than a hundred dollars left to her name—but she was free.

She was right about that first cockroach. The first night in the room, she met what appeared to be hundreds of the creepy, unwanted houseguests on her first nightly bathroom visit. These were tough, New York born and bred cockroaches, too. She tried everything to rid herself of the loathsome pests, spending precious cash for spray and roach hotels. The spray had zero effect; she drenched them until they turned white. Not only did they live, they seemed to thrive on the toxic fluid. She pictured them licking it off their backs as though it were a sumptuous meal prepared by a fine chef. If the spray was ineffective, the roach hotels were useless. The bugs treated them like actual guesthouses, checking in and out, after spending a night in their luxury suites. When all other methods failed, she tried beating the little bastards with the Sunday Times. This proved lame as well. These masochistic cockroaches enjoyed their beatings. They sauntered off unharmed when Montana's arm tired. She imagined their taunts: "Beat us, whip us, we LOVE it!"

One positive was finding work within the first week. After spotting a sign looking for bartenders, she went into the rundown neighborhood tavern to apply.

"What experience ya got?" asked Bing, the owner of The Drift Inn. Remembering his name was no problem because he looked just like a Bing cherry: round, red-faced, and bald.

"I have counter experience working at Scooter's Ice Cream in Buffalo." She wanted to be honest but instinct told her she would need familiarity with alcoholic beverages. "I know how to make drinks, though. While I've never been a professional bartender, I made cocktails for my moth...for my parents' parties."

Bing licked his lips, while his lascivious eyes scoured her young body. In the end, her looks took precedence over the flimsy experience. He hired her on spot, not bothering to ask for references. The pay was less than she'd hoped but Bing paid her under the table. She hoped the salary would cover rent and that tips would pay for food and other necessities. She could handle a frugal existence so she could move from the dreadful Shirley and start taking GED classes. She was eager to get a real career underway.

She was a quick study. Drinks weren't difficult in this 'shot and beer' bar, but it was a dismal place. It bore no resemblance to her fantasy of working in a rotating penthouse bar, high atop a towering skyscraper. The tips were a disappointment. This was no top shelf joint—the customers hunched in dreary failure on timeworn stools. They were barely able to pay for drinks, much less tip. The job was just enough to keep her in peanut butter and ramen. Even with the most careful budgeting, she had yet to save any money. School seemed more distant than ever. Had she just swapped one hell for another? Law school had never seemed further from her reach.

After several months at the Shirley, she had yet to speak to her neighbors. She hadn't made much effort. As far as she could tell, she was the only single woman. The men's strange accents and lusty stares frightened her. She kept her head down, inviting no conversation.

Don't feed the animals.

Her eighteenth birthday brought a new low. After bartending for the day, she returned to her dismal room. The thought of spending her eighteenth birthday alone depressed her. It was a *special* birthday and she was desperate for some fun. The problem was money. After buying toilet paper and toothpaste, she had less than two dollars remaining from her tips.

She glanced down and spotted the tiny solitaire on her right ring finger. It was no more than a diamond chip but the band was fourteen karat gold. A former boyfriend had given it to her as a promise ring before moving to California. It was her only piece of real jewelry.

She made a hasty decision, pulled on her coat and headed out the door. Down the block from The Shirley was a neighborhood jewelry shop. Montana gave the tiny ring a final glance and entered the store. Opulent jewels gleamed in their glass cases, which seemed to highlight the insignificance of her little ring. The clerk appeared to agree because he showed almost no interest.

"I have no money for food," Montana implored, her eyes shining with tears. "It's all I have left."

He appraised her. She was tall and beautiful, with striking eyes, and a body worthy of fantasy. A mane of wavy dark hair cascaded down her shoulders. Not immune to the tears of a beautiful young woman, he sighed and picked up the magnifier. He gave the ring a closer look.

"Okay," he said. "Thirty dollars."

"How about forty? It's a real diamond."

He looked at her pleading eyes. "Thirty-five and I shouldn't even offer fifteen. Take it or leave it."

"Thirty-five," she agreed, surprised at the sudden twinge of sadness. She had only vague memories of the boy who had once given it to her. After a perfunctory letter on each of their parts, they lost contact. Selling her only real piece of jewelry stung nonetheless. She shook off her soppiness and smiled. She needed a night on the town and it *was* her birthday

Back in her room with cash in hand, her spirits lifted. She put on the only cocktail dress she owned, a figure-hugging black mini that she'd bought for a fraction of its original cost. She knew it suited her because the two previous times she had worn it, every man gave a double take.

She usually wore only minimal makeup: a light dusting of powder, one coat of mascara, and a dab of lip gloss. On this special night, though, she took extra care with her appearance. She used a light foundation and faint blush on the apples of her cheeks. Tawny eye shadow made her blue eyes pop, along with eyeliner and lash-lengthening mascara. She brushed her hair until it lay in dark shiny waves and red lipstick finished her look. She gave an approving nod at her reflection in closet's full-length mirror.

She put twenty dollars in the zippered pocket of her clutch and stashed the remaining money in the padlocked closet. She grabbed her subway card and locked the door behind her. Six months after her arrival, she was heading out to enjoy her first night out in Manhattan.

Because it was a red-letter birthday, she decided to splurge on a drink at the Algonquin Hotel, a place that she had long romanticized. A voracious bookworm, she adored reading about Dorothy Parker and 'The Vicious Circle.' The 'Gonk' had been the group's weekly meeting place. It was a perfect choice for her special birthday celebration.

She tucked a fake ID into her purse. A smitten Drift Inn patron had it made for her when he learned she was not yet twenty-one. It proved superfluous, as the Algonquin's bartender gave her a wide smile and asked her to name her poison. She had never had a martini before but it seemed appropriate so she ordered one. The taste didn't quite suit her but it made her feel sophisticated.

As she relaxed, enjoying the soft lighting and ambience, her depression lifted. For this one night, she was the successful young professional of her dreams. So lost was she in her happy reverie that she didn't notice the tap on her shoulder at first.

"How much?" asked a seductive whisper from behind.

Startled, she turned to see a well-heeled middle-aged man smiling as though he knew her. She was certain they had never met.

"Wha... what?" She was perplexed. "What do you mean?"

"How much?" He beamed with confidence.

She stared at him, feeling stupid.

"How much do you charge?" he insisted.

Her eyes narrowed. She was perplexed; his question threw her off balance. Did he think she was a server? It was obvious she was a customer. She was drinking at the bar. She had always been quick but he confused her... until an unwelcome thought began looming.

"Aren't you working?" Now he was confused.

With sudden clarity, she realized what he'd meant. Her face and ears turned bright pink as outrage swelled.

"My God," she exclaimed. "You think I am a prostitute! How dare you? I'm a bartender—but when I save the money, I'm going to law school. I'll pass the bar exam and I'll be a great attorney. I assure you, sir, I am no prostitute. Can't I go out for a birthday drink without you insulting me?"

Her happiness evaporated—it was too much. Stinging tears streamed down her face generating uncomfortable glances from other patrons. She wasn't the weepy kind but the struggles of living alone in a Manhattan had been overwhelming. She'd just spent a third of her cash on *one* drink. She had so enjoyed the illusion of fitting in at one of the most storied bars in Manhattan until this bozo ruined it by insulting her.

He turned crimson, realizing how far off the mark he was.

"Oh dear, miss," he stammered. "I am so sorry. Please, don't cry. I was mistaken—that's all. You just look so pretty, sitting all by yourself and I, well, I just figured you were looking for work. I should not have assumed. Please don't cry, let me buy you a drink."

Steve, as she learned was his name, turned out to be a nice man. He hadn't meant to offend her. He was in New York on business and was recently divorced. He wanted a pretty girl to party with a bit. His initial assumption embarrassed him and he spent the evening making it up to her. He ordered them another round of drinks and a platter of appetizers to share.

Sitting together enjoying their cocktails, Montana told him of her struggles in New York. As her resentment faded, she realized how much she was enjoying herself. Here she was, sitting in one of the most beautiful hotels in the world, dressed up in special clothes, and talking to a man who hung on her every word. They talked until well after midnight.

After many cocktails, a light bulb flashed for Montana. She was broke—and wasn't he was looking for a girl? She was also quite tipsy. She turned to her drinking partner.

"Hey, Shteeeve, are you shtill intereshted in a girl for the night?" She hoped she was talking to the right one of the two faces before her.

"Oh honey," he shook his head. "No. You don't want to do that. You're a nice girl—I was completely out of line. Don't even start thinking about doing that."

At the sight of her disappointed face, he took out his wallet and put two fifty-dollar bills in front of her. She looked at him, perplexed.

"It's not what you think," he said seriously. "You are going home, but not on the subway, not in your condition. Take this money—consider it atonement for my earlier boorish behavior—a donation to the Montana Wylde getting home fund. Now let's go get you into a taxi."

On impulse, she kissed him on the cheek. She tucked the two fifties into her purse next to the ring money that she hadn't had to touch.

He led her, teetering on her stiletto heels, through the hotel's ornate doors. The door attendants rushed to help her into a cab. Steve gave the driver another fifty and instructed him to keep the change after making sure she was safe in her hotel for the night. Montana glanced back to wave to her benefactor but he had already disappeared.

Back at the Shirley, the dreary room was a sharp contrast to the Algonquin's stunning opulence. Her fairytale night was over, but she couldn't sleep. Her mind was awhirl with conflict and confusion. Without realizing it, Steve had shattered every stereotype she had of the kind of man who paid for sex. Their conversation started on a rough note but he was so kind once they cleared up their misunderstanding. The experience would change the direction of her life. As she counted out her nightly meager tips from the Drift Inn, she thought about her night at the Algonquin. An intriguing idea began forming. Could it be so easy?

How might she meet men like Steve—normal men just looking to relax with a pretty girl? Though she had no experience in the sex industry, she was no dummy. She was aware she'd be wading into dangerous waters.

She saw the evidence when she spotted occasional street girls hanging around the corner of the Drift Inn. They looked decades older than their chronological ages due to mean streets and crueler pimps. Steve would have no interest in those girls. Besides, that life was not for her. But what about the women tucked away in luxury apartments who saw men on their own terms? How did they manage to do it?

She would figure out how.

5

RELAXING AT THE LAZY TURTLE, Montana sipped a solitary margarita for almost an hour. She had arrived at 6:15, fifteen minutes late, knowing Suzette's tendency toward tardiness. By 7:00, a small knot of worry started forming in her gut. It was unusual for Suzette not to call or text when she was going to be very late—she was too considerate. Montana considered plausible explanations. Perhaps Suzette's phone had died or maybe she couldn't hear it ringing from the depths of her massive handbag. A waiter startled her, breaking into her thoughts.

"How's it going over here? May I bring you something else?" He nodded to the menu he had brought when she first arrived.

She forced a smile. "No thank you. My friend should be here soon."

"Probably stuck in traffic," he said sympathetically. "There's nothing like Friday night rush hour. Say, how about another margarita—you've just about killed that one."

"You're right about the traffic. You know, I will have another margarita." She picked up one of the menus he had brought when she first arrived. "I'll also take a combo appetizer plate."

"Excellent choice," he smiled, lingering a moment longer. She glanced up at him. He was tall and dark with striking green eyes—looks that attracted her—but she wasn't the least bit interested. She knew from experience he was looking for an opportunity to flirt. He didn't disappoint.

"If you'll pardon me for saying so, if you are waiting for a date, he's a damn fool to keep you waiting—rush hour or not. Heck, I'd make sure I was half an hour early." He looked pointedly at her unadorned left ring finger.

She wished she had thought to put on the simple gold band she often wore to avoid these situations. Flirtatious conversations made her uncomfortable because she wasn't ready to begin a relationship. She never initiated a conversation that would lead to someone asking her out for a date. There would be time for that later, after she passed the bar exam and the Coop was a distant memory. She ignored his inquiry about her friend's gender.

"Thanks much." She smiled up at him. "We'll order dinner when my friend arrives, so you can leave the menus for now."

"Good enough. I'll be back with your margarita and the appetizer platter. The nachos are particularly awesome. Our chef makes the guacamole fresh every day." He hurried off.

She glanced at her watch again. Something was off. She felt it in her bones—those intuitions that her Nana claimed were 'the sight.' She couldn't predict the future but she had often had compelling feelings about people or places. While she wasn't always right, she often was. Tonight her premonition was electric. Suzette was in some kind of trouble, she felt it in her gut. The question was how bad and what kind?

Still, it was too early to panic; the waiter had a point. Manhattan traffic was a nightmare, particularly on Friday at rush hour. Since Suzette had been on a daylong outcall, it was even reasonable she would be late. Nonetheless, as the minutes ticked by, her uneasiness grew, because while Suzette was often late, she would invariably call or text to let her know.

Another hour later, her second margarita was almost untouched and the appetizers had long gone cold. She had left Suzette two messages, three texts, and still not a peep. Montana was now very worried. She tried calling once more and it went straight to voicemail on the first ring. "Suzette. Please call me. I understand if something came up—but I'm worried sick. Just call or text to let me know you are okay. If you need me, I'm here—but just call."

The feeling that Suzette was in danger grew deeper by the minute. Her instincts were alight with dread. She recalled another night, before the Coop existed, when the escort service Suzette and she worked for had sent her on a bad outcall. The client had appeared normal, well spoken and courteous when he greeted her in his stunning penthouse apartment. Ten minutes later Dr. Jekyll turned into Mr. Hyde with a sudden murderous rage. She had been so certain he would kill her that it took weeks for the shock to wear off.

Had Suzette's client snapped in a similar way? Of course, there were major differences between the two. Suzette knew her client well—he was a VIP. She trusted him enough to go on an outcall, a privilege not allowed to all clients. That made the two situations very different because, by comparison, Montana's bad outcall had been with a new client—at least to her.

She tried Suzette's cell again and once more, it went straight to voicemail. She didn't bother leaving a message, but after hanging up, an idea struck her. Suzette might have lost her phone. She sent a brief text to Suzette's number: 'if you have found this phone, please call 212-555-1212 for a reward.' Maybe someone would call her back.

After three hours, she gave up. She waved to the waiter. "I'll take my check now," she said, forcing another smile.

"Of course," he replied. "I hope everything is okay."

"Me too," she answered. She counted out enough cash to take care of the bill and a twenty-five percent tip.

Rush hour was long over so she had no trouble hailing a cab. She twirled a length of hair as the taxi inched its way down busy 2nd Avenue. Plenty of boisterous revelers were out for Friday night—a stark contrast to Montana's dark mood.

After a seeming endless maze of honking cars and cursing drivers, she arrived at her Tribeca loft. It was her prized possession. Early in her career, a financial adviser client convinced her to buy property. After much searching, she found a stunning one-bedroom loft on the sixth floor of a converted warehouse. The primary selling feature was a spectacular view of the Hudson from her living room window.

She loved the neighborhood. Lower Manhattan had undergone dramatic transformations in the past fifty years. From the turn of the century to the 1950s, the area consisted of poor but safe ethnic neighborhoods, consisting of immigrants from all over the world. Most residents who lived in the Lower Manhattan owned or worked in small, family-run businesses.

By the 1980s, drugs and poverty drove out most of the existing residents who took their businesses with them, opting for the safer suburbs. Dealers sold heroin and crack from windows of a tenement's broken windows, giving the area a hard reputation. In those days, few taxis ventured to the Lower East Side. That was all before Montana's time in the city. She never saw the neighborhoods when they reeked of urine and desperation.

In the 1990s, Mayor Giuliani made dramatic changes to the city's culture. Determined to make the city a safer and more enjoyable place, he cleaned up the infamous alphabet city. New Yorkers branded the neighborhood such because of the A, B, C, and D Avenues. When Montana moved to New York, Lower Manhattan bore little resemblance to the drug-infested area it had once been. As rents in Manhattan skyrocketed, innovative developers transformed the old tenements while law enforcement drove the drug dealers out. Urban renewal replaced the drug dens with art galleries, expensive eateries, and edgy new clubs. While some long-time residents believed the changes had extinguished much of the city's character, these neighborhoods were now amongst the most desirable in the city.

Montana sat on her sofa sipping a glass of tasteless wine while she considered her options. Without Suzette's address book, she didn't know too many people to call. The two women tended to compartmentalize their lives. They kept their academic and theatrical pursuits separate from the Coop. Most of their colleagues had no idea what they did for a living. When people asked, they were vague in their answers, steering the conversation elsewhere.

They had always intended the Coop be a temporary means to an end. Suzette and she planned to close it after Montana passed the bar exam. Suzette had saved and invested her money wisely and she was eager to meet the right man so she could start the family she'd always wanted. She might even have met him already. Recently, Suzette's face had lit up when she spoke of a particular man she had come to know. When Montana probed her for more details, her friend was uncharacteristically quiet. Montana left it at that. When Suzette was ready to reveal more, she would. They never pried into each other's life.

Tired of her helpless paralysis, she decided to place a couple of calls. Her call to Hanky went to voicemail after a few rings. "Hanky—please call me back as soon as you get this message. Don't worry about the time. It's about Suzette—we were to meet at the Lazy Turtle and she never showed."

Next, she called the Coop's door attendant. He answered on the first ring. "Park Terrace Plaza, this is Nathanial. How may I assist you?"

"Hi Nathanial, this is Tana from 4E. I'm surprised to hear your voice—don't you work only Saturday and Sunday?"

"Hi Tana—that's right but this week things are kerflooey. Al usually works Friday nights but he worked today because Tony went to Florida on vacation. With Tony gone and Al working days, I'm filling in."

"That's right—Al was working when I arrived this morning. It didn't even occur to me that it wasn't his regular shift. I wanted to ask him if he had seen Suzy. We were to meet for drinks tonight and she didn't show up. Say, you didn't see her tonight did you?"

"I sure didn't. Are you sure she's not upstairs?"

"Positive, Nathanial—I was there all afternoon."

"Sorry I can't be of more help, Tana. You should talk to Al."

"You're right. Would you happen to have his number?"

"I sure do—Let me give it to you."

"No, don't do that—I shouldn't call him when he didn't give me his number. Would you mind asking him to call me, though? He'll be off for the weekend and I'd like to speak with him before Monday."

"No problem at all. I'll have him call you as soon as I get in touch with him."

Montana made sure Nathanial had her cell phone number, thanked him, and hung up.

Her phone rang as soon as she put it down. She peered at the tiny screen and saw it was Hanky returning her call.

"Hanky, thank God you called," her words tumbled out. "Suzette didn't show up at the Lazy Turtle and I haven't heard from her. We were to meet at 6:00 and she never showed up. I haven't heard from her—no calls, no texts—and you know that's unlike her. I've left messages on both her cell and landline but she hasn't returned them. I'm getting worried."

Hanky broke in, chuckling, "Girl, slow down a minute and breathe. She's only a few hours late—maybe she's tied up—perhaps in the literal sense." He tittered at his own joke. "Maybe she forgot about your date."

"No," Montana insisted. "She couldn't have forgotten because we made our plans only this morning. Even if something made her late, she wouldn't keep me waiting without calling or texting me. This is unlike Suzette."

"Yes it is," Hanky admitted. "But something legit could have come up. Maybe she doesn't have a signal where she is—say her car broke down. Could be that she's on a beach or in the Hamptons with that rich client right now. Maybe her phone died. It's only been a few hours, sweetie."

"You're most likely right. Maybe I'm jumping the gun, but I have a bad feeling. Something feels wrong."

"Was she at the Coop at all today?"

"Early—before I arrived. I talked to her while she was getting ready for a client—a VIP she was to spend the day with. That was when we made plans to meet. That was the last I spoke to her."

"Well, that narrows it down," Hanky said thoughtfully. "Do you have any idea who the VIP is?"

"You know we rarely discuss clients, especially VIPs, so I never thought to ask."

"If you don't hear from her by tomorrow, check the VIP files at the Coop."

"That's a wonderful idea—there aren't that many high rollers. I can narrow it down at least."

"See, girl? Now you have a plan. I have a feeling too. Mine says that Suzette is going to call you tonight or tomorrow and you'll feel silly about getting worked up."

"I sure hope so. Thanks for calling back so fast, Hanky. You always make me feel better." Hanging up, she did feel better. Hanky was right. Her phone would ring any minute, with Suzette's cheerful voice on the other end.

Just as she was pouring a strong shot of good cognac, her phone rang again. She didn't recognize the number. "Hello, this is Montana Wylde."

"Hey Tana, this is Al. Nathanial said you wanted to talk to me about Suzy."

"Thanks so much for calling back. I hate to bother you but I'm worried about Suzy. We were to meet for drinks and dinner and she didn't show up."

"That doesn't sound like Suzy."

"I agree. That's what's worrying me. Do you remember seeing her today?"

"I sure do. She left the building this morning about a half an hour before you arrived—around 10:30. She got into one of those fancy cars that has a driver. He opened the door for her and got into the backseat. Then they took off."

"Al," Montana hesitated. Suzette and she rarely spoke to the door attendants—or to anyone for that matter—about their business. "Did you happen to see who was in the backseat with her?"

"I sure didn't. The windows were dark—the kind celebrities use so no one recognizes them."

"I should have figured as much. Thanks again. If you think of anything else that might be important, please call me right away."

"Sure thing Tana—anything I can do to help. I think the world of you two. Don't you worry, though, honey. She likely just had a hot date and forgot to call you. I'd be willing to bet she'll call tomorrow to tell you all about it."

They said goodbye and Montana turned to the snifter of cognac. She sipped, mesmerized by the lights reflecting on the Hudson. They always drew her in—she could spend hours looking out the window. Tonight was different. For the first time ever, the dark gaps between the lights beckoned her instead of the iridescent neon of businesses' signs and the gentle twinkling of residential lights. New York had a million dark places that could swallow a person up. Which dark space had swallowed Suzette? Montana finished her cognac, washed the snifter, and put it in the drainer.

Despite her anxiety, she was bone tired. She doubted she would be able to sleep but she did so almost immediately. It was not restful. Nightmares of the evil that lurked in those dark places haunted her.

Before going to bed, as Montana sat gazing across the Hudson, a sleek town car pulled up to another young girl whose tight miniskirt didn't quite cover her bottom. Blissful with ignorance, like the others before her, she slid into the passenger's seat.

Unmindful of the malevolent presence beside her, she was busy using her rudimentary math skills to figure out how much rock cocaine she could buy for a hundred bucks.

6

DETECTIVE MAX CONSTANTINE was having a bad day. A little over an hour ago, a loony-tune had shot one of the city's best officers. The nut holed himself up in an apartment after grabbing a woman from the street. He was now holding her hostage. Max sent a SWAT team and his finest negotiator to deal with that mess.

If that weren't bad enough, he had to tell the Police Commissioner and Mayor about the CM's latest victim. A parishioner had fled in terror after finding a dead body propped up in a pew of St. Patrick's Cathedral. This made six victims in the killer's rampage. Same MO—a churchgoer looking for solace had found anything but that when she came across a woman's dead body propped up in a wheel-chair next to the back pew of the church.

The CM preyed upon drug addicted street prostitutes. The women moved stealthily through the murky shadows of their underground trade, trying to stay two steps ahead of the omnipresent vice squad. All were young—at least chronologically. The last victim was just a teenager but with such a ravaged face, the first responders initially appraised her to be over thirty.

The police had withheld other factors about the murders from the public, such as religious markings cut into the victims' bodies. The NYPD also withheld the manner of death. The CM embalmed his victims but first used a poisonous IV drip administered while they were still alive. The Medical Examiner's lab was still analyzing the latest victim's embalming fluid to see if it matched the previous cases. Bleach was a major component but there were other ingredients too. Max shook his head in disgust. No one deserved to die in that kind of hell.

The CM was no professional undertaker. If he were, it would be easier to start their investigation by looking at city-licensed morticians. He was strictly amateur; each process was a hatchet job. During the investigation, they found mounds of information on how to embalm bodies, even a wikiHow on the process. Who knew? There might even be one of those 'Embalming for Dummies' books out there.

Max and others on his team profiled him as a white man in his thirties or early forties—a religious vigilante who used his warped devotion to a demented God to rationalize his killings. He likely thought the streetwalkers deserved their fate.

If the CM were rampaging any other city, officials would have likely called in the Feds as an active part of the investigation but after the horrors of 9/11, the city had prepared its officers to be ready for nearly any threat. When the CM had claimed his third victim, Mayor Burke brought in the FBI's Behavioral Analysis Unit, known as the BAU. At first, the Feds served as consultants only, but after the fifth victim, the Mayor insisted they become an integral part of the manhunt. Murph Campbell, the BAU's lead profiler, and Max Constantine, NYPD's lead detective, headed the investigation. The rest of the team consisted of undercover detectives from vice and homicide. All had participated in successful in prior sting operations.

Serial killings are the hardest cases to solve. Generating leads can be difficult since the killers and their prey are strangers to one another. At least in the CM's case, law enforcement knew the population from which he selected his victims—and to an extent, the areas that he prowled.

It took three killings before law enforcement admitted the work was that of a serial killer. Only then did the news make the New York Times front page. Then it was a media heyday, sensationalizing the murders while hindering the NYPD's investigation. Soon after, civil rights groups cried foul and protests began. The public claimed the NYPD would have acted faster if the women weren't prostitutes. Adding to the pressure, it was an election year.

After the latest victim's discovery, Mayor James Burke—Jimmy to his friends—had contacted lead investigator Max Constantine and Police Commissioner Harry Durbin for a meeting before a press conference scheduled later that day. The three worked on the script aimed to reassure the public that law enforcement was doing everything in its power to keep the city safe. At the press conference, the Mayor introduced Max Constantine and Murph Campbell as the lead investigators in a newly formed CM task force.

Max had been a homicide detective for nearly ten years. In that time, he had come across a few serial killers. The police usually caught these sickest of perpetrators after their disorganization took over and they began making mistakes. Max prayed the CM's mistake would come before another hapless parishioner found the next victim in yet another church.

Max had been putting in twelve hours days and today was no exception. He'd arrived at the precinct at 7:00 a.m. Now it was well past rush hour, and he had yet to stop for the day. He went to the men's room and splashed water on his face, catching his reflection in the mirror. Most women considered him good looking, tall and athletic, with silver streaked brown hair and compelling green eyes. Today, heavy bags hung under his eyes and worry lines formed deep parentheses around his mouth. He shook his head at his reflection. No doubt, the job was prematurely aging him.

Even with the grim realities of his job and the hunt for this particular killer, no other job could fulfill him. Being a cop gave him a sense of purpose and pride. He was a fourth generation New York City cop and his family had always assumed he would become a cop like his pop and grandpop before him. It was in the Constantine blood.

His grandfather had become a legend in the city when he captured the notorious 'Sweetheart Killer' in 1946. Serial killers were a novelty, and the Sweetheart Killer led the pack. The press gave him the moniker due to the way he selected his victims. He sweet-talked lonely women posting personal ads in the New York Times. The innocence of the era made it easy because many women were desperate to find husbands. World War II had killed so many of their men and women were eager to escape the unmarried woman stigma. They were happy to meet a total stranger at their front door. Once he gained access to the residence, he raped, strangled, and robbed them.

The NYPD concocted a sting, placing a personal ad in the Times, hoping to trap him. It worked. The Sweetheart Killer wrote to the female undercover detective—also a novelty in the 1940s. As she waited in an apartment rented for the sting's purpose, a backup team listened at the apartment next door that had an adjoining shared bathroom. When the female undercover officer screamed, Alphonso Constantine burst in at the right moment. He stopped her executioner just as he was winding his trademark red silk scarf around her neck.

Alphonso Constantine, along with the undercover female officer, received New York's Medal of Honor, awarded to officers who performed extraordinary acts of bravery while putting themselves at great personal risk. The press hailed the senior detective a hero and applauded the young female officer's courage. Alphonso Constantine waved off the accolades. He was a modest man who insisted his sole purpose was in keeping New York safe.

Max practically grew up in the department. At fifteen, he worked in the mailroom, hearing legends of his grandfather. Max's own pop had followed his father's path and Max watched him rise through the NYPD's ranks. As expected, Max followed suit. He graduated with honors from NYU's School of Criminal Justice, after which he began training with the NYPD. He endured the same grueling drills as every other rookie and excelled. When the NYPD awarded him his badge and gun, he demonstrated the same Constantine bravery. The NYPD promoted him in record time. He worked as a beat cop for a year, during which time his superiors recognized his gift for investigation. He soon became the special assistant to the chief of patrol of the department's vice squad unit. Max appreciated the promotion but his heart was never in vice. Busting streetwalkers—only to see them back on the stroll the next day was disheartening. Pimps disgusted him. Their only use was bailing their moneymakers out of jail but they did that out of their own selfishness. Without their girls' money, where would they be?

Max despised bottom feeder pimps—scum who took advantage of the most vulnerable. They left the girls in their stables with a legacy of lost youth, drug addiction, and broken promises. Rounding up street-ravaged prostitutes was heartbreaking, but how Max relished busting pimps. Max was sympathetic to the girls' plights, believing they needed drug treatment and counseling more than jail. After a long three years working vice, his superiors again promoted him to his dream job: homicide. That advancement distinguished him as one of the youngest homicide detectives in NYPD's history.

Max loved the pride on his father's face when he brought home his gold detective badge. They had been partners for a year—and what a year it was, working under his pop's expert tutelage. He taught his son how to interrogate suspects and how to support the grieving families. But the most important lesson he instilled in Max was the duty to remember each victim as a person. They were never just victims— Max took the time to know each one personally and remembered every name. An early heart attack forced his father into retirement, which ended their partnership. Three months later, a second heart attack took his life. Max had his father's gold detective badge and gun and polished each regularly. He missed his father every day.

One of Max's gifts was a natural affability that helped him coax confessions from perpetrators who were resistant to other interrogators. He had integrity, walked a straight line, and inspired trust in his partners. Dirty cops who took bribes or shortcuts disgusted him. He loved homicide; nothing was more gratifying than taking a killer off the streets.

No case impassioned him more than capturing the so-called Church Murderer. He would take that scum down— or die trying.

7

THE WOMAN STRUGGLED to awaken from her drugged sleep. She was lost between oblivion and awakening. She fought through the fuzzy gray layers of unconsciousness and finally broke through. When she did, her limbs were weighty—as though made of iron. Her eyelashes felt coated with concrete, reminding her of past days of partying, awakening to sandy eyes, a dry mouth, and scratchy throat.

With great effort, she pried her eyes open but the world was still dark. Someone had blindfolded her. Where was she—and why was she here? Had she been in an accident— paralyzed? It was as though something had erased her memory. Her mouth was so dry it hurt to swallow. Shrugging off the remnants of her blackout, she became aware of the pain. All her joints and muscles ached. When she tried lifting her arm to rub her eyes, she discovered something was holding her down. The same was true with her legs; someone had shackled her legs as well.

When she tried speaking, she could not open her mouth. Something forced her lips and mouth shut. From nowhere, a distant memory surfaced. Duct tape. When she was thirteen, she had lain on a friend's bed talking about her favorite subject, boys. Talking nonstop about a crush she had on a particular boy, her friend had joked by putting duct tape over her mouth. This was the same feeling: sticky tape on her mouth, but this time it was no joke. Someone wanted her silent.

A door opened and she heard footsteps that grew louder until someone stood next to her. Jagged pain coursed across her eyes as someone ripped her eyebrows from their roots while tearing the duct tape off. She blinked, trying to adjust her eyes. An obscure figure took shape in the hazy light. He wore a mask.

A sharp twinge struck her inner arm and she looked down, noticing an IV drip. Another IV looking far less innocuous sat beside it. What was going on? Why was she on an IV? This was no hospital or clinic—and this was no doctor or nurse. He began fiddling with IVs, replacing the bag with the clear substance with another filled with ominous murky liquid. Terror arose as the gravity of her situation became unmistakable. As the drip from the new IV bag entered her blood stream, every cell within her shrieked in misery. Whatever the poisonous fluid—it was burning her alive. She knew with sudden clarity that she was going to die. In her final moments, snapshots from her life flashed before her. She had no time to think of a way to save herself—consciousness was slipping away again. Just before she passed out, the man lifted his mask.

She recognized him immediately.

Then everything was calm.

Including the man, who released his throbbing cock from the confines of his trousers. He slathered lubricant on his engorged member and began stroking it as he watched the life drain from her. As he watched her surrender to death, his hand moved harder and faster until his cock erupted in a furious orgasm. With utter calm, he checked her pulse.

With the precision of a surgeon, he selected a favorite knife and began carving the symbols into her body.

To identify her to the masses for the whore that she was.

8

THE NEXT MORNING, Montana's first thought was of Suzette. The combination of margarita, wine, cognac, and worry from the night before gave her a slight hangover. A dull throbbing ached in her head. If it were any other day, she would shut the blinds and enjoy the luxury of sleeping in on a lazy Saturday. Instead, Suzette's disappearance had infused her with urgency.

She checked her cellphone in case Suzette had called and she'd slept through it. She was disappointed to see no calls, texts, or phone messages. She tried Suzette's cell and landline again but both went to voicemail on the first ring.

Throwing off the bedcovers, she began brewing a strong pot of coffee. Caffeine would clear the cobwebs out of her brain. She made her coffee the right way: always grinding fresh beans. Soon its fragrance filled the apartment with some much-needed normalcy.

After a quick shower, she sipped coffee and dried her hair, her mind awhirl. She planned her day. The first stop would be Suzette's apartment to see if it held any clues. On most days, Montana was meticulous with her appearance but on this day, she didn't give it a thought. She applied light makeup, threw on jeans, a tee shirt, and a pale blue sweater. Spotting her beloved Nana's vintage paisley scarf, she wrapped it around her neck to give her strength. She laced her running shoes and headed out the door.

Walking out of her building, she spotted the familiar but unwelcome sight of a resident bag lady who had a penchant for wearing a bright orange fright wig. She sat, resolute, on the stoop of the next-door building, a grim reminder of Superstorm Sandy's devastation. Contractors had renovated or replaced most of the damaged properties in the neighborhood but this dark and vacant tomb stood in idle contrast.

The woman always wore her fright wig, its rebellious spikes sticking out in disordered rage. She looked like a deranged female version of Ronald McDonald: a smear of bright orange lipstick around her mouth, chin, and upper lip that perfectly matched her wig. The woman had never learned to color within the lines. Though she was used to the woman's barrage of insults, Montana still cringed as the bag lady shrieked out her customary greeting of expletives.

"You WHORE! You goddamn slut! WHORE," the woman screamed in self-righteous objection. As usual, passersby stopped to stare. Sometimes amusing and often annoying, the woman's invective was always embarrassing. Once, feeling particularly naughty, she had joked to Suzette, "How does she know?" They shared a silly giggle on that.

On this day, Montana didn't give the woman a glance. Instead, she strode to the curb and hailed a cab. Saturday's traffic would be light and she could avoid the crowded stench of the subway. As the taxi wound its way uptown, Montana recalled how Suzette and she met and how the Coop had come to existence.

It was after Montana's nightmarish outcall when a client had snapped. After the experience, she had isolated herself at home, nursing her bruised and beaten body. She ignored the incessant ringing of the phone until her voicemail would accept no more messages. Most were from the outcall service's greedy owner, Sandy, begging her to return. Montana knew Sandy's primary concern was getting a top moneymaker back to work. For days, she ignored all calls, lying numb on her couch as the outcall's nightmare replayed in a relentless loop in her mind.

Nearly a week later there was relentless knocking on her front door. She opened it to find a worried Suzette holding two cups of coffee. Suzette also worked for Sandy and was another one of her goldmines; men loved her golden haired beauty, curvaceous figure, and southern charm. Montana had occasionally done double dates with her, considering her one of the few normal women in the business. They both disdained pimps and neither had drug habits. Many of Sandy's escorts used cocaine, marijuana, and tranquilizers regularly. The two had hit it off right away. Suzette was refreshing in that she was a highly motivated actor and used the business as a means to an end, just the same as Montana did.

When Suzette had first arrived at her apartment, Montana's initial belief was that Sandy had sent her to urge Montana to come back to work. Seeing Suzette's eyes narrow in true anger as she listened to the story, Montana knew her outrage was genuine.

"That client did the same thing at least one time before," Suzette had said grimly.

"Whaaat?" Montana was shocked. "Are you saying that Sandy *knew* about that guy? How could she send me there? Anyone who would send an escort to a known maniac like him cares only for money and nothing about her workers."

Suzette told Montana about the previous escort Sandy had sent to the client. Just as he had with Montana, the client had tied and beaten her up, and then later seemed to enter a fugue state. He had offered the other escort the same profuse apologies and extra cash, just as he had with

Montana. Montana's outrage grew as she remembered the receptionist's innocuous warning, "He's a little difficult."

"We can't keep working for a woman like that," Suzette said quietly. "She cares nothing about us. Why should we give her half our money? We should go into business for ourselves."

Montana laughed. "If only we could."

"No." Suzette was serious. "Why not? I've been thinking about opening my own business anyway but I didn't like the idea of setting it up by myself. I've got money saved— enough for us to find a great apartment. We can make it luxurious and inviting and operate our business from there. It would also be safer for us."

Montana's eyes sparkled with excitement. "You *are* serious—and honestly it's a great idea. I have some money I could put into starting it as well. You know, my favorite mantra is 'nothing ventured, nothing gained.' Let's go for it."

The plan evolved. They would work for themselves, doing only in-calls—at least until they knew customers well. They would find a secure, door-attended building where they could screen all clients and meet them on their own premises and terms.

They found the perfect apartment in a 33rd Street high-rise between Lexington and Madison Avenues in the Murray Hill neighborhood. They used all their savings and creative juices to design a sensual, romantic environment. They did their own décor, gluing hundreds of mirrors to the front parlor's walls. That gave the illusion of more space while adding an erotic edge. They bought exotic plants, small gurgling fountains, and a large aquarium filled with tropical fish. With mood lighting, plush carpeting, and red and black lacy drapes, the apartment was sumptuous and inviting.

Suzette and Montana shared many similarities. They had both escaped abusive homes at a young age. Each was stunning in her own way. Suzette had warm brown eyes and naturally blonde hair, dimples, and a curvaceous figure. Her sweet disposition complemented her Southern belle charm.

If Suzette were the sun, Montana was the moon. Tall and lean, she had startling azure eyes contrasting her wavy brunette locks and creamy skin. People often asked if she was a model, one harried woman had chased her through a busy mall parking lot to thrust her modeling agency's card into Montana's hand. She had no interest in modeling. She wanted a career where she might make a difference.

The Coop was an immediate success. Sandy's outcalls had been lucrative but without splitting their money, it brought their incomes to new levels. They saved and made wise investments. They spent time and effort getting to know their clients, most of whom became regulars. They benefited from the advice of attorneys and financial planners who were eager to help.

Montana's reverie ended when the taxi reached Suzette's apartment. It was as far uptown as Montana's loft was downtown. The two neighborhoods reflected each of their personalities. Suzette enjoyed the sophistication of the Upper East Side while Montana loved the artistic edginess of downtown Manhattan.

She gazed up at her friend's apartment, heart pounding. What would she find? First, she wanted to talk to the owners of the building's ground floor coffee shop. They knew Suzette well, as she stopped by each morning for her usual double cappuccino. Since the shop looked right onto the street, perhaps they had seen something suspicious. The owners were well acquainted with Montana.

"Hey Vinnie, I'd love a double latte—in fact, make it a mocha—I can use some chocolate with my caffeine. I also have a question for you. When did you last see Suzette? We were to meet last night but she never showed up. I'm worried because she's not answering her phone."

Vinnie's brow wrinkled. "I'm sorry to say that I'm not much help because I've been gone this past week," he said as he worked on her frothy mocha. "I was in Boston for my Aunt Betty's funeral. I got back late last night. I'll talk to Bruno, though. He worked every day including yesterday so he might have seen something, although he sure didn't say a word about anything unusual to me."

"Oh goodness...I'm so sorry to hear about your aunt. Please accept my condolences and pass them along to your family as well."

"Thanks, Montana. She had a good long life but it's still hard on my mom. She and Betty were twins—not identical but as close as could be. I'll talk to Bruno and of course, I'll have Suze call you right away if she comes in. Standing you up seems kind of unlike her though, huh?"

"I agree. I'm going to go up to her apartment to check. Thanks Vinnie—again, I'm sorry about your Aunt Betty."

Montana had a key to Suzette's apartment just as Suzette had a key to her loft. They checked on mail and watered the plants when the other was out of town.

Everything was dark and quiet, the blinds shutting out the midday sun. Flicking on the lights, she called Suzette's name as she checked each room. Hearing only the echo of her own voice, the hushed stillness was off-putting. The hairs on the back of Montana's head rose. Montana had a bad feeling—there was a finality to her friend's vacant apartment.

Suzette's kitchen whiteboard where she would put reminders and shopping lists revealed nothing but a few grocery items. Nothing was noticeably amiss but the vibe was off. Montana looked in all the obvious places for notes or a clue but found nothing. Everything was in order. Suzette had always been the more organized of the two.

Montana sat at Suzette's desk and opened her friend's laptop. She typed in Suzette's password and the screen came to life. The email program seemed the most sensible place to start so she opened it first.

Montana knew her friend had three accounts: the Coop, another for theater, and a third throwaway account used for online shopping. She focused on the Coop account first, hoping to find clues about Friday's high roller outcall. The messages from the two previous weeks revealed nothing but there was a ton of correspondence to go through. She'd have to take the laptop home with her to go through the messages.

Opening the theater folder, she saw little correspondence from the last month. Suzette wasn't currently performing so there were no emails regarding rehearsal schedules and such. She had light correspondence with her agent from the week before but not much else other than upcoming casting notices. Montana gave the throwaway account a perfunctory glance before closing it down; it was obvious Suzette only used it for shopping. Because of the Coop, they both stayed away from Facebook.

Just as she was about to close the laptop, Montana noticed an icon labeled Personal. Opening it up, she saw it contained various folders. Nothing caught her eye until she spotted one marked 'Journal.' With growing excitement, she double-clicked on it but it didn't open. Instead, a small window asking for a password appeared. She tried the same password she'd used to gain access to the laptop. It didn't work. She then tried a series of passwords, entering the password backwards, different formations of Suzette's name, then using favorite roles, plays, and characters. None worked. Curious if Suzette had password-protected all her folders, Montana double-clicked on 'Bills and Banking.' It opened up without a hitch, as did all the others in her personal file. Why would Suzette password protect only her journal when anyone could get into the folder holding all her financial records? It didn't make sense.

She would need help getting into the folder; that much was clear. She was computer savvy but she was no hacker. She sat, head in her hands, wondering how a person could go about finding a hacker. Perhaps Hanky would have an idea. She would call him later on. He handled the Coop's surveillance cameras, which he ran through the computer system in their back room. If he couldn't open it, he might have an idea of who could.

The empty apartment was unnerving. She wanted to leave but dreaded the next obvious step: contacting the police. Doing so could have enormous ramifications. Once taken, she could not go back. Should she give Suzette more time? She considered what Suzette might do in reversed positions. She had her answer within an instant. Suzette would go to the police if Montana failed to show for a planned dinner and couldn't reached in any way. Suzette always stressed that their safety came first, which was why they'd hired Hanky in the first place.

Alerting the cops would require complete honesty. This could bring heat on the Coop, not to mention the potential damage to Montana's ambitions of succeeding as an attorney. It could also damage Suzette's lofty goals of making a name for herself in the theater.

Before shutting down Suzette's laptop, she googled 'file missing person report + NYC.' The first hit was the NYPD's missing person page. She clicked on the borough of Manhattan and a series of photos popped up—all were people who had disappeared. Each had captions telling their names, ages, when someone last saw them, and what they were wearing at that time. Each photo tightened the knot of dread in Montana's gut. The site had a link for a page called NaMus. She clicked on it and found the National Missing and Unidentified Persons System. Would Suzette's photo be with the rest today?

Both the NYPD and NaMus sites built their databases from missing persons reports that loved ones submitted. Montana would have preferred not to have to deal with the police in person; it would be better to handle this business online. She clicked several links on the page's toolbar but none held what she was looking for. After doing a quick site search, she decided she needed to stop wasting time and just go file the report in person.

Through the site, she found a precinct only five blocks from Suzette's apartment. She packed up her friend's laptop, picked up her own large handbag, and headed out the door, taking care to secure Suzette's apartment with both locks.

Walking to the precinct, she considered what to tell the police. She was nervous. Just the thought of talking to a cop about the Coop was disconcerting. While vice officers had never pressured their business, it *was* illegal. She decided to disclose everything. She was loathe to do so but the police had to know the truth if they were to help.

Suzette's introduction to New York had been even more harrowing than Montana's had been. She had arrived at Grand Central Station, fresh faced and innocent. The minute she got off the bus, a smooth talking pimp named Flash spotted Suzette's naivety.

He had seduced her into believing he would take care of her as her boyfriend. Nothing could have been further from the truth. After stashing her in a fleabag residential hotel, he introduced her to cocaine. Soon, she was dependent upon him and the lines, which she snorted from a mirror through a rolled up hundred dollar bill. Soon after, he forced her onto the street. Suzette soon realized what a mistake she'd made but by that point, she was dependent on him. She discovered many nasty traits, such as his hair-trigger temper. He became violent when she failed to bring home the money he thought she should have made. Suzette knew then it was time to escape but she was determined never to return to her sexually abusive uncle in Alabama.

Few street girls make it out of the business while they are that young. Even scarcer are those lucky enough to return to their hometowns—street battered but still alive. Their pimps usually discarded them when the drugs and age caught up with them. Some were destined to become part of New York's wandering homeless population. Jail and prison were other common destinations. Death was the most frequent finale. They were a vulnerable lot, for whom few championed. They were invisible, their lives disposable.

Suzette was different, though. She was no street girl. Even through the fog of drugs, she had innate intelligence. Without Flash's knowledge, she stopped snorting the lines of cocaine he offered. She would brush the fine powder into her hand and then wash it down the bathroom sink. Suzette was smart, talented, and beautiful. Flash had been lucky to score her for the short time he did—she was prime real estate for a low-level pimp like him.

He had underestimated her. She knew her ultimate survival began with money so she started hiding small amounts each day. In secret, she opened a bank account. She found a small business that rented lockers for sixty dollars a month. Her locker held the book from the savings account she had opened without his knowledge. It also contained a growing amount of cash that she stashed bit by bit, as well as a few pieces of jewelry that customers had given her. The first time she received earrings from a trick, she had shown them to Flash, only to have him snatch them and sell them for drugs. After that, she stashed all jewelry in the locker.

After a few months, she'd saved enough money to flee. She rented a small studio in Manhattan's Upper West Side, an area unfamiliar to Flash. She hid for a month but when her cash got low, she signed on to work at Sandy's service. After several months with no word from Flash, Suzette began breathing easy. Later, she wondered why she had ever become involved with a lowlife like him.

Suzette never again had a pimp and she despised them. A few years after escaping Flash, she started volunteering at a rescue shelter for street girls escaping abusive pimps and entering rehab programs. If the women wanted to continue with the business, Suzette tried convincing them to go solo so they could enjoy the fruits of their labor. She urged them to become legitimate and open bank accounts and file tax returns. She even encouraged them to start retirement accounts.

Montana arrived at the precinct feeling out of place and uncomfortable. Law enforcement made most people feel nervous but a woman in her business felt particularly so. Once she had pulled over on her way to the Hamptons when she'd thought the flashing lights and rollers on the police car behind her were signaling to stop. She pulled over and watched in amazement as the cop zipped past her in pursuit of whoever was his target in the first place.

Montana straightened her 5'9" frame, lifted her chin, and walked in the front door, giving herself a quick pep talk. She was an attorney—or almost one. She knew her legal rights. What advice would she give a client in her shoes? She'd tell the client that the police had no right to arrest her, nor could they close down her business without cause.

Still, she knew the cops could put plenty of heat on the Co-op if they wanted to.

The inner décor was as depressing as she'd expected. The institutional gray and unflattering fluorescent lighting didn't help. Then again, why would the NYPD want their precinct to look warm and inviting? They weren't in the comfort business, after all. Adding to the charm of the utilitarian design were the inevitable institutional odors of bleach, pine disinfectant and the hazy aroma of fear.

Although not yet noon, the place buzzed with activity. In the distance were screams from people sounding more in need of mental health help than jail. From behind the reception area's doors, she heard people shouting out claims of innocence or throwing derogatory insults at their captors. Still others demanded phone calls to their attorneys or loved ones. Others just raged about life in general.

Cringing, she walked to the front desk where a woman was texting furiously on her cell phone while snapping her gum.

Montana waited for several moments before clearing her throat. Then she tapped her fingernails on the counter until she finally broke in, "Um, hello—can you help me? I need to file a missing person's report."

"Does it look like I'm busy?" the woman sneered. "Well, yes, I guess it does."

Montana took deep breaths as she had learned in martial arts training. She willed herself to go Zen. She would be of no help to Suzette if she lost her temper.

Finally, the woman set her cellphone down and stared at Montana.

"How long has the person been missing?" The woman was indifferent.

"I last spoke to her yesterday, around this time."

"Is this a child, an elderly person, or someone with a mental disability?" The bored voice droned on.

Montana seized the opportunity to tell Suzette's story. "She's my best friend—about my age. We were to meet for drinks last night but she didn't show up, which is unlike her. She's not answering her phone—neither her cell nor her landline. I just returned from her apartment. It's empty. No one we know has seen or heard from her either."

"What's your name?

"Montana Wylde."

The woman sniggered. "Sure it is, sweetie. Everyone wants to be an actor. I'll be frank because you seem like a nice girl. We can't file a report for an able-minded adult until that person has been missing at least twenty-four hours."

Montana protested, "Well it could have been that long. It's been more than twenty-fours since I spoke to her."

"You said you were to meet her last night and she didn't show up." The woman's eyes narrowed. "That's not twenty-four hours."

Montana retorted, "But the last I spoke to her was around 9:00 a.m., which *is* more than twenty-four hours. You have to understand how out of character this is. She has to be in some kind of trouble. I would like to speak to an officer please."

The woman studied Montana a moment longer, snapping her gum a couple of times for good measure. She pointed to chairs lining one wall and shrugged. "It's up to you if you want to try but my guess is they'll have you come back tomorrow or the next day. Have a seat. I'll see if I can get someone to take a report."

"Thank you," Montana replied.

Soon she became engrossed in the precinct theatrics. In one corner, two well-muscled cops wrestled a drunk who was giving them a run for their money. Elsewhere, a uniformed officer led a disheveled group of women down the hall. It was obvious they were well acquainted. If not for the handcuffs, they might have been enjoying a raucous party.

"Honey," one laughed, "I can't wait to get outta this joint. My Boo just told me I lookin' fat when he visited yesterday. I'll tell you what—it's from eatin' this crap they call food."

Another piped up. "Giiiirl, I know what you mean. I been puttin' on the pounds my own self. Lord know I gots to get me back on that Jenny Crack diet."

"Don't I hear you honey. I need some Stem Fast my own damn self." The three howled with laughter.

The girls at the end of the line were talking business with one woman leading the charge. The others seemed in awe of her.

She was advising the surrounding girls. "You go for the gusto—just like our man say. Sides, you never know how much these mothers are gonna pay off. T'other night, a trick asked how much I charged. I told that motherfucker 'two hunnert dollars.' Well let me tell you, he look at me like I'm outta my ever-loving mind and say, 'you must think your pussy made of platinum.' Chile, let me tell you what I told that bastid. I look that mother in the eye and say, 'it is what it is mister, and right now, it is two hunnert dollars.' What do you suppose he say then?"

The apprentices, wide-eyed, shrugged their shoulders.

"He says, 'okay.' The woman leaned her head back and roared. "Just like that, I'm closing in on quota and it smooth sailing from there. You decide what your pussy is worth. Don't leave it up to the tricks because those bastids will cheapen you ever chance they get."

A pale man followed the women, his lips forming a rigid line as he spouted biblical rhetoric in a self-righteous but thin voice. "God can be your salvation. Jesus died for your sins, as great as they might be. Repent, harlots. Repent. Jesus died for your sins. Ask his forgiveness and enjoy an eternity in paradise because there will be no fire escape in hell!"

The cop leading the women turned around. "Give it a rest Samuel," he sighed. Let us do our job. You can't go beyond this point so you might as well turn around and go on home."

As the man turned to leave, he caught Montana's eye. He stared at her until she looked away in discomfort. He was disconcerting—something was familiar about him though she couldn't place him. It was mostly his voice. Perhaps he had called the Coop. God knew they got plenty of religious quacks calling to save them. He was no client, though. Neither Suzette nor she would open the door to someone with his appearance. Even as she stared straight ahead, his eyes burned into her. She watched out of the corner of her eye as he finally left. He was likely just one of the many religious zealots proselytizing on the city's parks and corners. He only spooked her because of her anxiety over Suzette's disappearance.

As she grew impatient, morbid scenarios ran through her imagination. She was more convinced than ever that Suzette would call if she could, and her not calling was a terrible sign.

"Montana Wylde?" A voice broke into her gloomy contemplation.

"That's me." She looked up to see a young uniformed officer.

"It's a pleasure to meet you." He offered his hand. "I'm Officer Darryl McCarty. Rhoda said you wish to report a missing person."

She shook his hand, "Yes, I would. Thank you for agreeing to meet with me."

"Let's go talk in my office—if you can call it that." As she followed him down the hall, he turned to her. "Let's see how well-honed my detective skills are. I'm thinking you are an actress and that Montana Wylde is your stage name."

She smiled despite herself, shaking her head. "You are wrong on both counts. Montana is my given name and I'm not an actor. My mother wished she'd been an entertainer though so perhaps she projected that onto me."

"Hmmm—projecting...are you a psychologist?"

Montana burst out laughing. "You are batting zero, I'm afraid. I just remember reading of Freud's concept of projection from a psychology class I once took. As I recall, it's when people impel their own desires and fears onto others."

"That Freud might have been on to something." Officer McCarty said.

Montana relaxed somewhat as she sized McCarty up. He was tall with thinning red hair. His kind eyes put people at ease and she could tell it would be easy for people to open up to him.

After what seemed an endless hike, they arrived at a tiny cubicle. Papers, folders, and empty to-go cups littered his desk in friendly confusion.

He motioned her to a chair across from his and smiled, "It ain't much, but it's mine." He pulled up a computer screen that held some kind of form on it. "So who is missing and for how long?"

"Her name is Suzette Peterson. It's been more than twenty-four hours since we spoke. We made plans to meet for drinks and dinner yesterday evening but she didn't show up. It might not seem that long to someone who doesn't know her but it is so out of character for her to disappear without calling or texting. She's the most reliable person I know."

Sitting in the small cubicle and talking about it, the reality of Suzette's situation hit her hard. She fought to rein in her emotions; she did not want to cry.

"Have you called her family, friends, and acquaintances?"

"Her family lives far away and they aren't close. I have called everyone I could think of and no one has heard anything. I've called and texted multiple times and she's not answering. Her cellphone and landlines go straight to voicemail—as though she turned her phone off or it went dead."

"Have you called her place of business? Perhaps work took her away from the city and she forgot to tell you."

Montana lifted her chin and met his eye. "We have our own...escort service."

If he was surprised at this revelation, he masked it well. Still, the ease of their previous conversation took a sharp turn. "You realize this casts a different light on the situation." It was a statement rather than a question.

"No, I didn't realize that." Montana face grew warm. "It seems that a woman in trouble is a woman in trouble, regardless of her line of work."

Officer McCarty cleared his throat, his cheeks growing rosy. "I'll be honest with you, Ms. Wylde. The NYPD requires adults be missing for at least forty-eight hours before we file a formal report. Even then, we would only add her to our database of persons reported missing. Only with children, the elderly, or if there is evidence of foul play do we start an active investigation. I'm assuming there's no evidence of foul play, since you didn't mention it."

"Interesting you didn't mention this hard and fast rule until I told you what she did for work. It seems like foul play *could be* a factor when someone reliable disappears for no reason. Especially when no one has heard from her and she's not answering calls. Maybe the real reason you won't investigate is because she's a prostitute."

"Don't put words in my mouth, Ms. Wylde. Try to view this from a larger perspective. Can you imagine how busy we would be if we pursued every missing call girl? There are many reasons why she could be missing and you have no evidence of foul play. Perhaps your friend smartened up and decided to go home? The road you two are on leads to nothing but legal hassles, disease, drugs, abusive pimps, and sometimes death..."

Montana cut him off. "Wow—way to generalize. We don't have pimps—and we don't do drugs. Nor do we have diseases. I'd bet that sex with either of us would be safer than most one night hookups from any neighborhood bar in this city."

"You may be smarter and luckier than most but the longer you stay in business, the more you press that luck. There's another thing you might not like to hear. Maybe she realized the road she's on leads to nowhere and decided to get out of the business. Have you considered she might not *want* you to find her?"

Montana stood and walked toward the door. "This is a waste of my time. You don't get it, officer. Don't you think I know my friend? Put your tired old stereotypes away and look at the individual before making such sweeping generalizations. If you knew her, you would understand how unfathomable it would be for her to vanish on her own accord without telling anyone—especially me. Thanks for nothing. I'll look for her myself."

He caught up with her as she headed out the door. "Look, I'm sorry your friend is missing but we have a lot of experience here—at least give us that much. Almost all missing adults show up after a day or two. Give it at least one more day and if you still haven't heard from her, come back and I'll file a formal report." He pulled a business card from his uniform pocket. "Ask for me so you don't have to go through the trouble of giving the same background information."

She felt frustrated and impotent but she still she put his card in a special pocket of her wallet. Her step was quick as she walked down the hall. She couldn't wait to get away from the oppressive environment of the precinct and breathe fresh air.

Officer McCarty considered Montana Wylde after she left. She was different from the other hookers he'd come across. Her eyes sparkled with intelligence and she spoke with the confidence of an elite professional—a stockbroker or perhaps an attorney.

A quick rap inside his cubbyhole doorway stole him from his musings. Max Constantine stood in the doorway, motioning down the hall with his head. He raised an eyebrow. "Whoa—who was that?"

"Name's Montana Wylde. She came to file a missing person's report."

"Did you file it?"

"Her friend has only been missing since last night. Her *call girl* friend I should add."

Max whistled. "She a call girl too?"

McCarty nodded. "The missing person is her business partner. Sounds like they run a high-end service. Makes you wonder what led her down that particular path. She has obvious intelligence—heck—she could choose any career she wanted. What a waste."

Max shook his head. "Not to mention what a shame it is. I noticed her as soon as I saw you two walking down the hall. I hoped you'd tell me that she was your single cousin. But I stopped by for another reason buddy. You ready for lunch?"

"Starving," McCarty replied.

"Let's head to Stripes and let Bobby cook us up one of his plate-sized burgers." Bobby was a former cop who went into the bar and burger business after a stray bullet found his leg in a gang shootout.

McCarty stood up and grabbed his coat. "I'm always in the mood for Bobby's burgers. Is Joey coming along?" Joey Malone was Max's partner.

"He's out for the day. He's chaperoning one of his kid's field trips so it's just us. Anyway, today's lunch won't be all pleasure. We're teaming up with the FBI's BAU to start a CM task force. Before they arrive this afternoon, I want to go over the crime scene reports and make sure we have all our ducks in a row."

"I heard the Mayor and Commissioner decided to call in the Feebs," McCarty groaned, "Don't know if that's good or bad but God knows we need all the help we can get."

"You heard right. The media is giving the Mayor ulcers, so I don't blame him. So, let's keep an open mind. The Feebs aren't all are bad. If they can prevent another girl turning up dead in a church pew, that's a good thing.

McCarty shook his head. "I don't blame the Mayor. He's been in the crossfire during the entire investigation. Meanwhile, every crackpot in New York is calling to confess to the crimes. Max, please tell me what would possess someone to confess to a crime he didn't commit?"

"Like Warhol predicted—everyone wants their fifteen minutes of fame." The two strode out into the midday sun.

9

H E CLOSED HIS EYES and sighed in deep satisfaction, savoring each memory of their encounter. It had been perfect—from the moment she had entered the car, until he'd snuffed the life out of her. Death brought out a woman's true beauty, when they were perfect in their stillness. He unzipped his pants, removing his swollen member as he relished each titillating detail of the experience.

The depth of his fulfillment surprised him. At first, he'd thought of himself as only a loyal soldier—fighting the good battle. What began as duty became much more...

Everything went according to plan. How imaginative and detailed his performance had been. He'd left nothing to chance, attending to every detail with no room for error. What a shame the public would never credit him for his masterful performance. How unfair life was. What a shame it was that no one would ever know—that no one *could* know of greatness.

His cock now engorged, he needed release and fast. Stroking his throbbing member, he recalled the shock on her sweet face—the terror as she comprehended her demise. How her eyes had pleaded for mercy until her final surrender. His hand moved faster, each stroke more furious until he screamed out in elated satisfaction as a violent burst of semen erupted. He wiped his cock, hand, legs, and pants with tissue. Then he leaned back and thought of the work ahead.

The police would never learn his identity. He had made sure of that. They were too incompetent and he was too brilliant. He was meticulous in keeping two steps ahead of them. It would remain that way. He knew he should move without haste onto the next phase of the operation but he desired to linger on her lovely face just a bit longer. Still, he had to hurry because the job was not yet complete. He gazed at her one last time in her current state as he recalled her pleading eyes—eyes that begged for mercy. In the end, he had shown her the same mercy she gave to all the men she had ever taunted, teased, and cajoled into loving her.

Which was none at all.

10

EETING WITH OFFICER MCCARTY left Montana frustrated and stressed. She glanced at the time on her cellphone; she could still make her weekly Taekwondo class if she hurried. Martial arts brought a balance that sheer cardio never produced. It was more than a workout—it was calming and empowering. Never did she need to relieve tension more than now.

She began training after the near deadly outcall years ago that had ultimately led her to Suzette and opening the Co-op. It started at the end of a ten-hour workday of nonstop outcalls. Nothing sounded better than a soothing soak in the bath, complete with candles and a glass of cabernet. As she was leaving her client's hotel to grab a cab home, her cellphone rang. She saw by the caller ID that it was the out-call service calling. She almost let the call go to voicemail but picked up at the last minute.

"Hello, this is Tana," she said, her voice weary.

"Tana, I'm glad I reached you. I have a call for you—a regular client who tips well."

"I can't do it," she protested. "I'm beat. The only call I'm answering is the one beckoning me to a hot bath, a glass of good wine, and a long sleep."

"Please Tana. He's a high-end customer who loves your type. Sandy will be appreciative if you take the call—if you know what I mean."

Montana did. Taking this call meant she would likely get high tippers for the next several outcalls.

"Okay," Montana sighed with reluctance. She had a bad feeling but chalked it up to exhaustion. "After this I'm turning my phone off."

"Thank you so much," the receptionist squealed. "I'll be sure to mention to Sandy how you went out of your way for us." She gave Montana the address.

"I'll drop off the money tomorrow," Montana said. "Not tonight."

"Sounds good," she replied. "And oh Tana? One thing I should mention. Sometimes he's a little hard to handle."

"What does that mean?" Montana regretted taking the call already.

"Oh, it's nothing. You know, some clients are a just little more demanding than others. Thanks again—so much." The receptionist hung up before Montana could ask more about him.

The mild warning hadn't worried her. Some escorts complained about difficult clients but Montana's experience was often different from theirs. She usually found that if she treated them well and gave them their money's worth, they weren't that bad. After all, she was in the business of fulfilling fantasies.

The client lived on the 38th floor of a spectacular Upper East Side high rise. Walls of windows showed off Manhattan's extraordinary skyline. High in the air, the city's magical lights glittered beneath them. The client impressed her as well. He was charming, attractive, and articulate. He poured glasses of champagne as they made small talk.

Things were so pleasant that his sudden turnaround was even more alarming.

Mid-conversation, he transformed from the pleasant calm man who had greeted her to a rage-filled lunatic. Marching over to her, he grabbed a fistful of her hair, pulling her up until her face was within an inch of his own. As she protested in shocked disbelief, he backhanded her with such force she hit the floor. She stared up at him, shaking her head, trying to comprehend what had just happened. Affable reality had become a terrifying nightmare so fast she was unable think straight.

The next several hours were a frightening eternity. Her stepfather's abuse had not prepared her for the vicious hatred erupting from this stranger. He produced a gun and dragged her from the living room to a bathroom where he forced her to strip and wash with scalding water.

"That's right," he hissed. "Wash your filthy cunt, you dirty whore."

As she whimpered in pain and humiliation, he lifted her hands over her head and secured them with a tight rope wound around her wrists. Then he fastened the rope to a hook hanging from the ceiling while she stood in terror, her feet barely touching the floor. Helpless before him, he grabbed a whip and thrashed every part of her body. Angry welts sprung up. Only her face was untouched.

As the mind-numbing pain rained down, her thoughts ran wild. He would kill her—she was certain of it. No one would ever see her again. She mourned her unfulfilled life. She would never go to school—would never become an attorney. She would never get married or have children. Only Sandy knew where she was and Montana was sure Sandy would never tell the police. The greedy woman would never risk her business for a dead call girl.

The night continued without mercy until dawn lit the sky. It reached the point where she wished he would end it—just kill her and get it over with—so great was her agony. She had rounded the corner of desperation and misery into hopelessness.

Then just as he had snapped earlier, he transformed again. His rage vanished and he was once again the charming, articulate man who had greeted her. He was dazed—seeming to have no memory of the assault because he looked at her in surprise when he saw her tied up and beaten. His head hung as he realized he was responsible for the torture.

"It looks like I got a little carried away," he murmured. "I'll give you something extra for your trouble."

The transformation dumbfounded her. She cared nothing for money at this point. All she wanted was to leave before his other evil personality emerged. She dressed as quick as her trembling fingers and aching body allowed. At the door, he handed her an envelope thick with cash. Numb with shock, she stuffed it in her pocket, not caring enough to open it until days later.

Safe in her apartment later, she sat on the floor of her shower, sobbing in helpless rage, releasing the hours of pent up horror. Never again, she swore... never again. As the water cleansed some of the shock and rage, she realized her dismal options. As naïve as she was, she knew better than to file a police report. All the evidence was now vanishing down her shower drain, for one thing. The police would do nothing to protect her. For all she knew, they would arrest her if she tried reporting him. Still she vowed that no monster would ever violate her in such a way again.

The experience was the catalyst for some much-needed changes in her life. Not only did she and Suzette open the

Coop, the experience forced her to take ownership of her own safety, which led her to Taekwondo.

She fell in love with the ancient martial art during her first session. It was empowering to know she could defend herself and it was a great workout in both the physical and mental sense. She had always been athletic and excelled in the class. Her progress was so swift the instructor encouraged her to continue beyond simple self-defense.

Within three years, she earned her first-degree black belt. She was now a fifth degree. Her excitement at going to classes had never waned. She always looked forward to it but today it was essential.

She came out of her reverie of that now distant night just as the subway reached the stop nearest her class. She was glad she would be on time; she hated being late for anything. It was one of the few incompatibilities between Suzette and her. Suzette was usually fifteen minutes late and Montana fifteen minutes early. They accepted each other's idiosyncrasies, as people do when they love each other.

She hoped this evening's class would help her find the balance she needed to start searching for Suzette. Each muscle was taut with tension that had been mounting since the night before. She was sick with worry and angry with the NYPD. She'd had a hunch the cops would not pursue a missing call girl. She didn't even care if he disapproved of the Coop—she expected as much from a cop. What outraged her was his utter dismissal of the seriousness of the situation. If Suzette were a Manhattan's socialite, Montana knew the full power of the NYPD would be at her fingertips. McCarty saw Suzette as just another prostitute, a throwaway life. She so needed to purge the mounting frustration, anxiety, and fury. What better place to do so than her taekwondo class?

She arrived with just enough time to change into her dobok, the traditional garment. She threw herself into the class, taking on several opponents. Stress and tension drained from her as the workout recharged her battery, just as she had hoped it would.

Although it was raining lightly, she walked the short distance to her loft. Montana noticed the strange bag woman with her spiky orange fright wig had lost her usual steam since she muttered rather than shrieked her usual insults and obscenities.

Upstairs, she collapsed onto the sumptuous sofa that was worth every nickel she had spent on it. Thirsty and famished, she gave an inward groan. Where was that cabana boy when you needed him? She forced herself up, went to the fridge, and opened and downed a half-full bottle of Pellegrino. She was famished. Thirty-six hours had passed since she had eaten a real meal.

Other than a few soggy appetizers, she'd only eaten a vendor hot dog while walking to the precinct from Suzette's apartment. Food had been the last thing on her mind the last twenty-four hours. Now biology took over; she needed food but was too exhausted to cook. That was no problem in the city: restaurants serving nearly every kind of food delivered. She pulled a large stack of menus from a kitchen drawer and scanned them.

An hour later, she feasted on a delectable Vietnamese dinner laid out before her on a blanket, picnic style. She splurged and opened a bottle of Napa Valley's Silver Oak. The young wine was full and round, bursting with fruit with an underlying oak finish. It was a perfect pairing with the spicy Asian food. She ate until she couldn't consume another bite. Sated, she wrapped the rest for later and then dragged herself back to the couch and watched the rain splatter against her living room window. Feeling a slight buzz from the wine, she closed her eyes. Within seconds, she was fast asleep.

She awoke to total darkness. Her automatic lighting had switched off the lights. She stared out at the city, the moonless sky making the night seem ominous in its slumber. Looking across the Hudson to the communities beyond, she saw only the barest smattering of lights. All the rest were dark spaces—strange how she'd not noticed them before Suzette's disappearance. Normally, the lights were what captivated her.

She'd been afraid of the dark since childhood when a monster appeared at her bedside each night. She would lay in terror dreading the inevitable approach. Malevolent deeds command the night's darkness. It hides the horrors inflicted upon the innocent by the depraved.

Montana stared out, transfixed, as the once magical lights now winked and mocked her, while in another scenario not far away, one more victim prayed as her captor cackled in cruel delight.

11

MAX CONSTANTINE'S CALL to Jimmy Burke dashed any hope the Mayor had of enjoying his weekend. The call verified his worst nightmare: another parishioner, stopping to light a candle for her mother, had found the CM's next victim.

Officers interviewed the witness as soon as they arrived on the scene. She had grown concerned when she saw what appeared to be an unattended person in a wheelchair near the back pew of the church. She told the police she'd not noticed the person when entering. When the witness approached the person in the wheelchair to see if she was all right, she realized the woman was dead. Her hysterical screaming brought the parish priest out from his back office. First responders contacted lead detective Max, who notified his partner Joey Malone. The two met at the scene. Their examination confirmed their suspicion: she was another victim of the CM. That was when they called Mayor Burke.

Even with this nightmare occurring in his city, Mayor Burke loved his job. He had always enjoyed challenges and this was his biggest yet. Before becoming Mayor, he had been a well-respected attorney. He had an altruistic streak. His philanthropic parents had raised him to believe in the importance of giving back. To that end, he provided pro bono representation for those who could not afford his fees.

He took on big ugly cases, such as fighting for compensation for the 9/11 workers who had become ill from the cleanup. He battled for better treatment of returning veterans, which worked out to the benefit of companies who gained tax breaks for hiring vets.

He won his first election in grand fashion and repeated the feat four years later in a landslide victory. Because of New York's new extended term limits, he hoped to win another four years in the upcoming November election.

Mayor Burke straddled the delicate balance of appealing to both genders. Men admired his judgment and integrity while women found him irresistible. He was tall and kept his natural athletic build finely tuned with daily workouts. Silver streaked the hair at his temples, complementing a full head of dark hair. His soulful brown eyes inspired trust. Having grown up in a household of sisters, he had a feminine side and wasn't afraid to show it. He was empathetic to the demands of women balancing careers and family.

His one real weakness was an insatiable appetite for beautiful women. He was the city's most eligible bachelor. Women vied for his attention. While he often had a beautiful woman on his arm, it appeared that none had captured his heart.

He rarely held weekend meetings but this one was born out of desperation. He needed all hands on deck after the latest CM murder. No one in attendance was complaining, either. Everyone understood the urgency of the situation. Beside the Mayor, Police Commissioner Harry Durbin, Max, his partner Joey, and the BAU's two top two profilers were also present.

There was a profound difference in both the attitudes and attire of the NYPD and the federal agents. Mayor Burke, Harry Durbin, Max Constantine, and Joey Malone were relaxed in jeans and sports shirts. The two federal agents looked stiff and uncomfortable in professional black suits. Standing guard near the door was the Mayor's primary diver, Charles Drinkwater.

Max studied his fingernails. He understood why Mayor Burke brought in the BAU. He appreciated anything that would generate leads for their stagnant investigation. Max had worked other serial crimes involving the BAU with mixed results. The collaboration solved one case but it came with a heaping helping of arrogance along with a side dish of condescension.

Adjacent from Mayor Burke's desk was a map of Manhattan and its surrounding boroughs. Pinned to it were colored pins that signified aspects of each victim. Each had her own colored pin. The pins showed up in three locations on the map. The first indicated the last time someone had seen the victim. The second established her last known address. The third marked the churches where someone found their bodies.

The FBI agents began the meeting by giving their profile of the CM.

"Good to meet all of you—I'm Special Agent Murph Campbell and this is my partner, Special Agent Cal Allen. Feel free to call us Campbell and Allen. We've met Mayor Burke and Commissioner Durbin..."

Max broke in, "Nice to meet you. I'm Max Constantine, the lead investigator on the case and this is my partner Joey Malone."

Murph Campbell looked toward the door, an eyebrow raised.

"Sorry," Mayor Burke spoke up. "This is Charles Drinkwater. He's been my personal driver for years and I asked him to come along with me when the good people of New York elected me to office."

Drinkwater nodded to the men in the room. He considered himself a bodyguard as much as a driver. He'd been with Jimmy Burke for over twenty years. They'd met when the Mayor was seventeen and Charles was twelve. Jimmy had been something of a big brother to Charles since that time.

Agent Campbell nodded at Drinkwater. "Okay, let's get started. We've examined your profile, Max—great job on that. Your ideas are in line with much of what we've also determined although we do have some additional traits."

Mayor Burke snorted, "My profile says he's a fucking psychopath."

"Psychopathy exists, but there is more to it," Campbell replied with all seriousness, sidestepping the Mayor's attempt at banter.

Max thought this was why he and the Feds didn't become friends. They had no fucking sense of humor. He was happy to work with them but he doubted they'd share a beer at the end of the day.

Campbell continued, "Not all psychopaths are serial murderers, nor are they destined to become ones. Now, the CM *is* a psychopathic serial killer. A psychopath may just dream of fantasies that never manifest. Some call sex lines or visit prostitutes to play out their fantasies. Psychopaths of this nature are usually harmless and fit in well in their communities. Many have spouses and families. They keep their psychopathy locked away and take their secrets to the grave."

Agent Allen spoke for the first time. "This unsub is different in that he has gone beyond psychopathy. He may have imagined murdering streetwalkers for years but only recently crossed the line from fantasy to reality. We theorize he reached a breaking point, where he could no longer control his compulsions. That was when the first murder occurred. He is a sociopath as well as a psychopath. That makes him far more dangerous. A sociopath doesn't recognize his victims as human beings; he views them as possessions."

Max Constantine interrupted, "Not to be rude, Agent Allen, but this is not our first rodeo here. Harry, Joey, and I have worked two serial cases before this one. We know how they view their victims."

Agent Allen addressed him, "I apologize if we're rehashing things you already know. Please bear with us, as we have other aspects in our profile that your dossier did not include. Any other questions before I go on?"

The men nodded and gestured for him to continue.

"Campbell, you'll take it from here?"

Murph Campbell stood before the victim map. "A few aspects make this unsub unique."

"No kidding he's unique. What kind of person embalms his victims and then props them up in churches?" Mayor Burke spoke with disgust. "Max profiled him as a religious sadist. Do you agree with that assessment?"

Campbell nodded at Max. "Indeed. He's a religious sadist but it doesn't stop there."

"He's one of the most complicated unsubs I've come across in my career," Agent Allen agreed.

"Religion is the most significant theme of his fantasy. He enjoys torture, which is why he carves religious symbols, such as crosses, ankhs, and eyes of God onto all his victims. Notable also is how he starts the process. First, he uses an IV drip to administer poison to the victim. That's what kills them. After, he embalms them using the same toxins he used in the IV to kill them—so in a way, he starts the embalming process while they are still alive. He may view their death as some kind of decontamination process. The crime lab's analysis found the embalming fluid contained a variety of toxins associated with cleaning. For example, bleach is the largest component.

"Religion is often a theme for serial killers. They often view themselves as saviors," Joey muttered.

Max rubbed his chin thoughtfully. "True enough. Gary Ridgeway—better known as the Green River Killer—was one of the most prolific serials in U.S. history. Although investigators weren't able to determine the total number of victims, it's thought it to be well over sixty."

"Spot on," Campbell agreed. "He went door to door proselytizing and became furious when people didn't respond to his religion. Like the CM, Ridgeway never viewed his crimes as abominable. He believed he was a vigilante."

Agent Allen nodded. "They also both preyed on street prostitutes. The CM views sexual needs as weaknesses. He doesn't perform overt sexual acts with his victims but some components exist. First, they *are* all prostitutes and he takes their panties for souvenirs and may take other items as well. The lab found only small amounts of semen on the victims, which leads us to believe he ejaculates onto their panties before removing them."

"True—he didn't sexually assault any of the women," Max agreed. "Maybe he can't get an erection with women— at least not living ones."

"A strong possibility," Agent Allen said. "Or he may find their sexual organs repulsive or beneath him because they are prostitutes. He selects from this population for three factors. Agent Campbell has compiled an analysis of these characteristics."

Campbell still stood by the map. "First, easy prey—heck the girls *want* someone to pick them up. Second is desirability, which has to do with victim traits. He prefers fledgling girls—the younger the better. Half his victims were under twenty-two and the others looked younger because of their petite stature. All had thin, even boyish frames."

Commissioner Durbin interrupted, "That could play into the point Max made. If the victims are boyish and he doesn't penetrate them, perhaps he's gay but still closeted."

"That's a possibility," Agent Allen concurred. "Coming to terms with his true sexual identity could trigger an extreme devotion to religion."

Agent Campbell spoke up. "The final factor is vulnerability. He chooses women who probably wouldn't turn down any trick, even if their instincts may tell them otherwise. All six were serious heroin or crack addicts, with multiple drug arrests. He has a smorgasbord of streetwalkers from which to choose but it's significant that his prey are all addicts. They're less likely to be able to put up a fight, too."

Commissioner Durbin looked at the two federal agents. "So he seizes the moment when the urge, opportunity, and desirability coincide."

"Exactly," Agent Allen confirmed. "He scopes out the strolls and studies his victims. He takes time selecting the right one and goes in for the kill—no pun intended."

Max shook his head. "So much anger—the way he marks his victims and then kills them—it has to be an agonizing way to die. I can't wait to take this bastard off the street."

Agent Campbell pointed his finger like a gun at Max. "Bingo. He's an angry, religious sexual predator. He finds satisfaction in punishing these women in the most miserable and degrading manner. You are right; their deaths have to be god-awful."

"Let's stop this bastard now," Mayor Burke said, pounding his hand on his desk to emphasize his point.

Max addressed the Mayor. "We're working on that now, Jimmy. The aim of our task force is to put highly trained female undercover officers on the strolls. We have a pool of effective officers from vice who are close to his physical preference. We disguise them as addicts—some have played this role in the past—to perfection I might add."

"So you're talking about a sting," Mayor Burke said thoughtfully.

"Yes." Max's eyes were on the victim map. "But we also hope they can get close to a few girls out there—get to know them as fellow streetwalkers—and pump them for information. They aren't going to talk to a badge but confiding in a fellow streetwalker is different."

"What information could they give you if they haven't come across the CM?" Mayor Burke asked.

Joey chimed in, "That's just it. They may have seen this maniac. You can bet these girls are talking about him. Maybe someone turned him down—or another went with him and escaped."

Mayor Burke cocked his head and addressed Max. "Why not call the anonymous tip line then?"

"They don't trust cops. We're the enemy," Max replied. "I do agree with Joey. It's possible he *has* encountered girls who turned him down. A streetwalker who doesn't have the desperation of an addict might not have liked his vibe. This goes along with the factors Campbell brought up: only the most desperate would go with him. He's been on the strolls. Others had to have seen him."

They group fell silent, all staring the sinister map of colored pins.

Mayor Burke stood. "I appreciate all of you giving up part of your weekend for this meeting. Let's move on this. I want this bastard caught yesterday."

12

THOUGH IT WAS 3:00 A.M., Montana doubted she could get back to sleep. Still, it was worth trying. She shuttered the blinds to block the morning sun. She slid back between the soft sheets, trying to relax but her mind raced. She tried her martial arts breathing exercises but it was fruitless. At last, she gave up, deciding to take advantage of the extra hours.

She brewed coffee then sat at her desk with the steaming mug. It was too early to call people but she could get a better look at Suzette's email correspondence. There likely weren't that many more people to call anyway. She'd already called all their mutual friends. None of Suzette's theater pals but Hanky knew about the Coop so Montana was ambiguous with what she disclosed to them. None had heard from Suzette.

At 8:00 a.m. desperation drove her to call Suzette's aunt and uncle on the off chance they'd heard from her, as unlikely as it seemed. She looked up their number in Suzette's address book and dialed.

"Yeah?" A woman's impatient voice answered, almost drowned out by the television blasting a preacher's voice in the background, expounding on the wrath of hellfire and damnation.

"Hello, I'd like to speak with Mrs. or Mr. Peterson. This is Montana Wylde, a friend of Suzette Peterson. I'm trying to locate her—we were supposed to meet for dinner last night and she didn't show up.

"We ain't heard nothing from her for more than a year. Susan is living a Godless life and if you're her friend, it means you must be living a life of sin yourself."

"Ma'am, I simply wanted to know if you had heard from her. You've answered my question. Thank you and have a great day." She hung up before the woman had a chance to respond. Their response to Suzette's disappearance was shocking. They seemed annoyed that Montana had interrupted their television viewing.

After the call, she went back to Suzette's computer and started looking at the Coop email first. This time, she read all the messages from the past three months. None appeared suspicious. The same was true going back several months with Suzette's theater account. Although she thought it was doubtful, she went through three months of her throwaway Gmail email but found no personal correspondence at all. Miffed, she shut the email program down.

Spotting the 'Personal' icon on Suzette's desktop, she spent two hours trying to hack into the account. She would need help with it. Hacking passwords was beyond her technical skills.

Feeling impotent and fuzzy from the lack of sleep, she rested her head on her folded arms at her desk. Then it struck her. She needed to head to the Coop. It could hold the key because that was where they kept all their client files.

They had two types of files: one for clients and one for pests. They created the pest file for wankers and lookie lou types. Wankers wanted free phone sex. When they called, the men whispered their fantasies in hushed voices. The wankers' goal was to keep the woman on the phone until they climax. The only deterrence was hanging up before they pleasured themselves.

The wankers were annoying but they took less time than the other major pest: the Lookie Lou. Too cheap to pay for a session, they still enjoyed the eye candy. They made appointments and showed up, hanging around as long as possible but never staying. Their lascivious eyes bored into the women as they licked their lips. They always left, claiming a forgotten visit to the ATM or some emergency text that would take them away.

Most useful were the client files, which had photos of everyone who made and showed up for an appointment. They included a list of the dates the clients visited, what their sessions involved, and how much they spent. They started the files with simple Rolodexes, before they had a computer. Hanky was now in the process of transferring all the files onto the computer but he hadn't finished that task so they still relied on the Rolodexes.

Hanky thought of creating the files when they hired him. It was his idea to include photos for each client, which he created from the surveillance video outside the apartment door. An unexpected bonus was being able to check that the photo on the card matched the client arriving for his next session. Again, Montana thought about how lucky they were to have Hanky. She recalled the incident that had spurred them into hiring a security man in the first place.

When the Coop first opened, the two women were their own security staff, scrutinizing each customer through the apartment's peephole. If they didn't care for his looks, they sent him away, saying they'd mixed up appointments. They never offered to schedule another one—instead telling the client to call back.

One day, they hadn't heeded their initial instincts. On that day, heavy clouds hung in a chilly sky. Only moments before the expected client arrived, pounding rain had drenched the city. As they looked at the sodden client through the peephole, Montana's first instinct was to turn him away but she was unsure. Dank clumps of hair stuck to his face, giving him an oily appearance. Still, it was hard to tell if he had just been soaked from the rain. She asked for Suzette's opinion. Peering through peephole, Suzette finally gave her thumbs up. It was raining after all.

Big mistake. *Huge.*

He was nervous from the start, further raising Montana's hackles. He failed to engage in the usual small talk in the front parlor. Something was distracting him—he was a ball of nerves.

When they asked which of the two he'd like to spend time with, he pointed to Suzette while his eyes zipped about the room. "I'll take her."

Then Montana's stomach had knotted with dread. Suzette, always the more trusting of the two, flashed him a wide smile. "Come on back, honey. Let's get this party started." He followed her down the hall, his head turning for a final glance at Montana before entering a back room.

Montana's first instinct had been on the money. Not two minutes later, he led Suzette back down the hallway, a knife to her throat.

"Give me your money. I'm a junkie...and I'm sick. I don't want to hurt you but I will if you don't cooperate. Just give me your money."

Without hesitation, Montana handed him a wad of cash from the tiny pocketbook hanging crossbody around her shoulders. Then she reached into Suzette's bag, giving him all her cash as well. The knife still at Suzette's throat with one hand, he snatched the cash with his other.

He barked out directions. "Sit and count to one hundred—don't you dare fucking move until you've finished. If you call for help before I am away, I'll be back to kill you—and don't you think I won't."

They sat terrified as he bolted from the apartment. They didn't call anyone—how could they? Theirs was an illegal business. The door attendants would come to their aid but it was also likely they would have to call the police. The Co-op was new and the women had no desire to get on the bad side of the building's management. At that point, none of the door attendants had a clue what was going on in apartment 4E, though over time they would.

Suzette had confided the incident to Hanky and had told him they wanted to hire a security person. Hanky, like most aspiring actors, was always in need of flexible jobs that paid well. When he suggested himself for the job, Suzette and Montana agreed he was the perfect choice. They'd never regretted bringing him on. Not only did he keep them safe, he was fun to have around. Today, Montana blessed him again for his idea of attaching the clients' photos to their cards. They might serve their most useful purpose to date if they could uncover clues from Friday's VIP client—the last person who supposedly saw Suzette before she disappeared.

She emerged from the building at 8:30 a.m., dressed for comfort in a featherweight gray cashmere hoodie and sweatpants. The resident bag lady was already in place wearing a yellow rain slicker: a bright contrast to the orange fright wig. At sighting Montana, she gave the familiar war cry. Montana tried a new approach by giving a cheerful wave and smile. This perplexed the woman, who stopped mid-obscenity. For once, Montana rendered her speechless. Might as well kill her with kindness she thought—the few times Montana had flipped her the bird seemed to agitate her even more.

She stopped at the deli across the street. They were enjoying a brisk Sunday brunch crowd. The inside was crammed and now that the rain had stopped, a few customers sat on chairs under big umbrellas in the outdoor area of the restaurant. It was a happy crowd; customers enjoyed huge sandwiches, creamy bowls of potato salad, and of course, the inevitable bagels and lox.

Montana wandered in to order her usual. Bernie, who worked the counter, brightened when he saw her.

"Hey—how's Wyoming today?"

Montana smiled. Every time she stopped in, he called her a different western state.

"Hi Bernie, I'm doing okay. How about a scooped out bagel with cream cheese?"

"You got it, beautiful." He scooped out the insides of the bagel with expertise. "Where's Blondie today?" Suzette often went running along with Montana on Sundays and they often had lunch at Bernie's after—usually outside if the weather permitted.

"Funny you should ask—I'm looking for her. I've lost track of her the last couple of days. Have you seen her?" It was a long shot but why not ask on the off chance that Suzette had looked for Montana downtown.

Bernie was perplexed. "No. I never see her unless she's with you. Doesn't she live uptown?"

"Good memory," she nodded. "You don't miss anything do you, Bernie?"

"Is she okay?" Bernie studied her. "You're worried—it's written all over your face."

"You *are* perceptive. Yes, I am concerned. We were to meet for drinks on Friday but she never showed up. I haven't heard from her and can't reach her. It's so unlike her."

Bernie came from around the counter and put his arm around her shoulder. "Honey, take the advice of an old man who has lived more years than you. Most worries turn out to be no big deal. Maybe she met someone special. Say she went to the Hamptons for the weekend or something like that. She's going to grab someone's heart soon enough— just as you will. In fact, it's time the both of you settled down with some nice young men. Didn't I tell you I have a nephew you'd like? He's an attorney just like you."

Montana laughed, "Not so fast Bernie, I'm not an attorney yet. Yes, you've told me about your nephew but I'm nowhere near ready to settle down. Finishing school is only the half of it—I still have to pass the bar."

"Doll, I'm trying to pass the bar too. Every night when I leave here I try to pass the damn bar and every night I go in." He roared at the same joke he told each time she mentioned passing the exam. "Honey, try not to worry and let me know if I can do anything to help. And I'll let you know if she happens to pop in. I'll give you a call." Bernie had her address and phone number since she often ordered deli deliveries.

The previous night's rain had washed Manhattan clean. It was a gorgeous day. She walked to Canal Street where she caught the subway to Murray Hill. She got off at 33rd and Park, just a block from the Coop.

She greeted the weekend door attendant, Jackson. She didn't know him well since they rarely worked weekends. In the early days, they were an important part of their business but these days they had so many workweek regulars that they now had the luxury of taking weekends off or just seeing high rolling customers.

Upstairs, she grabbed the Rolodexes. The client files interested her most. Their cards varied widely, depending on how long they had been clients and how often they visited.

Most clients had only one or two cards stapled together but long-term regulars had stacks of cards bound with rubber bands.

She started with the VIPs since one of them had made the Friday date with Suzette. Montana knew they had planned to meet around 10:00 in the morning. Beyond that, she had no idea what they had planned, but because it was an outcall, Suzette must have seen him for an in-call at the Coop at least twice. That was protocol—and it meant he ought to have a card.

They organized the cards alphabetically by first names since so few gave their last names. Though, surprisingly, some handed over their actual business cards. Only a rare client had no card at all, such as Suzette's few long-term regulars with whom she'd done outcalls before the Coop existed. They never visited for an in-call.

As she went through the cards, it occurred to her that she must do something about the upcoming appointments. She grabbed the thick appointment book from the coffee table. She was relieved to see only a few scheduled appointments. That wasn't surprising. Clients rarely booked in advance since desire usually occurred on a whim. Most called the day of the visit although a few busy regulars called in advance.

Montana had two upcoming appointments. She decided to honor those but would schedule no more. Suzette had three, all of which Montana canceled. She left one of Suzette's clients a voicemail and sent the two others emails letting them know Suzy had to cancel. She was vague about the reason and even more ambiguous about when her friend would return.

Next, she left new message greetings on their two phones lines. One was for regular customers, the other for new ones. On the private line, her message indicated they were unavailable for rest of the month and requested clients to call back in May. On the new client line, she said they were not taking new appointments until further notice. Then she canceled all ads on websites, magazines, and newspapers.

It had now been forty-eight hours since Suzette went missing so Montana decided to take McCarty up on his offer to file the report. She dug his card out of her handbag, calling his cellphone. Voicemail picked up after four rings with the message that he would call when available. She left a brief message requesting an appointment with him. Frustration bubbled to the surface once again. Based on what McCarty had said, she was certain the cops would do nothing but place Suzette in some large but useless database.

She glanced around, making sure she had finished her work before she left. She stuffed the Rolodexes into her handbag. She'd go through them thoroughly at home.

Before leaving, she called to update Hanky on Suzette. By now, he was as worried about Suzette as Montana was.

"At first, I thought she was just out on a long, fun date but you're right, she's gotta be in trouble. Does she have any upcoming appointments?" he asked.

"She only had three scheduled this week and none further. I canceled them all."

"What about you?"

"I have two—Paul and Otto—you know them both."

"Montana, I'm going to be there even though they're regulars. Until we know what happened to Suze, we aren't taking any chances."

"I cannot imagine they could have anything to do with Suzette, but I would feel better if you were here."

"I wouldn't have it any other way. What about her clients—are you gonna question them?"

"I'm most interested in talking to the VIPS—finding the one she saw last Friday could be critical."

He paused a moment. Are you going to see new clients?"

"Right now, I can't look beyond finding Suzette."

"I want to help."

"Thanks Hanky—I love you. Right now, I can't think of a thing you could help with but I'll call if something comes up."

"I love you too, girl—and I love Suze. You let me know the first you hear about anything."

"Of course."

She gave Hanky her appointment dates and times and they hung up. She turned off the lights and reset the alarm. The Coop spooked her—as though an innate evil were nearby. She had never felt this way about the apartment before Suzette disappeared. She fumbled with the lock, her fingers trembling. Rather than wait for the elevator, she ran down all four flights of stairs. She couldn't wait to inhale fresh air.

At home, she checked the cards' symbols to separate the VIPs from the regulars. Not only did the cards have photos and appointment dates, they had other identifiers as well. They used symbols on the off chance of a raid in which vice might take the files.

Checkmarks indicated the type of session expected. One checkmark meant the client was not interested in anything unusual. Two checkmarks specified something just a bit out of the ordinary, such as wanting a strip tease. Three checkmarks meant the request was unusual, like a shoe fetish. This also designated the client as one who was easy to deal with and who paid well. Four checkmarks showed the client was difficult or fussy. Five checkmarks meant he was eighty-sixed—no longer welcome.

Dollar signs identified how much clients spent. A single "$" meant the client was a cheapskate; he paid the minimum and no more. "$$" identified him as paying more than that, but not much. "$$$" meant he was above average by a good amount. They awarded "$$$$" only to the rare VIP. They were the *real* high rollers.

She pulled out all the $$$$ cards. At last, she felt she was doing something meaningful. Going through the files was better than the utter helplessness that had consumed her the last two days. The cards brought back so many memories. Some were strange but many were downright humorous.

A card belonging to a client, Edgar, made her laugh aloud. He'd been one of Suzette's most loyal VIP regulars. A meek accountant, he visited her at least once a month. Each time, he pulled a huge black dildo with a gold shiny vibrating tip from his ostrich valise. His fantasy was having a beautiful blonde penetrate him in his ass with the humongous dildo. On one unfortunate visit, things went terribly wrong. The dildo's golden head had become detached and lodged itself deep inside Edgar's anus. Montana had been in the front parlor when Suzette and Edgar came running from the back room in hysterics. Edgar came first, with Suzette on his heels.

"Montana," Suzette exclaimed. "The dildo is stuck in Edgar's ass. What can we do?" She did her best to contain her laughter, which Montana knew stemmed from nervousness. She knew her friend cared for the little accountant.

Edgar, on the other hand, was verging on a full-blown panic attack. "You have to get this out of my ass—my wife is gonna kill me if she finds out I was here. I can't go to the ER. You girls are the experts. You have to do something."

Suzette did her best to control her giggles. "Montana, you have longer fingers than I do. You give it a try."

"Oh for crying out loud." Montana rolled her eyes. "It's just a dildo head. No one is dying here, Edgar."

Montana's cool head prevailed. Seconds later, she greased a latex glove and slid two deft fingers up the accountant's ass. She pulled out the offending gold head.

Edgar had been so relieved he paid Suzette double her price and gave Montana a two hundred dollar gratitude tip as well. After he left, they both fell into hysterical laughter. Suzette doubted he would ever return but he'd made his usual appointment the following month. This time, with a new dildo—one with a permanent tip.

Another strange but harmless VIP was 'Joe the Egg Man.' He reminded Montana of Harvey the Pie Man; they were of the same ilk. Each visit, Joe brought several eggs, not that he needed them all, but to prepare himself in case one broke. He liked both women and varied his visits between them. His request was to have one of the women slide an uncooked egg inside her vagina. After letting it warm for several moments, she squatted over his open mouth and squeezed the egg out, letting it break open in his mouth while he masturbated.

With all the VIPs before her, Montana divided them into two piles: Suzette's and hers. Montana's all had photos. Two of Suzette's did not. These were likely Suzette's pre-Coop regulars because their most rigid policy was to make sure clients visited the Coop before *ever* doing an outcall. Now Montana wished that Suzette had insisted on a photo for them as well.

Montana checked Suzette's VIP dates but realized that was useless. She and Suzette filled out the cards *after* sessions because clients could change fantasies or give more or less money from the previous session. Suzette hadn't come back to the Coop last Friday—Montana knew that.

She decided to go through the wanker Rolodex but that she would concentrate on the very few she remembered who had seemed dangerous. Two brought chills to the women when they called. The first was a particularly judgmental caller with a high thin voice. From 'hello' a self-righteous tirade of preaching began. He demanded they give up their depraved lifestyles, to repent and allow Jesus into their hearts. For a moment, Montana flashed on the pious proselytizer at the precinct the day before. Extremists could go to great lengths. And there had been something about him...

The next one made Montana's blood run cold. He was full of rage when he called, screaming obscenities, declaring they were whores and worse. He never talked long but made his point in a few choice words. She remembered he had once threatened they would come to a bloody, ugly death.

Montana stared at the two cards, willing them to reveal more. Were these wankers dangerous? Was either capable of hurting Suzette? She had never taken the wankers seriously but now everyone was suspect.

None of the other wankers was worth setting aside. Besides, it might not be a client at all. Nuts snatched innocent women off the street all the time for no reason. Perhaps it was someone Suzette knew from the theater, or one of the many men who had asked her out on dates—most of which she had turned down. In a city of over eight million people, it could be anyone.

Contemplating how to search with so little to go on, her landline broke into her thoughts. She didn't recognize the number—could it be about Suzette?

"This is Montana Wylde."

"Ms. Wylde, this is Officer Darryl McCarty. I'm returning your call. Did something important come up?"

"Something important *did* come up, which we spoke of yesterday. Except now it is worse because she's been missing two days."

He sighed on the other end. "Ms. Wylde, this isn't my call; it is our protocol. Even if time *were* critical, filing your report early wouldn't make it through the red tape fast enough to make a difference. By then enough time would have passed to file the report according to our requirements."

"I'd like to file the report as soon as you'll let me." She hesitated. "And I would like to take you up on your offer. I don't feel like starting again from scratch."

"Sure, that's fine. Hold on and let me look at tomorrow's schedule." He paused for several moments. "I've got a ton of meetings in the afternoon but I can meet you early, say around 9:30 a.m."

Montana opened her calendar, scrutinizing the schedule. "I can make that."

"Good. Please bring in some recent photos of your friend.

"Will do."

The call renewed her frustration with the police. Feeling tense, she decided take a run on the trail and enjoy some afternoon sunshine. Out of the immense destruction of September 11, 2001, some beauty prevailed. The city built new trails along the Hudson for walking, running, or bicycling.

She pulled on running pants and matching hoodie. She attached her iPod to an armband and hurried out. Montana saw her nemesis, the bag lady, was in full stage makeup. She began her tirade with renewed vigor. Montana pressed her iPod's earbuds in place, rendering the woman silent. Now only in a pantomime of her displeasure, Montana reacted without thought and burst out laughing. This disturbed the bag lady even more. Montana, thinking better of her reaction, waved, and scampered down to the trail. After a quick stretch, she jogged, and then broke into a hard run to the beat of everything from Adele to the Velvet Underground.

Montana often ran to work out problems or pent up emotions. Today it helped with both. First, it released frustration with the NYPD but even better, she had a wonderful light bulb moment.

Why hadn't she thought of it earlier?

Part II
The Investigation

13

O F COURSE, she needed a private investigator. Back at her loft, feeling excited for the first time since Suzette disappeared, she fired up her own laptop. Doing a quick search of Manhattan's Private Investigators, she had hundreds of viable hits within seconds.

The first was a firm called B.J. Gold and Associates. Their link took her to a slick website, where they advertised areas of expertise including surveillance, background checks, missing persons, and insurance fraud. What caught her eye most was the black-outlined notice stating:

> **Available 24/7**
> **We *NEVER* Sleep!**

She grinned. Only in New York could one find a twenty-four hour PI service. She clicked on a link for 'Client Feedback' and read glowing reviews that heralded the agency's worth. While impressive, she was smart enough to know the company would never post negative testimonials.

She went through some of the other top hits but the number was overwhelming. None of the others had weekend hours so she kept going back to B.J. Gold and Associates. B.J.: the irony was not lost on her. Perhaps it was a sign. She made a hasty decision—after all, nothing ventured, nothing gained. She went to their page for contact information. Why waste more time?

When she searched her handbag for her cellphone, she couldn't find it. Dumping the contents onto the desk, she still couldn't find it. She tried calling the number to see if it was lost between the couch cushions but it went to voicemail after several rings. She thought hard. When had she last had it? Crap. That was all she needed—to lose her phone on top of everything else. Suzette might be trying to reach her.

Retracing her steps, she recalled putting her upcoming appointments into the phone's calendar. She must have left it at the Coop. *That* was why McCarty had called her landline—she just bet he had tried her cellphone first. She'd retrieve it later but she was now on fire. She used her landline to dial the agency's number. Just as she was thinking the office wasn't open 24/7 after several rings, a lyrical voice answered.

"B.J. Gold and Associates. How many I direct your call?"

"Hello, my name is Montana Wylde. I need to speak with a private investigator as soon as possible. Your website says you are open twenty-four hours a day. I can be there fast if someone is available. I need help finding a missing person."

"Just one moment. Let me see if someone can meet with you today."

A bastardized version of 'Hey Jude' then followed. Disgusted, Montana wondered why people would butcher such a great song by turning it into elevator music. The torture ended when the perky voice returned.

"Can you come in right away? If you get here no later than 4:30, Ross Bertolino can see you. Otherwise, you'll have to wait until tomorrow. We close at 5:00 today."

"Your Internet ad says you're always open."

"We offer twenty-four hour emergency services but those aren't free consultations."

Montana glanced at her watch. It was almost 3:30.

"Are you still at 547 Madison?"

"Yes, Madison and 40th. Suite 4401.

"I'll be there. Thanks much."

Usually she showered after running but there was no time for that. She washed her face, brushed her teeth, combed her hair, applied a touch of makeup, and then dashed out the door.

Madison and 40th was close to the Coop so she took her usual subway route—the fastest way to get uptown even on the weekends. The trains were obedient; a train pulled in within a minute of her arrival. She reached Times Square by 4:10 and took a brisk walk to the agency.

Her heart sank when she saw the 44th floor ultra-modern suite. Everything was white and plush, including the carpeting. The only contrast was gleaming chrome on the end tables and lamps. Montana sniffed. A familiar scent she could not quite place permeated the air. No question about it, this place was going to be expensive. An attractive redhead sat behind an immaculate desk holding nothing but a computer, a phone system, and an iPad—all in white. The only contrast to white and chrome was the woman's bright red hair and chic black suit. Montana knew her fashion. The job paid well or the woman had a gig on the side. That Tom Ford suit cost at least two thousand dollars.

"Hi, I'm Montana Wylde here to see Ross—sorry—I can't remember his last name—but I think it begins with a B. I called a short while ago. They said if I could make it by 4:30 he could see me."

"Just one moment," the woman dimpled. Montana recognized her lilting voice from the phone. She keyed numbers on the phone with nails so long Montana couldn't see how she could manage such a feat, much less conquer a computer's keyboard.

"Montana Wylde is here to see you." A short pause then, "I'll tell her."

"Please have a seat. Ross will be out in a minute. You know, I love your name," the woman gushed. "Montana Wylde sounds so romantic. Are you an actress?"

"No, but I play one on TV." She smiled at the woman's bewilderment. Montana sank into the plush sofa, hoping her running pants didn't have any Lower Manhattan grime on them.

In less than five minutes, a tall handsome man with dark brown hair and startling blue eyes greeted her.

"Ms. Wylde? I'm Ross Bertolino. Please come to my office where we can talk."

She shook his hand. "Thank you so much for seeing me on such short notice—it's unusual for a Sunday too."

"People may need an investigator at any time." His toothpaste commercial smile was blinding.

She followed him down a long hallway to a corner suite. He opened the door with a flourish. She gasped. This *was* high-end real estate. Floor to ceiling windows displayed a panoramic city view.

She was uneasy. It was all too slick and glossy; not what she'd had in mind. Her instincts were powerful and this wasn't 'the sight' as her Nana claimed. This was common sense. These were expensive digs and anyone leasing this real estate had to be paying a fortune. She was quite certain B.J. Gold and Associates didn't offer any sliding scales.

"Have a seat." He gestured to luxurious white chair.

"Thanks, Mr. Bertolino."

"Please, I'm Ross. So, Ms. Wylde, tell me who's missing." His smile was blinding.

"If you're Ross, call me Montana." She returned his smile. "My best friend and business partner has been missing for two days now. Her name is Suzette Peterson."

She gave him the same rundown she had given Officer McCarty. She brought the Coop up first so she could gauge his response. The sex industry brought judgment from many people and Montana wanted someone who wouldn't be self-righteous about their work. Ross Bertolino didn't blink an eye—but his job required that he conceal his reactions.

He addressed it right away. Montana thought that reasonable since he didn't know much about Suzette or their business.

"Not that I'm judging you but you do realize this opens up possibilities that other missing persons cases don't have. Of course, your confidentiality is safe with us. We aren't cops and our agency requires absolute discretion. If we do need to share something with the police, we will talk with you first, just to put that out front."

"I appreciate that."

"Given the complications of your profession, this investigation could take considerable time. We can address all those points if you decide to hire us. First, we should discuss our agency's fees and policies. If they're acceptable, we should move forward right away."

The early mention of fees turned her off. She had hoped he would give her an idea of how they would go about their investigation before she forked over money. It was clear money would need to exchange hands before a meaningful conversation would ensue.

"I understand your need to discuss fees. What might they be?"

"We will need an eight thousand dollar retainer to begin. We charge five hundred dollars an hour, plus expenses. When the hours come close to the charges against the retainer, we can revisit strategies."

The price punched her in the gut. While eight grand was higher than she'd hoped, the five hundred dollars per hour was out of control. It troubled her that he hadn't asked more questions about Suzette before talking money. It also occurred to her that mentioning the Coop so soon might have driven up the price. But how could she not? Another nagging worry was the agency drawing out the case. It could take months to go through all the Coop's files. The more she looked at Ross Bertolino, the less she trusted him.

"Your hourly rate is more than I expected but since this is new to me, I didn't know what it would cost."

"Our prices reflect our success rate, Montana. We are the leading investigative firm in the city. We have the highest success rate of any private agency."

Montana paused. "Your agency employs many investigators. Does your success rate combine the successes of all the investigators? Or would a smaller agency's top two investigators beat out your top two?"

His smile faltered, but only a bit. He started stammering, "I-I'm not s-sure what you are getting at..."

Montana continued. "I'm asking if your top investigators are the best in the city. Because this agency's huge number of investigators could skew the appearance of your success rate. If you're the *largest* agency in the city then it stands to reason that your success rate would appear higher than others if you are combining all your investigations."

She watched, fascinated, as a rash of hives began peeking above his crisp collar. Reaching into his desk drawer, he pulled out a glossy brochure.

He handed it to her. "Again, I'm not sure what you are asking. This brochure gives more information on our success rates in our various areas of investigation. Please take this copy."

At once, she remembered the scent of the conditioned air. Her mother had used lemon verbena to cover the smell of alcohol when Montana was a child. She looked around the room. The antiseptic décor and high-priced real estate turned her off. Ross Bertolino's disingenuous toothpaste smile didn't do much either. She was willing to pay people a decent wage for their work but everything about this place felt wrong. Then she saw it. The place had no soul. It was like a well-designed theatrical set. Impressive under the magic of stage lighting, costumes, and props but it had no substance underneath.

"I have no doubt your agency is successful. I'll look over this material and let you know what I decide. Yours is the first firm I contacted."

"I'm curious," he asked, "what made you call us first?"

"It was first on my search." She rose from her chair. "Plus you were open on Sunday."

"Take your time, Montana, but not too much. I realize this is an important decision but I'll offer you some free advice. Don't waste time making decisions. The longer people go missing, the harder it is to find them." He paused dramatically. "Clues vanish, people move, memories fade. Any police investigators will tell you they usually solve a missing person's case within the first two days. After... it gets a lot sketchier."

"She's been missing since Friday so it's close to that long now. I appreciate how fast you saw me and on such late notice. Thank you for your time."

"Sounds good." He stood, his smile still blinding.

Montana gulped big breaths of fresh air when she stepped out of the building. What a disappointment. Never had the scent of New York street grime smelled so good. She was going to investigate further to see if she could find a place less glossy... and less expensive.

She wanted nothing more than to go home but she had to stop at the Coop to pick up her phone. Suzette had Montana's cellphone number memorized but she wasn't certain Suzette knew her landline number by heart.

The sky was darkening and as it did, city lights flickered on. Since it was such a pleasant evening, she walked to the Coop. It gave her time to think about B.J. Gold and Associates.

When she reached the Coop, she was surprised to see Al. "What are you doing here? I saw Jackson earlier but I thought you didn't work weekends. Your wife is going to think you have a girlfriend on the side if you keep working these long hours." She winked at him.

"Hi Tana," he greeted her with a worn smile. "It's been hard with Tony gone. They didn't want to hire a temporary worker for only a week so we're all putting in extra hours until he returns. Besides, in this city, who can't use a few extra dollars? Believe you me, my wife would rather have the money than me at home." He looked at her with concern. "What are you doing here on a Sunday night?"

"I left my cellphone upstairs. I'll just be a minute."

"Seems we can't live without them these days," he said. "Who would have thought of having a mobile phone thirty years ago? I have to wonder if they've improved our lives or if we're now slaves to them."

"Hard to know," she agreed.

"Say, Montana, you did hear from Suzy didn't you?"

Her face darkened. "No. By now, I'm pretty sure something is wrong."

"Gosh, I hope not. Did you go to the cops?"

"I did but they're not much help in our situation, you know." Montana gestured up to the building. "I've decided to hire a private detective."

Al nodded. "That's the way to go—find someone who will devote all his time to finding her. You will find her, Tana—don't you worry."

She gave him a quick hug. "Thanks, Al. I appreciate all you do."

As soon as she stepped into the apartment, she heard noise in the back, which alarmed her. It didn't concern her that the lights were on because Hanky had set up automatic lighting that turned them on and off at various times of the evening so it was never apparent they weren't home at night.

The Coop had a gun. At first Suzette and Montana resisted the idea but Hanky persisted and after time, the women relented. She crept into the kitchen; an area only used for serving drinks. They kept the gun in a drawer closest to the apartment's entry. She opened it with a steady hand, searching until she felt the familiar cold metal. Picking it up, she transferred it to her other hand. At first, she had insisted upon keeping it unloaded but Hanky convinced her that an unloaded gun would be useless in a real emergency. Now she was glad he did. She was comfortable handling it since they had all taken gun safety classes. Hanky had insisted on that too.

With the loaded gun, she tiptoed down the hall. The noise originated from the security room and there were lights beneath the door. Faint music played in the background. Her heart pounded. Who was there?

The door ajar, her martial arts training was automatic. She kicked the door open, the gun ready for business. Someone shrieked. When she saw who it was, she dropped her hand.

"Hanky," Montana exclaimed, collapsing into a chair with relief.

"My God, Montana, you almost gave me a heart attack. Why are you here?"

"What am I doing here? What are *you* doing here?"

"I haven't been able to stop worrying about Suze. I decided to watch the surveillance tapes. I thought they might hold a clue." He looked miserable. "I can't think about anything else."

Montana stood and enveloped him in a big hug. "Of course you're worried. I'm so sorry I haven't updated you. I've been meaning to but things have been so hectic and stressful. I'm discombobulated. The cops are as useless as tits on a bull. The officer I spoke with refused to take a report yesterday and I doubt it will do any good when I file one tomorrow. They only run active investigations for children, the elderly, or those with mental issues. Without evidence of foul play, the NYPD has no basis for an investigation for a missing call girl. It's so frustrating"

"Did you tell them about the Coop?" he asked.

"I had to. If I'm not honest, how can they help? It likely affected the importance he placed on Suzette's disappearance, though. Maybe it was coincidence but right after I told him about it, he seemed to lose interest. I'll still file a report tomorrow. They'll take it but my guess is he'll just put the information in their database. He pretty much told me they wouldn't have any kind of active investigation. Those databases are only useful when they are trying to identify a dead body. In a small town it might be different, but not in Manhattan—not for a call girl."

"That sucks," Hanky said with disgust.

"I decided to hire a private detective. That's why I'm in the neighborhood. I was here earlier to pick up the client Rolodexes. I think I left my phone here so I stopped to pick it up."

"Smart thinking to hire a private investigator—but you're a clever woman. Did you hire someone yet?"

She shook her head. "I only checked with one agency that was open. I didn't like the feel of it at all. The office was slick—right out of a glossy architecture magazine—so we're talking expensive real estate. You should have seen their suite—plush white leather and chrome—designer everything. I was afraid to sit down after riding the subway. Of course, they pass that cost on to their clients. The investigator I spoke with looked like a model for a toothpaste commercial and he sounded like a sleazy politician."

Hanky laughed. "Ugh. That sounds awful. They were open on Sunday?"

"That was the main reason I went to them. I felt impotent so I decided to go for a run. While jogging, it dawned on me to hire a PI since the cops aren't going to do anything. It's weird, Hanky. I went through Suzette's computer and found a password-protected journal. Nothing else is password protected except that one folder. I need someone to help me get into that journal because it might hold some clues. Would you know how to do that? You're so good with technology."

"Sorry, Montana—I wish I could help but I have no idea how to hack into a computer. I know how to set up networks and can troubleshoot technical issues but my skills aren't that advanced. I'm sure you tried every password you thought she might use."

She nodded. "I spent hours working on it. That's why it dawned on me that I needed real help—someone who is being paid to help."

"I agree. What's your plan now?

"I want a hardworking detective who isn't all smoke and mirrors. I want someone who's down to earth—someone who'll work hard and not just for the money but because he cares about his work. Whoever it is can't be judgmental about our business. Mostly, I want a person who understands the significance of Suzette's disappearing without a word—who won't just blow her off as a flaky call girl. I'm also hoping to find fees more reasonable than B.J. Gold and Associates. They charge $500 an hour. My retainer would be gone in sixteen hours."

Hanky burst into uncontrolled laughter. "Oh, this is rich—B.J. Gold and Associates!" He held his belly, which got Montana going, and the two of them laughed until tears streamed down their faces. It was a much-needed emotional release. Although a grim subject, it was good to laugh.

"The irony was not lost on me either." She wiped away the tears of laughter. "I thought it might be a sign from God or something."

Hanky was now under control. "Sounds like with that first place you'd be paying for their designer duds—and you know how I feel about that crap." Hanky had grown up in a blue-collar family. "I'd rather go naked before wearing clothes with a designer's name plastered all over them. I'm probably the only gay man on the planet who doesn't like designer duds. I take it you're not going to go with the one you just saw."

"Definitely—I came up with lots of hits when I did a quick search. I do need to act fast, though. B.J.'s did offer one useful piece of advice, that time was important. He said the cops find most missing people within forty-eight hours—the successful ones, anyway. I'm exhausted so I'm heading home. You should do the same. Don't spend all night working. You look like you could use a good sleep."

He gave her another hug. "So do you—so go home and get some. We're gonna find Suze."

14

SHE ARRIVED HOME tired and hungry, but again, had no energy to cook. Normally, she enjoyed cooking. As well as a stress-reliever, cooking was satisfying. You could complete an entire job in a few hours. So much of her life involved long-term goals that worked on the promise of delayed gratification. She went through the stack of menus for the second night in a row. Comfort food called out to her. She ordered eggplant parmigiana, along with side orders of baked ziti and salad from her favorite neighborhood Italian restaurant.

While waiting for the delivery, she brought her computer back to life. B.J. Gold's site still filled the screen. She hit the back button and scrutinized some of the other sites. The first several looked almost identical to the slick B.J. Gold & Associates site. She clicked on the next page of hits and went in order down the list. None caught her eye until she saw a link for O'Malley Private Investigations—the name caught her eye.

In Buffalo, the O'Malley family ran the neighborhood corner market. That Mr. O'Malley had been a kind and gentle man. He'd known Montana's family was poor and probably sensed she had a tough home situation. When her mother sent her to the market, Montana was often short on money. Mr. O'Malley would offer a kind smile and say, 'That's close enough, honey.' He always threw a few pieces of candy in the bag, knowing she had no money for the goodies in the glistening glass containers. Since a name was as good as anything else to go on, she clicked on the page.

O'Malley Private Investigations
Former NYPD Homicide Detective
Specialties: Insurance Fraud
Background Checks
Missing Persons
Surveillance
We Offer Free Consultations
Sliding Scale Fees
tomalley@omalleyinvestigations.com
212-555-3781

The site was far from slick but it was clean and easy to navigate. The more she scrutinized it, the better it looked. It had a homey quality, as though he had designed it himself. Another promising thing jumped out at her. Even though she was furious with the NYPD, her gut told her that a former cop could have beneficial connections. She realized she had never even asked Ross Bertolino about his credentials. She dug the B.J. Gold pamphlet from her bag. One page listed all their investigators. With over thirty detectives, they had only one a former cop and he was in New Jersey.

O'Malley's detective agency listed missing persons as a specialty—another good sign—as well as sliding scale fees. He also offered a free consultation, which was what sealed the deal. She called right away even though it was a Sunday evening. She doubted he'd answer but hoped he'd call first thing in the morning. After several rings, his voicemail answered. No lilting voice here—the accent was gruff—and pure Brooklyn.

"Hello, youse have reached O'Malley Investigations. I can't take yah call right now but if youse leave yah name, numbah, anna brief message, I'll call youse back as soon as I can." Montana smiled at the strong accent. *Youse, numbah*—she liked his voice.

She left her contact information on his voicemail. As she considered calling a few other sites, her food arrived. Setting the containers on her kitchen counter, the enticing aromas changed her priorities, and she dug into the feast.

She turned on the television. The top story was another CM victim. The police had just released her name—Charlotte Candee was only seventeen years old. Even at that tender an age, she had quite an impressive arrest record for solicitation and minor drug offenses. Montana thought of her grieving family—did the media need to release that information? What relevance did it have to the murder?

Then Max Constantine took the podium. She recognized him from past press conferences. His mouth formed a line of grim determination as he spoke about the NYPD's urgency to solve the murders. He again seemed to withhold judgment on the victims—never once bringing up her profession or prior arrests.

He was good looking, no question about that. Tall and lean, his thick dark hair had just enough silver to give him a distinguished air. If not for a faint, jagged scar on his forehead, he would have been too pretty. The scar gave him a rugged look. He started to speak with the same confidence she'd noticed during earlier press conferences. She turned up the volume.

We're asking the public for leads," he pleaded. "We have a person of interest. He drives a late model, dark town car.

He's a white male in his thirties to mid-forties. I'm appealing to everyone, including those prostitutes he targets. Perhaps you or someone you know has already interacted with him. If someone meeting this description *does* or *has* approached you, do not get into his vehicle. Back away and call the number on your screen. I cannot stress this enough: we have no interest in arresting anyone who comes forward. Your information is confidential and it may lead to a Crimestoppers reward. We advise women to stay off the streets. If you do, we recommend you see only those customers you know well."

Deep lines creased his haunted eyes. She could tell the case was eating at him. His concern seemed genuine; he didn't seem judgmental. She wondered briefly if he were single—but shook off the foolish thoughts. When the story ended, she turned the television volume back down. Just as she was digging into another helping of food, her phone rang.

"Hello." She put a forkful of ziti aside.

"I'm lookin' ta speak with a Montaner Wylde." She smiled, having recognized who it was from his answering machine greeting.

"This is Montana Wylde."

"Did I catch you at a bad time?"

"Oh no—this is fine. Thanks so much for calling me back Mr. O'Malley. Your timing is fine."

"How did you know it was me?" He sounded surprised.

"I recognize your voice from your answering machine greeting. Mr. O'Malley, if you don't mind, I'll cut right to the chase since I'm in a hurry to find someone. I need a private detective and fast. Your site said you offered free consultations. How soon could you meet with me?"

"Please call me O'Malley—everyone does. What kind of service are you looking for? If you prefer to tell me in person, I understand."

"My best friend and business partner has been missing for two days now. I need someone to help me find her."

"Did you go to the police?"

"The cops can't help, which is why I need a private detective. It's a little complicated. I guess I'd prefer to explain further in person."

"I understand." She heard papers rustling. "Lemme see what I got tomorrow. Morning isn't good but I'm free in the early afternoon. Can you to stop by my office at 2:00 p.m.?"

She checked her schedule. She had a 9:30 appointment with Officer McCarty and an 11:00 session with her long-term regular Paul. Returning downtown by 2:00 would be no problem. "That works great. Are you still at 35 Worth Street? And is there a suite number?"

"My name is next to buzzers 1A and 2A. Buzz 1A. That's my office."

"I appreciate that you can see me that soon."

"No problem," he replied. "See you tomorrow."

Understanding that desperation often colored a positive first impression, she was still hopeful. Even over the phone, O'Malley's seemed a better fit than B.J. Gold and Associates. Another positive was that he was just around the corner. Perhaps she should have asked about his fees up front, but somehow, she doubted they would be as high as the ones Ross Bertolino had quoted. B.J. Gold, she thought, with a snort. Who would seriously name a company that—even if his initials were B.J.?

15

FOR THE FIRST NIGHT since Suzette had gone missing, Montana slept through the night and awoke refreshed. Sheer exhaustion, and perhaps an intuition that she was on the right track with O'Malley, had defeated her previous insomnia and she'd slumbered without nightmares. She was up early and eager to tackle the day.

She'd had the presence of mind the previous night to set her coffee on automatic brewing. Now the aroma filled her apartment. She filled a large mug, doctored with heaping teaspoons of sweetener and a generous dollop of cream.

She showered and chose a casual outfit. She pulled on a pair of indigo skinny jeans, topped with a crisp white shirt. She pulled on a pair of knee-high black leather boots and a butter-soft leather jacket. For good luck, she tied her Nana's vintage Hermès scarf around her neck.

Outside, the bag lady's orange fright wig greeted her as she rounded her building's walkway. The eccentric woman was going through a nearby dumpster. They'd become common in the neighborhood with all the reconstruction in Superstorm Sandy's wake. Jackhammers, saws, and whirring machinery created the cacophony of a street symphony.

As Montana started down the street, she caught an odd sight. For once, the bag lady hadn't shouted a single obscenity at Montana. She was busy harassing *another* young woman. Now this was a first. Until today, Montana had never seen the woman shriek at anyone else but now she hurled her usual insults to another young woman. One thing was certain. The woman could cuss with the saltiest sea dogs.

The bewildered young recipient was getting an earful too. "Slut! Whore! Yeah YOU goddamn it—YOU mutha-fucka muthafucka muthafucka. I'm talking to you, you WHORE!"

The young woman on the receiving end of this assault was not as seasoned as Montana. She hurried away, her face pink with embarrassment, while fear glimmered in her eyes. Montana gave her a sympathetic shrug. "It's not you. I live here and she screams at me almost every day. I think she's harmless."

"I'd rather not stick around to find out." She bustled off.

Montana wondered what the bag lady would do if she just walked up and introduced herself. Would it change the woman's opinion of her? She looked at the sad woman with pity. No one should have to call the street home. The pov-erty of the homeless population was a sharp contrast to the wealth that only the privileged few enjoyed.

During Montana's early days in the city, a deranged man had relieved himself on a street corner next to the Drift Inn. Horrified, Montana had urged Bing to call someone to help the man, who so obviously had mental problems. Bing had waved her off. "Ignore the loonies, Montana—ignore 'em and move on. You'll get used to them soon enough."

He'd been right. Soon she adapted to New York's tough environment. The homeless were invisible to most resi-dents. They were white noise—in the background but not noticeable unless they called attention to themselves like the resident bag lady. She noticed Montana just as she was rounding the corner and made a feeble attempt at harassing her, but Montana had already disappeared.

The bewigged woman sat on her usual stump, her eyes keen to warn others. Rosie had once been a beautiful young woman, perhaps even more so than the dark haired one she saw each day. Rosie had tried cautioning her—to warn her of the time thief that stole from the young as he had with Rosie. Time had taken her youth and beauty... and finally, it stole her hope.

Although Montana never realized it, the bag lady once spotted her after she'd gotten out of a limousine one night—a rare occasion when Montana had allowed a client to drop her a block from her home. She'd moved into her loft only a few weeks previously. The bag lady had seen the thick wad of bills that exchanged hands as Montana gave her client a hug goodbye. After that, the insults commenced. Rosie remembered when men did this for *her*, though they no longer did. It had been many years now but once she'd had lots of money until mental illness, alcoholism, and time had robbed it her of it.

Why didn't someone tell her that the sea of money would dry up? If they had, perhaps life would be different. That's why she screamed at the woman, cautioning her. Rosie's mission now was to warn others. She took a long swig from her small bottle of MD 20/20 and settled in for another day... watching and warning.

Montana arrived uptown with time to spare. The precinct was much quieter on a Monday morning than it had been over the weekend. She gave her name to a different receptionist. This time, Officer McCarty appeared within a few minutes and led her back to his cubbyhole.

Before they had a chance to begin the report, a sharp rap on cubbyhole's inner wall drew their attention. Montana was startled to see Max Constantine peering in. She hated herself for blushing but he was even better looking in person.

"Hey Darryl—those reports in order for this afternoon's meeting?"

"Almost, Max. I'll have them to you by noon. That okay?"

"Sounds good." Max glanced at Montana and then turned to McCarty with a pointed look.

McCarty took the hint and smiled. "Montana Wylde, meet Detective Max Constantine. Max, Ms. Wylde is filing a missing person report on her friend." He held out his hand. "I'm sorry to hear your friend is missing."

"Thank you," Montana shook his hand. Remembering about his marital status only the night before, her cheeks flushed with embarrassment. "It's nice to meet you." She still found herself checking if his left ring finger was unadorned. It was—although that wasn't conclusive evidence.

His eyes lingered on hers a moment longer. "Likewise—good luck." He turned to McCarty. "See you later, Darryl."

Montana cleared her throat, cheeks still pink. Reaching into her bag, she pulled a manila envelope out. "Here are some pictures of Suzette."

"I'd hoped you would have heard from her."

"I think it is unlikely," she murmured. "I don't know why this is hard for you to comprehend but if Suzette *could* contact me, she *would*—and long before now. I'd rather not waste any more time. Can we just fill out the report?"

He reached into a file cabinet, dug out a document, and pushed it toward her. "Let's get on it then. Fill out these first two pages until it says 'Official Use Only.' Then I'll scan the report into the database along with a couple of the photographs you brought us." He shook them out of the manila envelope. "It's great you brought in both head and body shots," he said, glancing through them. "That can be important."

In her neat handwriting, Montana printed Suzette's description and gave the demographic information. She was truthful about everything, including the address of the Co-op. Only the parts she didn't know did she leave blank, such as what Suzette had been wearing. She finished writing and handed the report to him.

He hesitated. "One thing I need to ask. You said neither one of you had pimps. Has that always been the case? If she *has* run into trouble, her old pimp may have decided it was time for her to return to him. In most cases where foul play is involved, someone close to the person is involved, such as an ex-boyfriend... or in her case, an ex-pimp. Are you sure she never had a pimp?"

Now Montana took a long pause. "She had one early on but she was only sixteen at the time. She's twenty-eight now so that was twelve years ago. She was alone and scared. She knew no one in New York so she did what many runaways do. She hooked up with the first person she thought might help and protect her. His name was Flash—her first and *only* pimp—but that was a long time ago. She's no dummy. She wasn't with Flash long. Even at sixteen, she knew he was trouble. So she escaped. She stashed a little money here and there and when she saved enough, she left him for good. She's never had another one."

"What if Flash saw her and tried taking her back?"

Montana was incredulous at the suggestion. "It was twelve years ago. Please see past whatever your stereotypes are. Suzette is a professional woman. We *both* are. You may not approve of our profession but we run our business the right way. Suzette left that creep Flash and she never looked back."

"What if he ran into her? Suppose he decided to give it to her good for leaving him." He gestured to the photos still scattered his desk. "Flash lost a moneymaker when she walked out. Maybe he holds a grudge."

Montana considered this. "That's improbable if not impossible. She doesn't even look the same. He would never even recognize her today."

"Well, that shoots down that possibility." McCarty glanced at the report Montana had slid across his desk. "This seems complete. As I mentioned, I'll put this into our missing person database. We'll take it from there. I'll let you know if anything develops."

His quick dismissal shocked her. "What do you plan to do to find her?"

He gave her a gentle look. "Montana, we'll file that report both here in the city and into NaMus, the national data..."

She cut him off. "I know what that is—I googled it yesterday. So you aren't going to *do* anything proactive to find her?" Her heart dropped. She realized that coming to the precinct—putting their business in danger was nothing more than busywork—the report was nothing more than an illusion to make her feel less impotent.

McCarty paused. "There's not much else we can do at this point. The report and photos will go into the database. I have to recommend that you shut your business down right away."

"So coming here was a waste of my time."

"No it's not. If we come across someone meeting your friend's description, this is how we'll identify her. And since she'll be in NaMus that means any jurisdiction has access to that information."

"That means when she turns up dead you'll be able to identify her." Montana tried to control her fury. "Seems like a poor way to run a police department—as though you're administering a flu vaccine to a person who already has pneumonia. The purpose of the police is to protect and serve *all* residents of this city. Does that only apply to those whose professions are palatable to the NYPD? Officer McCarty—will you give me an honest answer? If Suzette were a member of New York's Social Register, what would you do? Would you file the report away in your invisible database? Let's not kid ourselves. Your interest in Suzette took a downward turn when you learned of her profession." Her passion was clear.

He chose his words carefully. "Try to view this from our position. Hundreds of people go missing every day in this city. Most turn up. There is no evidence that she didn't leave of her own volition. We don't have the resources to investigate every missing adult unless there is evidence of foul play."

Montana was deflated—and defeated. The police were no use to her—that much was certain now. She prayed her face-to-face impression of O'Malley would be as good as the one on the phone. She needed someone on her side. It was clear she wouldn't find it within the ranks of the NYPD.

Montana stood. "I know it's not up to you personally. I suspected you wouldn't be able to do anything after our first meeting. Still, I had to try. Believe me on this, though, I'm going to find my friend with or without your help. I'm hiring a private detective even though I shouldn't have to. I pay *your* salary." Her eyes pierced into his shocked eyes. "That's right—I pay my taxes, which means *you* work for *me*. I expect better service from my employees." She gave her hair a good toss before leaving the maze of cubbyholes.

Outside the precinct, a sea of on duty taxis flooded the midday traffic. Her customary ballpark whistle got immediate results as a taxi pulled up to the curb. She turned off the annoying backseat television, wondering what genius came up with *that* idea. She tried to relax in the backseat, watching hundreds of busy New Yorkers bustling about their day.

Life was so different since Suzette's disappearance. Before Friday, she wouldn't have given the tangled labyrinth of people a thought but she now viewed them as an enormous human haystack. How could anyone find one missing person in the midst of so many? Still, as she had ever since Suzette disappeared, she scanned each passing face, hoping for a glimpse of the curvaceous blonde-haired woman.

The sheer number of women meeting Suzette's description left her gobsmacked.

16

HANKY WAS IN THE BACK SECURITY ROOM when she arrived at the Coop, focused on the surveillance monitors. Montana gave him a quick hug. She didn't have much time before Paul's appointment. She had almost scratched it altogether but he was such a longtime regular. She considered him a friend as well as a client. She didn't have the heart to cancel.

Paul wasn't the only client she thought of as a friend. While everyone, even regulars, paid for sex, in some cases their relationships evolved beyond that. Early on, she had realized many men not only want a *piece* but *sought peace* as well. The sexual element often took twenty minutes or less but Montana made sure her clients all got their money's worth. She started each session with a massage, coaxing her stressed clients into relaxing. She offered a sympathetic ear when needed. She was a good listener and people opened up to her. Clients told her about problems involving spouses, children, or work. Depending on the need, she was a psychologist, a sexual therapist, a confidante, and often, just a good friend; she was a chameleon.

She soon learned how 'normal' most clients were. Only a few were on the fringe, such as Harvey-the-Pie-Man—and even he was harmless, a successful attorney who just happened to have a fetish a bit stranger than usual.

Before she started the business, like most people, she thought only the desperate would seek out a call girl. She figured they'd have to be obese or foul smelling. She now realized with some irony how much her own early stereotypes mirrored those of Officer McCarty.

After a month of escorting, she realized how wrong she had been. Any client they allowed in the door was clean and attractive, as Steve had been from that long-ago night at the Algonquin. They were all successful. They had to be to afford the Coop's stiff prices. She thought most women would find the majority attractive and desirable.

At first, this confused her. Why would attractive and successful men seek the services of call girls? The reasons were as varied as the clients themselves. Some were married and loved their wives but the sex wasn't what it had once been. They weren't eager to start messy relationships with coworkers or friends so the anonymity of a professional appealed to them.

Montana had much insight into the human psyche, understanding the different views that men and women had toward sex. Women emotionalize sex—even casual encounters—and most men don't. Women make love with their minds as much as their bodies but men can enjoy a purely physical encounter. They enjoyed sex without the complications of love. Women tended to blur those lines.

As usual, Paul arrived on time. While he showered, she checked in with Hanky, letting him know everything was kosher. In a million years, she would never suspect Paul of harming her, but until Suzette turned up, she and Hanky would take no chances.

Paul was half-erect in anticipation when she walked into the bedroom. Montana had changed into erotic lingerie: a lace-up corset, a push up bra, thigh high black stockings, and red 'come fuck me' pumps. She dimmed the lights.

She started with a massage. A legitimate school had trained both her and Suzette and they'd obtained city licenses after completing their Associates degrees in massage therapy. They knew the importance of legitimizing their business and displayed their licenses in the front parlor in case inquisitive vice cops stopped by.

She poured a small amount of oil into her palms and rubbed them together. She began with his feet, caressing each toe, and then rubbing the known erogenous zone of the instep. She worked up his legs, over his buttocks, until she was rubbing his back with firm fingers, coaxing his muscles into relaxation. Then she teased him. She alternated between light butterfly strokes of her fingernails with rubbing his muscles. Soon, his tension drained.

After she finished his back, she nudged him to turn over so she could rub the front of his legs, arms, and chest. Her fingers danced down his body, tickling his chest and working toward his still-damp pubic hair. She stroked his engorged cock with one hand and began rubbing his balls and anus with the other. He groaned, begging her to take his throbbing member in her mouth.

She took her time, her tongue flicking in and out down his chest, her nimble lips kissing every inch of him. She deftly reached under a pillow to retrieve the hidden condom and put it in her mouth where she rolled it down over his cock without missing a beat. He was hard and stimulated. She worked him into a frenzy, flicking her tongue on the underside of his erection. Soft as a whisper, she skimmed the top with her tongue, enticing and tempting him until he groaned in unreleased agony. Finally, she took him deep down her throat.

When he could take it no longer, she took excruciating time lowering herself over him, inch by agonizing inch. He yelped in painful pleasure when she took him completely, riding him as a rodeo queen might tame a wild horse. At last, the agonizing pleasure was too much and he screamed in orgasmic pleasure at the release.

After, Montana nestled in the crook of his shoulder as her fingers played with his chest hair. He stroked her hair and held her close.

"How's the studying going?" Paul asked.

"Could be better," she admitted. "I've been distracted."

"Anything I can help you with, Montana?" He was one of the few clients who knew her real name. He took her chin in his hand and turned her face toward him. "You're worried about something."

"Just pre-exam jitters." She wasn't about to talk to any client about Suzette.

"Are you going to make the next exam deadline? I'll keep after you until you do."

"Believe me," she laughed, "I know you will." She kissed his cheek. "Thanks for everything, Paul. I mean that."

He was whistling when he left the Coop.

17

AFTER SHOWERING, Montana realized she had just enough time to make it downtown to meet O'Malley. Not wanting to risk noonday traffic, she took the subway. The train was right on schedule so she arrived at his office twenty minutes early. She stopped at the corner coffee shop and ordered a double mocha latté and a chocolate croissant. She was famished. She had eaten only two bites of a stale bagel along with coffee that morning. She sat at a high window table, enjoying one of her favorite city pleasures: people watching. New York was a never-ending sideshow.

At two minutes to the hour, she headed to O'Malley's office. The hearty brick building was an old stand-out from the years before developers glossed over Lower Manhattan. His building was a sharp contrast to the glossy chic of B.J. Gold and Associates.

She pressed the buzzer for 1A and waited. No response. She strained to remember—he had said 1A hadn't he? She pressed it again and heard it buzz so it was working. On the off chance she'd misheard him she pushed 1B. No luck with that one either. She squinted at her watch. She was exactly on time as always. Still, she understood most people were not as punctual. She paced the sidewalk in front of the building.

At fifteen minutes past the hour, she started becoming annoyed. She had tried not to feel too optimistic until they met but his tardiness disappointed her nonetheless. Being late to their first meeting wasn't a good first sign.

Just as her good feelings about him were evaporating, a disheveled man rushed down the street. He caught up with her in front of the building. Despite herself, she smiled. O'Malley wore a hat worthy of Philip Marlowe, askew in charming fashion. A cigarette hung from his mouth. If someone asked her to draw up a picture of a Raymond Chandler private eye, she would describe O'Malley. She towered over him in four-inch heeled boots.

"Would you happen to be Montana Wylde?" he asked, out of breath while holding his hand out for a shake. With his strong accent, it came out, *'Would youse happen ta be Montaner Wylde?'*

She put her irritation aside, shook his hand, and gave him a broad smile. True New York accents were becoming nonexistent. "I am. You must be Mr. O'Malley?"

"Like I said, call me O'Malley." He turned the key in the slot and looked back at her. "Mr. O'Malley was my pop, may he rest in peace."

With so little space between them, she caught a whiff of stale alcohol—the odiferous remnants of last night most likely. Although familiar, it wasn't comforting.

Inside, the office was small but neat—about as big as her bedroom. The primary furniture piece was a battered but magnificent maple desk that looked like a real antique. If someone took the time and energy to refinish it, it would be gorgeous. An ergonomic black leather chair sat behind it with two mismatched easy chairs on the other side. The far wall housed two large file cabinets and a studio-size refrigerator. The braided rug that took up most of the floor gave the office a homey feel.

He gestured for her to sit. She took one of the chairs across from his desk and studied his face. It told a story of harsh miles on a rough life journey. Angry spider veins burst against his pallid complexion. His eyes were a study in patriotic pride: red-rimmed whites against startling blue irises. Silver streaked what once had been dark red hair. He was of medium height but his paunch and poor posture gave him a stouter appearance. It was hard to tell how old he was since the booze had an obvious effect. She estimated he was around sixty. Still, the more she studied him, the more she liked his face. Beyond the bags and lines, his eyes were kind and warm.

O'Malley and his office were polar opposites of B.J. Gold & Associates. Moreover, comparing Ross Bertolino to O'Malley was a study in incongruity. O'Malley had no flash whereas Ross Bertolino of B.J. Gold exuded ostentation. Montana infinitely preferred O'Malley's hominess. She wasn't disappointed that his office was rundown or that the furniture didn't match but she was concerned about the alcohol emanating from his pores. That he was almost thirty minutes late for their first meeting didn't inspire much confidence either.

"Sorry to be so late," he said apologetically. "It took longer to get back downtown than I expected."

She appreciated his apology. It indicated consideration. He hadn't been *that* late—no more than Suzette often was. She had to admit that she was annoyed more easily during the last few days than usual.

"No problem. I know how city traffic can be." She decided to start fresh from that moment.

He reached into his desk and brought out a small device. "Do you mind if I record our conversation? It's easier than taking notes and this way, I can just listen and let the recording do the heavy lifting. I'll take a few notes for questions I have."

"That's a smart idea." It dawned on her that neither McCarty nor Ross Bertolino had done that. It was a good first sign.

Montana repeated the story. She brought up the Coop right away. As Ross Bertolino had the day before, O'Malley registered no shock but patiently let her complete the account of Suzette's disappearance. She ended by telling him about going through the emails, the client files, and VIP cards.

Finishing her story, she looked him in the eye. "At this point, I'm stuck. I pulled out all of Suzette's VIP client files from our Rolodex but I don't know how to figure out who they are. I also don't know how to begin going about finding her. Can you help me?"

O'Malley leaned back in his chair, studying the ceiling for a long pause. "If you hire me I'll do my best. I want to be upfront, though. Sounds like you know your friend and her behavior well. If she is as considerate and levelheaded as you say, she's likely to have run into trouble."

Montana stared at him as grateful tears filled her eyes. For all his tardiness and disheveled looks, he was the first person other than Hanky to think Suzette was in danger. Even reeking of cigarettes and booze, he could tell Suzette was no flake. O'Malley understood right away that she had not run off with a high paying customer nor had she returned home, as McCarty had suggested.

Sitting in his rundown office, she made a quick decision based on a hunch. O'Malley would be her private eye, based on nothing but instinct and a healthy dose of desperation.

"I agree," she said, her voice weak with relief. "She *is* in trouble—I feel it deep in my bones and I have ever since she was more than an hour late. I should have called you sooner. Can you start immediately? What kind of retainer will you need?"

"Hold on—let's talk about this a bit more." He looked uncomfortable. "Trust me when I say I have no judgment about your business but weeding out potential suspects could take time and I work by the hour. You know she was supposed to meet a VIP date but you have no idea if she saw that client. You don't even know who the client is. I just want to be honest with you about the potential hours your case could involve. I don't want to give you false hope, either."

"I do know she saw the client. I spoke to our building's door attendant who worked last Friday and he saw her get into a town car around 10:00 a.m. Other than that, there isn't a lot to go on but I'll pay you for your time—that's not my first concern. What *is* important is that you devote a good deal of time to this case—that you make it a priority. I'm worried too much time has already passed."

He leaned back again, staring at the ceiling once more. Though he would never admit as much to her, his business was slow. His drinking had gotten in the way since he'd first hung out his shingle. He mostly worked for insurance companies—catching those who tried to defraud them. The work was tedious, unlike the meaningful cases he'd had as a homicide detective. The insurance gigs and his police pension allowed him to live a comfortable, albeit frugal existence but the cases didn't motivate him.

He also didn't often draw clients who looked like Montana. His shabby office and appearance turned most off. He had enough self-awareness to know that the booze didn't help. Why was she was so anxious to hire him?

She was unlike most hookers he had met—and he had encountered more than a few. She was obviously intelligent—perhaps educated. Her vulnerability made him want to protect her—and they had just met. She intrigued him—and the case captivated him. For the first time in a long while, he was hungry to dig into a significant investigation. He wanted the gig—he just didn't want her to know how much.

"I usually charge one hundred and fifty dollars an hour. I'll be honest with you—an hour goes by fast when you're looking for a missing person in a complicated situation."

"Your website said you offered a sliding scale. How do people qualify for a lower price?"

"By being a low income client—and based on what you told me about your business, you wouldn't fall into that category." He looked at her curiously. "I have to ask—why ask for a sliding scale? You make good money—say, there are no drugs involved here are there?"

"Of course not." She was indignant. "Mr. O'Malley, I have money, just not unlimited funds. The money is good but I've made some significant investments so I'm not cash rich. Plus, I've shut down the Coop so I have no money coming in."

He rolled his eyes. "Like I said, call me O'Malley. Look, I don't mean to insult you but I need to know what I'm getting into before I agree to take your case. By the way, it's smart you shut your business down. It's the first piece of advice I would give you. If your friend is in trouble, your business could have led her to that trouble, which means you could be in danger. You must be careful from here on out."

Montana ignored his last statement when an idea hit her. "Mr... I mean, O'Malley, how about if you and I work together. I could do a lot of the legwork..."

"No way." He cut her off. "This is hazardous work. Plus you haven't any experience with investigations or the law."

"Yes I do." Now she cut him off. "I just finished law school—Columbia, as a matter of fact. I'm preparing for the state bar exam now."

While the Coop hadn't registered a blip on O'Malley's radar, his eyebrows now shot up in astonishment when she mentioned law school. He looked at her with open admiration. He'd known there was more than met the eye. He gave her a wide smile that lit up his face like sunshine on a hot summer day. When O'Malley smiled, the years of rough miles slipped away. The pallor and broken veins from his nightly indulgences disappeared. Like the kindness in his eyes, O'Malley's smile was genuine and warm. On spot, she decided she liked him a lot.

"Well ain't that something," he chuckled. "I didn't think anything or anyone could surprise me at this point. *That's* where the money has gone. I knew you were a smart girl—seemed like you had it together from the get go. I never thought you were a drug addict either—you don't fit that mold. Now I know why you don't remind me of a hooker. Because you're not a hooker—you're a lawyer although I'd be hard pressed to know the difference sometimes." He chortled at his own joke then became serious again. "But it won't work—I can't have you partner up with me. I would be liable if anything happened to you."

"I'll sign any release you need—and I won't do anything dangerous. You won't be liable. I'll do background work. I can save you time and me money. I'm a great researcher and I'm not too good to run errands or file paperwork. I'll help with your other cases if you spend more time on Suzette. I *do* know the law. Besides, I have to do something to help. Since I closed our business, all I do is worry. I haven't been able to sleep and my appetite is gone. I promise you won't be sorry."

He studied her pleading eyes. Montana took this as a good sign and continued. "The cops are worthless—oh sorry—you used to be one—but they haven't been helpful to me. I filed a joke of a missing person's report this morning. It'll only be useful if the cops need to identify her dead body—unless we find her first. The officer said that without foul play, they couldn't waste department resources. You're perfect. You used to be a cop. O'Malley—I need you."

"I don't know." He looked at her with doubt. "I never had a female partner."

"Hello, O'Malley, it's 2014," she exclaimed. "It's about time you did. Give me one week. If it doesn't work, I'll stop and pay full price. Give me one chance.

"Sheesh—you are relentless. The CIA oughta hire you to interrogate terrorists—they wouldn't stand a chance." He gave her another long look. "I'll tell you what. You can secure my services for a two thousand dollar retainer. We'll stretch that out with your help on paperwork and research." He raised his hand as he spotted the excited flush in her cheeks. "Now hold on—this is probationary status only. We'll see how it works and reevaluate as we go."

"Thank you so much. You won't regret it. I'll work harder than you can imagine." She beamed at him.

He rewarded her with a wide smile in return. "Oh—and one last condition."

"Name it." Montana grinned at her victory.

"When you're this big time attorney, I get free representation from you. Or at least you represent me on a sliding scale." He winked at her.

Montana laughed. "You got it. Where do we start?"

"We start by retracing her last steps. See, your instincts told you where you should start. We always start with who last saw the missing person. Since they hooked up last Friday, that would be the high roller you mentioned. Any way of knowing who that is?"

"None whatsoever. We rarely discussed our work—especially VIPs because we know those clients so well. In fact, we only do outcalls with regulars if we've seen them several times at the Coop first. I didn't question Suze on the client she saw on Friday because I understood that she knew and trusted him."

"You mentioned something about pulling Suzette's VIP cards. What are those?"

Montana told him about the Rolodexes, how she and Suzette labeled each card with a photos, checkmarks, and dollar signs.

"That was smart of your security guy to put photos on the cards. So that means we should at least have a picture of the Friday VIP."

"I was going to mention this next." She frowned. "Suzette has two VIP cards that have no photos. One client Suzette has seen for over ten years so he predates our business opening. That can explain why he has a card with no photo if he only does outcalls with her. The other card troubles me. His card only dates back four years so he should have come to our business at least twice—and usually three or four times. There's no reason he should not have a photo. The mandatory in-calls are an unbendable rule because I once had a client snap on a bad outcall."

"What if Friday's VIP snapped?" O'Malley was solemn. "It happens. We need to get in touch with him. Do your clients give their contact information?"

"Most clients give us a burner cellphone or a web based email address they can hide from their wives."

"I'll need the VIP files ASAP. I also need to see your friend's apartment. And I want a look at her laptop. I should go there right away. Can you meet me at Suzette's place tomorrow around noon? You can bring the client files then."

Montana checked her cellphone's calendar. "I have a 1:00 appointment so that won't work. Can we meet in the morning instead?"

"I'm not much of a morning person but I can make it by 10:00. Will that work?"

"It will." She snapped her fingers as a memory loomed. "Suzette's laptop is at my place but I'll bring it to her apartment tomorrow. I forgot to mention this but when I went through Suzette's computer, I found a password-protected file for Suzette's journal. It's under a non-protected folder she labeled 'Personal.' None of her passwords will unlock it—and that's another strange thing. I have passwords to everything: bank accounts, credit cards, computer logins— even her brokerage account. I can't figure it out."

"Perhaps I can hack into that file—and if I can't, I know someone who can."

As Montana was writing him a check for two thousand dollars, something else occurred to her.

"One reason your ad drew me was that you used to be with the NYPD. I thought that could be helpful. Do you mind if I ask how long you were? Also, why did you go off on your own?"

His demeanor took a nearly imperceptible shift at her questions. He stood and took his time walking to the front window of the office. When he spoke, his voice was low and somber.

"I was with the force for twenty years," he replied. "When my wife died, I needed a change so I decided to strike out on my own."

Montana was perceptive—she was no stranger to men who held secrets. There was more to his story but she wouldn't pry. She rose to leave. "Well good enough, then.

I'm so glad I found you, O'Malley. I feel better already. Thank you—for everything. Is there anything I can start on?"

"Think of anything that might lead us to the identity of her last outcall."

"I'm already on it, boss." On impulse, she kissed his cheek—out of relief and gratitude.

He walked her to the door. "Now I have a question for you."

"Shoot," she said.

"Did you interview anyone else before me?"

"B.J. Gold and Associates," she replied.

He snorted. "What made you choose me?"

"You are the only person I've talked to who seemed to grasp the danger Suzette is in. You got that she didn't run off to Europe with some big spender or go home to her abusive family. It helps that you don't have any attitude about our business. Also, I once knew a kind man named O'Malley." He *did* remind her of the Mr. O'Malley of her childhood—the one who let a little girl slide when she was a couple of dollars short—and who always slipped some candy in her bag.

He opened the door for her. "See you tomorrow, partner."

Montana walked back to her loft since it was so close. Rounding her corner, a whiff of something delectable reminded her how hungry she was. The aroma beckoned from a favorite neighborhood food truck, Philadelphia Phil's Cheesesteak. It was a popular spot for the local lunch crowd. The food was legendary and had placed third in that year's prestigious Vendy Awards. Montana waited with her usual patience in the long line. Fervent foodies were always willing to do this for exceptional fare. She ordered the truck specialty: a twelve-inch hoagie piled with thin-sliced roast beef, dripping with tangy cheese and onions. She took her food to a picnic table behind her building and enjoyed watching people against the backdrop of the Hudson River. She ate every bite, enjoying the satisfaction of hiring O'Malley as well as eating with real hunger for the first time in days.

When she got home, she again focused on Suzette's VIP cards. Suzette had thirteen such clients, including the two without photos. Of those thirteen, all but four had either an email address or a telephone number.

She spent the next hour talking to, leaving messages, or emailing the VIP clients. Of the four she spoke with, their unabashed surprise at her call convinced her that none of them had seen Suzette last Friday. As she emailed the others, she received three return phone calls within an hour. It was obvious that each of these clients cared for Suzette. All expressed concern and astonishment when they learned Montana had not heard from her for several days. Whether it was premonition or just common sense, Montana was certain none of the clients she spoke to was Friday's high roller.

She scrutinized the information on the two cards without photos. 'John' was likely a pseudonym. His card contained nothing but the mandatory symbols as well as a list of dates, cities, and names of high-end hotels. She glanced through the list: St Regis, Rome, Four Seasons, Florence, Claridges, London. Montana strained to remember the vacations Suzette had taken in the last few years. She'd gone on at least one client trip to Italy last year but she'd not said much about it and Montana hadn't thought to ask. The card contained no contact information.

Suzette had labeled the other photo-less card with a single letter, 'J' without any other identifier to his name. Beneath that, she had written 'VVIP-NYC.' All high rollers were VIPs. What made this particular client a VVIP? The extra V meant nothing to Montana. She couldn't recall Suzette ever talking about someone who would deserve such status. Listed below this obtuse information were rows of dates in Suzette's tiny crimped handwriting. The first date entered was June 12, 2010. Their final outcall was exactly a month before Suzette's disappearance.

She stared at the card, willing it to reveal more. Something was off—the dates, the lack of information, the VVIP status. Just as she was about to give up, she noticed a pattern. Excited, she opened her computer's calendar and scrolled through the months and years. There *was* a pattern. Suzette saw this client every second Friday of the month. She grew more excited when she realized that Suzette's last outcall was the second Friday of April. If Suzette and the client stayed on the same pattern then they would have had a date on the day she vanished. Her instincts were now afire. She was now almost certain that whatever happened to Suzette had something to do with the card before her.

She separated this card from the others to show it to O'Malley the following day. She was wound up, anxious and unsettled. The loft was stifling and bending over the client files had cramped her muscles. She needed air—and exercise. Nothing got rid of tension like a good, hard run. The fresh air in her lungs and oxygen in her blood would clear her mind. It was later than she usually ran. It was getting dark but there would still be others on the trail at this time.

She changed from her comfortable pajamas into cropped running pants and a fitted shirt and zippered light hoodie. It had a built in arm pocket, into which she slipped her smartphone and keys. She laced her shoes and rushed outside, eager for an invigorating run.

Outside, she gulped deep breaths of air. The bag lady was no longer keeping watch; she must have moved on to another spot.

But someone *was* watching as she disappeared down the path leading to the Hudson River trail. He congratulated himself for having the foresight to cover his tracks. He also applauded his brilliance at making certain he would stay a step ahead of everyone else, including the brunette slut and the incompetent NYPD. It was of utmost importance. Anyone engaged in war knew that one must know the enemy's move before they did. And as in every war, there has to be collateral damage.

Everyone knows that.

18

O'MALLEY HADN'T EATEN before meeting Montana. Heck, he never ate breakfast, unless you considered a black cup of Joe armed with two shots of Dewar's a meal. In fact, before their appointment, he'd been at The Corner Bar—its real name—to calm his trembling hands. This was starting to happen too much lately. But as usual, the double-shot and beer back did the trick. He managed to steady himself as much as possible after his previous night's bender.

He spent the rest of his afternoon continuing to reclaim his equilibrium by sipping black coffee spiked with Dewar's Scotch—just enough to soften the edges. The sun was setting as he finished writing the expense reports and invoices for two cases he'd closed. His grumbling stomach reminded him that he needed to eat.

New York's best pizzeria, Stromboli's, was six blocks away so he decided to walk. As he strolled, he considered Montana Wylde. She intrigued and impressed him. It was clear she was no dummy—working her way through law school was extraordinary. And he'd be willing to bet she'd pass one of the country's toughest bar exams on the first try.

In his own way, O'Malley was as perceptive as Montana. It was why he'd been such a good homicide detective. He wasn't all that surprised that she made money the way she did. She was, after all, a beautiful woman. What astonished him was that she hadn't drowned in the dangerous waters surrounding such a profession.

Even more extraordinary was working her way out of the business. She shattered all the stereotypes. It seemed that Suzette Peterson had as well, which made her disappearance even more troubling.

The first immigrant male O'Malley offspring, Sean, started the family tradition of being a cop with the NYPD. Sean joined the force when Theodore Roosevelt was the Police Commissioner. Since Sean's tenure, every O'Malley male had followed his lead, each rising to the top. Tommy O'Malley always knew he would be a cop. And as his relatives before him, NYPD superiors promoted him earlier and more often than most of his peers.

By thirty, O'Malley had earned his gold detective badge. Soon, he led the homicide division of the organized unit, as had his father before him. The mob tried every tactic to bribe O'Malley but his integrity was unquestionable. No one could buy him. He and his team brought down many of the newest generation of the Mob, including high-ranking soldiers from both the DeLuca and Granada families. But had he known the enormous price he'd have to pay, he would have quit the force—family tradition or not.

One terrible April night, O'Malley came home and found his beloved wife Sylvia and their two young daughters dead. Although the NYPD could never prove it, mob soldiers had shot all three, execution style. No one who had information would name the killers. Witnesses dreaded mob retaliation far more than they feared the cops. Those who hadn't already been murdered or arrested took no chance at ratting out the bosses or their fellow soldiers. New York's District Attorney never even made an arrest. It was a constant festering wound in O'Malley's heart. Every time April rolled around, the pain was all consuming.

After finishing his huge slice, Stromboli's owner, Giuseppe asked where he was heading next. O'Malley told him The Corner Bar, resulting in their usual banter—a takeoff on Abbott and Costello's famous comedy routine, 'Who's on First.' The Corner Bar was O'Malley's favorite non-NYPD haunt. While he sometimes enjoyed the camaraderie of cop bars, he often preferred the company of civilians. Tonight he needed time alone to think about Montana Wylde's case.

The Corner Bar's patrons consisted mostly of functioning alcoholics. Like O'Malley, some wanted a quiet place to ward off their demons. If Montana and O'Malley compared notes, they would see striking similarities to the Drift Inn and The Corner Bar. In both, customers were acquaintances rather than friends.

They were 'white noise' people—whose presence was a calming background influence but who never intruded on one another's personal space or thoughts. They couldn't become close because most didn't remember their previous conversations. Each night was a different take on the same scene, their shared elucidation found in a shot glass.

O'Malley nodded to some of the regulars as he took his place on his usual stool. The bartender brought him a shot of Dewar's and beer back automatically. Taking his first soothing sip of scotch, he pulled Montana's client files from his briefcase. Soon lost in stories about Harvey the Pie man's fetish and Edgar's lost dildo head, O'Malley threw his head back and roared. Laughing was good—especially in April.

19

ONTANA WAS AGAIN PROMPT for her meeting with O'Malley at Suzette's the next day. Again, he was late but this time, it didn't surprise or annoy her because she expected it. When he rang Suzette's buzzer at 10:20, he didn't look as healthy as he had the day before. Still, she'd seen his intelligence and competence at their first meeting. Until his behavior demonstrated otherwise, she was going to stick with him.

She peered at him. "Jesus O'Malley—with those bags you don't need luggage."

"Huh?" He held up his hand. "I told you I'm not a morning person. You were the one who wanted to meet at the crack of dawn."

She rolled her eyes. "It's hardly the crack of dawn." She looked closer and saw a troubled portrait of alcoholic behavior—one she knew well. The gray pallor, spidery veins, ruddy cheeks, and red nose all indicated there was more than social drinking going on.

As he walked into the apartment, she caught a whiff of stale booze and cigarettes—reminiscent of her childhood. Too many mornings Montana would awaken to find her mother passed out on the couch, with empty whiskey glasses and overturned ashtrays next to her. Montana hoped

O'Malley's malodorous greeting wasn't an indication of early morning drinking but she nonetheless suspected his thermos held more than coffee. She'd known this upon hiring him, though. He'd smelled boozy the day before and was still sharp, wasn't he? Besides her gut still told her he was the right man.

"Let's sit for a minute." She motioned to Suzette's dining room table. "I may have discovered something important last night—a clue as to who Suzette's Friday high roller might be. That is, I think I found his client card."

O'Malley rubbed his temples as he watched her dig in her bag. "You sure are perky. I haven't had such an eager partner in years. Course, I haven't had a partner in years."

She pushed several cards toward him, "Check out these cards. They have checkmarks, dollar signs, and letter symbols. Dollar symbols distinguish how much cash clients spend, checkmarks symbolize the type of session they enjoy, and the abbreviated letters give more information. See—they all have photos."

He thumbed through several cards. "Yeah—you explained the reasoning for taking the photos—smart girls." O'Malley gave her an admiring look.

"Credit Hanky, not me. It was his idea."

"Still impressive."

She pointed to one card. "See this one? The dollar symbols indicate he's a high roller and the two checkmarks means he likes normal sex. The letters on his card say something too. The L stands for lingerie, BJ means the obvious, and OS signifies he likes giving oral sex. So, we know that he's a big spender, who likes lingerie, blow jobs, and giving oral sex."

She pulled another card from a separate zippered pocket of her handbag. She handed it to him.

O'Malley looked at it and then turned it over. "Where's the photo?"

"That's just it—two high roller cards have no photos. Remember, I told you about those yesterday. As I mentioned before, one makes sense because Suzette's seen him for longer than the Coop's existence. Now look at this other one. According to the dates, Suzette has known this client four years. This means he should have been to the Coop several times and he should have a photo on his card. This is standard operating procedure and we *never* break that. The absence of the photo means he's *never* visited our business. I can't figure that part out because Suzette created these rules herself. Also strange, she's identifies him only with the one initial, 'J.' Then below that Suzette wrote VVIP. Why put two V's in the VIP? We don't identify clients that way."

O'Malley studied the card. "Maybe the camera wasn't working when he came in."

She shook her head. "That's unlikely. He'd have to have been to the Coop for at least two in-calls before going on an outside date and it's doubtful the camera could fail twice when as far as I know it's never happened before."

"Obviously he's a *very* important VIP." O'Malley's brow wrinkled as though willing the card to reveal more. "I wonder why she thought it was important to identify NYC below his name."

"That confuses me as well. We've never placed importance on where they live. It must mean something but what?"

"What makes you think this card is for Friday's high roller? The last date listed is March fifteenth."

She winked at him. "I wanted to see if you noticed something. I studied this card a long time because of its irregularities. That was how I caught the pattern of dates for their outcalls. Look—Suzette met this client on the second Friday of every month for the last four years: March 11, February 11, and January 14. It goes back to the same second Friday of the month for four years. Last Friday was April 8. That falls into the four-year pattern."

"Of course she would have updated the card after their date."

"Yes. Always after the session because clients can change what they want, how much they pay—anything."

O'Malley stared at the card. "You girls are smart, no doubt about it. The problem is that we still don't know who he is. Without a photo or meaningful contact information, he could be anyone in New York." He noticed her forlorn face. "Hey—don't get yourself down." This time he winked at her. "I've cracked harder cases with less information. We're just getting started."

"How do we know how to start looking?"

"We retrace every step she made on Friday. You talked to her that morning. The door attendant saw her getting into a fancy town car." His brow wrinkled. "Where do clients pick you up for outcalls?"

"At the Coop. Another hard and fast rule is never to give clients our home addresses."

"We need to speak with Al again—as well as Tony when he returns. Maybe they can help identify him. I'm a bulldog, Montana. We're going to find him."

Beyond the red-rimmed eyes and alcoholic breath, Montana saw a confidence that inspired her. "I believe you. Great idea to ask Al and the others what they've seen. After four years of outcalls, they could very well have useful information."

"Agreed," O'Malley nodded.

"But even if we do find him, I have a hard time believing this high roller would hurt her. I think something happened after their date and before we were to meet."

O'Malley shook his head. "I agree that it's doubtful but we can't rule him out. People go off the deep end all the time in your business. You all have been lucky—and you run a smart business. But don't assume Friday's high roller isn't involved."

"You may understand our business on a cop's level but I know our clients. Our regulars are loyal, particularly someone who's seen Suzette for four years. Several clients have fallen in love with her. I just can't believe a client who has been a regular for four years would harm her."

"Having customers fall in love with her—that's dangerous. The two greatest motives for murder are love and money—not always in that order. What if he *had* fallen in love with her and she shot that notion down, telling him there could be no future? Maybe he snapped. Obsessive and unrequited love can be damn deadly."

The hair on the back of her neck began rising. "I never considered that," she murmured.

"Why doesn't he have contact information like the others?" O'Malley shuffled through the cards as if he was about to deal them, Vegas style. "Most others do."

"That frustrates me too," Montana replied. "Lots of things with this card don't fit protocol. I was so excited when I found the pattern but now it seems worthless."

"No, this is good. There are clues—valuable ones. We have the initial J then VVIP and a list of dates. It gives us a starting point."

"True."

"Montana, investigations take patience. It's tedious. Now our next step is to crosscheck her computer to see if someone with the initial J sent her an email."

She pulled Suzette's laptop out of its case and handed to him. O'Malley fired it up as Montana pulled a chair up beside him. "What's her username and password?"

"The username is suzettep and her password is psuzette, all lower case.

"Not exactly genius," O'Malley muttered. "Have you girls heard of identity theft? Any burglar could get into this thing with that brilliant username and password—he doesn't even need to know how to hack. Once he's in, he drains her bank accounts, gets her credit card information, and may even steal her identity."

"We'll tell Suzette that when we find her," Montana said drily. "I've been through a lot of her email and there didn't seem to be anything significant in those but I didn't go back that far. More intriguing is that password-protected journal."

"I'll go through the emails later then. What folder did you find it in?"

Montana pointed to the shortcut for 'Personal' on Suzette's desktop. "It's in there."

O'Malley opened the folder and began clicking away. As he worked, Montana walked around the apartment. Suzette's absence was profound. Montana sensed her everywhere—could almost feel her spirit in the apartment. She sent out a telepathic message asking her friend to give them a clue.

As she stood staring out the kitchen window that overlooked the adjacent apartment, she saw Suzette's neighbor brewing coffee. He smiled and waved when he saw her. She gave an absent wave back. Although they'd previously met, she didn't remember his name.

O'Malley called from the living room. "Say, Montana—can you come here?"

O'Malley was shutting down Suzette's laptop. "What's up?"

"I can't crack this code with my skills but I know someone who can—in probably less than five minutes." He fished in his briefcase and pulled out an external hard drive. "I'm going to make a backup of her hard drive. That way, you can just plug it into your computer and access her files. I hope my buddy can crack the password-protected journal because that could be important. Tonight, I'll crosscheck her VIP clients against her business emails from the last several weeks to see if I can come up with anything more about last Friday's date."

"Sounds good."

"Another thing—do you have the surveillance tapes from last Friday?"

"Not from the Coop's cameras. Since, Suzette was gone for the day and I saw only regulars, Hanky wasn't in."

"Your security guy must not make much money. After ten years aren't most of your clients regulars?"

Montana made a seesaw motion. "While we do have many regulars we always have new clients just like any business. Not all clients become regulars—and some stop coming by for one reason or another. Hanky works part time for us but he's also a personal trainer at the gym down the street. Hanky's real ambition is to make it in the theater. That's how Suzette met him—they were in the off-Broadway show, *Bring on the Cheers* together."

"I heard of that show but never saw it. I'm not much of a theater guy."

Montana smiled. "Your loss—they were both great."

"Now back to the cameras—does your building use surveillance? Many do after 9/11."

She snapped her fingers. "You're right. It does. The door attendants run them."

"We need to talk to the attendants ASAP. Most cameras run a loop of several days—maybe a week—before overwriting the film. I'll give your building's door attendant a call later today to see if they still have last week's film. Why don't you ask them to hang onto the tapes from last week and let them know I'll be calling so they aren't surprised. Since the high roller picked Suzette up at your business, those tapes could be valuable."

"This is why I hired you. I should have thought of that myself," Montana said with admiration.

"I'd still like to talk to Hanky and maybe go through some of his past tapes. They could be useful. Do you know how long he keeps them?"

"No idea," Montana replied. "You'll have to ask him."

"Let's head over to your business."

Montana glanced at her watch. "I can't. I have an appointment with a regular. In fact, I need to get moving or I'll be late. Can you meet me at the Coop after my appointment? You can talk to the door attendant about the surveillance tapes while you're there. You can talk to Hanky too unless he has an audition or training session. He'll do anything to help. He's loves Suzette too."

"Thought you said he didn't come in for regular clients—and also didn't you say you'd shut the business down?"

"It's open for only two more clients and they are exceptions. As far as Hanky being there for a regular, before last Friday he wouldn't have come in. Since Suzette went missing, Hanky and I both think he should be present for these last two appointments, even though I know both well. We don't know who to trust until we find Suzette."

"Gotta say it again—smart people." He winked at her.

"That's right," Montana winked back.

"So, I gotta question for you."

"Shoot."

"You keep referring to the Coop, which I already assumed is a name for your business. Let's see how good my detective skills are—Coop stands for chicken coop—you know, as in chicks?"

Montana laughed. "Chicken coop? No. You'll get to know us better. We would never name our business after a chicken coop. Coop is short for 'cooperative.' We called it the Co-op at first but after a while it just became the Coop."

O'Malley returned her laugh. "Co-operative. More women in the business should follow your lead. Hey—maybe when you retire from your law career, you can write a self-help book for call girls. You can call it, "A Call Girls' Guide to Wealth and Education."

She burst out laughing. Although she had known this man for only twenty-four hours, it felt as if they had known each other all their lives. Again, she was certain she'd made the right call in hiring him.

They agreed to meet three hours later. O'Malley was on his way to meet his computer whiz friend at his old precinct, while Montana hailed a cab for her date with Paul. She relaxed in the cab. Her gut told her she'd made the right choice with O'Malley. Before, she had been alone and anxious. It was comforting to have someone with such experience and background in solving important cases. Even more compelling was a notion that Montana couldn't shake: O'Malley had a deep and urgent need in him to solve this case.

20

SHE MADE IT TO THE COOP with only ten minutes to spare before Otto was to arrive. He was a long-time client or she would have canceled. He visited the Coop as much for companionship as sexual gratification. In fact, sex with Otto was almost nonexistent. Not that he was impotent or unable to become aroused like some clients with medical conditions. Otto achieved an erection each time she saw him but he refused to have intercourse with anyone other than his wife. Montana was a form of organic Viagra. She aroused him, which in turn, allowed him to perform better with his wife, which made her happy. Otto considered it a win-win situation for all. As they say happy wife, happy life.

Hanky was in the back room when she arrived. She asked him to stay after Otto left, explaining that O'Malley wanted to talk to him about the security system. As she expected, he was happy to help.

Al, who was working the door, called to let her know that Otto was on his way up. Montana and Suzette tipped the door attendants well for their discretion.

Otto's thing was watching Montana dance. Aside from that, he was all about romance. He never failed to bring Montana a gift. On this day, he didn't disappoint and greeted her with an exquisite vase filled with two dozen long-stem white roses.

"Hi sweetie." He kissed her cheek.

"Otto, these are gorgeous," she exclaimed.

"Not as beautiful as you." He studied her face. "You feeling okay, honey?"

"Just a little stressed—I've not been getting enough sleep lately but I have plenty of energy for you. Come on back," she winked at him.

"Where's your beautiful sidekick?" Otto asked. He sometimes saw Suzette if Montana was unavailable.

Montana led him to his favorite room. "Suzy is taking some time off." She left it at that. O'Malley was certain she made the right call in not telling clients anything about Suzette. He viewed everyone as a potential suspect.

One of the Coop's policies was that clients shower before their sessions. They enforced this rule except for a small number of exceptions. Otto was one such because they never engaged in any sexual act.

While Otto relaxed on the bed, Montana dressed in another room. She chose a red and black lace corset with a matching garter belt. Sliding the silky stockings up her legs, she attached them to the belt, and then stepped into a pair of black and red stilettos.

Opening the door to Otto's room, the mellow glow of candlelight cast a sensual ambiance to the room. She pushed a button and seductive jazz filled the room.

She began with an erotic massage, pouring oil onto her palms, caressing every inch of Otto's body. She worked the tension out of his shoulders with strong, nimble fingers. She massaged his arms and felt his muscles relax. She rolled him over, finishing with his legs, inner thighs, and buttocks. Turning him over again, she teased his stomach, thighs, and pubis with light touches from her long fingernails. Otto's breathing became rapid. When she finished, he was erect.

She began the show while Otto sat up on the pillows watching as his hand worked on his erection. She shook her hair from its loose bun allowing the dark waves to caress her shoulders. She touched herself, rubbing her erect nipples peeking above the corset's demi-bra, delicious dark berries against creamy skin.

She undid each hook sensually, revealing more of her well-shaped breasts until they bounced free. The corset hit the floor and she began an erotic dance, teasing and caressing her body. She removed her garter belt, stockings, and stepped out of the tiny G-string. Wall mirrors cast her reflection around the room. At last, she stepped up to a pole in the middle of a small stage, its audience the person on the bed. She climbed it, twisting her body over and then sliding down. Her legs opened wide, revealing every inch of herself. Around the pole she twisted, moving up and down, her legs splayed out. Her body stroked the pole—as though she were making love to it.

After, she moved to the bed and lowered herself within an inch of Otto's face. He cried out in delight as she worked her fingers in and out of herself. She moaned and gasped, pulling her fingers in and out, rubbing them against herself. She worked herself into a believable sounding orgasm and then moved off the bed.

Montana clicked another button and the music stopped. She turned the lighting up just a bit, signaling the session had ended. She gathered her discarded clothes, allowing him privacy as he dressed.

"That was a great show as usual, Tana. Thank you."

She blew him a kiss. "I'll be back to collect you in a few minutes. Take your time—no one is waiting for the room."

Several minutes later, she walked Otto to the door. Before leaving, he pressed an envelope into her hand. Like Harvey-the-pie-man, he had earned the privilege of paying after the session.

Although Otto hadn't noticed it, worry about Suzette distracted Montana during the session. She was thankful to have no more scheduled. She put a new message on the answering machines, letting customers know the Coop was on vacation.

Hanky joined Montana in the parlor, where she was ordering two corned beef sandwiches from a neighborhood deli. Though she hadn't had an appetite since the past Friday, she needed to eat. Just last night she could slide her skinny jeans off without unzipping them. She had also noticed her collarbones protruding. Even Otto commented on her thinness. She still wasn't hungry but her stomach growled—a reminder that she needed fuel to keep up her strength. She'd not be of any help to Suzette if she collapsed from exhaustion and hunger.

She showered while waiting for the delivery. The timing was perfect. Just as Al called to say the delivery was on its way up, she finished dressing. As they ate, Montana filled Hanky in on O'Malley, the surveillance videos, and the Rolodexes.

"Sounds like he knows what he's doing." Hanky took a big bite of sandwich.

"He's good. I googled him. The city gave him a ton of commendations for his heroism and service while with the NYPD. I learned more about his personal life too, and it's so sad. Someone murdered his wife and daughters about ten years ago. The reports were clear that it was the mob because they were execution-style hits and O'Malley had worked homicide with the organized crime unit. The NYPD never arrested anyone because no one would go against the mob. That had to have devastated him. I think it's why he drinks. He quit the force as soon as he'd made his twenty."

Hanky gave her a side eye. "While it *is* tragic about his wife and kids, a drunk private detective doesn't sound like a good idea."

"I didn't say he was a drunk. He drinks—most likely too much and perhaps even during working hours. It's hard to tell. He reeks of it in the morning but I think it's from the previous night. He's good, Hanky—he knows what he's do-ing—and I liked him right away. He's comfortable and down to earth—not one bit of pretentiousness. He's quick, despite the drinking. The bonus was that he's the only one, other than you, who grasped the severity of this situation. He knows she's not some flaky hooker. Moreover, he's not judgmental about the business.

"That way the cop made you feel." Hanky shook his head.

"Bingo." She aimed her finger at him.

"Did you tell him about law school?" The last of the sandwich disappeared into Hanky's mouth.

"I had to. I wanted to help him with the investigation and he wasn't having any part of that until I told him I went to law school." She laughed. "It was pretty funny. The Coop didn't register a blip on his radar but when I told him I was studying for the bar exam, his jaw hit the floor."

"What are the cops going to do with the report?"

"Nothing. What a waste of time. The officer just reiterat-ed how they can't do anything without signs of foul play."

Al interrupted them to say that O'Malley had arrived.

"Thanks, Al, Please send him up." She shrugged. "You can judge for yourself."

Montana opened the door for O'Malley, who greeted her with a lopsided grin and fresh whiskey fumes. Montana had an unblocked view of Hanky from his position on the couch. She pantomimed bringing a glass to her lips while rolling her eyes. Hanky stifled his laughter and smiled back at her.

They spent the next two hours talking, with O'Malley recording it all. He explained to Hanky that his memory wasn't precise and that his handwriting was illegible. He brought up another interesting point: he said he recorded people to see if they changed stories. If they did, he could refer to a recording. Montana thought that was a brilliant idea. She looked at Hanky as if to say, 'see?'

Hanky led O'Malley to the security room and gave him all the existing recordings he had. It amazed Montana that he kept all tapes for two months.

"Why so long?" she asked.

"Now that everything is digital, it's easy. Today, you can record years because computers have so much memory. Now I wish I had kept the tapes longer. If she's been seeing this same high roller on a particular date each month, we could have checked back for years."

"Your tapes might not be helpful for Friday's high roller, though," O'Malley interposed. "His card has no photo so we have to assume he's never been here. But those tapes could still be useful. We can't assume Friday's high roller had anything to do with her disappearance. It could be any one of your customers or just some nut on the street. Can you burn me copies of the recordings?"

"No problem," Hanky replied. "It'll just take a minute."

Montana looked at O'Malley. "Did you ask Al about the surveillance tapes from last week?"

"I did. We're in luck because Tony overwrites the tapes each Monday. That would have been yesterday but since he's on vacation no one thought to change the film. He gave me all the tapes he has. If we're lucky, we might get a glimpse of the high roller. We need that kind of lucky break."

"That would be awesome. So, where do we go from here?"

"I go through her computer files to look for emails that might match the faceless 'J' from the high roller card, since we assume he *was* her Friday date due to the dates on the cards. I'll also review the surveillance tapes—both Hanky's and the building's since she met the client here."

"Yes, this is another firm policy. With outcalls, clients must pick us up from here. We never give our home addresses to anyone. If we have a late night outcall, they drop us off near our homes but not at our address. You know, I just thought of something. Suzette's building has a small coffee shop—you may have noticed it this morning, O'Malley. We should talk to Bruno and Vinnie—they own the shop. Maybe they saw something or somebody suspicious."

"I'll check that out," O'Malley replied.

"Another thing I should mention. When I left to go to the Lazy Turtle, I noticed an empty gift box on the kitchen counter. It was from an expensive store. It had to have been for Suzette. I threw the box away but I wish I had kept it. If we had figured out where the box came from, we might have been able to contact the store to see if they remembered anything about sending a gift to this address."

"Try to remember the name of the store or company from the box," O'Malley said. "All we need is the name—at least to start."

"I'll try to remember it." Montana shook her head. "It was a glossy white box, with black and white layers of tissue. Oh, and if you want to talk to Vinnie and Bruno, I can give you their number."

"Nah—you always want to talk to people in person. It's hard to know if people are being truthful on the phone. When you talk face to face, you gauge body language, facial expression—all that. I'm not saying Bruno or Vinnie would have any reason to lie but it's a firm policy of mine. Most people aren't good liars when someone looks them in the eye."

Hanky handed a jump drive to O'Malley. "Here you go, boss."

O'Malley nodded up at him. "Thanks. We'll see what comes up. I have a buddy at the precinct who works the photo lab. I can get his help if I need it. If I see a clear image of Suzette with last Friday's client, I'll have him run it through the database for a match."

"Facial recognition software," Montana nodded.

"That's right," O'Malley said. "Today's technology is amazing. I was working when 9/11 happened. After that, Homeland Security scrambled to develop all kind of software to identify terrorists. Now, anyone with an arrest record is in that database—and it's an international one."

"That's great news. Anything I can do? Remember, we're partners."

"Try to identify that box. Go through the conversation you had with Suzette again and try to remember anything else that could be useful."

"I'm already on it, boss."

O'Malley looked at her with the kind eyes that first drew her. "I know you are." He was almost to the door when he turned around. "Oh—I almost forgot. I gave a copy of that password-protected file to Frankie—a pal from my old precinct. He said he'd have it cracked by the end of the night. The journal interests me a lot."

"Me too. It's funny, but so many things I keep learning about Suzette surprise me."

"Each person has a deep well of secrets, Montana."

"I think you're right."

After she let O'Malley out, Hanky took off as well. She did a final check of the apartment, the duty of the last person to leave. As she walked through to shut off lights, the Coop was suddenly stifling. She couldn't wait to leave. Her Nana would say a ghost had breezed in. Shuddering, she locked the front door. Too antsy to wait for the elevator, she skipped down the four flights of stairs until she reached the ground floor and ran outside, gulping fresh air. The Coop hadn't felt like home since last Friday.

Montana hailed a cab even though it was almost rush hour. She didn't feel like dealing with a crowded, smelly subway. Luck was on her side because a taxi pulled up as soon as she lifted her arm. She slid into the backseat, oblivious of the man watching her casually from across the street, his face hidden by an open newspaper.

After she disappeared into one of myriad of yellow cabs, the man watching her mused on how he planned to stay a step ahead—of everyone. He had no worries about the incompetent cops and their investigation, not even with bringing in their federal cohorts. He was already in position to keep abreast of that investigation.

The tall dark haired slut and pudgy investigator could be a problem though—for a less intelligent man. He had several ideas of how to keep them in check. He would monitor their movements just as he had with Blondie. It would require more disguises but that was what he was born to do. Broadway might not appreciate his talent but it was handy nonetheless.

He threw the newspaper in the trash and then got into the car. Before he sped off, he looked up a name on his smart phone and punched dial.

21

ONTANA WAS OUT OF SORTS—lonely. Without Suzette's presence, she now saw how dependent she
had been on their friendship. Spending years in
college and then law school, she'd not allowed her classmates to peer into her life. The loneliness would have been
unbearable had it not been for Suzette. Now without her,
the solitude was as profound as it had been during her early
days in New York.

Up in her loft and gazing at the trail lining the Hudson,
she knew how to clear her troubled mind. She changed into
her running clothes, dashed out the door, then scampered
down to the trail. With her earphones in place, she was
oblivious to the bag lady's interminable ranting.

She stretched her leg muscles, using the railing as support. Warmed up, she began at a slow pace and then increased speed until she reached a rapid sprint. Endorphins
flooded her system buoying her spirits. O'Malley had already made a lot of progress. Hiring him had been a good
call. After years in an industry that required finely honed
people skills, she was rarely wrong about people.

After thirty minutes of hard running, she dropped to a
steady jog, and then slowed to a walk. Before she went back
to her loft, she paused to admire the joyous burst of a fiery

sunset against an indigo sky. The remnants of sun sprinkled diamonds on the Hudson. The kaleidoscope of colors reminded her of life's everyday beauty that she too often took for granted. Through the growing depth of despair, the magnificent sky gave her a flicker of hope. She had O'Malley and he had a plan.

Before going home, she picked up some much needed groceries, which made her think of Suzette. Each Tuesday they shared a homemade dinner, taking turns on hosting. This week, Montana would have prepared dinner at her loft for the two of them.

The bag lady was back at it when she returned. Even with the harassment the woman heaped on her, Montana couldn't help but feel sorry for the strange woman. If the woman weren't so abusive, Montana would have handed her a few dollars on most days. Perhaps because it was so late in the day, the woman's weary tirade didn't have the same malice.

"Whore," the woman said in a feeble voice.

Montana smiled, waved, and nodded. Yep, that's right.

Upstairs, she changed into soft gray sweatpants, a light tee shirt, and her favorite leopard print fuzzy slippers. She laid out the groceries she would use for dinner and put the rest away. She worked on the salmon first, seasoning it with olive oil, and dressing it with dill, lemon, and salt and pepper. She put it in the oven to bake. She cut off a section of the baguette and warmed it in her toaster oven while she made a salad. In honor of her friend, she whisked up Suzette's favorite vinaigrette. Cooking was soothing. As she was taking her dinner to the coffee table in front of the couch to eat while watching some television, her cellphone rang.

"Hey O'Malley," she said amiably.

"I just sent you a file—Suzette's journal, no longer password-protected. Remember, I told you Frankie was a genius."

"That was fast," she exclaimed. "I'll dig into it right away. I sure hope it sheds some light on what might have happened to her."

"Yeah, I read a bit of it but it's hard for me to know a lot about what she's talking about because she uses a lot of abbreviations and I don't know who's who. One thing popped out right away that you never mentioned. "

"What's that?"

"Your friend was in love, or at least falling hard for someone."

"You're kidding." Montana was shocked.

"Read for yourself—maybe I'm wrong but it sure sounds like it to me."

"Wow."

"You okay?"

"Yeah... just surprised." She was flustered. "Thanks O'Malley—I'll look at the journal now. And please thank Frankie for me too."

O'Malley's revelation suppressed any appetite Montana had. She left her food untouched and went to her desk to open her laptop. When it came to life, she downloaded O'Malley's message with the file. She had a knot in her gut—one that had been growing with each piece of surprising information about Suzette's life. Her best friend had far more secrets than Montana could have ever imagined. Montana had her own secrets but none that she kept from Suzette.

The secrets hurt, but even worse, they scared her.

22

MAX CONSTANTINE was up to his eyeballs with the CM case—and it showed.

His partner, Joey Malone, cut to the chase. "Max—go get some sleep."

"Don't you start—I already got one lecture from my mother at our weekly dinner last night. I don't need another."

Joey shrugged, holding up his hands, indicating that he was backing off. He was right, though. These kinds of cases always ate Max up, especially late at night when he couldn't shut out the haunting eyes of the victims. He'd worked two serial investigations since his promotion to homicide and both had become personal. Nothing angered Max more than the most vulnerable of victims who could never stand a chance with their attackers. His mother always mused about his white knight syndrome, telling him he wanted to save the world. He didn't want to save the world—just future victims.

Those who were murdered were never mere statistics. He remembered the humanity in each. He knew each of their names, spoke to their loved ones, and learned who they were in life. He didn't back away from looking into a mother's pleading eyes and or allowing a father to unfetter his fury. He worked doggedly to give closure to the loved ones. The CM case was no different. It wasn't his job to judge the victims' occupations.

Mayor Burke's meeting had been productive. The task force included the finest of the NYPD and BAU detectives, as well as several undercover vice officers. The team included two seasoned vice cops, Sheila Prowse and Linda Collingswood. Both matched the victims' profiles—around the same weight and height. Makeup and wigs gave them the right coloring. They posed as streetwalkers on the strolls the CM frequented most. They were fitted with wires and had two backup units to protect them. They'd been out for several days, hoping to lure the CM into a sting. While they hadn't yet had a nibble, they'd just started to fish.

A phone call from Commissioner Durbin interrupted Max's thoughts. It wasn't a welcome one—yet another parishioner had discovered a victim. She was at the Trinity Catholic Church. Same scenario but a different venue where the maniac had left the victim in a wheelchair near the back of the Church. Like the others, she was in full stage makeup wearing an elaborate wedding dress. Max cursed as he hung up. He called to Joey and they agreed to meet at the scene.

Early responders had already taped off the church when Max arrived. A swarm of hungry investigators were dusting for prints and photographing the scene. Max shook his head in disgust. The CM had big balls to involve churches in his murders. Even nonbelievers were wary of tempting a possible vengeful God with their eternal fate.

Max approached the victim. Rigor mortis had set in, her limbs were stiff and unyielding. The extravagant dress had tiny buttons from hem to collar. Max gently undid enough of them to expose her rib cage and free her arms. He found the needle mark the creep used for placing the IV of poisons into her arm and the same type of crude incision he'd later used to embalm her. He snapped a few quick pictures on his phone for comparison to the others, later.

She had high cheekbones and good bone structure—was probably was once good looking but with all that makeup, it was hard to tell. It masked the ravages from the street. He rolled up her sleeve. No needle marks but that didn't rule out addiction. Many of the victims were crackheads. The toxicology report would render its final verdict on her drug of choice. If she worked the street, she most likely had a monkey on her back. Those without habits worked in safer, more pleasant environments.

"Hey Max." Joey walked up, nodding at the woman's body. "This fuck is amping up his rampage—just as the BAU said he would."

"Sure looks that way," Max replied.

"Where's our primary?"

"At the hospital. She was having a full-blown panic attack when the first cops arrived. Must have been one hell of a shock—you hope for a sanctuary and come across this instead." Max gestured to the body in the wheelchair. "When the hospital has finished treating her, someone will bring her to the precinct."

Joey still had his eyes on the victim. "I bet she's pretty without all that makeup. I wonder who she is—or was."

"We'll find out soon enough. Anyone who works the street has a sheet."

Max's phone rang. He answered and spoke for only a minute. "The witness is on her way from the hospital to the precinct. Let's book on out of here—we'll get her statement while it's fresh."

The two detectives walked out. "The world gets sicker every day, Max."

"That it does, partner, that it does."

23

MONTANA READ until long after midnight. Much of the journal was opaque because she didn't know many of the people—or couldn't figure it out. Suzette was prone to using abbreviations and other shortcuts. They made the journal difficult to interpret.

O'Malley had been right. Suzette *had* been falling in love. From what Montana could decipher it sounded as though the romance was just beginning to blossom. This new love interest surprised her. She and Suzette had both resolved not to involve themselves in intimate entanglements until they closed the Coop. They had talked about settling down at some point—but not now. Of course, life—and love—doesn't always heed our wishes. Sometimes, love happens when you least expect it. Aside from surprising her, the relationship bothered Montana on another level. Why would Suzette keep such important news to herself?

Montana's method for avoiding relationships was to thwart them before they had a chance. Suzette had tried to do the same, at least in the beginning. From what she had written, her paramour was not eager to become involved either. Suzette alluded to how they both were keeping the relationship secret, at least for the time being.

Suzette never referred to her love interest by name—not so much as an initial. Suzette referred to him as 'My Love' or 'Him.' For others, Suzette used the initials. Some were easy to interpret. For example, Montana was MT and Hanky was H. It took her a moment to understand that BOTC was Suzette's off-Broadway show, *Bring on the Cheers*. Suzette had been scared of someone, though—or was anxious about him at least. Suzette gave him the stark initial of C and Montana had no clue who this was. She surmised he was a theater acquaintance because of several passages in the journal.

> *C getting under my skin. Shouldn't have been so nice at BOTC auditions. Mistook friendliness 4 more. Not interested but C keeps pushing our shared theatre bckgrnd. Says it's destiny. WTF? Not attracted 2 him then or now. We have no destiny but I don't wnt to be rude, particularly bcuz of his connection to My Luv. C doesn't seem 2 get normal social cues.*

Montana racked her brain trying to think back to those auditions. She remembered them well because Suzette had made it so far into the callbacks and of course, had ended up in the cast—one of her first big breaks. But she couldn't recall anyone named C that Suzette had mentioned. There was another passage about her trepidation of this person as well.

> *Uh-oh. C not hppy abt My Luv and I finding each othr. Jealous? Could be. C is just creepy now. Doesn't seem to get I wasn't looking then and still am not.*

So, there was a person who was jealous of a love interest. Could that person have become so obsessed as to want to harm Suzette?

She also realized why Suzette hadn't told her about her love interest when she came to the passage that alluded they were keeping things on the QT.

Wasn't planning on love but He & I can no longer deny it. Just happened. Want to tell MT but My Luv swore me to secrecy. 4 now, we must hold off 4 one more (long) year. Then who cares what ppl think. This may b the performance of my life."

Montana read the passages several times, straining again to think who C might be. Could he be involved with Suzette's disappearance? Who could her love be? Suzette had revealed just enough to make Montana's growing knot of dread worsen.

Then it dawned on her to talk to Hanky. He'd been in *Bring on the Cheers* with Suzette so perhaps he would know. She'd make it a point to call him first thing in the morning.

She glanced at the clock—after 2:00. She was exhausted—and hungry. She warmed her untouched dinner in the microwave and watched the lights continue shutting off across the river. At this hour, there were again more dark spaces with the lonely and intermittent twinkling lights in the background. Which of those dark spaces had swallowed Suzette? Montana raised her glass of cabernet in a wordless prayer. Still, she couldn't shake off her fear that something horrible had already happened.

She cleaned up, poured herself another glass of wine, and curled up on the couch. Tension began easing from her neck and shoulders. For five days, she had swallowed raw emotions—fearful that if she released them she would be unable to regain control. The wine loosened them now and the past week's full force hit her hard. Heaving sobs shook her to the core. The anguish was visceral but also cathartic.

Each sob released some of the festering dread that had been just under the surface since last Friday.

It was good to cry. She seldom did and hadn't cried in front of another person until she met Suzette. When Buffalo's Child Protective Services removed Montana from her mother's care when she was six, her paternal grandmother had become the major anchor in life. Her Nana's influence ended far too soon, when she had beomce too old and ill to care for her. The state then returned an eight-year-old Montana to her unstable mother. When her beloved Nana died six years ago, in the assisted care facility that Montana paid for, Suzette had comforted her.

Suzette held and rocked her. "Let it all out, honey—just let it go. Sometimes we all have to hunker down and just blow snot bubbles."

Montana let it all go. Deep primal sobs erupted from her inner core. She cried until no more tears could come. As the pain subsided a bit, she hiccupped and gulped deep breaths. She lay, exhausted, staring across the Hudson. She poured a snifter of cognac and took it to the bedroom, hoping it would ease her to sleep. Before she had could take a whiff let alone a sip, slumber overcame her.

For a few blissful hours, she slept without dreaming.

24

WHEN MONTANA AWOKE, her first thought was of Suzette, as it had been every day since Friday. It was now Wednesday. Tonight it would be six days. *Six days.*

She went through her morning routine on autopilot, brewing coffee, toasting half a bagel, and squeezing grapefruit juice. She took her coffee and breakfast to her desk and speed-dialed Hanky. It went to voicemail. Most likely he was in a training session with a client. Hanky hit the gym as early as 5:00 a.m. to accommodate his busy clients' schedules. She left a message that she had sent him Suzette's journal and that they shuld catch up later after he'd read it.

She took her coffee over to the couch and just as she took her first sip, the phone rang. The name on caller ID made her smile. She hit speakerphone.

"I thought you weren't a morning person, O'Malley? What's up with the early call?"

"Your case," he said indignantly, "and several things we need to discuss. I'd like to hear your take on the journal but I also went through the surveillance tapes, your notes, and I discovered some interesting things."

She set down her cup, heart pounding. "What did you see?"

"Lemme show you. I want to see if you can identify something."

"A client?"

"I don't think so but there's a car that appears several times. It's hinky—you know what that means?"

"Of course. I've read plenty of cop books. What about the car?"

"It's a town car—the kind rich people use when hiring someone to take them to the airport," he replied.

"You said there were a few things. What else do you want to discuss?

"Too complicated to go into over the phone and besides, I need to show you. When can you get here?"

"I just woke up. Let me get dressed." The clock read 8:55 a.m. "I can be at your office in less than an hour—but you said you had a few things. What else did you find out?"

"Let's talk in person—and hurry—I'm going to need more coffee soon."

"I'm on it boss," she responded.

Montana dumped her coffee in the sink. Then she brushed her teeth, tossed her hair into a ponytail, and washed and moisturized her face. She applied a touch of makeup, threw on running gear, and sprinted out door.

Outside, she considered her options. O'Malley's office was nearly a mile from her loft. Running would be fastest. After a quick stretch, she dashed down the street amidst the morning traffic.

Fifteen minutes later, she arrived. O'Malley buzzed her in right away.

"That was quick. Why are you out of breath?"

"I ran," Montana replied between gasps.

"You ran—literally?" He pantomimed sprinting with his arms. His strong accent colored his words, *'Youse ran—litrally?'*

"Sure did." Montana gave his arm a playful punch. "Oughta try it yourself—a day at the gym wouldn't hurt."

"Fuhgeddaboudit—I hear that from my doc. Besides, we ain't here to discuss my health. Lemme show you what I found. I went through Hanky's tapes first—the ones from outside your apartment door. Those tapes aren't of much use—at least from what I see now—just shows Suzette, Hanky, you, and your clients coming and going. Oh, and some of the other residents who walk by your apartment door."

"But you said you saw something...?"

He held his hand up. "Patience, grasshopper. While *Hanky's* tapes yielded little, Al's tapes showed some interesting—and troubling—footage. Look." He slid a DVD into his laptop.

Montana watched the clip. "This is just street traffic."

"Hold on. Look at this car." He stopped the video, pointing to a car across the street from the Coop.

"So what?" She was impatient.

"Just keep it in mind for a minute," O'Malley said. "Now look at this." He consulted a pad and fast-forwarded to another spot.

Montana snapped her fingers. "It's the same car."

"Now you got it, Sherlock." He chuckled and winked at her. "Or Watson—since I should be Sherlock. Now look." He again looked at his notes and fast-forwarded to another location. "See here?"

"Looks like the same car." Montana frowned in concentration. "What does this mean?"

"Hold on—there's more." Montana watched Suzette walk out from under the building's canopy and then disappear from the camera's view.

Montana gasped. "That's Suzette—is this from last Friday?"

"No, from last Wednesday, two days before—you know. Now look here." After another quick consultation, he fast-forwarded again. "This one's from last Tuesday—watch."

The tape showed Suzette and her leaving the building. A moment later, the town car across the street took off.

"Yes, Tuesday. I remember," she said softly. "We take turns cooking dinners once a week. Last week was Suzette's turn. How often is the same car across the street?"

"I only have tapes for three days last week. On two, the car takes off right after Suzette leaves. And on Tuesday when you walk out together."

"Where is Friday's tape? That's the one we need."

"Bad news there I'm afraid. That tape is missing. So is the weekend surveillance. As Al told you, Tony, is on vacation and he normally works days. Al doesn't know what happened to Friday's or the weekend's tape. My guess is that someone forgot to run the camera on Friday and it went unnoticed until I asked Al about it."

"But Friday is the important one."

"True, but we're fortunate to have these and even luckier that no one overwrote them. Al said they usually overwrite the tapes each week, starting on Monday. It's a damn good thing Tony was on vacation or we wouldn't have this."

"But how can this help if Friday's surveillance is missing? This is just a car parked across the street that leaves when Suzette does. We can't even see who's driving. It's odd but not much to go on."

"Al noticed Suzette get into a town car on Friday. I want to show him these pictures and see if this car might be the same one. I'll talk to Tony when he returns because it's possible he's noticed more because he works days. He might not have seen last Friday but perhaps he's seen Suzette get into the same car at other times. It may shed a light on who that Friday client is."

"I still don't understand how this video can help—seems worthless to me," Montana said, dejected.

"Not worthless. This is how investigations work, Montana. We're piecing a puzzle together and that takes time. This tape is just one piece but it may help form a sketch of what happened last Friday. A piece here and another there and if you're lucky, a picture emerges. There's something else too—see that license plate?"

She studied the frozen tape. "Huh? It's impossible to read. Can you make the photo larger?"

"Sure but with my photo editor it's still unreadable." He maximized the screen until a blurry close-up of the plate emerged. He was right. She couldn't make out the numbers.

"I see what you mean—I can't read the numbers."

"The tapes aren't good quality—plus the car is across the street. But look here on the bottom of the plate—just below the number."

Montana gasped with excitement. "Does that say official?"

"Bingo—and the only official plates are those belonging to New York's city government."

"Government—whoa—could the Coop be under surveillance? That would explain why a government car would park across the street, although we have never..."

"No." O'Malley cut her off. "I worked vice for a time. They would never drive a car with official plates—that would tip off potential busts. Plus, the NYPD isn't going to waste their resources busting a place like the Coop. There's a ton of crime in this city. The cops would never prioritize the Coop."

Montana felt fuzzy. "I need caffeine. I only took a sip this morning so I could get here fast. Can I have some of yours?" She nodded at his thermos.

O'Malley gave her a crooked smile. "It's a bit stiffer than your normal brew. Tell you what—let's hit the coffee shop on the corner. I'll treat."

Walking along, Montana was thoughtful. "If the car isn't vice, I wonder whose it is."

"That's the million dollar question. I wish your building kept tapes as long as Hanky does because we can't establish any patterns with only three days of film. Don't lose heart, though—I have a couple irons in the fire. I also want your interpretation of that journal. I'm hoping you can shed some light on that."

"Ugh—the journal. I had a hard time deciphering her codes and abbreviations but Hanky may be able to help because that's how he and Suzette—doing theater—and I'm almost certain that she met her love interest in the theater—although I have no idea who he might be. What kind of irons do you have in the fire?"

O'Malley opened the coffee shop's door for her. "Let's grab a coffee and go back to the office. I'll lay out my ideas there."

Montana ordered a double mocha latte. O'Malley shook his head. "Here I was gaining respect for you, thinking you're a broad who's not all fluff and cotton candy. Then you disappoint me with a sissy drink."

Montana rolled her eyes. "O'Malley, no one says 'broad' to refer to women any more. Wake up and smell 2014."

"Oh yeah." He smiled at her. "Sorry honey. Is that better?"

She had to laugh as he turned and handed a thermos to the young barista behind the counter.

"I'll take an extra-large black coffee," he said, ignoring the pseudo European names printed on the large chalkboard. 'And my friend will take a... what did you say it was?" He turned to Montana.

"I'll have a large double mocha—thanks," Montana filled in.

Back at his office, she sat while O'Malley hung up his coat and hat. Then he sat behind his desk, opened the right hand drawer, took out a silver flask, and dumped a generous serving into the thermos. He took a grateful sip and smiled at her. "I have good news. I know another guy who works in my old precinct's photo lab. He's a genius at making poor quality photos better. I'm going to ask him to clear up the lettering on the plate. If we know the numbers we can figure out which office uses that car."

"That sounds great. What can I can do?"

"Talk to Hanky about that journal. If it involves her theater friends, talk to them. Rack your memory for conversations the two of you had about her high rollers or anything she might have said that connects to the person she was dating during that time. We need to figure out who the 'J' client is and find out what happened after their date was over."

Montana sipped her brew. "I sent Hanky the opened journal and asked him to call me. I hope he can enlighten me because I don't know those people. In fact, I don't really know her theater friends but ask Hanky might know something more."

"Sounds good."

"What can I do until then? How can I speed things along? Remember I also said I'd help with other cases if you need me to."

"Nah—don't worry about it. Any extra time you have, you study for your exam. You should have already taken it if you graduated last summer. Don't let fear hold you back from your dreams, Montana. I have no judgment on you or the Coop. You have my respect regardless, but you are too good for your current business—high end as it may be. You're a straight up chick..."

She rolled her eyes. "Referring to women as chicks is also derogatory."

He smiled sheepishly. "Whoops—I know you broads—damn—sorry again—hate that type of talk, but you have so much more to offer. Until you hear from Hanky let me do the legwork and you study."

"I can't concentrate. The words have no meaning."

He stood up and rolled his chair around the desk so he could look her in the eye as he sat back down. "I'm going to do my best to find your friend. You need to accept that we might not find her or if we do, it could be the worst way to find her. Your life has to go on no matter what. Read and then reread the material until it sinks in. I'm counting on you to take the July bar exam."

"You know the dates?" she asked with incredulity.

"Damn straight. People sabotage themselves—I'm an expert, believe me. Let me do my job—you do yours."

"Okay," Montana sighed. "I'll give it my best shot."

O'Malley paused a moment. "Montana, when I worked as a homicide detective, I often went on hunches. Sometimes they were nothing but they often saved my life or the life of my partner."

"I know what you mean. My Nana—my grandmother—always said I had 'the sight.' She said it ran in the maternal blood of the Wylde family. What's your hunch telling you?"

"You be careful. That car parked across the street waited for Suzette to leave the Coop at least three days last week and then followed her. That person knows who you are. We have no idea what he's up to but the fact that Suzette isn't here to tell us is enough to send off all kinds of warning bells—concerning you. You need to watch yourself. You need to BOLO—"

"Be on the lookout," Montana chimed in, "but O'Malley, I doubt I'm in danger. I don't feel it at all."

"I'm serious. I have a hunch here—even if you don't."

"Okay... okay... I will BOLO my ass off wherever I go. Promise. So, now that we know that I'll be spending the day studying, what are you doing?"

"I'm going to figure out who J is and see how the car fits in. I'm going to my old precinct to drop off the photos and a copy of Suzette's hard drive to my buds. Then I'll talk to Bruno and go back to the Coop to talk to Al again."

Sounds like a plan. Can I come with you?"

"What did I just say," O'Malley declared, exasperated. "I need a good attorney. You need to pass the bar. Go study."

Montana saluted. "Aye-aye, Captain."

25

H E HAD BEEN IMPATIENT all day waiting for the story to break. He knew it would. He paced the floor with his television cued to the local news. The five o'clock broadcast finally rewarded him. It was the top story—of course. He reveled in the newscaster's account of the whore's death. One of the faithful had found the cunt in the church where he'd left her. They were not revealing her identity until the NYPD had contacted the family.

He was elated but not anxious. The cops were no threat—not at this point anyway. His superior intelligence and creativity, along with his brilliant planning would keep him a step ahead of all of them. He threw his head back and laughed in wicked delight.

The coverage of the whore's death was extensive. Pleasing him more was that the story had made the national news. People were bloodthirsty bastards, regardless of their feigned horror. Everyone was hungry for the gory details.

He sat riveted by the television, watching as grim faced medical personnel wheeled the slut's lifeless body out on a gurney. What a shame to conceal her with a body bag. No one could see his brilliant makeup and staging. It would be more satisfying if the public could appreciate his expertise. How he itched for recognition of his superior mind but secrecy was imperative. He must remain an unsung hero but he couldn't help but wonder how He would feel about the devotion he'd shown to Him.

He had disguised them both for this incredible performance piece and found immense enjoyment in this. Once he had dreams of making it on Broadway—perhaps even Hollywood.

The theater bug had bitten him at a young age, rescuing him from the solitary existence of always being the odd boy out. The popular boys shoved him into lockers and picked him last for every team sport. His was a miserable existence until the magical day the high school drama coach urged him to perform in the annual talent show. No one could doubt his talent as he performed. His comedy routine had featured spot-on impersonations of some of Hollywood's greatest actors and comedians but that wasn't his peak moment. His impersonations of the school's most eccentric teachers brought the house down. His imitations were flawless. With every roar of the crowd, he grew bolder—even taking on some of the jocks who were the worst of his bullies.

His ego proved greater than his talent when he knocked on Broadway's—and off-Broadway's doors. While he'd been good, perhaps even great, by a public high school's standards, he lacked that elusive charisma that gives most actors the unique shine required for true stardom.

His failures recharged the fury of his middle school and junior high school days when he'd been the favored target of wedgies and other public humiliations. He hated them all—the ones who could have changed his life. They had the power to lift him to stardom but they were too dim to see his enormous talent. Each rejection brought another icy crystal that frosted his soul until it was hard and ready to crack.

He began dealing small amounts of heroin and crack but failed because he was his own best customer. After several minor stints at Riker's Island, the last arrest was a 'third strike' and he was looking at serious time. Instead, a compassionate judge sentenced him to treatment instead of jail. He overcame his addictions but never shook off the bitter failure of his theatrical dreams.

Rejected by Broadway—and even off-Broadway, he created his own theater. Tonight, he had been the writer, director, and star of his show. He was the lead story in every evening newscast.

He had disguised them both for this incredible performance piece and found immense enjoyment in doing this. God knew he had greater talent than any Tom Cruise or Brad Pitt. Preparing their disguises had taken great expertise, but he had a knack for creating elaborate makeup. First, he'd done the whore's makeup. Her costume and makeup took far less time than his own did. He'd painted her face loud and garish, befitting of the tramp she was. Once her face makeup was complete, he disguised her body, dressing her in an elaborate vintage wedding dress. Then he placed her in an old model manual wheelchair and bowed her head so it would appear she was deep in prayer. He crossed her hands, wrapped in a rosary, in her lap.

After completing the slut's transformation, he'd gone to work on his own disguise. In less than an hour, he went from a vibrant man in the summer of life to a much older version of himself. Keeping his identity secret was of utmost importance—if anyone learned who he was, everything would turn to chaos.

He had been gratified to see a light rain had shrouded the night in murky shadows, working to his advantage. He had placed a couple of raggedy shawls around her head, face, and upper torso. Before walking out the door, he had paused by the full-length wall mirror, pleased at their final reflection. They were perfect: a doting husband wheeling his infirm wife into church for a late night prayer. Out into the misty night they had gone where the wheelchair equipped van waited for them.

He had been prepared in case something went wrong. He'd hidden a stolen handgun in his overcoat pocket but it proved superfluous. Everything was as smooth as a sheet of glass. The end, in fact, had been anticlimactic. As he'd suspected, only a handful of the faithful remained at the church when they'd arrived. He'd waited for them to leave, growing more impatient by the minute. Finally, with only two parishioners left, deep in prayer, he'd made his move. He removed the shawls covering the slut and walked out into the murky might.

He would savor her ending not only in his memory but also through the videos that he'd had the foresight to tape. He'd filmed every aspect, immortalizing her forever. He fast-forwarded to her death scene, becoming aroused. Then, on second thought, he ejected the DVD showing the whore's magnificent death. Instead, he put on a headset and scanned the bookmarks of favorite porn sites. He logged into his favorite, quickly picked a girl, and bought the cheapest session. His release wouldn't take long. He undid his pants and freed his burning member.

"Hi honey," the woman on screen drawled, "what's your name and what's your fantasy?"

"Don't talk," he ordered. "Play with yourself. We don't have much time. Just stick a dildo up your cunt. Fuck your nasty hole and scream when you come."

"It's your fifty bucks mister," she pouted.

She played with an erect nipple with one hand, while the other traced her mound of Venus. She opened her legs, revealing her wetness, as she rubbed her finger against herself. Then she rammed two fingers in and out of herself, pulling them out, and then popping them in her mouth to suck. She masturbated with a frenzied rhythm. It might have been a good acting job but she sure looked excited. His cock responded.

"The dildo," he moaned. "Get the dildo."

She brought out a huge dildo, slathered it with lubricant, and rubbed the head along her vagina lips. Then she began pushing it in and out, repeatedly. Each time, she went deeper, pulling it out then plunging it in again. She stuck a finger up her anus, continuing to move the dildo at a furious pace. The two were in harmony, matching thrust for thrust.

Up and down and in and out they went, breathing in unison until they each erupted in furious orgasms. As soon as he came, he stopped the session and shut his laptop in disgust. He no longer wanted to see the dirty whore. He looked down at the mess—the nasty spunk covering his hands and legs. To purify himself, he took a scalding shower and cursed the bitch who'd bled him of his manhood and money.

Goddamn her—and He would.

26

O'MALLEY AWOKE FEELING a heck of a lot better than he did most days. April was rough for him. April 12 marked the eleventh anniversary of his wife and daughters' deaths. Each April, he became lost in an abyss of despair, renewed guilt racking his conscience. His usual approach was a month long bender but not this year. Without meaning to, Montana had stopped this destructive pattern when she brought him her case. Her quiet dignity and vulnerability drew him right away but it wasn't just that. Her case had real meaning—far more than busting horny wives or catching people cheating insurance companies.

His commitment to the case had inadvertently improved his health and his quality of life. He wanted to give Montana his best. Last night he'd had only a couple of shots and a few beers. He'd fallen asleep rather than passed out and was rewarded by awakening alert and without his hands trembling. That hadn't happened for a long time. Without wasting an entire morning nursing a hangover, he remembered how productive a day could be. By 8:30 a.m., he'd already completed several invoices and had written the reports for several cases he was finishing up. By 9:00, he was on his way to his old precinct ready to dig into the case.

Each time he stopped by his old precinct it reminded him how fast time had passed since he was on the force. He barely recognized anyone these days but one familiar face lit up as soon as he walked in. Marsha still worked the information desk, as she had been two days before when he'd stopped by to hand Frankie the password-protected file containing Suzette's journal. With surprising agility, she moved her considerable girth from behind the desk to envelop him in a deep hug.

"Well I'll be," she exclaimed. "Twice in one week. Something must have lit a fire in your belly again. Great seeing you again so soon—and if you don't mind my saying, you look a sight better than you did two days ago."

"I'm feeling a sight better too," he grinned.

"What brings your bad self here this time—other than to flirt with me?" She winked at him. Marsha was the precinct mother who never failed to bring her famous sticky buns and towering canisters of soup for hungry officers.

He kissed her cheek. "I have another favor I want to call in. Would Nicky Rinaldi happen to be in today?"

Marsha consulted a screen she pulled up on her computer. "You're in luck. He's here. Want me to ring him up?"

"Nah—let me surprise him." He stepped back to look at her and gave a low whistle. "Marsha, you get more gorgeous every year. You epitomize what connoisseurs say about fine wine and fine women: you improve with age."

She waved him off but glowed with pleasure nonetheless. "Pfffft. How you do go on."

Inspired by Montana's glowing health, O'Malley bypassed the elevator and climbed three flights of stairs to Nicky's office. Breathless when he reached the top, he reminded himself to lay off the late night Reuben sandwiches.

When he reached the photo lab, he popped his head in and grinned. "Hey Nicky—how ya think those Yankees are shaping up this spring?"

Nick turned around in surprise and grinned. "O'Malley, you old bastid," he boomed. "We're gonna take you bastids down *again* this ye-ah." Having grown up in Boston's North End, Nick was a lifelong Red Sox fan and had the accent to prove it. "What brings ya gnarly ass back he-ah?"

"You owe me one if my memory is accurate." O'Malley dug several photos from his briefcase. "Tell me you can clear these up."

Nicky let loose a low whistle. "These are some lousy shots. I didn't think it was possible to take such crappy photos these days. Where'd you get these?"

"Surveillance tapes—got the originals too." He fished a jump drive out of his pocket. "I blew these up. It only does so much if you know what I mean."

"What are you looking for?"

O'Malley pointed. "See the plate on that car? Can you clear up those numbers? It's an official city car—you see that?" He pointed to the word below the numbers. "I want to find out whose plate that is."

"No problem—I can fix that," Nicky said. "I should have the information by the end of the day. Is your cell number still the same?

O'Malley handed him a business card. "This has all my updated information. You can either email, call, or text. Thanks buddy—I knew I could count on you. Now we're even."

"No worries, but O'Malley?"

"Yeah?"

"I still owe you one."

"Fuhgeddaboudit." O'Malley grinned. "Great seeing you, Nicky. Let's get together for a beer soon."

"Sounds good. I'll give ya a call later."

Finished with his precinct business, he headed to Suzette's apartment building. When the cab arrived, he spotted the coffee shop Montana had mentioned.

"How's it going?" he asked, walking in. "I'm looking for Bruno?"

The man sized him up. "Who's asking?"

O'Malley handed him a card. "O'Malley. I'm a Private Detective, working for Montana Wylde, who..."

The man cut him off. "If you're working for Montana, I'm at your disposal." He came from around the counter, wiped his hands on the towel tucked into his belt and held his hand out for a shake. "I'm Bruno. What do you need?"

"Montana talked to your partner last weekend—not sure if he mentioned it to you. Suzette Peterson, who lives upstairs, disappeared last Friday. Do you remember seeing her that day? Montana told me she usually comes in for coffee before heading off to work."

"Whoa—Vinnie didn't mention she was missing... wondered why I hadn't seen her. I figured she'd gone on vacation. I do remember last Friday because it was different. She came in early—for her anyway—around 7:00 a.m. Usually she stops by in the late morning—sometimes even noon. In fact I commented on how early it was for her."

O'Malley pulled a photo from his briefcase and showed it to Bruno. "You ever see Suzette get into this car?"

Bruno shook his head. "Nah. I never saw any fancy limo picking Suzy up—that's a small limo isn't it?

"It's a town car," O'Malley replied.

"Nah," he said again. "She takes the subway. Suzy's no snob—she'd never have a limo—or have a fancy car take her to work."

"Do you remember seeing Suzette out on dates with men?"

Bruno wrinkled his head in concentration. "The only guy I've seen her with goes by the name of Hanky but I think he plays for the other team if you know what I mean." He gave O'Malley a conspiratorial wink.

"You sure you don't remember seeing her with anyone else."

"She keeps to herself. We only see her in the mornings and then she goes straight off to work. Between her job and her acting career, I think she keeps pretty busy."

O'Malley held out his hand. "Thanks Bruno. You've been helpful."

"I have?" Bruno looked surprised but shook the outstretched hand. "Sure doesn't feel like it. I hope you find Suzy—what a sweetheart. Gorgeous inside and out. They're both great girls—always tip so well." He paused. "Say would you like a cup of coffee?"

"That sounds great—thanks." O'Malley handed him his thermos. "Mind putting it in this?"

"No problem. Room for cream?"

"Good idea."

"Condiments are over there." Bruno motioned to a condiment counter.

"How much I owe you?"

"No way—it's on the house. You find Suzy."

"Gonna do my best." O'Malley walked to the condiments but ignoring the offerings. Instead, he pulled out a silver flask and gave the thermos a generous dollop. Bruno smiled, shaking his head, saying nothing.

Next on the docket was the Coop. O'Malley gave a cabbie the address and sat back to enjoy his coffee and the never-ending sideshow playing out on every street.

At the Coop's building, the attendant's station had large windows overlooking the street. Anyone working the desk would have a great view of the street. A heavyset man wearing a uniform sat behind the desk reading a magazine.

"How's it going, Al," O'Malley gave him a congenial smile.

"Don't tell me—you are...?" His brow wrinkled.

"O'Malley." He stuck out his hand. "I was here to see Montana yesterday. Remember—you gave me last week's surveillance tapes."

Al snapped his fingers. "That's right. My memory's not so hot. You're investigating what happened to Suzy. I sure hope she's okay. I figured she'd show up by now. Tana must be sick with worry—those two are as thick as thieves." With Al's accent, it came out, '*tick as teeves.*'

O'Malley nodded. "She's worried."

Al shook his head. "I watch them crime shows with my wife—she's crazy about them. They say the longer a person is missing, the less likely it'll come to a good end. My wife has these crazy hunches—probably from watching those shows. She thinks something bad happened to Suzy—that she came across some sicko. But don't tell Tana that."

"Of course not," O'Malley replied.

"We know what goes on in 4E." Al winked at him. "Hey I don't judge. They're good girls. Never had a problem with them—no drugs, pimps, or lowlifes. They class the joint up if you ask me—looking like movie stars. Still, you have to wonder about the people they might come across."

O'Malley pulled some photos from a manila envelope. "Question for you Al—does this car look familiar?"

Al frowned in concentration. "That sure looks like the car that picked Suzy up last Friday."

"This came from the surveillance tapes you gave me. I know you can't make out the numbers on the plate—I can't either—but look below the numbers. You see that?" O'Malley tapped a spot on the photo. "Says 'official,' which means it's a city government car. Do you recall if last Friday's car had official plates?"

"Jeez—I don't remember. My eyes aren't so good anymore—probably need to get them checked. Anyway, my eye was on Suzy thinking what a lucky bastard that guy was."

"Someone was in the backseat?"

"Sure was."

O'Malley felt the old thrill of being close to something to something significant. "Do you remember what he looked like?"

"Jeez, no—the windows were dark and like I said, my eyes were on Suzy."

O'Malley continued. "This photo is from last Thursday. A similar car appears on three separate days last week—the week Suzette went missing."

Al frowned in confusion. "You mean the car was waiting for her?"

"Maybe. Someone parked this car across the street. The tape showed it leaving as soon as Suzette left the building. Same thing happened on Tuesday when both Montana and Suzette left. As soon as they disappear," he motioned to the awning outside the building, "the car takes off. I'm trying to figure out if that was a regular occurrence. I can't tell because we only have a partial week of film—only three days."

"You think he was stalking her?"

"Could be," O'Malley replied. "I'd like to talk to the person connected with that car. I hoped you might shed some light."

"You need to talk to Tony—he'll be back on Sunday. If it happens regularly he would have lots of opportunities to notice."

"I'll do that."

"Tana hasn't been in lately—what's going on with her?"

O'Malley shook his head. "You'd have to ask her." He pulled a card from the bundle in his pocket and handed a few to Al. "If you think of anything about the car—anything you think might be important—give me a call. And pass along my cards to the other attendants in case they noticed anything."

"You bet I will," Al nodded. "Anything I can do to help."

"Thanks. Here are more photos of the car to show the others as well. Ask if anyone remembers this car—it could be important in finding Suzette."

"Please give my best to Tana. We're all here for her."

O'Malley paused, "Say, would anyone happen to be up in 4E? Either Montana or her security guy?"

Al's face brightened. "Yes, as a matter of fact, Hank went up about an hour ago. Didn't say what for."

"Would you mind ringing him and telling him I'd like to speak with him?"

"No problem."

Hanky opened the door for O'Malley just as he was about to knock. He gave a glance at the hall and entryway. "Where's Montana?"

"Hopefully studying for the bar or deciphering Suzette's journal. She said she sent you a copy—did you get it?"

"That's why I'm here. Have a seat." Hanky gestured to the parlor. "I couldn't open the file on my own computer. Call me old-fashioned but I'm a Word Pro guy. ThinkPad—back when they were good—used to give a far better bundle than Office, including the best word processing software—and that's Word Pro. I wasn't able to open this Word file so I'm reading it on the computer in back."

O'Malley sat in an overstuffed chair while Hanky took the couch. "What do you make of the journal?"

"Hard to believe it but it sounds like Suze was in love—or was falling in love anyway. Who with—I have no idea.

She never mentioned a word to me but I'm very surprised she didn't say anything to Montana. I wouldn't have thought Suze would keep anything from her. It's a total mystery. She's careful not to write his name—I noticed that—not even his first."

O'Malley's face fell. "No help at all?"

"I'm not finished reading it yet—but there *is* something. At the *Bring on the Cheers* auditions, one puny dude had it bad for Suzette. Of course, Suzette *was* nice to him—but she's nice to everyone. He might have read too much into her kindness. She told me he creeped her out. She was glad he didn't make it past the cattle call and first callback. I can't remember his name but this C character might be him."

"Would the director keep a list of those who auditioned?"

"No idea, man—I was always on the other side of the stage."

"Maybe Suzette said something about him to Montana but she doesn't remember."

"It was a couple of years ago. Montana might not remember a lovesick actor who came on to Suze, but it's mighty weird that she didn't tell her she was falling in love."

"All these secrets bother Montana. Suzette kept a lot of things from her."

"It shocks me too. I'd have never believed Suzette would keep such a big thing from Montana. There must be a good reason why she kept it quiet."

"You and Montana should keep trying to think of anything that Suzette might have mentioned, as small as it might have seemed at the time."

"I'll talk to Montana about the journal as soon as I'm finished with it. Maybe together we can come up with more than each of us alone."

"Sounds good," O'Malley said. He paused and said, "One other thing. I want to show you something." O'Malley pulled the car photos from his briefcase."

Hanky looked lost. "This looks like the street out front."

"It is but look here." O'Malley tapped on the town car. "Have you ever seen this car parked across the street?"

"If I have then I don't remember."

"Al thinks it might be the same car Suzette got into last Friday. It's a government car, see?" He tapped the photo again.

"Whoa—you're right."

"A buddy of mine is clearing up the numbers so we can figure out what office the car is from."

"As I said, I never saw it, but again, I'm on the other side of this stage. If you know what I mean."

O'Malley stood and gave Hanky's hand a shake. "Thanks for your time. How far into that journal are you?"

"About halfway—it's not that long. While she kept the journal for a long time, her entries weren't long and she wrote mostly in abbreviations. I should be done by the end of the day."

"Anything you can glean—anything at all—call Montana or me right away."

"Of course." Hanky's face darkened. "I'm starting to get *worried*. Something is wrong—Montana felt it first and I feel it now."

O'Malley saw himself out and walked down the four flights of stairs. He bade Al goodbye on his way out the door.

His stomach rumbling, O'Malley spotted a hotdog vendor on the corner of 33rd and Park. He ordered his favorite kraut dog, munching along as he walked down the street. Mid-bite, his cellphone rang.

Nicky Rinaldi had some interesting news.

27

MAX AND JOEY along with a handful of cops and the BAU agents sat in a precinct meeting room. Max continued as lead investigator. He assigned Sheila Prowse and Linda Collingswood to pose as prostitutes while covering the strolls. They were seasoned professionals with several years in vice under their belts. They knew how to lure men when it was time to clean up the strolls. This time their objective was to pull the CM into a successful sting. Also on the task force were four NYPD officers: two in uniform, two in plainclothes. They stood by in a backup van and had complete oversight on all potential encounters. The tech department had wired the undercover cops so they could monitor and record all communication.

A large corkboard held a map of the boroughs where the CM had gone on his murderous rampages. Like the one in the Mayor's office, each victim had colored pins to identify her on three locations on the map.

Max spoke gently about each victim, wanting the officers to know the humanity in each. He told the group a bit about each woman and her loved ones who suffered from their loss. He breathed life into each victim, so the officers would carry this bit of compassion with them.

He pointed to the newest—a purple pin. "Someone found this victim at the Holy Trinity Church last night." He passed pictures around to the group. "We don't yet know her identity. This is a computer-generated sketch of what she looks like based on the photos taken at the crime scene. Those photos wouldn't help much because her makeup was so garish, but we think this sketch might let someone recognize her."

Max looked around. "Any other questions before we head out?"

Some shook their heads while others murmured that they did not.

"Okay then," Max stood up, "you know the drill. Let's catch this son of a bitch. Be smart, stay safe, and keep in touch."

28

WITH O'MALLEY FOLLOWING UP ON LEADS, Montana stayed home with every intention of studying. The problem was concentration. Her computer was on and the prep book open but her mind kept wandering. The case had her transfixed, unable to concentrate on anything else. She shut her computer lid in frustration after realizing that she'd stared at the same page for twenty minutes and hadn't comprehended a thing. She wished O'Malley had let her come with him.

To kill time, she ran errands. Walking down the pathway leading to the front sidewalk, she saw the bewigged bag lady on her usual stoop. She looked at Montana with suspicion and disgust. Montana decided to take a closer look at her oppressor. The nearer she got to the woman, the stranger she appeared. She was of an indeterminable age due to the elements of harsh weather and the brutality of street living.

Perhaps because of their close proximity, the woman remained silent. For once, she didn't scream obscenities at Montana. Instead, she gazed reproachfully at her. Montana dug into her handbag, producing a twenty-dollar bill. Even though the woman was a constant source of antagonism, Montana couldn't help but feel compassion. She had the insight to recognize that fate often turns on a dime, depending on a single choice—or circumstance. Montana's own life might have taken a similar turn if she'd not had the wits, opportunities—and yes—looks that she was fortunate enough to possess. Timidly, she approached the peculiar woman.

"Hi there." Montana held out the cash as though it were an olive branch. "It's cold today. Maybe you should go somewhere to warm up. You know, get some hot coffee—something to eat."

The bag lady stared at the money as though it were a poisonous snake. She appeared fixated but made no move to take it. Montana pushed it closer but the woman wouldn't budge. Just when Montana was ready to stuff it back into her handbag, the woman's long dirty fingers snatched it. She grabbed her cart and scurried down the street. Halfway down the block, she looked around and then scampered away in a hurry. Montana smiled. It was a marked improvement. At least the woman hadn't shrieked at her.

Feeling an odd sense of accomplishment, Montana began taking care of tasks she'd been neglecting. She dropped a bundle of clothes at the French laundry down the street and picked up the fresh clothes awaiting her. She lunched at Destination Bakery, one of her favorites, where she enjoyed a chicken salad stuffed croissant. It was hearty, with chunky chicken, sliced grapes and slivered walnuts. She'd come across the tiny bakery the day she'd begun law school. The name seemed a good premonition. Before leaving, she picked up a crusty baguette, still warm from the oven.

Sated, she did her shopping. She chose seasonal fruits and vegetables from the colorful display at her favorite produce market. At the neighborhood's best gourmet shop she stocked up on Greek yogurt, eggs, coffee, cream, and a block of velvety brie cheese.

After putting away her groceries and laundry, she paced the living room. She was edgy—her gut told her that O'Malley was close to something important. Everything seemed to be falling into place: the pattern of dates on the 'J' client card, the city issued town car—they were narrowing in on Suzette's Friday date. Watching the sun start to go down, she could stand it no longer. She phoned O'Malley. He answered right away, sounding more lucid than she'd ever heard.

"I'm glad you answered," Montana burst out.

"Of course I answered. I knew it was you and not the IRS." He chortled at his own joke. "Caller ID is a pain in my ass, although it can come in handy. Did you get a lot of studying done?"

"Not a lick. I can't concentrate. Don't keep me in suspense. What did you find out about the car? Do you know to which person—or office—the city issued the car?"

"Whoa—slow down. It's been a productive day but I still have a ways to go. I have a few more things to do today but we should talk soon. Can you meet for lunch tomorrow? I know the best Italian joint in the city. It's right around the corner from my office, too."

"Italian is my favorite. Which place is it?"

"Posto Pinella. Let's meet at my office at 1:00. We can walk from there."

Montana swallowed her disappointment. "Sounds good," she conceded. "I'll see you tomorrow."

With disappointment lingering, she hung up the phone, almost willing it to reveal more. As if on cue, it rang. She was so certain it was O'Malley calling her back that she answered, "Please say we can meet today instead, O'Malley."

Puzzled by the silence on the other end, only then did she glance at the caller ID. It wasn't O'Malley. She didn't know *who* it was because the screen indicated it was a BLOCKED caller. Someone *was* on the phone—she could hear the breathing. .

"Hello, who are you looking for? Sorry for my hello but I was expecting someone else. This is Montana Wylde. Can I help you?"

Someone was listening... she heard faint breathing on the other end.

"Who is this?" Now she was getting annoyed. "Hello?"

She hung up the phone, puzzled. It was probably a crank call—heck, there are bound to be plenty in a city as big as New York. Still, it spooked her. The hairs on the back of her neck tickled—a common reaction when her intuition kicked in.

She had a restless evening, alternating between pacing the floor of her loft and gazing out the living room windows, willing some force to reveal Suzette's whereabouts. Last Friday, the universe had thrown her life into a nightmarish spiral. For over ten years, she had felt in command of her life but now that control was slipping away. She was so grateful to have O'Malley.

Dreading a long and sleepless night, she remembered the seldom-used Valium in her medicine cabinet. Usually used only for long flights, she reasoned that tonight was an exception. She fished one out of the bottle, dropped it into her mouth, and washed it down with a shot of cognac.

As soon as she lay her head on her pillow and turned to the window to count stars, the pill worked its magic.

She counted six before a dreamless but still blissful sleep took over.

29

MONTANA AWOKE groggy from the Valium. Three cups of coffee took care of that. Now awake, she had five hours to go before meeting O'Malley.

She decided to go for a run on this picture perfect spring day. The sun was making its morning rise and she stopped to admire the fluffy clouds bouncing against a watercolor sky. The sun's warmth felt good on her face.

Then something jostled her intuition and she looked across the street. The deli was just opening. She felt the stare before she saw it. Scanning the deli's front, the employees hadn't yet set up the outdoor seating. The chairs were still on the tables except one where a solitary figure sat staring at her. He was slim with a full head of dark hair and a full beard and mustache. And he *was* staring at her—his eyes burned into her. She turned around to make sure his gaze was on her. There was no one else in the direction. When she looked back, he'd hidden his face in a newspaper. Had he been looking at her? She shook her head at her silliness and started down the trail. She was just jumpy—that's all. He was likely just enjoying the fresh spring morning sitting in a comfortable spot.

Then she remembered the strange call she'd received the day before. O'Malley had her spooked—warning her that she could be in danger. That was just nonsense. Still it sure seemed he'd fixed his intense glare right on her. On her way down the trail, she glanced back but the building was now out of view. Again, she shook off the notion and scampered the rest of the way to the trail. She leaned against the railing and stretched her limbs. She was ready for a hard run.

Forty-five minutes later, renewed by her vigorous exercise, she took a long, hot shower. She washed and conditioned her hair and shaved her legs for the first time in a week. Pampering herself, she rubbed soothing creams into her body until she glowed. She scrunched her hair with her fingers while blowing it dry, until glossy waves fell around her shoulders and back. She applied light makeup and dressed for the day. Whip slim in black jeans and a sleeveless black turtleneck, she topped her outfit with a pale pink cashmere cardigan. Her only jewelry was a gold Tiffany key pendant Suzette had given her for her last birthday. She fingered it, hoping it would unlock the mysterious disappearance of her friend.

With a half an hour remaining before their meeting time, she took a casual stroll to O'Malley's office. When he answered the door, she noted that once again he greeted her with clear eyes and a healthier complexion. Even in such close proximity, he looked and smelled more sober than usual. Giving him a side-eye as they walked down the street, she considered his new state. O'Malley, for whatever reason, was drying out—or so it appeared.

Posta Pinella was two blocks from his office. It had red-checkered tablecloths and roses on the tables, typical of many Italian restaurants. Montana was familiar with most Italian eateries in Lower Manhattan so she was surprised she hadn't yet heard of it. Delectable aromas wafted from the kitchen, making her mouth water as soon as they walked in. The maitre'd tinkled a bell, which fetched a robust man wearing kitchen whites and a big chef's hat. From the heartfelt hugs on both their parts, it was clear that the chef and O'Malley were old friends.

"O'Malley, you old son of a gun," the man exclaimed. His accent was even thicker than O'Malley's was. "I didn't know you had a gorgeous daughter." Montana had to smile at the strong dialect: *youse old son of a gun. I dint know youse had a ga-jus dortah.* He winked at Montana and slapped O'Malley across the back. "I know she ain't your girlfriend cuz what would this knockout see in an ugly old coot like you?" He threw his head back and roared with laughter.

O'Malley grinned. "Montana Wylde, this is Sal Pinella, owner, head chef, and chief pain in the ass of Posta Pinella. All kidding aside, Sal serves the best Italian downtown. Sal, meet Montana Wylde."

"You must be an actress or a model." Sal beamed at her.

"Nah, she's got big brains, Sal. She's a lawyer," O'Malley replied. Sal's accent brought out the Brooklyn in O'Malley as well: *Loy-yah.*

"Brains and beauty—well light me like a firecracker and blow me to kingdom come. What a combo."

Though she rarely drank during the day, she ordered a glass of red wine to go with her eggplant parmigiana. O'Malley ordered his usual Dewar's with a beer back to go with his veal scaloppini. As they sipped their drinks, Montana relaxed.

"Yesterday was productive," O'Malley began. "There just might be something to this waking up early crap. More hours in the day, that's for sure."

"Productive?" Montana raised an eyebrow.

"I talked to Nicky Rinaldi—the photo ace I told you about. I gave him the photos."

"Did he clear them up?"

O'Malley held up his hand. "Not right then—but patience. When I finished there, I stopped at Suzette's building and talked with Bruno. Suzette *did* come into his shop on Friday—said he remembered because it was so early in the morning. He said she grabbed coffee at seven o'clock, which was rare for her."

"True." Montana nodded. "We aren't morning people. That's why we open the Coop at noon and close it late in the evening."

"After talking to Bruno, I headed down to the Coop to talk with Al some more. I showed him the blurry pictures of the car—Nicky hadn't had a chance to work on the photos yet. I wanted to jostle Al's memory about the town car. He had some interesting information."

Sal arrived with heaping platters of steaming food. O'Malley hadn't kidded her about the food. Platters of eggplant parmigiana and veal scaloppini loaded with sauce and gooey cheese filled the table, along with two orders of baked ziti. They dug into their food in silence for ten minutes. As they filled up, O'Malley continued.

"When I showed him the town car, he thought it looked like the one Suzette got into on Friday."

"That's great. Did he see who was in the backseat?" Montana took a big bite of eggplant.

"Nah, unfortunately, he didn't. He also didn't know anything about the plates but he seemed sure it was the same car. Course all those cars look the same." He told her about his visit to Hanky as well. Montana sat listening, enjoying her food while digesting O'Malley's information.

Forty-five minutes later and stuffed to the max, a waiter whisked their dishes away. The portions were so generous that Montana requested a couple of to-go containers for the remainder of hers. Then Sal made another beaming entrance, carrying a tray with two tiny cups of espresso and two enormous servings of tiramisu.

Sal winked at Montana. "This is my sainted grandmother's secret recipe, may she rest in peace. Mind youse, it's the best you've ever had." He gave O'Malley a pointed look. "The coffee is mostly for your sake. It's my civic duty to counter all that booze you lap up."

"Yeah, yeah. Don't I hear enough from my doc that I have to hear you yapping about it too?" O'Malley laughed good-naturedly. Sal rewarded Montana with another big grin before heading back to his kitchen.

"Did you ask Hanky what he made of the journal?" Montana took a bite of tiramisu.

"He wasn't finished reading it but like you, he had no idea who Suzette could have been falling in love with." O'Malley went on to tell Montana what Hanky said about Suzette's want-to-be paramour at the *Bring on the Cheers* audition. "Do you remember anything about that?"

Montana's brow wrinkled in concentration until she shook her head in frustration. "No. I don't. So many people have had crushes on Suzette. She told me about some of her auditions but I can't think of one where some guy creeped her out. Let me think on that some more, though. That was a while ago."

"This one stood out enough so that Hanky remembered him."

"I'll talk to Hanky about it—maybe he can jog my memory."

"That's what he said too—that the two of you together might be able to come up with more."

"But O'Malley, you made great headway on several fronts. I wish we could have learned what those license plate numbers were though."

"Hold on—I'm not done." O'Malley held up his hand. "When I finished talking to Al and Hanky, Nicky calls me. This is where it gets interesting."

"What?" Montana's spoon stopped in midair.

"Not only are the plates city-issued—but the city assigned that very town car to the Mayor's Office."

Montana was speechless. "So are you saying that someone from the Mayor's office could have been stalking Suzette?"

O'Malley shrugged. "Not at all, though it's possible. That's a real stretch at this point. I imagine the Mayor's office has access to several vehicles. We also need to keep in mind that the city issued the car to his office, not to him personally. Very possible he's not the only one who uses it. Maybe he doesn't use it at all."

"How can we learn who uses that exact car and when?"

O'Malley lowered his voice to a whisper. "This is the highest level of city government. We must tread lightly. The Mayor appoints the police commissioner. Before we head down that road we should talk to the Tony—the Coop's regular daytime attendant."

"You're right."

"I'll talk to him as soon as he returns. If the pattern of dates is correct, then Tony worked the door on most, if not all, those Fridays. Al saw the car only once and he remembered it. Tony's worked your building over fifteen years. If he's observant, he could have valuable information for us."

"Like what?"

O'Malley shrugged. "He might be able to tell us who the backseat passenger is. He might not know his identity but he could give us a description. With that, we can have *another* friend of mine—one who happens to be a police artist—compose a computerized sketch. It pays to have NYPD connections. That way, we could figure out his identity.

These days, everyone is identifiable." O'Malley stood up and Montana rose with him.

"So what's next?"

O'Malley shrugged. "I'm going to continue trying to discover who Friday's client was and who was driving the town car last week."

"I thought you said we needed to talk to Tony."

"We can't count on that. Maybe he's not so observant—maybe he has a poor memory. There are other ways to skin that cat."

"Can I tag along?"

"You need to study. Just dig into that prep book and don't let this case distract you. After you've studied for a few hours, give Hanky a call. He thought he'd finish reading the journal by this afternoon. Then, you two brainstorm about the guy who pestered Suzette at that audition."

She sighed. "I hope I'll have better luck studying today. I'll call Hanky and let you know if we figure anything out."

They parted ways, with O'Malley promising he'd call if anything important came up.

Montana took her time walking back to her loft—she couldn't move at a faster pace if she'd wanted to. She couldn't remember the last time she'd stuffed herself that much. Her head felt as full as her tummy—bursting with questions. So far, the answers they'd gotten had led to more questions: a journal that had been password-protected, a town car that appeared to stalk Suzette—perhaps the same one issued to the Mayor's office. Then someone who had worried Suzette enough that she'd written about him in her journal...

Rounding the corner to her building, she saw the bag lady had moved further down the block. Now she sat on the stoop of a building under construction. The two caught each other's eye at the same time. The woman had a wary eye on Montana but didn't utter a word—insults or otherwise. For the first time since Montana could remember, she was able to slip into her building without a verbal assault. Perhaps the twenty-dollar bill had made some progress after all.

Upstairs, she turned on her computer and gave a cursory glance at the prep books still piled beside it. *Ugh.* She still wasn't motivated to study. Instead, she plopped down on the couch and picked up the remote to see if she could escape for a few hours by watching a movie.

Before she could click on the On Demand menu, a breaking story about the Church Murderer had preempted the station's regular daytime programming. Montana watched the screen switch from a serious anchor's face to a sketch of a woman's face. There was no mistaking who she was.

Part III
The Dead

30

AFTER A LONG AND UNSUCCESSFUL NIGHT on the sting, Max allowed himself the luxury of sleeping a few extra hours. Instead of his usual 6:00 a.m. alarm, he set it for 8:00 since it was sure to be another ten-hour day. He arrived at the precinct by noon. Just as he opened his laptop, he heard a light rap on his door.

"Got a minute?" Joey asked.

"Make it a quick one. I'm already behind and the day is just starting. What's up?"

"You know the last victim—the one from Holy Trinity?

"Yeah?"

"There's no mug shot for her; her prints aren't in any of our databases."

At this, Max's head shot up. "You're kidding."

"Would I kid about this?"

Max felt the beginning of a headache and began rubbing his temples. "Run her prints through the national base. She's not that young. She's got a sheet somewhere."

Joey shook his head. "Way ahead of you partner—nada—no prints anywhere. Maybe she's not a prostitute?"

Max leaned back in his chair. "That's a possibility I never considered. Say she isn't one but the CM thought she was. Because if she was working and didn't have a sheet, it would make her the luckiest streetwalker in the world—or was until she ran into this lunatic."

Joey shrugged. "Maybe the dude is branching out."

"Jesus Christ, I hope not. I never thought I'd say this—but I hope she *was* a prostitute—or at least that he *thought* she was—because if the CM now views all women as prostitutes, we're in deep shit. It would mean that *every woman* is a potential target. That could bring on a full-blown panic—the last thing we need."

"Agreed. So, what's next, genius?"

"Keep showing the sketch—make sure it's on every newscast. Somebody knows this woman. If she's not a hooker then her family and friends are probably worried sick."

Joey stood. "Will do. After that I need to catch up on paperwork."

"Ugh," Max commiserated. "Why don't they ever show that on CSI?"

"No one would watch," Joey said with a laugh.

Just as Joey was leaving, an upset Darryl McCarty rapped on the door.

"What's up?" Max inquired.

"I think I know who that last victim is."

This got Max's attention. "You're kidding."

McCarty thrust printouts of Suzette Peterson's report and photos across the desk. "Look at these. Tell me they aren't the same woman."

Max scanned the report and examined the photos. Then he swung his chair around to face the victim pictures on his back wall. His head ping-ponged back and forth, as we looked from McCarty's photos in his hand to the computer-generated sketch pinned to the wall. Then he swung his chair back around.

"Where did these come from?"

"Montana Wylde—you met her briefly. She filed a missing person's report and you popped your head into my office. Beautiful woman—you had a hard time believing she's a call girl. She and her friend run a high-end Murray Hill apartment. Or did run."

Max snapped his fingers. "That's right. She was upset that day if I recall."

"She's gonna be a lot more upset now." Joey grimaced.

"Darryl, I'd appreciate it if you would call and ask her to come in. Also ask her to bring something that would have her friend's DNA."

"I'm not looking forward to it. She said this woman was like a sister. But I'm on it, Max."

"This is good detective work, Darryl." He looked again at the fresh faced, smiling girl in the photos. "If it's not her, then she's got a twin."

"This would explain why there are no prints in the database," Joey mused.

"It sure would," Max agreed.

McCarty turned to go. "I'm on it now."

After they left, Max brought up the photos from the morgue and crime scene and compared them to the ones McCarty had brought in. If he were a betting man, he'd put a bundle on the odds that Suzette Peterson's DNA was going to match.

He thought about Montana Wylde—and wished they were meeting again under better circumstances. He remembered how her eyes had sparkled with intelligence and defiant anger, as well as the willful thrust of her chin. She had to be made of strong stuff to avoid the usual pitfalls of such a wretched business. She intrigued him. What was her real story? He wanted to know.

31

ONLY WHEN SHE FELT SHE WOULD PASS OUT did she remember to breathe. She sat, still as a statue, arm outstretched with the remote still in her hand. She heard the clicking of her grandfather clock as the horrible reality settled in. She stood, sat back down, and then stood again, unsure of what to do next. It was as if someone punched her in the gut—hard. Once when she'd played kickball as a child, a bigger kid had run full force into her, knocking the wind out of her. She had the same feeling now. Her brain felt as scattered as autumn leaves blowing in a frenzied windstorm. She stared dumbly at the telephone. O'Malley. She needed to call him. Her hand shook as she picked up her cellphone and speed dialed him.

"You should be studying." He answered on the first ring.

"Can't," she said in a voice that sounded as though it belonged to someone else. "Suzette."

In an instant, O'Malley went from his joking, jovial mood to being dead serious. "What are you saying, Montana?"

"The t-television—picture—S-suzette." Each word took effort. "S-she's d-dead."

"Are you home?"

"Yes." Her voice was so muted he could barely hear her.

"I'll be right there. Is your name on the buzzer?"

"Yes." Her voice dropped to below a whisper.

"I'm not far—I'll be there as quick as I can."

She hung up and stared at the nonsensical images on the television screen.

The television was still on when O'Malley arrived twenty minutes later. In the short time that he'd left her, she looked like a different woman altogether. Her face was devoid of color and her eyes that normally sparkled blue with intelligence had become a foggy gray. He picked up the remote and clicked off the television, as the breaking news had now returned to regular broadcasting. Instead, he sat at her desk, booted up her computer, and found the website for the channel she'd been watching. Within a few minutes, he saw the sketch that had shocked Montana. Although O'Malley had only seen pictures of Suzette, the montage on the screen left little doubt who it was. He returned to the couch.

"Montana... honey... we need to get you to a hospital or an urgent care center." O'Malley looked at her with concern. "Maybe they can give you something to help."

"Suzette..." Her voice was weak but resolute.

"Honey, we can figure all that out later. Let me take you to an urgent care. There's a place a few blocks from my office." O'Malley insisted.

"No." Her voice had regained some of its usual determination. "No urgent care... I'm fine."

O'Malley's looked at her doubtfully. "You've just had a huge shock. You need a doctor."

"No," she said vehemently. "I want to look the story up on the Internet—to find out what happened."

O'Malley went to Montana's desk, brought her computer over to the couch, and angled the website he'd just viewed between the two of them. He took a healthy swill of Dewar's from his flask and then offered it to Montana. She shook her head no.

The screen showed a smaller version of the computer generated sketch of Suzette. They read the story underneath. The police wanted the public's help in identifying the unknown victim.

Montana's cellphone, still in her hand, rang.

"Hello." Her voice was dull, lifeless. She listened a moment and replied, "Yes, I just saw the sketch." More quiet as she listened. "What would you like me to bring?" Another pause, then, "We'll be right there."

O'Malley raised his eyebrows. "Who was that?"

"Officer McCarty—he took Suzette's report. He said the lead investigator on the case wants me to come to the precinct to talk to him. They also want something with Suzette's DNA on it."

"I'll go with you." He put his arm around her.

Montana didn't argue.

They hailed a taxi to Suzette's apartment. The cabbie waited while Montana grabbed Suzette's toothbrush. Due to the late afternoon rush hour, the ride to the precinct was endless.

O'Malley again pulled the flask out of his jacket's inner pocket and took a swig. He offered it to Montana but again she shook her head no. She had already had a glass of wine with lunch and she wanted to be in control of her emotions. She was grateful for O'Malley's presence, his protective hand over hers. During the short, intense search for Suzette, their relationship had progressed. She realized how much she had come to value O'Malley's friendship.

Walking into the precinct was almost an out of body experience for Montana. She recognized the female dispatcher from her last visit. This time, Montana got straight to the point. "I'm Montana Wylde and this is Private Detective

O'Malley. Officer McCarty called to ask me to meet with Detective Constantine."

The woman punched some keys on her desk system. "Montana Wylde is here to see you." She looked up. "He'll be out in a minute—have a seat." The woman gestured to the familiar chairs lining one wall.

Just as they sat down Detective Constantine strode out to greet them. His face serious, he held his hand out to Montana first.

"Thanks for coming in on such short notice. I'm Max Constantine, lead investigator on the Church Murderer investigation. We met briefly when you came in to fill out your friend's report."

"Of course," she replied, her voice barely audible. "This is Thomas O'Malley, the private investigator I hired when you all refused to look for Suzette. I've asked him to be present for our conversation."

"I have no problem with that." Max held his hand out for a shake. "Mr. O'Malley, it's a pleasure to meet you."

"Make it O'Malley," he replied, shaking the detective's hand.

"And please make it Max. Let's head to my office."

Following the same maze Montana had undergone twice before, they arrived at Max's slightly larger office where Officer McCarty was waiting. Max removed files from the third chair across his desk and gestured for Montana and O'Malley to sit.

Montana, who sat next to McCarty, got down to business right away. "Why did you need a computer-generated sketch when I gave you several photos of Suzette when I came in to fill out the report?"

Max answered for him. "That's a fair question. Officer McCarty is a member of the CM task force. When we released the sketch to the media, he hadn't connected Suzette as a CM victim because she didn't fit the profile. When we arrived at the crime scene, she was unrecognizable from the photos you brought in. She was in full stage makeup. We were on a different track at that point since all the previous victims were streetwalkers. But when her prints didn't show up in any database and after receiving photos from the ME with her face scrubbed clean, Officer McCarty was astute enough to recognize her from those photos."

"Suzette doesn't work the street. How can she be connected to the Church Murderer?"

"Two days ago, a woman found your friend propped up in a wheelchair near the last row of pews at Holy Trinity Church. The same has been true for every victim of the CM—the abbreviated name for the Church Murderer."

Montana brow wrinkled. "Are you saying that this Church Murderer—the man who kills street girls—is responsible for Suzette's death?"

"Yes." Max nodded. "It's the same MO, though I cannot and will not go into details we've kept from the public."

"But Suzette doesn't work the street."

Max consulted his computer. "According to your report, Suzette Peterson worked the street with a pimp named Flash when she first arrived in New York."

O'Malley cleared his throat. "Detective—Max, that was over ten years ago. She was a kid then—fifteen or sixteen. Correct me if I'm wrong, Montana."

"That's right," Montana nodded. "She moved here when she was fifteen to escape her uncle's sexual abuse. She was alone, broke, and scared—on her own for the first time. Flash was a lowlife predator who took advantage of her. She was smart, though. As soon as she figured out how, she hid money from Flash—a little at a time until she could escape. She worked for Flash only a few months and she's not worked the street since. We're not stupid; our business is a cooperative. No one makes money but us."

"Maybe she was padding her wallet without your knowledge," Max said evenly. "Or perhaps the CM saw her picture from your Internet ad and followed her to your place of business. Or perhaps he's branched out. Maybe he's decided to upgrade to escorts."

"We never do outcalls unless we know a client. She would never agree to an outcall unless she had seen the client at the Coop first."

"The what?"

"Coop. Our business. It's derived from cooperative."

"Maybe he grabbed her off the street," Max suggested.

Montana frowned. "It seems unlikely he could grab her without someone noticing."

"Look—there's no point in speculating about this now. What we know so far is that nearly every aspect of your friend's murder is the same as the others."

"Where is she?" Montana's voice dropped again.

"At the morgue—the ME is still conducting its investigation. I have some photos from their office, taken postmortem. I hate to ask you to do this but I'd like to show you those pictures for a positive ID. Would that be okay?"

She couldn't speak but gave a near imperceptible nod.

Max pulled up a photo on his laptop and turned it around to show her. "Is this your friend?"

Montana's diminutive yelp answered his question. Montana hated it but fat tears began rolling down her cheeks. "I want to see her."

"That's not possible. You've already given us a positive ID. Plus, whatever you've brought that has her DNA will confirm her identity."

"It's not such a hot idea anyway, honey," O'Malley concurred.

Montana retreated to a familiar place of numbness—one she'd often drifted to as a defense against her stepfather's abuse.

"I guess I'll have to let her family know," she said finally.

"If it's easier for you, I can do that," Max offered.

"No. Someone who loved Suzette should tell them."

Max's voice was gentle. "I need to ask you for whatever you brought with Suzette's DNA."

Montana dug in her handbag and pulled out a large zippered baggie. It contained Suzette's toothbrush.

O'Malley, his hand over hers, looked at her with the compassion that had first drawn her. "Honey, let's get you back home—you're in shock."

"Can I give you a lift?" Max stood up.

"Thanks." Her voice was monotone. "I'll take you up on that."

Max pulled a couple of business cards from his case and handed them each one. "This has my private number." He turned to O'Malley. "Can I give you a lift too?"

"Thanks. You can drop me off at my office—it's only a half mile from Montana's loft."

"Sure."

She and O'Malley waited outside while Max went to get his car. The day had become surreal —a badly scripted movie. Montana expected that a harried director to burst in yelling 'cut!' Then Suzette would jump out, thrilled that she'd pulled off such a great punk on her friend. But this was no script, there were no directors or actors. This was not a film. Someone had silenced Suzette's boundless energy and sunny disposition forever.

Outside, the cheerful sunshine mocked her. Why wasn't it raining? Or at the very least, overcast?

O'Malley's worried face searched hers. "I should stay with you for a while, Montana. This is no time for you to be alone."

"I need to be alone—to process everything."

O'Malley hesitated. "If you need me, I'm only a phone call away."

"Thanks," she whispered.

Max pulled up. With rush hour still ongoing, the ride downtown was torturous.

After what seemed an eternity, they arrived at O'Malley's office. He opened the door. "Appreciate the ride, Max." Before getting out, he turned to Montana. "Remember to call if you need to talk—even in the middle of the night. I'll be up, believe me. If I don't hear from you tonight, I'll call you in the morning."

She nodded, afraid that even a single word would produce the anguish begging for release.

Max opened his door. "Let me walk you to your door."

O'Malley shrugged. When they reached the steps, O'Malley turned to Max with a raised eyebrow. "What's up?"

"I'm sure Montana appreciates the work you've done but it's just as well to let this case go. Her friend is no longer missing and the NYPD and BAU have formed a task force to handle the CM investigation. You should let us take over now."

"With all due respect," O'Malley responded, "Montana is my client. She's capable of making her own decisions. Don't underestimate her. She left an abusive home at seventeen, moved to this city knowing no one, and put herself through school—all the way from earning a GED to graduating from Columbia's School of Law." Without giving Max a chance to reply, he slipped his key in the door and disappeared behind it.

Max's jaw hung open. There was more to Montana Wylde than he'd imagined. He squinted at her profile through the car's window, sitting erect and proud with her chin thrust out in defiance. He looked on with admiration. What a woman.

It took less than five minutes to reach her loft. Max turned to her. "Anything I can do before I go?"

"Find the crazy son of a bitch who killed Suzette."

"I will or die trying—believe me on that." He hesitated. "There's one other thing I must tell you before I leave. It's my job to do so. If your friend wasn't working the street— and I'm still inclined to believe she was—then her death has broadened the scope of victims. Do not continue with your business until we find this creep. You could be in danger yourself."

"You don't have to worry," Montana replied in the same dead tone. "I don't work the street, and the Coop is closed."

Upstairs, she first dealt with the unpleasant task of breaking the news to Suzette's family. Suzette had spoken of her family's dysfunction but the aunt's reaction still shocked Montana. The woman didn't sound a bit sad or up-set—not even when Montana told her about the murder. Instead, her voice quivered in self-righteous disapproval. "It's not surprising. As I told you when we last spoke, Susan lived a sinful life in a satanic city."

Her primary concern was Suzette's will, telling Montana that she and her husband would take over their niece's af-fairs. Then she went into a long whining tirade about how they couldn't afford the airfare or hotel. To get her off the phone, Montana offered to wire the money, cursing herself as she did. How she dreaded their inevitable meeting.

The call left Montana wishing that Suzette and she had discussed their end-of-life issues. But it hadn't seemed ur-gent. There was all the time in the world... until there wasn't, of course. Suzette had once talked of starting a foundation to help girls get off the street. After hanging up with the aunt, Montana decided she'd do a thorough search of Suzette's apartment on the slim chance she'd left a will. The thought of the greedy, horrid relatives getting a dime from Suzette was loathsome. Still, even if the relatives did manage to sink their talons into Suzette's estate, Montana was determined to start that foundation in her friend's honor anyway.

The second call was tougher but not nearly as unpleasant. She wished she could tell him in person but he deserved to hear the news from her rather than the way she did.

"Hanky..." Her voice broke, and with it, the dam did as well.

"Montana—Montana, what's wrong?" Hanky demanded. "What is it? Is it Suzette?"

"Y-y-yes-s." It was all she could manage.

"Oh my God, No! Not Suzette." Between the two phone lines, their grief mingled. They clutched their phones, weeping in shared sorrow.

When she got herself under control enough to speak, she gave Hanky the bare bones of what she knew of their friend's death. This brought outrage from Hanky and fresh tears from both. After talking of their memories and the what-ifs, they hung up, promising to talk soon.

Once finished, she took her landline off the hook and turned off her cell phone. Still numb from the day, without her awareness, a tiny flicker of doubt began sprouting in her mind. It was all wrong.

32

GRIEF HIJACKED HER. She cried until the day faded to dusk and then she wept some more. The emotions she'd suppressed at the precinct now came unglued. Great sobs shook her to the core. Never had she experienced such profound pain, not even when her Nana had died. This was worse because someone had robbed Suzette of so much of her life.

She wailed, pounding the floor, and cursing God. She sat for hours in her rocking chair, alternating between tears of anguish and staring out at the darkened dead spaces across the river. The lights twinkling in between those dead spaces now seemed to mock her grief.

Deadly thoughts danced in her brain. How long had Suzette suffered? How much agony had she gone through? How fast had the end come? Relentless images spun through her too-vivid imagination. After an indeterminable amount of time, another too cheery sun rose. It was incongruous to the raging storm within her. For the first time ever Montana drew the blinds down, shutting away the magnificent view.

Along with pain and anguish was an enormous anger at the incomprehensible apathy of the NYPD. She blamed its black and white system. Its bureaucracy viewed people as categories rather than individuals. Why had she waited *two days* to file Suzette's report only to learn there would be no real search. Had she known, she'd have searched for a private detective sooner. It never occurred to her that a police officer would just toss the report into a meaningless database. What might have happened if she'd had those two days?

She would never know.

Suzette as a victim of the CM didn't make sense. Instead of closure, this scenario raised even more questions. Her instincts were still burning, too—telling her that she and O'Malley had been onto something. Suzette didn't fit the profile of the other victims. How could she be one? It didn't make sense.

She pondered her own situation. For more than a week, working with O'Malley had been a lifesaver. She'd felt she was doing something meaningful. Now that Suzette was no longer missing, there was no case. O'Malley's job was finding Suzette. It seemed irrational but she didn't want the case to end—and her gut told her it wasn't supposed to end—not this way.

O'Malley. In less than a week, she had become closer to him than she had nearly anyone other than Suzette and Hanky. She felt she'd lost two people. While she recognized the selfishness of this, she was unable to stop feeling that way. O'Malley liked her—but he owed her nothing. Their relationship—brief as it was—would end with Suzette's death. Still, his compassion at the precinct had been real.

She'd not slept for over twenty-four hours—even though she was in desperate need of it. She went to the bedroom, discarding clothes along the way. After a restless half an hour, she went to the medicine cabinet and shook a Valium into her palm. After a moment of hesitation, she fished another from the bottle and threw both into her mouth. She cupped her hand under the running water to wash them down.

Back in her comfortable bed, a blue, mellow calm allowed an escape into another dreamless sleep where no killers, no dead friends, and no dark spaces could exist.

33

S HE HAD FALLEN ASLEEP with the bedroom blinds open and now an angry morning sun glared its greeting. She cursed it. Worsening the situation, someone was pounding on the door. Slamming the blinds shut, she willed whoever it was to disappear, but he or she was relentless. Ironically, it reminded her of Suzette the day she'd come to see her after the nightmare outcall.

Now shouts accompanied the pounding. Groaning, she threw off her bedsheets and gave up. If she didn't answer, a neighbor was bound to call the cops. Still groggy from the Valium, she threw on a bathrobe and cursed the day again. Just as she approached the door, she heard a click.

Someone was trying to get in.

Suzette was the only one with a key. Tiptoeing to the kitchen, she looked around. The only gun was at the Coop because she never dreamed she would need one at home. It was her sanctuary—her escape. Now O'Malley and Max's warnings about potential danger took hold. She took a frantic look around her kitchen and spotted the knife rack. She grabbed the largest one. As unsteady as she was, she tried preparing herself mentally as her taekwondo master had instructed.

One final click took hold, then the only thing stopping the intruder was the door chain. Whoever was there opened it with one hard kick. After screaming, she nearly fainted in relief.

"O'Malley," she exclaimed. "What are you doing here? You about scared me to death."

He looked at the knife in her limp hand. "Whaddaya gonna do with that thing? But the better question is why aren't you answering your phones? Your landline is busy and your cell goes straight to voicemail—it's full by the way. I've been pounding on your door for ten minutes. I'm worried about you," he yelled.

She lay the knife on the counter, walked to the couch, and plopped down. "I heard a key in the lock—how did you get it?"

"This isn't your key."

She raised an eyebrow. "How'd you open the door?"

"Tricks of the trade." He sat beside her on the couch and showed her a ring holding different sized picks and other tools. "These belonged to my pop. I inherited them when he passed away. They've come in mighty handy, like now."

"I'm glad we're friends."

"Me too. That's why I'm here."

"If you're my friend, you'll leave me alone."

"As your friend that's the last thing I'll do. You've holed yourself up for two days—I've been worried sick. I've called dozens of times. This was my last resort."

"I haven't felt like getting out of bed."

O'Malley gave her a hard look. "You aren't going to feel better until you eat something. You're downright skinny—must have dropped ten pounds since we met." He got up and opened the refrigerator, inspecting an egg carton for dates. Satisfied, he set it on the counter.

She sat up from the couch. "What are you doing?"

"Making you breakfast." He pulled some cheese and veggies out next. "Take a shower—that always makes people feel better. When you're finished, I'll have breakfast whipped up for us."

She stood and almost staggered. O'Malley rushed to her. "Hey—are you okay? You're as white as a sheet."

"I just got up too fast and the blood rushed from my head. You're right. I need to eat."

Twenty minutes later, she emerged from the shower with wet hair, wearing soft pink sweat pants and a matching tee shirt. Freshly brewed coffee and other breakfast smells made her mouth water. O'Malley transferred the second cheese and veggie omelet from the pan to a plate and brought them both to the dining table along with a stack of buttered toast. He poured them each a steaming cup of coffee, even attending to her requisite sugar and cream.

"That smells good."

"I'm a good cook. Don't you eat too fast or it's gonna upset your tummy. Take it slow."

When they were finished, O'Malley cleared the table while Montana dropped back onto the couch. O'Malley joined her there.

"Talk to me, Montana. What's going on?" O'Malley's gruff voice was gentle.

She rubbed her temples. "It's rough. I'm just haunted by all the 'what ifs.' I can't get it out of my brain. I should have sought out your services much sooner. I knew something was wrong—and so did you when you heard the story."

"Regret is the most useless emotion because it doesn't change anything. Be realistic. One day wouldn't have made a difference. Being mad at yourself isn't going to do a bit of good, either. It's not gonna bring Suzette back. Don't let your grief sabotage your goals. You need to get back on track—start studying for that exam. It will give you a sense of purpose again." He turned her face toward his. "Suzette would want that."

At the mention of her name, Montana burst into tears. When they subsided, she nodded her head. "She encouraged me so much. She celebrated every victory with me. When I felt like giving up, she wouldn't let me." She buried her face in O'Malley's shoulder and wept again. He rocked her as he would a child. When her outpour turned into sniffles and hiccups, he spoke to her in earnest.

"Don't make the mistake I made. When I lost my wife and daughters, I dishonored them. Even worse, I dishonored myself."

"I read about your wife and daughters. After I hired you, I googled you and read about the murders."

"You googled me *after* you hired me?" He gave a grim chuckle. "It's supposed to go the other way around, you know? Let me tell you a bit about my story. You should hear it. I loved my wife and daughters more than anything. Coming home hot and tired, with the stench of crime surrounding me, beautiful Sylvia lifted my spirits—she made me see the purpose of my work. How she loved me!"

"Sounds like an amazing woman."

"She had a gift to see the best in everyone. Helping others was second nature to her, particularly those who were most vulnerable. She worked at the soup kitchen near our home. She always thought of others before herself."

"I can't imagine the hell you went through."

"Something fundamental in me changed when I watched Sylvia give birth to Bridget. Holding that tiny baby in my arms, I vowed to protect her until my final breath. She was a daddy's girl—the apple of my eye. When Sylvia became pregnant with Katie, I worried I wouldn't be able to love another child as much. But that all changed when Katie came along. My heart expanded. I called her 'my weasel' because she weaseled her way into my heart."

O'Malley was now lost in his own pain. Lines etched onto his face made him appear older than he was. "When those bastards killed my family, the guilt tore me apart because I put them in danger. Had I known, I would have quit the force in a second."

"I'm so sorry," she murmured.

"I ain't looking for your sympathy. I'm telling you this so you don't do what I did."

"What was that?"

"I drank—morning, noon, and night. I didn't sleep, I passed out. When I woke up, I'd be in the same crumpled suit I'd worn the previous day. Always hungover, I started taking a little hair of the dog in the morning. Then I'd need a pick me up during my noon breaks. I reeked of booze but my superiors looked the other way because of what I'd been through. Plus, I'd been a decent cop for eighteen years. Since I was useless working an actual investigation they coaxed me into a desk job for two years. They did that so I'd make my pension."

"I bet you hated that desk."

"You know it. I pulled the pin the day I hit twenty. Then I went on a month long bender that just about killed me. Can't remember most of it—it's just a boozy blur."

"How did pull yourself out?" She thought of the two valium she'd taken the previous night, understanding O'Malley's rationalization for using booze. She'd done the same with the valium. Forced slumber could be addictive.

"No one comes out of something like that without help, Montana. People cared—like I care about you." He gave her a stern look. "For me, it was my former partner, Frankie. When I wouldn't answer the phone, he came rapping on my door. I was so boozed out I didn't even hear him. Frankie didn't have my nifty tool ring but he kicked my door down. What he told me saved my life. If I'd kept on like I had been I'd have been dead in less than a year."

"What did he do?"

"First he made me release the pent-up pain. I sobbed in his arms for at least an hour—maybe more. Each tear washed away a small bit of anguish. What really got to me was what he said about Sylvia. He told me how disappointed Sylvia would be if she saw me. Hearing that was like a sharp slap. I stopped pitying myself and slowly pulled myself up out of that deep vat of depression. If I were to write a perfect ending, I'd tell you how I found God and quit drinking altogether. But this ain't a perfect world. And, as you know, I still drink." He patted the familiar bulge in his inner right hand pocket. "But I manage it enough to get out of bed in the morning and work."

"So you started your own agency then."

"That was Frankie's idea."

"I'm glad he gave you that idea. You've been a godsend."

"Don't put me on a pedestal, Montana. I don't belong there. I'm not the hot shot PI you read about in books. Mostly, I handle insurance fraud, which is about as interesting as watching an empty fishbowl. Your case was different though. It sparked a fire in me—I'll admit it. The case breathed life into my career." He paused, his face filled with sadness. "I wish I could have given you a happy ending."

"You did a great job—Suzette's death is in no way *your* fault. You made a lot of progress in a very short amount of time."

"*We* made a lot of progress. Look, I'm gonna give you back most of your retainer—I only did one real day of work."

Although she'd known this was coming, the words still assaulted her. For all his drinking, lateness, and trembling hands, he had helped her through the worst time of her life. It struck her how much she had relied on him.

"They haven't caught him yet," she countered.

"But they know who he is. What's more, they have an entire task force devoted to capturing him."

"But you could still help, couldn't you?" She thrust her stubborn chin out.

"I wouldn't know where to begin looking for him—and their task force doesn't need me tagging along. I won't let you waste your money. You're going to need it when you open up your first law practice. Let the task force do their work and you do yours, which is studying for the bar. You need a break from this case—it's eating you up."

"I know," she said miserably, "but I can't even concentrate right now."

"Try—learn from my mistakes. Let me pass along some of Frankie's wise words. He said, 'Tommy, even if you don't feel like getting out of bed, do it anyway. When you don't feel like smiling, fake it. Fake it until you make it.' So I did that. I faked it even when I felt like a complete phony. Then one day I realized my smile was real. I laughed because something was funny, not because I thought I should. Sounds corny, I know. But it works. Time heals. It will help heal you."

She tapped her head, "I know you're right up here. Still, it's hard, knowing her killer is on the loose." She shuddered as she looked across the Hudson.

"They're gonna catch him. I have a lot of faith in Max Constantine. You should too."

"I'm going to miss you." Fresh tears sparkled in her eyes.

"No you ain't because I'm not going anywhere. We're friends—you call me whenever you need to talk. And let's have dinners weekly like you and Suzette."

"I'd really like that, O'Malley."

"I would too." His voice was gruff. "It's still light. Why don't you go for a run and get the last bit of afternoon sun. But until they catch the CM, don't you dare run at night. No walking alone. You call a car and have it come to you— no hailing a taxi on your own. You got that?"

She smiled in spite of herself. "Yes sir." She gave a captain's salute.

"When you get back from running, eat a hot meal, and then study for the exam."

"If not tonight, I promise to crack the books tomorrow."

"Good, because I'm counting on you to be my lawyer."

"I'm going to need all the clients I can get. O'Malley?"

"Yeah?"

"Thanks for being my Frankie."

She walked him to the door, obeying his instructions to double-lock the door. She took his other advice and pulled on running clothes. She opened the living room blinds and saw that she had an hour of sunlight left. She planned to take advantage of it.

Montana stood in front of her window attaching her iPhone to an arm carrier. Looking up, she noticed how the sunlight hit the water, again creating the effect of a million glittering diamonds on the water's surface. Taking in the beauty of the view, a tiny speck of something other than grief began flickering. From an endless field of sorrow, a tiny seed of gratitude sprouted.

Walking out the door, she spotted a photo of Suzette and herself on a rare vacation together. They'd cruised the Caribbean on a small luxurious yacht, loaned from one of Suzette's high rollers. How grateful she was that they'd shared that trip. How wonderful that she'd known Suzette as long as she had. She picked up the photo, studying it. They had their arms looped around each other in camaraderie with wide smiles on their tanned faces. Was such pain worth knowing Suzette?

Unequivocally yes.

34

THE MAN HID behind a newspaper, watching from the corner of his eye as she exited the building. He had kept an intermittent eye on her building during the last several days. He planned to stay on watch too. He needed the perfect opportunity to present itself—and that would take patience. He had to be careful. She'd already spotted him a few mornings ago. He knew she'd seen him because of the way her eyes had glowered into his. Good thing he'd been in disguise and he'd remain so. This time, she hadn't noticed him at all, but then she was bound to be out of sorts after she'd learned of her slutty friend's demise. He smiled at the memory of snuffing the blonde tramp's life out. It was good to purify the world from such filth.

The brunette whore stretched her legs on the railing that guarded the trail. What a shame it was still daylight—not the right time. His patience would pay off—and that was one of his strong suits. If he remained alert and kept careful watch, the right break would present itself. This afternoon there were far too many people on the trail. Someone would likely intervene. He needed to catch her off guard, under the cover of night.

It would take vigilance in the next few days because he had to deal with her soon, that much was clear. She'd already proven to be the type who wouldn't give up easily. He reassured himself that he still had time on his side because the foolhardy police were still chasing their tails—their impotence was pitiable. They had no clue who they were dealing with. The brunette whore and her devoted drunk detective were far more of a threat. Nevertheless, he planned to take care of her soon so she could join her slutty girlfriend in Hell. All he needed was to continue on his watch.

He'd already picked out a church in her honor...

35

SHE STOPPED AT THE RAILING for a quick stretch. Her body felt tight, unused. She'd not been to her taekwondo class for a more than a week and hadn't run for several days. No wonder she felt out of shape.

As she warmed up to a slow jog, uneasy questions lurking in the recesses of her brain came to the forefront. With the shock wearing off, things didn't make sense. How did Suzette encounter the Church Murderer? The NYPD's rigid belief that Suzette was walking the street was ludicrous. There was just no way.

Still, Max Constantine was sure the Church Murderer had killed Suzette because of how she had turned up. He'd also claimed there were other details that convinced him but that he hadn't released to the public. Still, how could have Suzette come across the CM? Too many questions and not enough answers—but something was off.

O'Malley had been right to suggest the run and she realized he was also right that she wouldn't run after dark until they caught the bastard. As she walked the short distance from the trail to her building's entrance, she was too lost in thought to notice the same bearded stranger who had stared so intently at her a couple of days before.

Upstairs, she soaked in her bathroom's Jacuzzi until her fingers looked like prunes and she felt waterlogged. Climbing out of the tub, her reflection in the full-length mirror shocked her. She stepped on the scale— eight pounds gone in less than two weeks. The anxiety and grief diet, she thought with irony—it worked for me.

She'd decided to remedy that. Sorting through a stack of menus, Hunan Chinese called out to her—something spicy to awaken her senses. Besides, the capsaicin in hot peppers was supposed to be a painkiller. She could use some relief for her aching heart.

Other than the need to fill the emptiness in her stomach, she hadn't thought she was hungry. But when the aromatic food arrived, it caused her stomach to growl and her mouth to water. She made a heaping plate filled with savory dumplings, onion cakes, and curried chicken. Even though her stomach had shrunk, she managed to put away half the food. She stashed the rest in the fridge for later. Then she opened up her fortune cookie.

'Don't ever give up.' She stared at the tiny slip of paper between the two broken halves of cookie. It was a *fortune cookie*, for goodness sake. Still... *don't ever give up.*

The thought kept returning, as she spent the next few hours channel surfing. She couldn't concentrate on anything. She got up, restless and dissatisfied. It was getting late but she wasn't the least bit tired. Of course, the magic bottle in the medicine cabinet could take care of that but she'd used more of the little blue pills in the past week than she had in the previous six months. She mustn't start relying on them.

She decided to watch the late news. It was just starting, and again, the hot story was Suzette. Montana almost clicked the television off—she'd had quite enough of that story. But just as she picked up the remote, a montage of victims' faces filled the screen. She set the remote down again. Suzette's beautiful, smiling face amongst the rest of the women was too incongruous. The other photos were from their mug shots whereas Suzette's was one Montana had provided to McCarty. Her well cared for hair, teeth and skin stood in contrast to the others' sad and ravaged faces. Montana sat transfixed at the collage. Something was wrong. Troubling questions had been tickling her brain all day and at once, those doubts became clear. She glanced at the clock. It was now quarter past eleven but she knew what she had to do.

She replaced her tank top and shorts with a pair of old gray sweat pants and a matching hoodie. She laced up her sneakers, tucked forty dollars into her credit card case, and zipped it into her pocket. Grabbing her cellphone and keys, she dashed out the door.

Outside, she glanced around the street. It was almost deserted save for a few stragglers wandering home from a late dinner or on their way out to a club. She gave a cursory search for an 'on duty' taxi but decided it would be faster to run. O'Malley's office was less than fifteen minutes if she ran quickly. Rather than waste time stretching her legs, she decided to warm up by walking at a brisk pace and then to increase speed until she reached a full run. After a block of power walking, she increased her pace to a steady jog.

A quarter of the way to O'Malley's building, she noticed someone following her—at least he sure seemed to be. She sensed the presence of another person before she heard the footsteps. If she'd worn her earphones as she usually did while running she might not have noticed him at all. She turned her head around to look. Halfway down the block was another jogger. O'Malley's stern warning hadn't crossed her mind as she'd started out. She'd been too preoccupied with her mission to think of it. Now his forewarning was front and center and her heart began pounding.

Contrary to popular belief, some parts of New York City *do* sleep at night, particularly the small side streets that zig-zagged their way to O'Malley's office. She picked up her pace, her ears now tuned to the foot patter of the person behind her. And he *was* following her—she was certain of that now. When she picked up the pace, so did he.

She hadn't much further to go until she would reach O'Malley's office. She broke into a fast run. Now only five minutes away, and panting from the exertion, the terror from his footfalls drove her even harder. She thought of the ways she could deploy her often practiced but never used martial arts training.

She rounded the corner to O'Malley's office at a furious pace. And, it paid off. Her pursuer didn't have her running chops; she'd gained some ground. He was over a block away but he'd catch up once she stopped as O'Malley's door.

Frantic, she banged on O'Malley's outer door while pressing her fingers on the buzzer. She alternated between ringing the back apartment first and then his office. She looked around wildly, the runner now less than a block away. She was sure he was after her. Was he the Church Murderer? Would she end up like Suzette and the rest? Her heart beat in wild trepidation as she pressed the buzzers and prayed. Just as she began shouting, a bewildered O'Malley opened the door, his annoyance turning to worry as he saw her panic.

It almost sobered him up.

"He—he's behind—that's him," she cried, pointing her finger down the street. Only, it was now deserted. She squinted her eyes and thought she saw the remnants of a person's legs disappearing into an alley halfway down the block.

"Who are you talking about? What the hell is going on?" He ushered her into the building. "Come back to my apartment."

She gulped big breaths of air, trying to steady herself. "Someone was following me. He took off almost as soon as I started running here." Her words came out in a rush. "I sensed someone behind me and then I heard his footsteps. If you hadn't answered the door when you did I would have finally put my taekwondo training to use."

"I told you not to go out alone," he roared.

"I wasn't thinking. I'm sorry, but I had to come see you."

"Are you sure he was following you? Maybe it was just a late night jogger."

She was still shaking. "No. Every time I increased my pace, he did too. And he disappeared into that alley halfway down your block when you answered the door."

O'Malley went to a small cabinet, grabbed a bottle of cognac, filled a healthy portion, and handed it to her. She gulped it down and then coughed and looked at him gratefully. If her own reflection had startled her earlier, O'Malley's was a shocker. He looked like a different man than the one who had visited her previously—he looked like death microwaved a few times over. His ruddy face was sallow beneath the broken veins on his cheeks and his nose. His eyes were so red they looked ready to bleed. He must have been drinking since he left her place. For the first time, she stepped out of herself to realize that O'Malley had his own private demons to deal with. He'd told her about them just that day. He picked up his glass of scotch with a trembling hand.

Her own agony had been too consuming to see how rough things had been for him also. Now it was all too clear. He'd more or less told her that her case had been his salvation from his annual self-condemnation of guilt and grief. With Suzette's case in the hands of law enforcement, he'd reverted to his normal mode of coping. Drinks and more drinks.

She gave him a hard look. "O'Malley, you look as fucked up as a soup sandwich. How much have you been drinking?"

"Soup sandwich—ha—good one. Don't I just feel like one." He set the booze down. "Hold on and let me get my hangover juice before I ask just what the hell you're doing here."

Montana watched him mix vodka, tomato juice, hot sauce, horseradish, and Worcestershire sauce into a tall glass. Then he dropped a raw egg into the whole mess, gave it a vigorous stir, and gulped it down. He set the glass down, belched, and shook his head a few times as if clearing out the remaining fog. Looking on in amazed disgust, she almost gagged.

"That's better." He motioned for her to sit. "Now *why* are you here?"

"You need to continue the case."

As he shook his head in protest, Montana cut him off. "Just hear me out, okay? You said I still have money on the retainer. If it isn't enough, I have more."

"Not gonna take it—it would be like stealing. It's not a wise use of your money—or your time and energy. The task force is all over the CM case. As for me, I don't have a case because there isn't a missing person."

"But there is," she exclaimed. "Friday's client—he's missing. When I went running earlier, I started thinking about that client. We were on the verge of figuring out who he is. Also, there's the matter of this so called Church Murderer killing Suzette. I don't see it. I know the cops are certain he did it but I need to understand how that happened. So, we need to find Friday's client and ask him if he saw Suzette. If he did, we need to ask him where and when he dropped her off. You won't be interfering with the cops' investigation because you aren't looking for the CM *and* you're not looking for Suzette. You're looking for the high roller. That person has answers. I need to know what he knows."

O'Malley hesitated. She took advantage and pressed on.

"You'll just be investigating the last few hours of Suzette's life. There can be no closure for me until I know how she wound up in the clutches of that creep. Be honest—do you have a sense of completion?"

"It was a good lead," he admitted. He took a long thoughtful pause. "Okay, but this is how it goes. We find the high roller and talk to him. After that, our work is over—and we pass on any pertinent information to the police. After that—we're done with this, Montana. And after we talk to him, you study like hell for that exam. Do we have a deal?"

Montana jumped up and kissed his cheek. "Yes—I agree. Thank you."

He gave her a gruff hug. "Okay, partner, we start up on the case again tomorrow. Now let me call you a taxi—no more running. If you want to run then use your treadmill. No more going off on your own, not on the trail—and not even in the daylight."

Montana shuddered. "Believe me, you have nothing to worry about."

36

AFTER DUCKING INTO THE ALLEYWAY, he pounded his clenched fists against the building's brick wall as he cursed himself. It had been a perfect opportunity—one he'd waited for with such diligence. He'd almost been ready to give up for the night but something had told him to wait until midnight passed. He'd been ready to go home for a few hours of sleep when he'd been amazed to see the filthy slut leave her building. As soon as he saw her, he'd tightened the laces on his running shoes—thinking he might get his chance because she loved to run so much.

Then he'd blown it. *Goddamnit.* His head hurt in disappointment with the now defunct chase. He'd *almost* had her. She was strong; something he'd need to keep in mind in the future. This one would put up a fight. Next time, he wouldn't be so obvious. He'd have to catch her off guard. He'd gotten a bad feeling when she'd turned around to notice him following her. If only he'd been quieter—or taken a side street and then faced her head on. He hadn't been sure where she was headed—although retrospectively, he should have known she'd run to the drunk detective for help. Where else would she go? Few people would dirty themselves with her presence but that well-oiled detective seemed dedicated to her and the dead blonde slut.

What were they up to now? Why meet so late at night? He'd have to remain on guard—one of His soldiers. Another opportunity would come if he stayed the course. He had His Work to do.

God would help him get that miserable bitch. He would pray to Him tonight.

37

ONTANA HADN'T SPOKEN TO HANKY since she'd told him about Suzette. Today they were to meet at the Coop. Montana planned to give him his final paycheck along with a generous severance package. It was time for both of them to move on. She'd always planned to stop but with Suzette's death, the inevitable end had just come sooner. While she'd miss seeing Hanky so often, they would remain lifelong friends.

She had other business at the Coop as well. She planned to forward their two business lines to two burner phones she would purchase that morning. She'd thought of it while lying awake after returning from O'Malley's apartment. She'd called him to run the plan by him earlier that morning and they both thought it wise to track the Coop's calls. Suzette's killer was still on the loose and no one knew how they'd crossed paths. The Friday high roller was also on Montana's mind. He might not even know of Suzette's death. Now that the NYPD had released Suzette's name, he might call the Coop.

She bought the phones at a Duane Reade and then stopped at the corner coffee shop where she bought giant lattes for Hanky and herself. When she approached the Coop's building, Tony, the regular daytime attendant, hurried up to greet her.

"Tana, I heard about Suzy." His eyes were wet as he wrapped her in a warm hug. "I just can't believe it. How could anyone hurt such a sweetie?" He gave her a close look. "How're you holding up, honey?"

"I'm okay," she said trying to stay calm, but tears were always close. It took little to set off her raw emotions. She wiped her eyes. "I wanted to let you all know I'll be moving out. I won't renew our lease when it comes up next month. I'll let the management know in the next day or two, and I'll be moving things out later this month. I'll miss all you guys, though. You've always been so good to us."

"I understand," Tony nodded. "We'll all miss you and..."

She cut him off, giving him another squeeze. "Thanks again for everything."

"Let me know if there's anything I can do." Tony opened the door for her.

"There might be," she said, thinking of O'Malley. "A Detective O'Malley will be coming to see you in the next few days to ask you a few questions. It would be great if you talked to him."

"No problem, Montana—and in fact Al told me about him. I'll be here all week working my regular hours."

"You're the best, Tony. Thank you."

The empty Coop was an eerie ghost town. It gave her the creeps. She couldn't wait until Hanky arrived. Her heart was pounding—irrationally she knew—as she flicked on the lights, trying to bring life to the place. As they came on, mirrored reflections of herself greeted her. For the first time, it was unnerving. Her instincts were on fire. Ever since the chase to O'Malley's apartment, her inner instincts were alight, scanning everyone and everything with a critical eye. She had no desire to meet her stalker for one-on-

one combat. As irrational as it was, the Coop seemed evil. She hoped Hanky would arrive soon.

Within a few minutes, his usual 'shave-and-a-haircut-two-bits' knock, followed by his key in the door, alerted her of his arrival. She jumped up to greet him where they indulged in a long mournful hug. Tears of grief flowed, clinging together as if they were on a storm-tossed lifeboat. It was soothing to share the love and mourn with another person who had loved Suzette as much as she did.

After their tears had subsided, Montana filled Hanky in on what she knew of Suzette's death.

He shook his head. "I don't get it. How did she run into this guy? It makes no sense. What about the car parked across the street with the government plates and the high roller card? Wasn't that detective onto something? Something is off here."

"I have a hard time with all this too. What would Suzette be doing near a stroll? That's where they say he picked up his victims."

Hanky scoffed. "Suzette would never be anywhere near a whore stroll."

"I agree, but Constantine said that everything about her death fits the CM's profile—even things they haven't let the public know."

Hanky shook his head again. "So, is O'Malley now off the case?"

"No, but I had to talk him into it. In fact, I begged him to continue."

She told Hanky about talking to O'Malley the previous night, leaving out the part about someone chasing her—no sense in worrying Hanky about that. "He agreed to focus on the high roller but he told me the CM is off our radar. I still think that Friday client plays a role here—or at least knows something. I get the feeling O'Malley agrees with me."

Hanky nodded. "Go with your instincts. You're the smartest chick I know."

"Another thing I need to tell you," she murmured. "I'm not working anymore."

"I figured as much—the cops know all about this place now."

"I hadn't considered that," Montana said, "but that's not the reason. I just can't do this anymore. It's time to move on—it was almost time anyway."

Hanky hugged her. "I'll miss seeing you regularly but this isn't goodbye." He balled a fist, she did likewise, and they bumped knuckles. "You have a brother for life. You need me—you just holler. Don't you forget it."

"Thanks Hanky. I love you." She reached in her bag and pulled out a thick envelope. "This is three month's salary plus a bonus. You always made us feel safe—not to mention how much fun it was having you around."

Hanky pressed the envelope back into her hand. "No— you don't need to do this. You aren't working—at least not until you're a fancy-shmancy attorney. Save your money to get your practice going."

"I'll be okay." She forced the envelope into his shirt pocket. "I have money saved. Nana didn't raise any fools."

"Damn straight," he agreed.

After he left, Montana played each phone's messages, starting with the regular client line. Of those messages, nearly all calls were hang-ups, which made sense since regulars rarely left messages. They called to make appointments and usually stayed on the line only if someone answered.

Three regulars did leave messages; all wanted to schedule appointments and left their contact information. She scribbled their names and numbers to call them later. Halfway through the messages, the nature of the calls changed.

These had to have come in after the media had made Suzette's name and profession public. Some left brokenheart-
ed condolences, sincere in their sorrow. But one particular
message made the hair on the back of her neck rise. It left
her unnerved. She wasn't sure if the caller was male or female as whomever it was had used something to alter their
voice—it sounded muffled and distant. While she didn't
know who it was, she had no trouble understanding its
menace.

'If she profanes herself by whoring, she shall be burned with fire.'
After a long pause, it continued. *'Ask yourself this, you slut. You
may live with riches but you're a filthy whore and will never be
more than that. Are you next? Filthy whores get what they have
coming. Be forewarned—no one mocks the Lord.'*

Her hand shook as she replayed the message. Someone
was after her—she had no doubt—the frightening run last
night had convinced her. But this message was no random
call by a self-righteous religious nut. It was a direct warning: *'Are you next?'*

Since the call had come in to the Coop's landline, she
recorded it on her cellphone; she wanted O'Malley to hear
it. On edge now, she looked around the room, half expecting a bogeyman. Did the Church Murderer leave the message? It came in to their regular client line—the one new
clients didn't have. Could he really be a client? She shuddered at the thought of his presence in the Coop.

The new client messages offered no leads, they were either wankers or hang-ups, but she listened to each one so
she wouldn't miss anything important. Finished, she clicked
the speakerphone off.

She followed the directions for forwarding calls to another number. Identifying the two burner calls by color, she
chose red for new clients and blue for regulars. Once done

with that chore, she bolted—she couldn't wait to get the hell out.

Downstairs, she gave Tony another hug and let him hail her a cab. When she arrived home, her building's front entrance was tranquil. Still, with the previous night's narrow escape fresh in her mind, she gave the area a long suspicious look, paying particular attention to the outdoor deli. The bag lady was elsewhere. Satisfied that no one was following her, she went upstairs to call O'Malley and fill him in on her day.

"How you feeling today, honey?"

"Much better—thanks to you. You'll be happy to know that I've been keeping a close eye around me. That scare last night made me believe I really might be in danger."

"Listen to a former New York City cop, Montana. If I say BOLO, you damn well better BOLO. Glad to hear you're taking that to heart."

Montana looked at the phone as though it was a rare dinosaur bone. "O'Malley, you sound downright perky today. It's hard to believe I'm talking to the same man I saw last night. That disgusting concoction must work magic."

"It *is* magic, thank you—and I'm feeling much better. You oughta try it—although you're smart enough not to drink so much. So what's up, Watson?"

"I went to the Coop this morning." She told him about listening to the troubling message.

"Play it for me now."

She did.

"I do *not* like the sound of that call. Whoever it is was threatening you. I need to say this again—you must be careful from now on. We don't know how Suzette came across this nut."

"Do you think the CM left that call? It fits in with his religious theme."

"Impossible to know. Everyone knows Suzette's identity now. You advertised the Coop on social media. This means every lunatic has access to your phone lines—and there are a ton of religious zealots in this city."

"That call came into the regular client line, O'Malley—we don't advertise that number. We only advertise the new client number."

"That's even more troubling. You know, Montana—you may think you know your clients but you don't—not really. It's hard to say what lurks in the psyches of people. I've captured enough normal looking lunatics to know this firsthand. You know, I'd like to hear that call in person because your cellphone distorts the sound quality. We should get together soon, anyway—to talk about our next move."

"When can you meet?"

"Anytime—now—whenever you can come."

"I can be there in half an hour."

Aromatic coffee filled the office when she arrived. O'Malley poured them each a big mug and handed her one. He didn't spike his coffee, which surprised and pleased her. It was the first time she'd seen him forego that ritual.

"Thanks for my midday boost of caffeine—and for buying real cream and sugar."

"Pfffft." He rolled his eyes. "Sissy coffee. I'm on my fifth cup—been up since 9:00 a.m."

Montana laughed. "I have to say it's a little weird to see you this perky. Color me impressed."

"Yeah... I got up early and thought why not get started early. Amazing what you can get done."

"Thanks O'Malley—I'm grateful you agreed to continue. Also, thanks for going with me to the precinct the other day."

"No problem on that. I do want to stress something. I know you have questions and I believe you deserve answers. I'll do what I can to find the high roller but you need to prepare yourself. We may not learn anything. Our leads are flimsy at best. Just as I warned you that we might not find Suzette, I can't promise we'll find the high roller."

"I know," she murmured.

"Let's start with what we know. A town car issued to the Mayor's office stopped by the Coop and picked Suzette up at approximately 10:00 Friday morning. A passenger was in the backseat."

"Unless he hadn't been picked up yet," Montana countered.

"No, Al said there was someone in the back seat. He said—and I quote, 'I was thinking he was a lucky bastard to be with Suzy.'"

"O'Malley, do you really think someone from the Mayor's office would hurt Suzette? I have a hard time believing that."

"I tend to agree. Suzette had seen that client for over four years. It's too unlikely—in too many ways. If I had to guess, I think someone grabbed her after her date let her off. It might have been while she was on her way to meet you."

"How could someone grab her? She would scream. Besides, if someone grabbed her against her will, someone would stop the person."

"He might have drugged her—the other victims had powerful sedatives in their toxicology reports. He could have subdued her that way."

Montana nodded. "She'd never go willingly."

"That's one theory."

Montana digested this. "Even if he drugged her, don't you think someone would stop someone who was dragging an unconscious woman to a car?"

"People get lost in crowds. Dozens of crimes occur every year during the Times Square New Year's Eve celebration. Even if they notice something, people don't like to get involved, usually for fear of their own safety. I saw it all the time as a cop. People we *knew* had witnessed a crime would clam up. People justify their lack of good citizenship too—by believing she must be drunk if someone lugged her over his shoulder."

"I never considered that."

"I have another theory, too. Everyone assumes the CM is operating alone, but what if he has a partner? It takes a lot of strength to move a dead body."

She eyed him with admiration. "The NYPD lost a good cop when you left. I never considered that possibility."

"But our eye isn't on the CM, right? Let's get back to the high roller."

"How do we sleuth that out?"

"We talk to him. I'll know if he's telling the truth." He gave her a sly smile. "They used to call me the lie detector."

"Well we know the city issued that car to Mayor Burke's office..."

"Which means our next logical next step is to talk to him," he finished for her.

"You think he'll talk to us?" she asked.

"Good question," O'Malley nodded. "Probably not unless he's motivated to do so—and that means we need to compel him to speak with us. I say we be up front with what we know: tell him we know that a car issued to his office picked Suzette Peterson at 10:00 a.m. on the day she went missing. We can suggest that we'd hate to go public with this information but we have questions that need answers—and that those involve him."

"That sounds like blackmail," she said with distaste.

"No, not blackmail. We'll promise him confidentially—although we'd have to break that if he should happen to be involved in a crime—we'll soothe him by saying we don't want to shake up the city."

"We don't have all that much on him."

"Ever played poker?"

"We played at the Coop sometimes when it was slow—Suzette, Hanky, and me. The winner paid for dinner or drinks. We weren't serious."

"I'm a good poker player—and part of winning is guessing how good the other players' hands are. Burke has no idea what cards we hold so we tease him by showing him one card—say we show him the photos of his office's town car parked across from the Coop. Then we add that the same car picked Suzette up the day she went missing. We'll gauge his reaction to that. It might spook him enough to talk—at least to tell us who drove the car."

"You're one smart detective."

"Yeah, yeah—you're gonna give me a big head. So let's go fishing." He winked at her and then pulled out his phone and slip of paper from his pocket. After dialing, he hit speakerphone so she could listen. Several rings in, a mature sounding woman picked up.

"Mayor James Burke's office. How may I assist?"

"This is Detective O'Malley calling. I'd like to speak with Mayor Burke."

"Is he expecting your call?"

"I don't believe so but it's imperative I speak to him right away. It's an urgent matter."

"What was your name again?"

"O'Malley. Thomas O'Malley."

"Please hold while I check his availability."

A bastardized version of Bob Dylan's *Like a Rolling Stone* emanated from the phone's tiny speaker. Montana stuck her fingers in her ears and made a face while O'Malley laughed. A few minutes later the woman rescued them.

"Unfortunately, Mayor Burke has meetings all day."

"When can I make an appointment?"

"What does this concern? The Mayor apologizes but he doesn't recognize your name." The woman remained pleasant but firm.

"It's personal in nature, ma'am—something I'm sure he'd prefer remain confidential."

"I'll pass that on to him. How may he reach you?"

O'Malley gave her his number and email address before they exchanged amicable goodbyes.

"Well played." Montana punched his arm. "If it were me, I'd be dying to know what you had to say."

He considered this. "If you had nothing to hide would you talk to me?"

"Of course," she replied. "I'd be curious why you wanted to talk to me."

"What if you had something to hide?"

"I'd want to talk even more—to see what you know."

O'Malley winked at her again. "I agree. Although if he doesn't want to talk to me it doesn't mean he's concealing anything. He might be too busy for a small time detective like me."

Montana shook her head. "Nothing small time about you."

"I got you fooled." He rose from his chair. "Say, would you like to escort a hungry old man to a late lunch? Ever heard of Katz's deli?"

"Of course I know Katz's," she exclaimed. "It's the best deli on the Lower East Side."

They enjoyed a short walk to the Houston Street deli. Even at two o'clock in the afternoon, the place was bustling. O'Malley ordered a Reuben sandwich while Montana got the Rachel. Both came with a side of potato salad and a soft drink. When their number came up to indicate their orders were ready, they brought their lunch to a corner table.

They concentrated on their sandwiches and creamy potato salad before restarting their conversation. Even in the corner, they had to shout over the din in the crowded place.

"The next bar exam date is in July. You gonna be ready for that?"

"Geez, you don't let up do you?"

"Nope and I'm not going to either. What kind of law do you want to practice?"

"Criminal law. It's always fascinated me. I'd love to open my own practice but I'm not sure if I'll be ready for that. I might apply to the city—maybe become an assistant DA. Perhaps I'll prosecute cases Max Constantine solves. He can bust them and I'll break them."

"I'm pretty sure he wouldn't mind," O'Malley chuckled. "You'll be a great prosecutor—smart, logical, tough—just what a criminal attorney needs to be."

"Now *you* stop," she blushed.

As they finished, O'Malley's phone rang. He raised an eyebrow and showed her the Caller ID. After listening a moment, he said two things, "No, we need to meet in person,' and 'I can do that.' The call took less than twenty seconds.

"You were right that he'd talk to us." O'Malley put his phone back in his pocket. "I'm meeting him tomorrow morning."

"Did he sound guilty?"

O'Malley chortled. "You watch too many crime shows. How could he sound guilty in such a brief call? He didn't *sound* off if that's what you mean—but you can't tell much by phone. As I've said, it's better to talk in person."

"I want to go with you."

He appraised her. "I guess that's okay—might even make sense. I wouldn't mind getting your read on him."

O'Malley insisted on seeing her into a cab even though she wasn't far from her loft. When she arrived, the bag lady caught her attention with a reproachful look. At least she wasn't screaming. Ultra-aware of her surroundings since the late night chase, Montana saw another man sitting at the deli. Like the bearded stranger the other day, he stared at her with malevolent intent—or so it seemed to her.

What was going on? Was she getting paranoid? But he *was* intent in looking right at her—unfazed—even when she met his gaze with a defiant glare. Anger flushed her cheeks as she decided to introduce herself to the man and ask if they'd met. After all, she'd be safe since a crowd swarmed the deli. This time, they were on even ground—she wasn't alone and afraid on a dark street after midnight. He jumped up as he saw her weave her way in and out of the stopped traffic. Before she reached the other side, he disappeared into a taxi. Frustrated, she looked around, hoping to spot another cab so she could follow him but by the time another taxi was within sight, he'd disappeared.

A cold chill went up her spine.

38

ONTANA AWOKE early the next morning, excited about the meeting with Mayor Burke. She and O'Malley decided the subway would be fastest during rush hour. Although subways were the best way to get around New York, they weren't for the faint of heart. Each train was a diverse symphony of visual, audible, and olfactory stimuli. Stepping outside after riding, even Manhattan's grimy streets smelled good.

City Hall had always had extensive security but since 9/11, things were even more intense. After the horrible day that rocked the nation, New York's city officials started having the NYPD, FBI, CIA, and homeland security work together regularly. A metal detector scanned Montana's bag and O'Malley's briefcase while a diligent security guard kept a watchful eye as they walked through a metal detector. Once through, they stopped at a reception area where a middle-aged woman tapped away at her computer.

She was a drab bowl of oatmeal—gray and beige—from her washed out hair to an anemic complexion. She was what Hanky called a 'flavorless nightmare.' Only when Montana gave a loud, exaggerated cough did she look up.

"Can I help you?" she asked in a bored voice. It seemed Oatmeal's demeanor matched her lackluster attire.

"I'm Detective O'Malley and this is my assistant, Montana Wylde. We have a 9:00 appointment with Mayor Burke."

"One moment, please." Hearing Mayor Burke's name changed her disposition. Oatmeal awarded them a ferret-like like smile that somehow made her overall appearance much worse. Now her voice was crisp and full of self-importance as she spoke to someone on the phone. "A Detective O'Malley and his assistant are here for their 9:00 appointment." She listened a moment. "Thank you. I'll tell them."

She hung up the phone and motioned them to chairs lining one wall. "Please have a seat. Someone will escort you to Mayor Burke's office when he's free."

Fifteen minutes later, an attractive woman in a shape-hugging dress came out. If the receptionist was oatmeal, this woman was red velvet cake.

"You must be Detective O'Malley." She smiled at him and then glanced to Montana.

"This is my assistant Montana Wylde."

Montana shook her hand. "It's a pleasure to meet you."

Red Velvet gave another beaming smile. "Please follow me."

They followed her down the hall until she opened the door to a corner office with floor-to-ceiling windows that boasting an expansive city view. The office décor suited the Mayor's image: luxurious but with rugged masculinity. Diffused lighting by Tiffany lamps—or at least good replicas of them—created a warm inviting ambiance. Around the desk were overstuffed leather sofas and chairs. It was confident without being overbearing. After Red Velvet introduced them, she slipped out the door.

Montana recognized the Mayor from his press conferences and interviews. He appeared taller and was even more handsome in person. Silver streaks shot through a full head of dark hair. His was a chiseled face complete with a cleft chin. He greeted them with warm and friendly eyes, and gave them a wide smile.

"Pleased to meet you both." Mayor Burke held out his hand for a shake. O'Malley shook first.

When the Mayor turned to Montana, surprised recognition flickered across his face as he took her hand, though he quickly concealed it. She saw why he was successful; he made each person feel like the most important in the world.

"Montana Wylde—what a beautiful and unusual name. Are you an actress?"

She blushed and hated herself for doing so. No question the man was striking. "No, but you aren't the first person to ask. It's a pleasure to meet you."

O'Malley's demeanor was warm as he began, "We appreciate you meeting us on such short notice—I'm sure you're busy."

He gestured for them to sit. "O'Malley, I'll admit that I did some checking on you. You served twenty years with the NYPD and received more commendations than ten other cops combined. The city thanks you for your service. So, how may I assist you two?"

"Thank you, sir. It was an honor to serve the city." Then he wasted no time pulling Suzette's photo out of his briefcase. He thrust it across the desk. "Do you know this woman?"

Color drained from Mayor Burke's face but in an instant, he regained his composure. "Pardon my shock. It's just—isn't she the Church Murderer's last victim?"

"Yes." Montana looked him straight in the eye.

"Such a tragedy." He wore a confused look. "Why would you think I know her?"

O'Malley spoke up. "Suzette Peterson was Montana's friend and business associate. She hired me when Suzette went missing. Their building's door attendant saw Suzette get into a car with official plates—plates issued to this office." Montana remembered what O'Malley said about poker. He could make a fortune in Atlantic City if he decided to give up investigating.

The Mayor chose his words carefully. "The city issues several vehicles to each department, including this one. If someone saw your friend get into a city car it doesn't mean it involves me." His eyes had authentic sadness as he spoke. "I'm sorry about your friend. Be assured that our task force is doing everything possible to capture this man—and we will. We'll make sure your friend and all the others receive the justice they deserve."

"We know the city is working hard on the case," O'Malley replied. "We're looking in a different direction. We're trying to determine how a well-paid call girl ended up as a victim of the Church Murderer. The attendant saw Ms. Peterson getting into a car issued to your office the day she went missing. We'd like to know who was driving that car and who the passengers were."

"Mayor Burke," Montana pleaded. "I'm just looking for closure. I can't understand how Suzette could have run into that maniac. That man preys on streetwalkers and Suzette couldn't be further from that. I need to know how she went from your car to being a victim."

"I'm sorry but I can't help you."

"Let me put your mind at ease," O'Malley cut in. "We're only interested in finding out who drove the car that Friday."

Mayor Burke would never make a good poker player. His face showed every conflicting emotion. After a long pause, he sighed and repeated. "I can't help you." He stood up, walked to the window, and stared out at the stunning view.

O'Malley pulled another photograph out of his briefcase. "This might refresh your memory. Not only was this the car Suzette got into but someone parked this same car across the street from Suzette's and Montana's business several days during the last week of her life. The building's surveillance photos show this car and the door attendant swears that it's last Friday's car. Doesn't that concern you?"

"Of course it concerns me. I'm troubled when any of our residents come into harm's way but I don't have any information on who used what car on any particular day. My staff handles that. Now if you'll excuse me, I'm going to have to cut this meeting short."

"Mayor," O'Malley said as he rose from his seat. "You said your staff handles the designation of cars to drivers. I assume that means there is dispatcher. Could you put us in touch with that person?"

"Of course." Mayor Burke sat back down and consulted his laptop then scribbled a hurried note on a pad. He handed it to O'Malley. "Annie Davis is the city dispatcher. This is her number and extension."

O'Malley held out his hand. "We appreciate your time. One more thing—would you call Ms. Davis to say we'll be calling?"

"I'll send a memo now." Mayor Burke watched them walk down the hallway. As soon as they disappeared around the corner, he pulled out his personal cellphone and punched a number.

"We need to talk," he said.

39

ON THE STREET, Montana couldn't contain her excitement. "I've never met Mayor Burke but I swear he recognized me as soon as I shook his hand. Only for a split second, but I saw the recognition in his eyes. Did you notice anything?"

"It's possible your looks knocked him out. He sure did a double-take when we walked in." He burst out laughing as Montana screwed up her face and crossed her eyes. "Except when you're doing *that*. I sure did notice his discomfort upon seeing Suzette's photo. I'd bet *his* large bank account that he knew her—and not from the recent news."

"I agree. Particularly because that photo isn't one from the media."

"I did that on purpose—used one he wouldn't have seen from the news."

"Smart thinking, O'Malley."

"I doubt he would recognize a victim other than Suzette at first sight like that—but who knows. He tried masking his emotion but he recognized her. My gut says he was lying."

"My gut goes with your gut. Something more is going on."

O'Malley stopped in his track. 'J,' he shouted.

"Whaaat?" Montana whipped her head around.

"J from the J client card—with NYC-VVIP underneath it."

"You're losing me." Confusion wrinkled her brow.

"J as in *James* Burke. J Burke. It also explains the VVIP underneath."

Montana's eyes lit up. "I see what you're saying. That makes sense. It also explains why she marked another V in VVIP on his client card and why she went rogue on following the Coop's protocol. I couldn't figure out why she went against rules that she herself set up, such as doing an outcall without him without seeing him in the Coop first—and why she never told me about him. Suzette was serious about confidentiality—she would never break that trust, not even with me. Maybe Mayor Burke *is* the high roller."

"Our evidence is mighty weak."

"True. He sure didn't confess to anything—and we need to keep in mind that this is an election year. Why would he admit to something that could derail his hope for another term? Especially now that the media is painting Suzette as a streetwalker." She sighed in disgust.

"Don't lose hope. We still have cards to play."

"Such as?" she asked.

"Finding out who drove that car on Friday, April 10." O'Malley pulled the pad from his pocket. "Let's give Annie Davis a call, shall we?" He punched some numbers and then hit speakerphone. He handed her the notepad. "Take down names or any useful information she might give us. I'll just concentrate on the conversation."

An automated voice system answered and seemed to drone on forever. It offered twenty different time-consuming options: 'Press 1 for our location and hours of operation; Press 2 if you are a driver looking to speak with the dispatcher,' and on it went. At last, the robotic voice announced, 'If you know your party's extension, you may press it in at any time.' O'Malley keyed in the digits. A pleasant sounding woman answered on the first ring.

"City dispatch. Annie Davis speaking."

"Hello Ms. Davis. I'm Detective O'Malley. I just spoke with Mayor Burke who passed along your number. I'm investigating a car and driver from April 10, which was the Friday before last. According to Mayor Burke you're in charge of those records."

"Yes, I keep a log of cars, drivers, and destinations. Do you have the driver's name?"

"No but I have the car's plate number."

"Are you sure it's a city car?"

"Quite. The bottom of the plate reads 'official.' The number is L-33208."

"Would you mind holding a moment? And what was your name again?"

"O'Malley—Thomas O'Malley—I was with the NYPD for twenty years."

The Muzak spared them Bob Dylan but replaced it with a horrific rendition of Billy Joel's fine song *The Piano Man*. Again, Montana had fun with it, pantomiming gagging while O'Malley laughed. Just as it switched to another awful tune Annie Davis's cheerful voice returned.

"Sorry to keep you waiting but I had to check your identity—I'm sure you understand why. The Mayor said he'd meant to call me but that he hadn't gotten around to it just yet."

"I can appreciate how busy he must be," O'Malley demurred.

"According to the schedule, Charles Drinkwater drove that day. Charles is Mayor Burke's usual day driver. Of course, there is a chance the logs may have some inaccuracies because drivers sometimes switch shifts on occasion.

I'm not even sure if Charles drove that particular car that day. He hasn't submitted his log for this month. Until I get his log you'd have to check in with him on the exact dates."

"Thank you, Ms. Davis. You've been very helpful." O'Malley ended the call.

"Why didn't you ask for his phone number? How will we reach him?"

"All I need is his name." O'Malley winked at her, consulted his phone, and punched out a number." He put the call on speakerphone.

"Detective Bill Cavanaugh."

"Billy," O'Malley exclaimed.

"I'll be damned if it ain't O'Malley. I'd know that voice anywhere. What's up?"

"I'd like to call in a favor—don't know if you owe me or if I owe you but it's important."

"Lemme guess. You need help in tracking down some fraudster on an insurance claim?"

"Not an insurance claim, but it's for a case."

"No problem buddy. Who you looking for?"

"Charles Drinkwater. I need his home address. You spell it just like it sounds, Drink Water. He's one of Mayor Burke's drivers.

There was a long pause as they heard tapping on a keyboard. In a moment, Billy's voice returned. "Here ya go, buddy. Charles Drinkwater—employed as a city driver. His address is 1361 E. 66th St. Brooklyn.

"Thanks a million Billy. I got it straight now—I definitely owe *you.*

"Fuhgeddaboudit, O'Malley. You can always call in a favor."

O'Malley hung up. "Ya wanna know why I didn't ask for his phone number?"

"Oh, I know now that I thought about it," Montana said slyly. "When we first met you said it was always better to take people by surprise and interview them in person. You want to surprise him. Am I right?

"Bingo. You catch on quick, which is why you'll make a great attorney. Are you free to tag along to Brooklyn this evening?

"Of course." Montana was pleased O'Malley assumed she'd want to go. "Taxi or the subway?"

"Neither. We'll drive. I'll pick you up at 6:00."

"You have a car?" Montana was surprised. "Why do you always take taxis or the subway?"

"I hate driving—especially in Manhattan. I don't need the legal hassles—as you know, I often spike my coffee. My last DUI cured me of the habit of driving under the influence. I use the car for work outside Manhattan and sometimes for pleasure."

"O'Malley, thanks for asking me to come with you."

"I want your take on him. You have a keen eye for people—another trait of a great attorney."

After they parted, Montana was glad to have some time to think. The last couple of days had her wound up and on edge. She looked longingly at the trail, but that would have to wait. The close encounter had driven O'Malley's point home that she could be in real danger. Instead, she thought she'd spend forty-five minutes on the treadmill.

Only then did she realize that she'd forgotten to tell O'Malley about the *other* strange man sitting and watching her from across the street. She dismissed calling him; she'd tell him on their drive to Brooklyn.

Heading up the walkway, Montana smiled at the bag lady. Today, the woman was dressed to the hilt, wearing what looked like a tattered prom dress caked with mud and dirt. Her garish makeup and bright hair looked even crazier with the glittering tiara sitting askew atop the colorful wig. She sat on her perch and watched.

A rock trio played a few feet from Montana's building. They had their music cases open, hoping for donations from sympathetic passersby. When the bag lady spotted Montana, she came to life in a dramatic pantomime. Montana couldn't hear what she was saying because the music drowned everything out. The woman was making wild gestures to her throat, her finger making a slashing motion. Montana shrugged and shook her head again, to indicate that she couldn't hear. The woman's eyes narrowed as she made another violent slashing motion to her throat. Montana gave her a last helpless wave before heading into her building.

Upstairs, after working out, she enjoyed her quiet sanctuary. She reheated the Hunan food and sat in front of the television, bypassing the regular programming in favor of the Three Stooges. It felt good to laugh for a change. That killed time until O'Malley arrived. When he buzzed, she headed down to meet him and broke into a wide smile when she saw his car. It was a fully restored 1967 Mustang.

"Whoa," Montana exclaimed. "What a beauty."

He rubbed the dashboard with obvious love. "You like her huh? I'm the original owner—bought her in '67. She's gorgeous but like most beautiful women, she's high maintenance. I only drive her when I'm heading out of the city. I don't take her out that often but when I do, my troubles seem to disappear."

"I can see why," Montana said with appreciation.

They rode in silence. O'Malley maneuvered his way onto the Brooklyn Bridge from Centre Street, his car a stark contrast to the taxis and SUV's. Once on the bridge, Montana broke the quiet.

"I forgot to tell you something—it's probably nothing. Probably just my nerves."

He gave her a worried look. "What?"

She told him about the new man who had watched her from across the street from her building. She explained that she had crossed the street to confront him but that he'd disappeared into a taxi.

O'Malley exploded in a fury. "Why were you going to confront him?"

"Because he was scaring me and I don't like being afraid. I wanted to know what he was doing."

He shook his head. "What if he'd pulled out a gun on you?"

"Like he's going to pull out a gun in broad daylight," she scoffed.

"This city has as many crazies as any ten asylums. Let me tell you a little story. There was a burger joint—in the 1970's when there *were* burger joints instead of those big tasteless chains that serve cardboard hamburgers today. My uncle was on the force then and he told me this story. Two men stood in line in one of those joints, arguing about who was first in line—big argument. So, one of them takes out his gun and shoots the other guy—killed him dead. The guy who shot him *was* first in line then—but what did it matter? He went straight to jail. Never did get his damn burger. "

"I don't see how this fits in..."

"It fits in because people are fucking crazy—scuze my French." He shook his head at her. "At this point, we have far more questions than answers. Did you get a good look at him? Are you sure it wasn't the same guy?"

"I'm positive he wasn't the same man. This man was heavyset and balding—the other was slim with a full beard and moustache."

"You may just be a bit paranoid at this point, Montana—but if something hinky pulls at you, don't ignore it—that's my advice as a former cop. Tell you what—next time you enter or leave your building, have the camera on your phone ready to shoot. If we have a photo, we can run it through the facial recognition software at my old precinct."

"Maybe I was just being paranoid..."

O'Malley shrugged. "You have good reason to be after that chase the other night. We still don't know how Suzette got into the CM's car. And I want you to promise me again that you will not run, walk, or do anything by yourself. Don't even stand waiting to hail a taxi. Call for a car."

"I promise." She laughed and pointed to the GPS. "I'm saved from further lecture." She navigated. "Charles Drinkwater lives in the next block on the right hand side of the street."

Parking luck was on their side—one of the more difficult aspects of owning a car in New York. Bumper to bumper cars packed the street but O'Malley was able to slide his Mustang into a corner spot that someone had just vacated.

O'Malley rang the bell of Drinkwater's modest Brooklyn duplex. They saw lights and a figure sitting in a chair through the front room's lace drapes. After a moment, O'Malley rang the bell again.

A pale thin man got up and walked to the door—what they could see of him anyway. With the door still chain-locked, they could see only an inch. "Who is it?"

"I'm Detective O'Malley and this is my assistant, Montana Wylde. We'd like to speak to Charles Drinkwater." O'Malley flashed a badge. "Would that be you?"

"Are you the police?"

"I'm a former New York City cop who now works privately."

"What do you want?" he whined.

"We'd like to speak with you about a city car you drove the Friday before last. May we please come in? We spoke with Mayor Burke earlier today. He gave us your dispatcher—Annie Davis's number. When we asked who drove the Mayor's town car on Friday, April 10, she said it was you. May we please come in? This shouldn't take long."

Montana sensed his hostility. His porcine eyes glanced back and forth between Montana and O'Malley with open hostility. Unlike Mayor Burke, if he was familiar with Montana—or O'Malley, he concealed it well."

"I'm Charles Drinkwater," he sighed. He unlocked the chain and opened the door. The three crowded the tiny entryway.

"May we sit?" O'Malley asked.

"I guess," Drinkwater sighed again, then gestured them in.

They sat on a flowery couch that reminded Montana of her Nana's stuffy furniture. In fact, the décor was suited more for a grandmother than it was for a single man. He was nervous, sitting ramrod straight in the matching chair. He was a mouse of a man, timid and washed out with a pallid complexion. Worse, he had an unfortunate, weak chin and balding grayish hair. He bit his nails as he watched them. Montana was full of pity. His childhood peers must have been relentless in their bullying.

Again, O'Malley wasted no time. He reached into his briefcase and pulled out the same photo of Suzette he'd shown Mayor Burke.

"Do you know this woman?" Montana studied Drinkwater's face.

The man barely looked at the photo. "No."

"Take another look," O'Malley insisted, shoving the photo under his face. "Are you sure?"

Drinkwater sighed again and put on a pair of reading glasses. He peered at it for a moment and then shook his head. "No," he whined, "I don't know her."

O'Malley gave him a long look. "Annie Davis says you were scheduled to drive Mayor Burke's town car on April 10, which was the Friday before last. That car picked up this woman." He continued holding up the photo of Suzette.

"The Mayor's office is busy." Drinkwater's tone had become haughty. "I can't remember what the schedule was then or if I drove that day."

"Annie Davis said drivers are required to keep logs of their routes and destinations."

"I turn those in monthly."

Montana spoke for the first time. "But the month hasn't yet ended so wouldn't you have your log still?"

"I don't have it here."" Drinkwater's cheeks flushed with anger.

O'Malley pulled out another photo and showed it to him. "You were scheduled to drive this car on Friday, April 10." He nodded at the photo. "Your car stopped at this building on 33rd between Lexington and Mad and picked up a woman. We have witnesses that saw the car. Did you pick up this woman from this building on April 10?"

Drinkwater's eyes narrowed as he looked at the photo. "My memory isn't that good. I could have possibly been there. It's hard to remember. Also, while I'm Mayor Burke's usual daytime driver. I am not his only one. Sometimes I drive for other city officials too."

O'Malley persisted. "I need a copy of the entire last month of your schedule."

"I'm not obligated to give you anything," he intoned. "I am speaking to you out of courtesy to the Mayor. I'm not *required* to answer your questions. You aren't the police—you are only a private detective."

"We've come as a courtesy too." O'Malley's tone was amicable. "Our questions need answers. We'd prefer not to involve the media but we will if we must. And you know how the media are—their obligation is to conduct investigative reporting."

"You've not told me what this is about." Drinkwater finally asked the one question Montana thought he should have asked first.

"We are investigating the day Suzette Peterson went missing." O'Malley pointed to the photo that he'd shown Drinkwater when they first arrived. "On April 10 a door attendant saw Suzette Peterson get into a town car with an official city license plate—issued to Mayor Burke's office. Several days later, a parishioner found Ms. Peterson's body next to a pew in the Holy Trinity Church—a victim of the so-called Church Murderer."

Drinkwater was defensive. "I don't know anything about all of that. As to the car, the attendant is likely mistaken. After all, how many of those cars like that must there be in this city? Now if you'll excuse me..."

O'Malley cut him off. "He was quite sure it was the same car—one issued to Mayor Burke."

"You have no proof it was the Mayor's car that picked up that woman," Drinkwater snapped. "A task force is already working that case. You shouldn't interfere with their investigation."

Montana spoke up for the first time. "We are not interfering with anything because we are not investigating the Church Murderer. All we want is to speak to the person who drove the car that picked up Suzette Peterson on the morning of April 10."

Drinkwater stood up. "This conversation is over. I'm under no obligation here. You were once a cop but you aren't now."

"You're right." O'Malley shrugged. "You don't have to speak with us. I just figured it would be better for everyone if we didn't go to the press about Mayor Burke's involvement with Suzette Peterson."

A light coat of perspiration broke out on Drinkwater's pale face. He spluttered denials. "That's not true. Mayor Burke would never have anything to do with her. There's no story for the press."

"There *is* proof to counter that, O'Malley said mildly, "but we'd prefer to handle this privately. We've no desire to see the city rocked by another sex scandal. That doesn't help anyone. We don't want to but we'll go to the press if we have to."

"D-don't g-go to the press." Drinkwater stammered. "I'll g-get you a copy of my schedule. You need to give me a couple of days."

O'Malley's face was inscrutable. "Thank you. We have no interest in hurting the Mayor or the city but Ms. Wylde deserves answers." O'Malley pulled a business card from his pocket. "You can email your schedule to the address on this card. We hope to keep the media out of it if at all possible." The pungent threat lingered.

"Mr. Drinkwater," Montana pleaded, "If you know anything, please tell us what it is. I won't say a word to anyone. I want to protect Suzette every bit as much as you want to protect the Mayor. I just need to know—did you pick her up that day? Please tell me if you did."

Drinkwater hesitated, seeming on the verge of speaking, and then snapped his mouth shut, his lips forming a defiant line as he stood. "This interview is over. I said I'd send you the schedule." He opened the door, and watched them leave.

Peeking from behind the lacy drapes, Drinkwater watched them get into the vintage Mustang. As the car pulled out, he pulled his cellphone from his belt holster. "They just left."

He listened for a moment. "No problem," he responded right before hanging up.

40

"HE WAS LYING," O'Malley declared.

"I agree. But he might just be protecting Mayor Burke. "

He chuckled. "He looked ready to lose his lunch when I showed him the photos."

"I understand why he'd lie to protect the Mayor. I just wish I could make him understand that defending Suzette's reputation is as important to me as protecting the Mayor is to him. I don't think he understands that."

"Thought you had him for a minute there," O'Malley said. "He seemed ready to spill when you told him you only wanted to know what happened."

"He sure clammed up in a hurry, though."

"He's loyal, and as you said, it's an election year. The last thing Burke needs is a scandal."

"It will be interesting to see if he gives us the schedule," Montana mused. "If he doesn't, there's nothing we can do."

"Let's see how it goes. My sainted grandmother had a saying. 'Don't trouble trouble until trouble troubles you.' Let's give him a chance. My guess is that he'll call the Mayor and tell him we paid a visit. Then he'll do what the Mayor tells him."

"Can't blame him for that but I'm even more certain Mayor Burke *was* her client. We just need to find out where he—or another driver—dropped her off."

O'Malley nodded. "I agree. That might tell us how Suzette ran into the CM. It might even help with the task force's investigation. If he doesn't cough up the schedule, we'll need to talk to Burke again and put a little more heat on him. We can use the 'going to the media' line with him—he might just spill."

"It's worth a try," Montana replied.

They arrived at Montana's building, agreeing to talk the next day. He insisted on walking her to the door. On an urge, she hugged him.

"Thank you. For everything." Her eyes were misty.

"No problem." He gave her a gruff hug and watched until the outer door shut behind her.

41

SHEILA PROWSE was working undercover. Her non-cop friends would never recognize her in her current getup. Her crop top was a mere band covering her breasts and her skirt barely covered the junk in the trunk. Sheila's lone presence on the stroll was an anomaly. Most girls' pimps marked and protected their territory. Usually, those working the street would not allow a newcomer on their turf. They'd either chase or bully the newbie into giving up a sizable chunk of her cash. If she proved weak enough, the pimp would try to sweet-talking the newbie into joining his stable.

Sheila didn't have to worry about this. Her regular partner, Rodney, was on the task force as well. He was posing as her pimp and no one would say 'boo' to him. He was 6'6" and 260 lbs. of pure muscle. One scrawny pimp had already tested him. When the pimp began hassling Sheila, Rodney stepped out from behind his post. One look at the chocolate colored giant and the lowlife pimp vamoosed.

The task force had wired Sheila to give and receive messages. Her pleather skirt had a belt with a tiny transmitter wired into its underside, capable of giving two signals. Pressing one button indicated a possible interaction with someone fitting the CM's description. She'd press that button twice to alert the backup team that she was in the town car with a likely suspect. The other button was the warning button—one press meant she was sure she had the right guy and two presses told them she was in real trouble. The signals connected to apps on the phones of Max Constantine, Joey Malone, and a quartet of two NYPD officers and two BAU agents. Their van was halfway down the block. Another van parked in the opposite direction held a six-man swat team.

Sheila hoped the sting would be a success. She wished to get this scumbag off the street more than anything but she also hoped for a promotion along the way. So did fellow undercover officer Linda Collingswood. While the feminist movement had made leaps and bounds within the police force, women still had a ways to go. The NYPD promoted men more than women—even those male officers with less time and fewer qualifications. Sheila and Linda hoped their roles in the operation would shorten the ladder to the department's glass ceiling. Like most officers, they wanted their gold detective badges.

Law enforcement knew precious little about the CM. As far as they knew, no one had survived an encounter with him. If a woman had escaped, she hadn't filed a report. That wasn't too surprising since street girls viewed cops as their enemy. The task force was going on Max Constantine and the BAU's profile: a white male in his mid-thirties driving an expensive dark town car. They knew that much only because two of the victims' pimps had told officers they'd last seen their girls getting into a car fitting that description. It wasn't much to go on.

Sheila and the team had been on the scene for several hours and street business was booming. They were considering going for a coffee run when a car meeting the CM's description caught Sheila's attention. He'd circled her corner several times, going slower each time. He was studying her. She keyed the first button once.

Sheila was relieved to hear Rodney say, 'Got ur back baby,' through the tiny bud buried in her ear.

Murph Campbell monitored the signals and conversation from the backup van. Sheila heard his voice next. "We have strong signals for the computer and GPS. You're covered Sheila. You won't be out of our sight." He gave his colleagues the thumbs up.

The car came to a stop the next time it circled Sheila. As the man unrolled the passenger's window Sheila sauntered up to him. She bent down low enough to give him a good view of her breasts.

"Hi honey," she drawled.

He stared straight ahead. What an odd duck—showing no interest in her at all. When he did speak, he wouldn't look at her.

"How much?" If she were really working the street, her gut instinct would tell her to get the hell away from this bastard as fast as possible. He was disconcerting—his unsmiling face staring ahead. The hairs on the back of her neck gave an uneasy tickle.

"What you are looking for?"

"A hundred bucks for half and half." His voice was gruff.

"Sounds good to me, sweetie."

He continued staring straight ahead. She was near certain he was their man.

"Get in," he ordered.

She said a silent prayer for everything to go as planned as she slid into his passenger seat. As they drove off, she tapped the first button twice, letting the team know she was in a hinky car. The vans holding the backup and swat teams started their engines. Rodney jumped on his motorcycle in case they needed more flexibility. When Sheila and the trick drove a half a block away, Rodney roared off following them. The two vans took off next.

Years of working vice had street-seasoned Sheila but something about this man made her blood run cold. He drove fast—unusual for a trick. Most customers slunk around, giving the girls sneaky glances as they looked for the nearest dark alley. The goal was sex. Period. They weren't interested in massages or pole dancing—they wanted to take care of business, fast and simple. A hundred dollars was far more than most streetwalkers got for a date. They worked based on quantity rather than quality; most got a trick off in as little as five minutes and then moved on to the next man on the prowl.

Sheila glanced at inner door. Her heart dropped.

The handle was missing.

At once, she was certain she was with the notorious Church Murderer.

She pressed the warning button to signal the team that she was likely with the CM.

Driving along, adrenalin flooded Sheila's system. Ten years of training kicked in. She was calm even though she had never been in such a precarious situation. Her ability to chill under pressure was a big reason Max had chosen her.

"Mister, where are we going?"

He turned to her for the first time, his eyes devoid of emotion. "Shut the fuck up," he hissed.

"Will you let me out of the car please? I'm not feeling well." She used another agreed upon strategy: if the man let her out of the car, he wasn't the CM but if he insisted she stay, they most likely had their man.

"I said *shut the fuck up.*" This time he didn't bother a glance.

Again, she singled punched the warning button. A second single press told the team she was certain she had her man.

Max Constantine monitored Sheila's GPS; the signal was strong. Rodney had the car in his sight as well. The team planned to follow Sheila to the final destination. They would pull him over only if they felt Sheila was in imminent danger. They needed evidence, and hoped he'd lead them to the murder scene. Sheila's hinky feeling and a missing door handle was nothing as far as prosecution went. They needed real evidence.

Sheila thought about the terrified women before her. She had a team of professionals at her disposal whereas they'd had nothing but their wits. Regardless of how the public judged the streetwalkers lifestyles, nobody deserved to experience this mounting terror and brutal death. Every twenty seconds, she would hit the warning button once, telling the team that she was still with him but okay.

He drove out of Brooklyn, taking the Battery Tunnel to Staten Island. Sheila stole a look. His lips still formed a rigid line. When he slowed at an impending red light, he reached into his pocket. It happened too fast for Sheila to fight or message the teams. Before unconsciousness took hold, the last thing she saw was the metallic glint of a needle. Then it plunged deep into her neck.

The teams became frenzied when Sheila's communication stopped. The task force knew the CM drugged his victims. Max considered turning on the rollers and pulling the plug on the sting but his gut told him to let it play out. He was certain the car would lead them to evidence. Sheila's GPS signal was still strong and the team was at a safe distance. Rodney could overrun him in a minute if he needed to.

As the town car turned onto a private road, Constantine recognized the location. A dilapidated set of buildings called The Farm Colony was at the end of the long driveway. Throughout New York's history, horror stories had sprung up about its existence. Much was urban legend but it had also been the place of at least two known murders. No doubt, there would be more to its infamy after tonight.

The man dragged Sheila's limp body from the car and threw her over his shoulder. As he made his way into a large barn, the backup and SWAT teams arrived with their lights off to avoid detection.

Max gave the signal and the swat team exploded out of their van, catching the man off guard. He dropped Sheila and Rodney pulled her to safety. Two officers with paramedic training checked her vitals and health status. Max ordered the man to show his hands. Instead, the man ran for his car but the swat team was too fast—too experienced. In under a minute, they wrestled him to the ground. As he fought them, an officer tased him as another cuffed his hands behind his back.

As soon as it was over Max called Commissioner Durbin. His message was brief. "We nailed the bastard. Halle-fucking-lujah."

Part IV
The Encounter

42

EXHAUSTED, Montana finished the last sip of her cabernet. Just as she was about to scrub her face, brush her teeth and crash for a good long while, her phone rang. She glanced at the clock. It was late. She picked up her cellphone and accepted the call when she saw it was O'Malley.

"Are you watching the news?" He sounded more excited than she'd ever heard him.

"No. I was about to go to bed."

"Turn it on," O'Malley demanded. "They caught the bastard."

"What?" Montana's tired brain was foggy.

"They caught him tonight, Montana—the Church Murderer," he exclaimed. "Suzette's killer is in custody."

That woke her up in an instant. She picked up the remote and turned on the television. Even after midnight, the story demanded news coverage. A fatigued Max Constantine stood at a podium giving the barest details about the sting to a group of reporters. A smaller window appeared on the upper right portion of the screen showing a video of the team of CSIs as they sifted through the crime scene evidence.

Montana was so riveted to the television that she forgot O'Malley. She picked up the phone. "Are you still there? Sorry, I got lost in this news."

"That's understandable."

"You know, I should let Hanky know. He's been beside himself since we learned about Suzette."

"No problem, honey. I thought I should let you know right away."

"Let's talk tomorrow—and thanks letting me know."

She punched in Hanky's number from her speed dial list. His groggy voice answered on the third ring. "H'lo?"

"Hanky, sorry to wake you but I thought I should let you know. I'm guessing you didn't catch the late news."

"Nah—I went to sleep early. What news are you talking about?"

"They caught the Church Murderer."

"No," Hanky exclaimed, now wide awake.

She waited while he turned on the news and they watched together. The story was mesmerizing so they barely spoke. The group of hungry reporters kept shouting out new questions when the Police Commissioner and an elated Mayor Burke joined Max at the podium.

"Thank God they caught that bastard. I don't normally believe in the death penalty but in his case I'd consider it," Hanky muttered.

"It's a moot point. New York abolished the death penalty some time ago. At least he'll never be able to hurt anyone again. But I can't feel all that happy because none of this brings Suzette back to us."

"I miss her every day." Hanky's voice choked with tears.

Montana started crying with him. "I miss her too. I still expect to get a phone call or a text. I'm sorry I woke you up but I thought you'd want to know right away."

"No, I'm glad you did." His voice sounded distant.

"You okay?"

"Fine—just thinking about the news but I probably should go back to dreamland—if I can that is. I have a 6:30 training session tomorrow."

"Ouch. I should have waited until morning to call."

"No," he insisted. "You did the right thing."

Neither was able to sleep for quite some time. Montana sipped a glass of cognac and watched the lights flicker out across the river.

Hanky was preoccupied. When the press conference ended, he turned off his television and went to his desk. When his computer booted up, he found the same news site that he and Montana had watched. He watched it once and then hit the replay button. Halfway through his second time watching, he stopped the tape at the point where the group of cops and city officials surrounded the Mayor at the podium. Something—someone—in the photo tickled his memory.

A sudden urge made him pull a box of photos from the top shelf of his bedroom closet. He rifled through the box and found the stack he was looking for. He took the photos to his desk and compared some to the video stopped in mid-play—the shot of the Mayor and his surrounding group. Try as he did, he couldn't put his finger on just what bothered him.

He yawned, remembering the alarm that would be going off in less than three hours. Nevertheless, before he turned in for good, he printed out the video's screen shot.

He'd probably figure it out after a good night's sleep.

43

ALTHOUGH she'd only had a single glass of wine, Montana awoke with a killer headache. It felt as though a sledgehammer was pounding on her brain. Then she remembered O'Malley's call, the cognac, and the late breaking news.

She started feeling human after her second cup of coffee. When the phone rang, she was full of curiosity. Max Constantine's name was on her caller ID.

He wasted no time. "Montana, I'm sure you've heard the news by now but I wanted to call you myself. We caught him. I know it doesn't make your loss easier but I hope this will bring you some peace."

"Yes, O'Malley called me last night. Thank God, that maniac will never hurt anyone else. I'm still processing it all. Do you know who he is?"

"John Raymond Duncan, but he goes by Ray. He flew under our radar because he has no rap sheet. Not even a DUI. His family has overseen The Farm Colony for years. Ray took the helm when his father died in '08."

"The Farm Colony?"

"It has a notorious history—much of it urban legend—though some is true. This will add to its grim legacy."

"I've never heard of it."

"It's no tourist attraction." He hesitated. "I'm calling for another reason as well. Mr. and Mrs. Peterson—Suzette's aunt and uncle—arrived this morning. They want to go to Suzette's apartment and I wanted to warn you about that. One of our officers will accompany them, but I thought you might want to go with them.

"Should they go there? Isn't her apartment under investigation?"

"Yes and no. At this point, we don't consider it an active crime scene. We've cleared it for entry for loved ones with the accompaniment of an officer. I wanted to warn you because the Petersons, well frankly, rub me the wrong way: their focus is on the status of their niece's estate. I thought you might want to go with them as well."

"Thanks for letting me know. Yes, I would like to go with them. Where are they staying?"

"At the Hancock. It's one of those boutique hotels. They're coming to the precinct at 1:00. "

"Um, Max?" Calling him by his first name still felt uncomfortable. "Would it be possible to speak with you for a couple of minutes before we go to Suzette's?"

"Stop by at 12:45. I wish I could give you more time but I'm swamped."

"I understand. Do you mind if I bring O'Malley?"

"I was going to suggest that," he replied.

Montana then called O'Malley. Before she could ask if he'd go with her, he insisted that he would come along. He wasn't about to let her meet the Petersons without protection.

She went through the motions of showering, washing, and drying her hair. On autopilot, she applied makeup and dressed without thinking much about it. She chose dark jeans, a crisp white shirt, and a tailored blue suede jacket. She topped the outfit off with high brown leather boots.

Her only jewelry was a sleek gold watch on her left hand and her grandfather's 18 kt. gold ring she wore on her right thumb. She grabbed Suzette's keys and threw them into an enormous brown calfskin bag.

Montana had hoped she could go through Suzette's file cabinets alone or with O'Malley. She wanted to look for Suzette's will without the relatives. One thing was clear: she'd tear the place apart to make sure there *wasn't* a will before she allowed the greedy relatives to get their grubby mitts on anything.

When she got into O'Malley's waiting taxi, she gave him a good look. He looked like ten miles of backroad trying to get on the freeway. His eyes made *her* peepers hurt and the hundred proof fumes emanating from his breath almost knocked her out. He must have celebrated the CM's capture a bit too much the previous night. Montana hugged him nonetheless. They'd been through a lot in the past two weeks.

He asked the cabbie to wait for them at a coffee shop along the way. Inside, O'Malley filled his thermos, leaving room for a generous dollop of amber fluid. Montana stuck with her usual light and sweet coffee and ordered an enormous sticky bun.

"Good to see you eat," O'Malley said, as they slid back into the taxi. "You're too skinny."

"I know." She swallowed a large bite. "But changing the subject, I want to ask if you think we should tell Max about talking to the Mayor and his driver?"

"I've been thinking about that too. Finding this creep changes everything. Even if Mayor Burke were the high roller, what good would it do to expose that now? It won't bring her back—and would Suzette want that?"

"No," Montana agreed. "If he *is* the high roller, Suzette went to great lengths to protect him. She even kept it from me. We should do what she'd want—and that would be to protect her client."

They arrived at the precinct ten minutes early. The same woman worked the dispatch desk, her furious fingers working her smartphone.

"Can I help you?" She didn't bother looking up.

"I'm Montana Wylde and this is Private Detective O'Malley. Detective Constantine is expecting us."

With a reluctant sigh, the woman set her phone down. "I'll let him know you are here. Have a seat."

Within a couple of minutes, a haggard Constantine appeared. He led them to his cramped office.

"So what did you want to talk to me about?"

Montana was blunt. "What do you know about Ray Duncan in relationship to Suzette? Has he said anything about her?"

"Nothing so far—but we've only started interrogating him." He gave them a rundown of the sting and subsequent arrest. It was nothing Montana hadn't already learned from the news.

"Are you sure he killed Suzette?"

Constantine looked at her with surprise. "The lab reports are back. The toothbrush you brought in is a direct match to her DNA. We're going through the crime scene where her DNA is bound to show up. We're in the beginning stages of the investigation and there is still a ton of evidence to go through. We've found Ray Duncan's souvenirs and his home embalming setup."

"Home embalming?" Montana was horrified. "He embalmed Suzette?" She shuddered, angry and heartbroken all over again, knowing her best friend had suffered so.

"There is a lot of ugliness we kept from the press. Unless you have a strong stomach, I advise you to stay away from the news because I'm sure the media will sensationalize everything. Let's just say this case will go down as one of the most gruesome killing sprees in our city's history."

"How much has he talked?" O'Malley wondered.

"Unfortunately he just lawyered up. Don't worry, though—there's a ton of physical evidence even if he doesn't say another word. He's never getting out of prison."

"Thank God you caught him." Montana shuddered.

Constantine's phone buzzed. He spoke for a moment and then turned to them. "The Petersons are here. I'll escort you out."

"We appreciate it," Montana said quietly.

Suzette's overwhelmed and bedraggled relatives stood in the precinct lobby. It was hard to believe they shared Suzette genes. The aunt was around fifty-five but she could pass for seventy with her wiry gray hair and dried out skin. Her husband appeared even older. What hair he had was entirely white and he walked with a cane. They were a study in inherent despair. They reminded Montana of the Drift Inn's regulars who sat hunched on their stools every night. Thank God Suzette had escaped.

Montana already knew too much about them from Suzette. She disliked them on sight but vowed to hide her feelings for Suzette's sake. She clenched her jaw. "Mr. and Mrs. Peterson, I am so sorry about Suzette." She opened her arms to embrace the aunt but the woman stopped her cold by stepping back. Montana recovered and held her hand out for a shake.

"I'm Montana Wylde. I am... was... Suzette's best friend. This is Detective O'Malley. I hired him to find Suzette when she went missing."

The aunt ignored the outstretched hands. She didn't give O'Malley as much as a glance. Her eyes traveled from Montana's expensive boots to her designer jacket, her steely disapproval evident.

"Her name was Susan. I don't recall her mentioning you." The aunt looked like she'd sucked on a lemon.

"She did mention you." Montana looked her straight in the eye. Suzette had been their cash cow—only hearing from the two when they were low on cash. Suzette always sent it, perhaps out of misplaced duty or maybe because of her sweet nature.

Mrs. Peterson ignored Montana and turned to Max. "Can you tell us what happened to Susan's belongings?"

"I have no idea, Mrs. Peterson, but if you work with Montana, I'm sure she'll discuss all that with you."

The woman had no interest in why her niece had died. Her sole focus was money. "We know Susan had bank accounts. We hope we won't require a legal team to locate them."

"She did have bank accounts," Montana confirmed. "I'll be straight with you, Mrs. Peterson. Suzette trusted me with the keys to her apartment and all her filing cabinets. Nothing will leave her apartment until I go through everything."

"We'll relieve you of that responsibility," Mrs. Peterson replied. "It's best if family takes over now."

Montana was resolute. "No. Suzette trusted me with her belongings. I promised to watch over her things. I keep my promises, Mrs. Peterson. I will head any search of her apartment."

"That's my job too," O'Malley chimed in. "Montana hired me to oversee these issues."

"We need to protect ourselves." Mrs. Peterson turned to Constantine for support. "Can you provide an officer to watch these two? We have to make sure Susan's belongings are safe."

Montana flushed with anger. "Mrs. Peterson, Suzette was the sister I never had. I would never do anything to dishonor her."

O'Malley was hot as well. "I don't like the sound of this. Montana wouldn't take advantage of Suzette. She hired me to find her—with her own hard-earned money."

Mr. Peterson spoke for the first time. "So you don't know if she had a will?"

"No, I don't know." Montana was now exasperated. "We'll find out soon enough. There's no purpose in speculating."

A vein was working on O'Malley's temple. "Mr. and Mrs. Peterson. Your niece's belongings are safe. I'll be accompanying you and Max can verify that I'm a former NYPD cop."

"Detective O'Malley is right. He was one of the best officers on the force. We were sorry to lose him." Max then looked at O'Malley and snapped his fingers. "As a matter of fact, as a former NYPD detective, you can accompany the Petersons to their niece's apartment. I was going to assign an officer but since the apartment is not part of the crime scene, I'll approve you accompanying as a representative of the force." He then offered his hand to the Petersons. "Now if you folks will excuse me, I have a meeting. I'll leave you in Ms. Wylde and Detective O'Malley's capable hands."

Montana turned to the pair, "We can walk from here. It's only a few blocks."

They trudged along in uncomfortable silence. New York's fast-walking residents contrasted with the sluggish pace of the Petersons. Montana and O'Malley kept waiting for them to catch up every half block or so. New Yorkers walk fast, with a sense of purpose—the opposite of the Petersons. They ambled along, their mouths agape and heads up, staring at the looming skyscrapers. Montana thought they must be a pickpocket's dream.

"New York must be a culture shock." Montana tried for congeniality again. "When I moved to the city, the sheer number of people overwhelmed me."

Mrs. Peterson's pious eyes turned to her. "I'll be frank. We are religious people. Detective Constantine informed us that Susan worked as a prostitute. That's *why* she was murdered. We raised Susan to worship the Lord. She was to spread His Gloried Word but instead she ran off to conduct her sinful business." She sneered at Montana. "You must be a prostitute yourself since you were business partners."

"We were more than business partners. And I'll tell you this—I've never met a Christian who was kinder than Suzette."

"Vengeance is mine, sayeth the Lord," Mrs. Peterson cried out in self-righteous indignation. Her eyes rolled back in religious fervor. "The Lord sent me a vision to pray for Susan's depravity."

"I had a vision too." Montana's patience was nearing its end. "Mine told me that the Lord prefers loving atheists to hateful Christians."

The aunt's face crinkled in furious distaste. "You work in a shameful profession," she hissed before giving O'Malley a pointed look. "A former police officer should understand how shocking this is—the shame it brings to our good name."

Montana's anger now boiled over. "That's not how Suzette described your hellhole—unless your personal brand of religion includes sexual assault." She gave Mr. Peterson an accusatory look.

Montana's blunt honesty finally shut the woman up—for a moment. After a lengthy pause, Mrs. Peterson spoke in earnest. "Susan would be alive had she not been a whore."

O'Malley was now angry. "Mrs. Peterson, no one can say how Suzette came across that nut. We don't know if she'd been safe if she'd been a receptionist."

"If she profanes herself by whoring, she shall be burned with fire," Religious fury filled Mrs. Peterson's eyes.

Montana's head whipped around. She had heard that phrase before...

Finally, they reached Suzette's apartment building. A crushed Bruno rushed out to greet them.

"Montana—oh my God—I'm so damn sorry. I can't believe Suzy is gone. I keep expecting her to bounce in here for her morning latte. You must be devastated."

As Montana hugged him, her eyes filled again. It was appalling that Suzette's death meant more to a coffee shop owner than it did to her relatives. "Thanks, Bruno."

They rode up the elevator in uneasy silence. Montana turned the key to Suzette's apartment and opened the door. She stood motionless and gasped, the key suspended in midair.

Someone had ransacked Suzette's apartment.

44

O'MALLEY PULLED MONTANA back into the hallway. He held a finger to his lips. The Petersons stood dumb and dazed, their niece's trashed apartment finally shutting them up. O'Malley produced a small handgun from a side holster hidden by his jacket—a surprise to Montana. He entered the apartment, motioning the others to remain in the hall. He went from room to room, listening at each door before opening it. Several moments later, he returned.

"Whoever did this is gone." He examined the door. "No sign of forced entry—and she has good locks. A skilled pro might be able to pick them but most could not. My guess is that the person had a key." He paused a minute. "Hold on— I want to check something else." He returned a minute later.

"I thought someone might have gained access through the fire escape in back but that's not possible. She has gates with good locks on her windows. Montana, do you know if anyone else has a key?"

"Not as far as I know."

"You are the only one with a key?" Mrs. Peterson's accusatory eyes narrowed.

O'Malley had wandered into another room. He came out, ending a phone conversation.

"Cops are on their way. We'll meet them in the coffee shop."

The aunt shook her head. "No. We should ensure the remaining valuables stay safe.

O'Malley put his hand up. "Not gonna happen. This is a crime scene. We can't touch anything until the cops arrive."

He herded the Petersons down the hall while Montana locked the apartment door. Still shaken by Suzette's death, she felt she was in a windstorm, uncertain where life would toss her next.

"I wonder what they took." Mrs. Peterson grew more sullen by the minute.

"This isn't a burglary," O'Malley explained. "That television is right there—as well as an expensive stereo system. Thieves don't upend file folders unless they believe they contain valuables. Whoever did this was looking for something."

Within fifteen minutes, three of New York's finest arrived. Arriving that fast was almost unheard of but since the break in occurred at the home of a CM victim, they were quick to arrive. O'Malley being a former cop made the scene a priority as well. The crew included an older cop in plainclothes, a young uniformed officer, and a CSI with a camera slung around his neck and a black equipment bag. The older cop and O'Malley recognized each other right away.

"José you old dog—nice to see you." O'Malley rose to greet them. "This is Montana Wylde. She hired me to investigate Suzette Peterson's disappearance—she was the CM's last victim. These two just arrived. They are Suzette's aunt and uncle. We came over to check for legal documents and found the place ransacked."

The older cop turned to the Petersons. "Wish we could have met under better circumstances. I'm José Rodriguez. I'll be leading this investigation. Hank Johnson is our CSI, he'll dust for prints, look for evidence, and take photos." He nodded toward the younger uniformed cop. "Del Gomez works this beat." He turned to O'Malley. "You're the last person I thought I'd run into today. Been a long damn time. What's your take on this, you old geezer?"

"It's not a burglary but someone gave it a good tossing—wait'll you see the mess."

"Let's take a look. O'Malley, you can come up but the others can't."

O'Malley turned to the group. "Montana, I'll call you later. It's gonna take some time—so no sense in hanging around. Besides, don't you need to study? Mr. and Mrs. Peterson—go relax at your hotel. We'll call when we have more information."

"That's a good idea," Montana said. "I'll get the Petersons a taxi."

"We should keep watch," Mrs. Peterson insisted. "I intend to make sure Susan's belongings stay safe."

"Mrs. Peterson, what are you suggesting? Nobody here would take anything from your niece." O'Malley anger was palpable. "You can't contaminate the crime scene. Help us by letting us do our jobs without interruption."

"He's right," José broke in. "You can't touch anything until we're finished here, Ma'am. Go back to your hotel."

Montana stepped up to the curb and gave a perfect Yankee Stadium whistle. A taxi careened across three car lanes and screeched to a halt. She gave the driver some bills and directed him to return the Petersons to the Hancock. Then she faced the detectives.

"I'm coming up," she informed them. "I won't contaminate anything."

"Miss, that's not a good idea," Jose objected.

"José, she's okay," O'Malley interjected. "She'll be quiet. She's a lawyer. Might be good for her to stay because of those nutty relatives—they might decide to sue us—and I'm only half kidding. Also, she may help us figure out what someone's motive might be for tossing the apartment since she knew Suzette better than anyone."

José gave a low whistle as he sized her up. "I'd sure hire you. If O'Malley says you're okay, I'll take his word. Don't touch anything, though."

She held up her hand. "No problem."

Sitting on the couch, Montana watched them work. The place was a mess, with overturned cabinets and the drawers removed and emptied.

O'Malley pointed to an overturned trash container. "Right there says this is no burglary. Burglars aren't interested in trash."

"True," José concurred.

The CSI snapped photos and dusted for prints. O'Malley returned from one of the back rooms and sat with Montana on the couch.

"So, if this isn't a burglary, what the heck is going on?" She gestured to the surrounding chaos.

"That's the big question," O'Malley replied. "I have to wonder how this figures into everything else. Who could have done this?"

Montana paused. "Doesn't it seem a strange coincidence that the CM kills Suzette and right after that her place is ransacked?"

"It's hinky. It's either a helluva coincidence or something else is going on."

"Hey O'Malley," José muttered, coming out of the bedroom, "the perp must have been looking for something specific—and not valuables. She has a jewelry box full of expensive stuff. There's also cash tucked here and there—not well hidden. A big TV might look too conspicuous, but any thief would take the jewelry and cash."

The others joined José in the living room. The CSI spoke up, "We're about done here, but it's still a crime scene. You'll have to break it to those relatives that they can't come back until the tape is gone."

"They aren't going to like that," Montana said.

"Blame it on the cops—it's a crime scene—out of your control. Their niece's estate comes after the investigation." O'Malley answered.

José turned to the group. "Okay folks, everyone has to clear out. We're got to secure this entryway with tape—we'll talk to the manager on our way out."

Montana shook the officers' hands. "Thanks for your help."

"That's our job, Miss." José gave her a winning smile then turned to O'Malley. "I'll be in touch, you old bastard. And don't be a stranger."

O'Malley and Montana left the officers to secure Suzette's place. Outside, dark clouds were moving in their direction. A storm was moving in.

"Ugh, now to deal with the Petersons," Montana said with distaste. "Would you mind calling them to say they can't come back until the investigation is finished? They're more likely to listen to you. They hate me."

"They hate everyone—but sure, no problem. Where are they staying again?"

"The Hancock," she replied.

O'Malley pulled out his phone and frowned. "Damn. My phone is dead. With all the excitement last night, I forgot to plug it in. I'll call them when I get home—try to remind me okay?"

"Will do—and thanks. I appreciate it. The less I have to do with them, the better."

"So you didn't care for them?" His voice dripped with sarcasm.

She punched his arm. "About as much as you."

"I could use a drink—how about you?" he asked Montana. "It's been one helluva day. Besides which," he pointed to the threatening sky, "it's gonna start pouring any minute. Whaddaya say—you wanna go for a drink?"

"Best idea I've heard today. If ever an afternoon drink was deserved, this is it."

Walking out, a bolt of lightning streaked across a fast-darkening sky while a clap of thunder roared in the distance. Moments later, light rain splashed against the sidewalk. "Do you know where we're going?" Montana asked. "I hope it's close because it's going to start pouring any minute and I don't have an umbrella."

Just as the rain started coming down in earnest, O'Malley led them to a nondescript building with an old art deco sign: *New York Tony's Jazz Club*. He opened the door to reveal a dim and musky club with the telltale odors of old booze and stale cigarettes. Montana spotted ashtrays on the table. New York Tony's obviously disregarded New York's antismoking laws.

The club was a holdover from a different era, the bar a testament to the beautiful woodworking of past generations. It even had a footrest. An ornate art deco mirror reflected the gleaming bottles of alcohol surrounding the horseshoe bar. A small dance floor was in front of a tiny stage filled with musical equipment.

"Tony's is one of the city's best kept secrets." O'Malley watched Montana's delight as she took it all in. "The original Tony is no longer alive but his grandson, T.J. runs the place now. Not only does he serve an honest drink, he offers his space to young jazz musicians trying to break into the music scene. Some of the greats played here back in the day. You name 'em—Miles Davis, Etta James—hell, this place predates Duke Ellington."

"It's awesome." Montana looked around in appreciation.

A man with coffee colored skin and a cropped head of tiny black curls peered out from behind the backroom door. "Hey there—I thought I heard someone come in. Welcome—we don't usually get people until later."

"T.J. wouldn't happen to be in, would he?"

"Nah, he's off today. Bout time too—he never takes time off."

"Just like his dad. Do me a favor—when you see him tell him O'Malley stopped by to say hello."

"Will do. Nice to meet you O'Malley. I'm Jerome." He stuck out his hand and shook O'Malley's hand. He turned to Montana with a raised eyebrow.

"Nice to meet you Jerome. I'm Montana Wylde."

"*Very* nice to meet you." He shook her hand. "So what's your poison?"

O'Malley ordered his usual Dewar's with a beer back. Montana, inspired by the club's ambiance, ordered a sidecar.

"Why not just have a Coca Cola if you want something so sweet?" O'Malley shook his head and laughed. "You broads sniff your noses at a straightforward drink like Dewar's but get all excited at a frou-frou drink with a pink umbrella."

"O'Malley," she exclaimed. "How many times do I have to remind you that real men don't refer to real women as 'broads'? Besides, I'm not a girly girl. I prefer wine to any 'frou-frou' drink but this place reminds me of another era. Thanks for taking me here."

"I thought you'd like it," O'Malley beamed.

She paused. "What do you think about what we walked into back there? Why would someone trash Suzette's place without taking a thing of value?"

Jerome brought their drinks. Her tiny martini glass filled with high-end brandy had a rim of sparkling sugar.

O'Malley took a long swallow of his beer. "First tell me what *you* think."

She gathered her thoughts. "

"The CM broke didn't break into her place. That break-in has to do with something else."

O'Malley nodded. "I agree. No other victim had her place broken into. We would have heard about it had it occurred." He sipped his scotch. "I'll run my own theory by you now."

"I knew your wheels were spinning back at the apartment. I could see it." She sipped her sidecar. "Shoot."

"Whoever broke in was looking for something. Think about it, Montana. Suzette's home is a prime hit for worried former clients. You said something that has stuck with me. You said that clients fell in love with Suzette all the time. A man in loves often sends flowers, gifts—or a note—you following where I'm going? My gut says a jumpy client wanted to make sure there wasn't any incriminating evidence at her apartment after news of her death broke. Is it the Friday client? Maybe or maybe not. She had lots of clients other than Friday's."

"But we didn't give out our home addresses. Any client would have sent gifts to the Coop. I never gave a client my address."

"We know now that Suzette didn't always follow protocol. Maybe she did give some of them her address. The Coop would be harder to ransack because of the high security and door attendants. Of course Suzette's building has that coffee shop underneath but they wouldn't be focused on who was going in and out of the building."

"You're right. You know, I haven't been to the Coop since I met Hanky there a couple of days ago. Maybe I should check to make sure it's safe."

"You stay away from the Coop. Have one of the door attendants or management check the place."

"But they caught the CM."

"That's true and chances are you aren't in danger but we just agreed that whoever broke into Suzette's apartment wasn't the CM. We don't know who it is. You need to continue being vigilant."

She gave him a flippant salute. "Aye, aye." Then she turned serious. "So what's up now—things sure have moved fast the last couple of days."

"Now that they've caught the bastard it changes things. There's no purpose in outing the Mayor even if he was Suzette's high roller. You don't want to ruin Suzette's reputation any more than it has been I'd guess. A scandal would hurt this city. No good would come of it. As to the break-in, let the cops to figure it out."

"While a part of me believes the public has a right to know what elected officials are up to, I would never go against Suzette's wishes. She went to obvious lengths to keep this client's identity a secret. I have to honor that."

"Good. It's time for you to step away from all of this. The trial will likely answer many of your questions. For now, let it go. Let the NYPD and courts do their jobs and you do yours—and that's passing the bar exam."

"You're right. You know, I'm going to miss you."

"As I told you before, you ain't gonna miss me because I plan to stay in touch. You know, I sometimes work cases where I need an attorney. Now I know one. I'm expecting big things from you."

"Thanks. Thanks for taking the case and for letting me tag along."

"I had misgivings at first but I'll be honest with you, you helped keep me on the straight and narrow. You've also inspired me to want to take on more investigative cases and fewer insurance frauds. And I don't feel like going on a bender every night—although I won't say I'm quitting drinking."

"Really, O'Malley?" Montana's face flushed with happiness. "I'm so glad positive things came out of this for you."

He gave her a one armed hug and then glanced at his watch. "So, what do you think? You think the rain has let up?"

"Only one way to find out," she replied.

Outside, a fresh blue sky was breaking through the still darkened clouds.

Montana pointed. "Look—a rainbow. Those are always a good sign—especially in the middle of the city."

45

THE CHURCH MURDERER'S CAPTURE was the most sensational story of the year. For those addicted to grisly crimes, it was a feeding frenzy. The depravity of the crimes drew sensation seekers like sharks to blood. The media was happy to give the bloodthirsty ghouls what they craved. They didn't overlook any gut wrenching details of the victims' suffering.

Max Constantine became an overnight star, riding the waves of success on the CM's capture. Every major network wanted to interview him: Dateline, Primetime, 48 hours. Not much for attention, he handled the spotlight with dignity. He always downplayed his own role, giving credit to the task force's bravery and commitment.

Someone leaked the Coop's existence, adding another layer of intrigue. Because Suzette was so beautiful and her lifestyle so different from the others, she received the most attention. The week's hot topic was how a woman as beautiful and successful as Suzette could wind up in the path of the CM. The press contrasted her luxurious lifestyle to the drug-infested poverty of those victims who'd been street-walkers. Suzette shared nothing with them except the unwanted distinction of being one of the CM's victims.

Worse, when reporters broke the news about Suzette's long ago relationship with the lowlife pimp Flash, Montana's phone began ringing. They wanted all the details. Did she know her high-end partner was moonlighting on the side by working the street?

Montana couldn't have been more frustrated. Regardless of what she said, the media twisted her words. She felt as though she were trying to punch her way out of bubble-wrap that was stifling and distorting her every word. When she informed reporters that Suzette had *not* been working the street, they continued pressing on. None cared about the truth—only about the sensationalism.

The investigation was just starting but CSIs had already uncovered a mountain of evidence. They found souvenirs from many victims. Killers often kept mementos and the CM was no exception. Most grabbed a pair of panties or took a lock of hair but the CM was bold. Investigators found shrines dedicated to each victim, with pictures and videos detailing their rape, torture, and death. They also found smaller souvenirs. The CM labeled each victim's shrine: 'Lottie Day 1,' 'Lottie Day 2,' with 'Lottie Purified' as a sad endnote.

Most ghastly were the homemade snuff films. The most malevolent in the porn industry made these black market films to pleasure the sickest offenders. They began as typical porn until the final scene when an actual murder occurred. The director didn't stage the deaths; they were real. Such films commanded a fortune on the black market. Investigators didn't believe the CM sold the films; he kept them for his own depraved pleasure.

Max and Joey were busy poring over the photos and DVDs, diligent in matching each photo to the ones on the victim map. After several hours of matching photos, Max stood and rubbed his lower back.

"Joey, how do you think Suzette Peterson came across this nut?"

"We've already gone over this, partner. Either she was working the street or he thought she was—or maybe he was branching out to higher end girls. While it's true that she didn't have a drug habit or a pimp, she was still a hooker. A trick in a fancy car pulls up and offers some big change and she's going to go with him. Look, someone found her in a church wearing the same type of clothes as the others. She had religious symbols cut into her skin, the same needle marks on her inner arm, and the same type of crude embalming incision. Not every detail is the same but there are far more similarities than differences."

"One thing bothers me—a lot." Max shook his head.

"Only one thing bothers you?" Joey's chuckle was grim. "Heck, everything about this case bugs the shit out of me."

"Of course but remember the ME's initial report. Whoever carved into Suzette Peterson did so after she was dead. All the others were tortured alive with those carvings. Why change his MO with Suzette?"

"That's a difference," Joey admitted, "but it's not a huge difference. Maybe she put up a fight and he had to kill her before he got the chance to start his artwork. Maybe he's getting disorganized."

"I'll still be interested in seeing that final tox report," Max muttered. "We know she had sedatives and poisons in her system but I'm sure interested to see if they match the others."

"I'll bet you a dinner at Stripes that the ME is going to find the same stuff—maybe different amounts—but the same stuff."

"You're on. Although I hate betting against you on this—I hope I'll be buying that dinner.

"You have a point," Max conceded. "Something just feels off to me."

"Thank God we got this sick fuck off the street." Joey shook his head in disgust.

46

A FTER PARTING WAYS with Montana, O'Malley spent the rest of his afternoon doing tedious legwork he'd neglected. He went to the bank, submitted invoices to several companies, and picked up two weeks of mail from his post office box.

It was good to focus on something other than what was gnawing at him. While he'd told Montana she should let the case go, he was having a hard time doing so. Something was off, though he couldn't quite put his finger on it. The case had ended up in a different direction than he'd expected but that wasn't what bothered him. Too many loose ends weren't adding up.

When he finished his errands, he was hungry and thirsty. With nothing to eat all day, he knew just the remedy. He'd go get one of Bobby Finney's famous burgers from Stripes. He could already taste the burger made of the finest ground beef, topped with three slices of cheese, two trips of bacon, tangy sauce, and a double-fried onion ring on top. That, and some double dipped French-fries would fix him right up. A cold draft beer would also go down well.

Bobby and O'Malley went back a long way. They had met as recruits and shared an Irish heritage as well as a Brooklyn background. Bobby had to change careers when a gang shootout left him with a gimpy leg. He'd worked a desk job for a while but like O'Malley, he'd hated it. Stripes had been the perfect solution. He still had the camaraderie and he loved cooking. He kept a well-stocked bar with an enormous selection of Irish and Scotch whiskeys. If you wanted an eighteen year old McCallan or Laphroaig, Stripes had it. If you wanted a less expensive option such as a shot of Dewar's with a beer back—this was the joint for that too.

O'Malley had been MIA for almost a month and the crowd roared a hearty welcome as soon as he walked in. On cue, Bobby poured a double shot of Dewar's and an ice-cold beer back and brought them to O'Malley who sat in his regular corner perch.

"You son of a bitch," Bobby exclaimed. "I've been talking about forming a search party to find your sorry ass."

O'Malley gave him a good-natured shrug. "What can I say? I've been busy."

"Those insurance companies keeping you busy stopping scumbags from defrauding 'em?"

"They do, but I haven't been working any of them lately. I've been busy with a missing person investigation but that ended when she turned up dead a few days ago. I'm sure you've heard of her—it's been all over the news. She was a victim of the CM."

"Did her pimp hire you?" Curiosity filled Bobby's face.

"She didn't have one. Her business partner—well more than that—hired me."

Bobby snapped his fingers. "You're talking about the high end hooker who had that upscale joint near midtown. Why was she working the street?"

"She wasn't." O'Malley replied. "I'm sure of that and so is her partner. Their business was top shelf."

Bobby nodded. "She sure was beautiful—I saw that from the news photos. So different from the rest of those girls."

"Yeah, and her partner, Montana Wylde, is another look-er. She was frustrated after the cops wouldn't do much. You know how it goes—without foul play they weren't going to chase down a missing call girl." O'Malley shook his head. "We only met a couple of weeks ago but it seems like I've known her for years. She's one helluva dame—or woman, I should say." O'Malley chuckled, "She doesn't like being called a dame."

"Montana? A hooker name if I ever heard one."

"Nah—it's her real name, crazy as it sounds. I ran a back-ground check the day she hired me. There's more to her than meets the eye—and as I said, she's some eye candy herself. She has a BA from NYU and she recently finished Columbia's School of Law. They don't let dummies into that joint. She's getting ready to take the bar exam—in fact I hope she's studying now. I'd be willing to bet she passes on the first go-round." O'Malley's face beamed with pride.

Bobby's brow wrinkled in confusion. "Law school? I thought she was a call girl."

"*Was* a call girl. She was pretty close to leaving the busi-ness when all this came down. When her friend—Suzette—went missing it made her leave faster. I was so impressed with her that you'll never believe what I did."

Bobby stopped wiping the bar. "I can't imagine."

"I let her partner with me. And she was a damn good one."

"You're kidding." Bobby gave him a side-eye. "That doesn't sound like the O'Malley I know. She must have been on the straight and narrow—no drugs I bet."

"Nope." O'Malley was firm. "She never touched that stuff. Her mother was an alcoholic so she doesn't even drink much. She runs and does taekwondo."

"A health chick." Bobby nodded knowingly.

O'Malley laughed. "Haha—don't call her a chick. She doesn't like that any better than dame."

"Sounds like you're stuck on her, you old dog. I can't blame ya."

O'Malley burst out laughing as he shook his head. "You dirty old man. She's half my age. I'm old enough to be her father. Heck, I *feel* like her father—God knows she never had much of one." He paused for a minute. "You know, she's had a rough few days. I'm gonna ask her to join me for a burger—she needs fattening up. Plus, she'll class this joint up—and likely raise the IQ."

O'Malley frowned as he pulled out his dead phone. "Damn—that's right—my phone's dead. These last two days have been so hectic I forgot to charge it."

"Use mine." Bobby slid his across the counter.

"You think I know her number? The biggest benefit to these electronic appendages is their ability to store numbers." He downed his shot along and the rest of his beer. "I'll be right back—as soon as I charge my phone enough to get her number I'll ask her to meet me here—I should be back in a half an hour, tops."

Bobby poured another shot and refilled O'Malley's beer. "I have your drinks waiting so I'm holding you to that. What does she drink?"

"Any frou frou drink will make her happy," he called out walking out the door.

47

MONTANA RETURNED HOME feeling out of sorts. The case was over but she was antsy—dissatisfied. Things *still* felt unresolved—or was she kidding herself? Was she unwittingly hanging onto the case as a morbid way to stay close to Suzette?

Her rumbling stomach reminded her that she needed to eat. For two weeks, food was a necessity rather than a pleasure. A full-blown shopping run was in order. The gooey sticky bun from the morning was long gone so she overbought, breaking a steadfast rule never to shop when hungry. Tonight, she didn't care.

She ordered a farm-raised filet mignon from the butcher and picked up fruits and veggies from her favorite produce market. She stopped by the Wine Cask and picked up a few bottles of favorite wines. Her final stop was Destination Bakery where she picked up a still warm baguette and a strawberry cheesecake tart.

The bag lady was on her regular stoop when Montana returned. Montana was gobsmacked when the woman raised a tentative hand to wave. She waved in return. They weren't ready yet for a girls' night out, Montana thought, but the relationship had taken an upward turn.

Relaxed at home, she put La Bohème on the stereo, turned up the volume, and poured a glass of merlot as she conducted a make-believe symphony with chopsticks. She washed and side-cut the veggies for a stir-fry side while letting the meat rest at room temperature. Cooking was therapeutic.

She was about to put the steak on the grill pan when her cellphone rang. She debated letting it go to voicemail after she saw 'unavailable' on Caller ID. While she dithered, it stopped ringing. Then her landline rang. Also 'unavailable.' Her curiosity now piqued, she answered.

"Hello?"

"May I speak to Montana Wylde?" a familiar voice asked, though she couldn't quite place it.

"This is she."

"This is Mayor Burke."

The minute he said his name she recognized the voice. It was deep and confident—a memorable voice. His call stunned her. She stopped cooking, spatula suspended mid-air.

"Mayor Burke? What a surprise. What can I do for you?"

"It's what I can do for you, Ms. Wylde. I've been thinking. We need to meet as soon as possible. We need to talk about Suzette."

At the mention of Suzette's name time froze. She heard each sound in her apartment, no matter how minute: the ticking of her antique clock, the freezer's automatic icemaker, and the fan whirring inside her laptop.

"What about Suzette?" she whispered.

"We need to speak in person. The phone won't do."

"I can come by your office first thing in the morning."

"Are you free tonight? It's quite important."

She looked at the food resting on her counter. Her appetite was long gone.

She was confused. "Mayor Burke—what is this is about? What could be so urgent?"

"Please believe me that it's important—I must talk to you in person."

She hesitated but for only a moment. "Well...okay. Shall I come to your office?"

"My car will pick you up. We'll be there in ten minutes."

"Give me twenty," she replied. "I need a little more time."

"Twenty minutes then. My car will be waiting in front of your building. When we buzz, just come down." A dull click silenced his smooth voice.

She turned off the grill pan and then wrapped and loaded the meat and veggies into the refrigerator. She corked the rest of the bottle, and dumped her glass in the sink. She wanted a clear head when she met the Mayor.

She threw on a chambray shirt and comfortable faded jeans tucked into brown leather boots. Noticing dark circles under her eyes, she dabbed on a touch of cover up. She finished with a light application of blush on the apples of her cheek, a sweep of mascara, and a dab of pink lip-gloss.

The doorbell buzzed and just as she was stepping out the door, she thought of O'Malley. Mayor Burke's call had so unnerved her that she hadn't the presence of mind to consider him—but they *were* partners. He'd want to be present for such an important meeting—and certainly, the Mayor wouldn't object to stopping to pick him up.

Her call went to his voicemail after the first ring, which made her remember his dead phone from earlier. She tried his office and home landlines but they too went to voicemail. She left messages on all asking him to call her right away. Perhaps he could join them if he called soon enough.

When door buzzed again, she grabbed her handbag and keys, her curiosity buzzing as she left to meet the Mayor.

In her rush, she'd left her cellphone. Had she remembered it, she would have heard in person the message that Hanky left on her voicemail ten minutes after she left.

48

O'MALLEY BUMPED into a chair in his dark office. "Damn it," he swore. He turned on the light, plugged in his cellphone, and within a couple of minutes, a lightning bolt came on, indicating it was charging. The battery was so dead the phone refused to come to life. Then he noticed the messaging light on his phone system blinking twice, indicating two messages. He turned on speakerphone to listen. The first call was from the Petersons. He had promised Montana he'd call them later but had forgotten all about that. He'd call to update them tomorrow. The second call—from Montana—surprised the hell out of him.

"O'Malley, your cellphone must still be dead because my call went straight to voicemail. You won't believe what happened. Mayor Burke just called me at home—he insisted that we meet right away—that he needs to speak with me about Suzette. I hoped I'd catch you to come with me but I'll fill you in later."

Dread knotted in O'Malley's gut. He didn't like the sound of her message at all. What could be so urgent? Why would the Mayor insist she meet him right away?

He cursed his still-dead phone and willed it to come back to life. When had she left the message? The messaging machine time was useless because he hadn't reset it the last time his building lost power. The electronic voice droned on 'Sunday, 12:00 a.m.' as each call came in. Funny how little things like that came back to annoy you.

He considered his options. He wished he'd written her number down instead of relying on his cellphone's memory. He racked his memory but he couldn't come up with it. Perhaps she called right before he walked in. There was a chance he could still catch her at home. He grabbed his briefcase and locked his office door, hoping he'd beat Mayor Burke to her door.

Things started out well when he saw an on-duty taxi driving up his street. He ran down the steps, calling to bring it to a halt. Climbing in, he gave the driver thirty dollars and told him to keep the change if he could make it to a Tribeca address in five minutes or less. The cabbie roared to life, dodging cars and minor traffic jams like a true professional. They made it to her building in record time at which point O'Malley pulled another twenty from his wallet.

"Wouldya mind waiting a few minutes, buddy? Keep the fifty and remember the normal cost of this jaunt would be about ten bucks including tip."

The cabbie took the twenty. "Been a slow night, buddy— your money is my time—literally. Don't worry, I'll wait right here."

O'Malley moved faster than he had since he'd been on the force. He trotted up her walkway and pressed the buzzer to her loft. No answer. He pressed again. Still nothing. Then a light bulb flashed and he wondered why he hadn't thought of it earlier: the NYPD had her phone number. As he reached for his cellphone, he cursed in mounting frustration. It was still charging back at his office. He hurried back to the waiting taxi. Surely, the driver would have one he could use.

He'd almost made it back to the cab when an odd figure approached him. When she was within a couple of feet, he remembered her. It was the bizarre bag lady with the nutty orange wig—the one who screamed obscenities at Montana the first time he'd been to her building. Now that she was close, he could smell the ripe odors of urine, alcohol, and God only knew what else.

"You looking for her?" the woman wheezed.

She sure was weird, reminding O'Malley of the old Bette Davis and Joan Crawford movie, *Whatever Happened to Baby Jane*. A former child star, Baby Jane Hudson—played by Davis, had worn garish clown-like makeup just like this creepy old bag lady. Only the bag lady looked ten times crazier than Baby Jane Hudson ever had.

"Who?" He was in a hurry—impatient. Why he was wasting time with this nut?

"The whore who lives here," the bag lady hissed. "She stole my corner."

O'Malley reached for the woman's arm but she backed away and brandished a small penknife from one of her pockets.

"Wait," O'Malley said. "I'm not going to hurt you. Are you talking about the woman who lives here?" He pointed to Montana's building. "She's tall, long wavy black hair, and blue eyes—pretty." He hunched down so he could meet the woman's eyes. "Look, it's very important that I find her. Did you see something?"

"She got in the car." The bag lady eyed him, penknife still in hand. "The one that sometimes waits. Tonight it picked her up. "

"What car?" O'Malley almost shouted.

"The black car," she replied.

O'Malley reached into the waiting taxi and pulled a photo from his briefcase. "Is it this car?"

The woman nodded and put the knife away.

He tapped on the license plate. "Did you notice the license plates? This is a city car. See below can see it where it says 'official?'"

The woman sneered in suspicion as she backed away. Something had set her off.

"The *officials*," she shrieked, "*will kill her too*." She turned so quickly that she almost tripped. She looked at him, full of suspicion, before she went scampering down the street. Halfway down, she turned around and screeched, "The whore. I tried to warn her. The car took her that way." She pointed downtown.

O'Malley slid back into the taxi. "Hey bud—my cellphone is charging back at my office. I need to talk to the cops right away. Can you loan me yours?" He pulled another ten from his wallet.

The cabbie laughed and shook his head. "Don't worry about the ten bucks. Here." He handed him the phone. "That was some old hag lady—one of the weirdest I've seen and I've seen some doozies."

O'Malley ignored him. He was too busy digging through business cards. Finding the one he'd been looking for, he dialed Constantine. Max answered on the first ring.

"This is O'Malley," he broke in abruptly. "I'm worried about Montana. She left a message on my landline—my cellphone is dead but that's another story. She's gone to meet Mayor Burke—and..."

Max cut in, "You aren't the only one who's worried. I've been trying her cellphone and landline and she's not answering either. Where are you? We need to talk."

"Outside her apartment but she's not here."

"Can you head back to your office? We're not far from there."

"No problem." O'Malley pushed end and handed the phone back to the driver, "Thanks guy. Take me right back to where you picked me up."

"You got it." The driver tore down the street.

49

MAX AND JOEY were waiting on O'Malley's steps when the taxi pulled up. O'Malley hurried up to greet them.

"Thanks for getting here so fast," Max shook his hand. "You remember my partner, Joey Malone?"

"Nice to see you again." He nodded at Joey and then turned to Max. "Why are you worried?"

"We're now almost positive the CM did not kill Suzette Peterson."

O'Malley realized the news didn't surprise him. "What changed your mind?"

"The murders are similar but there are significant disparities. We knew of one major difference a few days ago, as soon as we got the ME's original but incomplete report. The CM engraved religious symbols and quotes onto his victims while they were alive. This was not true in Suzette Peterson's murder. While she also had engravings on her body, they were postmortem. We knew the symbols and other carvings were different but the similarities far outweighed the differences. However, just a couple of hours ago, we got a more detailed toxicology report. The sedatives and poisons used to subdue and embalm Suzette were far different."

"Holy Christ." O'Malley paled.

"There's more." Max was grim. "The CSIs have by now gone through a ton of evidence. They found DNA for all the victims except Suzette. We are now operating on the belief that there is another killer out there. Maybe a copycat. That means Montana could be in real danger."

"I think Montana had problems believing the CM killed Suzette but you were all so positive. I'll be honest with you. We were continuing our own investigation until the successful sting. Montana needed to know how Suzette came across the CM. We've been looking at Suzette's final out-call—the date she had on the Friday she went missing. We believe Mayor Burke could be that client."

Max's jaw dropped. "You're kidding."

"No, I'm not." O'Malley realized they were still on his stoop. "Look, come into my office."

They stood inside the small office while O'Malley hit play on his answering machine. They listened. "See what I mean," O'Malley said, "Something about that message isn't right. All of a sudden, Mayor Burke has an urgent need to meet with her. What could be so serious that they *had* to meet tonight? Does any of this pass the smell test with you, Max?"

Max said, "Could be he just wants see what she knows and to see how much it could damage his career. It's an election year after all. Maybe he'll offer her a little hush money to keep her from going to the press."

"He might offer it but she'd never take it," O'Malley said, his voice defensive. "She has integrity. Her only purpose in meeting him would be to find out what happened that last Friday."

"It is odd he'd insist on meeting her tonight—on such short notice. Are you sure it was the Mayor who called?"

O'Malley hit the play button again and stopped it at the point where Montana said, 'Mayor Burke just called.' Then he addressed the detectives. "Montana's business at the Co-op relied on her ability to remember details about her clients. She told me she tried memorizing her clients' voices so she'd recognize them when they called. The Mayor has a distinctive voice—one I'm sure she'd recognize. More worrying to me is that if everything is kosher, why isn't she answering her phone?"

Max thought a minute. "Maybe it died like yours or she forgot it at her house. I have Mayor Burke's private number. Let's give him a call."

Max called, turning on the speakerphone so everyone could hear. Max swore when voicemail answered. "Jimmy, this is Max. It's imperative you return my call as soon as you get this message."

O'Malley looked at Max and Joey. "Let's go to his house. He might not be home but maybe someone knows where he is."

They piled into the car. Max drove, Joey rode shotgun, and O'Malley slid into the backseat. Joey grabbed the detachable rollers from the car's glove box and attached them with one arm onto the car's roof. Max then turned on the sirens so they could bypass traffic. A flood of taxis parted— a yellow version of the red sea. Several blocks before arriving at Mayor Burke's home, Max turned them off. The Mayor's home was aglow although that didn't mean he was home. Most residents in the Mayor's upscale neighborhood had automatic lights programmed to turn off and on to deter hungry burglars.

A woman in a crisp uniform answered the door and allowed the detectives entry as soon as Max and Joey flashed their badges. Within a minute, Mayor Burke greeted them with a baffled look. He was comfortable in lounging pajamas and a robe.

"Max?" Mayor Burke looked puzzled. "What brings you here?"

O'Malley blurted, "Where's Montana?"

Mayor Burke's eyes widened. "What?" He shook his head in authentic bewilderment, spluttering. "Why would you think she'd be here? I-I've not seen her since you two were in my office." He nodded to O'Malley. Mayor Burke's surprise was genuine.

Max studied him. "Jimmy, Ms. Wylde left a message on O'Malley's voicemail saying you requested she meet with you tonight. I heard it myself."

Mayor Burke grew more confused. "I have *not* spoken to her—not since she was in my office with you." He looked at O'Malley again.

O'Malley countered, "That's strange because she left two messages—one on my cell and the other on my landline. She said that *you* had called saying you wanted to meet because you had information about Suzette Peterson." O'Malley brought out his somewhat charged cellphone and hit play on his voicemail. "See?"

"But I did *not* call her." Mayor Burke was vehement.

"She was very clear. She said she talked to *you*," O'Malley insisted.

"I'm telling you I *did not* call her." Mayor Burke sunk into a chair as his shoulders slumped in defeat. "I might know who did, although I hope to God that I'm wrong."

O'Malley watched fascinated, as New York City's most important man looked down, wrestling with whatever demons that held him hostage. He looked up and faced the three probing stares.

50

A DRIVER STOOD by the town car when Montana emerged from her building. He held the door open for her. It was a quiet night, unusual for Tribeca. The bag lady was almost a block away pushing her shopping cart. The minute she saw Montana, she began yelling but it wasn't her usual barrage of cuss words. Montana couldn't understand her—it had to be nonsense anyway.

"Hello. I was expecting to see Mr. Drinkwater." Montana nodded.

"He works days." The man smiled. He was an older man dressed in full livery gear. "At least most of the time. We sometimes switch schedules. I'm James—pleased to meet you." He held the back passenger door for her.

"Pleased to meet you as well." Montana glanced into the back and saw it was empty. She looked at James. "Where's the Mayor? He said he'd be picking me up."

"He's finishing an important meeting. He has so many headaches with the capture of that dreadful man—the one they call the CM. He asked me to pick you up."

There was something familiar about the man but Montana couldn't quite place it. "I see." She slid into the car, feeling uneasy. Her instincts were afire but she told herself she was being silly. After all, she *had* spoken to Mayor Burke. The break-in at Suzette's just had her spooked.

Montana's head buzzed with curiosity. What could be so urgent? Would he confess to being Suzette's client? Perhaps he wanted to clear his conscience, but why the hurry?

They drove even further downtown, in the opposite direction from City Hall. Just as she was about to ask where they were going, he stopped in front of a building under construction. Confused, she watched him get out and come around to open her door.

Montana, full of uncertainty, faced him. "Why are we here? Where's Mayor Burke?" she demanded. The block was dark, with streetlights at a distant corner.

"Superstorm Sandy damaged these buildings," James replied with confidence. "You can see they are under construction. Soon, they will be new city offices. Look up to the top floor to the right—see those lights? A few finished offices are in the back. Mayor Burke is upstairs waiting for you."

Montana hesitated. After honing her perceptive skills for years, something was amiss.

"It's so dark," she protested. "It looks uninhabitable."

He took her arm and led her to the side of the building. Lights *were* aglow on the top floor. "See? That's where his office is."

This made her relax a bit, but her apprehension remained. "It's strange he would want to meet here."

"Let me tell you a secret." James gave her a conspiratorial wink. "These days the Mayor needs time away from City Hall since it is swarming with the media. He thought it more discreet to meet here."

The explanation made sense. Was she paranoid? The last two weeks of shock had left her fragile. She studied his face.

In the dim illumination of the distant streetlights, his face took on an eerie glow.

Something was wrong. Her primal intuition demanded she leave at once. Each time she had disregarded that sixth sense—whatever her Nana believed she had possessed—she'd been sorry.

As she turned to run, James pushed an ether soaked rag over her nose and mouth. She fought—but only for a moment.

The drug's effect was immediate and strong.

51

WHEN SHE AWOKE, she was in darkness. Pain was the first sensation; her joints ached as her head pounded. Her throat was bone dry, making it difficult to swallow. A concrete slab was her bed. Sluggish memories began returning... until the full realization hit her.

Mayor Burke had conspired with one of his drivers to bring her here. Could Mayor Burke be Suzette's killer? As she considered what had just happened, the more terrible sense it made. Suzette had never been the CM's victim. She'd known it in her heart and gut; O'Malley hadn't fully bought that theory either.

Survival mode kicked in as she assessed her condition. How long had she been unconscious? It was impossible to know if it was day or night because her eyes were taped shut. She felt the tape's sticky discomfort on her eyelids. James had restrained her arms and legs, and taped her mouth shut as well.

She cursed her naiveté in agreeing to meet the Mayor alone. No one even knew where she was. She should have insisted that O'Malley accompany her. But the last two weeks had been the most desperate of her adult life and she'd been too anxious to hear about Suzette. Even

O'Malley could not have predicted Mayor Burke's role in Suzette's murder. They'd been way off base there.

She *had* left him messages though—on all of his phones. He would know she'd gone to meet Mayor Burke and he was a smart detective. He'd figure it out—she just hoped he'd have enough time.

She sensed another presence that broke the room's stillness. Footsteps grew closer until they were right next to her. She smelled hot sour breath on her face.

"Hello Montana," Mayor Burke's silky voice purred.

Her heart sank. It *was* true. Mayor Burke was the killer.

Stinging pain produced immediate tears as he ripped the tape from her eyes. A lantern glowing sinister yellow provided dim light in a far corner but at first she couldn't quite see who was before her.

She blinked, adjusting her eyes to the dim light. Once focused, confusion scrambled her brain as she saw *Charles Drinkwater* standing before her. Where was James? Even more important, where was Mayor Burke? She'd *just heard* his distinctive voice. Just as she thought things couldn't get any more bizarre, Mayor Burke's upper-crust voice came out of Charles Drinkwater's mouth. If it weren't taped shut, her jaw would have dropped in astonishment.

"Comfortable, my dear?" he asked, delighted with himself. "Surprised? It *is* a good impression if I say so myself." It was surreal, hearing Mayor Burke's voice come from Charles Drinkwater's mouth. He switched to his normal voice. "Acting is a hobby of mine—one I once hoped to make a career of. My imitations were always perfect. Don't you think this one is?"

"Where's James?"

Drinkwater lifted a deflated latex mask and taunted her with it. He waved it back and forth, speaking in a singsong voice. "Why here he is," Charles cried out in delight. "And would you like to meet another man who's watched your slutty ass for the last week?" Drinkwater picked up another limp bundle of hair and latex. "Here *he* is." He laughed in wicked amusement.

His eyes gleamed with madness. He was insane but he'd been clever enough to hide it from most people. She wondered what the Mayor really knew about his daytime driver. Just as questions began looming large, Charles Drinkwater filled her in.

Using his own voice, he lectured, "Were you so stupid to think that the Mayor of this fine city would want to meet with you? For someone who graduated from a top-level law school you are quite dim. Why would Mayor Burke risk his career and reputation for a whore like you? He almost jeopardized it for that blonde slut. Of course, I could never allow that.

He pulled a folding chair next to her cot. "It's story time," he said in his singsong voice. "So gather 'round, children. Once upon a time, the Mayor of the greatest city on earth had *everything* going for him. His constituents loved him—his opponents admired him. Even his enemies respected him—the few that he had that is. Unfortunately, this powerful man had a most unfortunate weakness. Do you know what that was?"

Montana was spellbound. She shook her head no.

"It was his penchant for beautiful women. They weren't a problem—not much of one anyway—until your slutty friend came along. At first, she was no trouble. For years, they had their occasional dalliance, which would have been fine had it remained that way. Then disaster hit. Do you know what that was?"

The restraints wouldn't allow her much movement but she again shook her head no.

He slapped her across the face—hard, his face within an inch of her own. "He fell in Goddamn love." In his rage, angry drops of spittle sprayed her face. "I tried telling him. You *fuck* whores. You don't *marry* them. That was his plan— one he confided to me. After the upcoming election, he was going to make that nasty slut his wife. Of course, I could not allow that to happen. I spared him *and* this great city from what would have been an epic travesty. What I did was for the greater good."

Drinkwater pranced around the room, filled with self-righteous gloating. "Then the so-called Church Murderer came along—the perfect solution. I paid attention to *Him* from the beginning. The name 'Church Murderer' didn't do him justice. He was a *Purifier*. How I admired him. In time, my admiration turned to adulation. The Purifier revealed my true calling so I studied under him as any good pupil would. He followed God's plan and I followed his. Just as the Purifier eradicated the filth from this fair city, I rid Mayor Burke of the indecent tramp he thought he loved."

He pulled up the chair, sneering at her. "She thought she was better than the street whores—just as you do—but you are *not*. The only difference is price."

How Montana loathed this narcissistic and delusional monster who had killed Suzette. He continued his pious rant.

"I needed a solution. As Jimmy's driver, I was privy to most meetings involving the CM and task force. Without knowing it, the police taught me his craft. I learned how he cleansed the whores through first injecting them with purification water and then embalming them. I learned that he decorated them with symbols of their conversion. The first tragedy was tricking The Purifier into capture. Now vermin will once again roam free on the streets of this city. The second misfortune is that he'll not learn of my respect for him. I can never let him know because to do so would put Mayor Burke and this city at risk. I'm not selfish enough to do that."

Drinkwater danced around the room, the lantern's dim light making wild shadows on the walls. He picked up an object from a table in the back. Montana squinted, trying to make out its shape. As he grew close, she saw the knife. She felt a sharp slice of pain as he traced its tip across her cheek. Then wetness—a trickle of blood—coursed her cheek like a teardrop.

The pain caused the fog to lift. She assessed her chance of a successful escape. As he had danced in maniacal delight spouting his narcissistic hyperbole, Montana had kept busy working to free her right hand—the one furthest from him. If she didn't get away, she'd die trying.

Nothing ventured, nothing gained.

She had one advantage over Suzette. Although she had urged her friend to take self-defense classes, Suzette hadn't shown interest. Even though Drinkwater wasn't a big man, Suzette wouldn't have had the skill to fight him. But Montana was an able opponent: a fifth degree black belt in taekwondo. With her hand freed, she might be able to knock him out with a well-placed punch to his neck. As he droned on, she continued working the cuff binding her hand.

"You brought this all on yourself," Drinkwater's haughty voice intoned. "I would have let it go with your friend's death but you and your detective got too close. I have out-witted you, Miss Future Attorney-at-Law. You're what the hawk politicians call collateral damage—but that doesn't mean I won't enjoy your death."

The wound on her face wasn't deep but it was bleeding profusely as facial cuts do. Blood dripped onto her hand making it slippery to work the binding loose. Drinkwater didn't notice; he was too enamored with his one-man performance.

Her wrist was almost free. She needed only a few more minutes and some luck. She prayed for him to continue his rant just a bit longer. Egomaniac that he was, he obliged. He was happy for an audience—even a captive one.

"What a pity I can't purify *you*. I would have preferred taking you to the basement chamber I built. That's where I took your blond-haired slut friend. We had lots of time for fun before I started her cleansing." He winked at Montana.

"I don't have the luxury of time here. If I had managed to capture you when you were running to your drunk detective's house, we could have enjoyed a couple of days of *fun* just as your tramp friend had. You're a strong runner, I'll give you that. If I'd caught up with you, you could have also undergone purification. But any hope of your cleansing ended with the capture of my mentor. Therefore, you'll just vanish—fast and neat. I considered that end for your tramp friend but copying the Purifier's work was too great a temptation. As his apprentice, how could I resist? So, no purification for you—no press coverage, no fifteen minutes of fame as Andy Warhol promised. They'll never even find you," he hissed.

Her right hand was now free. She was ready to make her move but stopped when she saw the gleam of metal. She'd been too busy to notice that he'd picked up a gun.

He pointed it at her head.

52

MAYOR BURKE LOOKED UP AT THEM. "I believe I know who called her."

"Who?" The three detectives chorused.

"My driver, Charles Drinkwater."

"Oh good Christ," O'Malley exclaimed. "I had a hinky feeling about him and so did Montana. Wait—that doesn't make sense. She said she talked to *you*—not to your driver."

"Allow me to explain. Charles and I have known each other since childhood. At first I was a protector rather than friend. He was a scrawny kid—the type bullies victimize. I met him when I volunteered at the YMCA one summer. One day, a gang of young thugs was beating the snot out of poor Charles. I intervened. After, he followed me around like a puppy. I felt sorry for him—still do, I guess. His father was a drunk who left when Charles was in diapers. After he left, his mother became a religious fanatic."

Max lost his patience. "How is this relevant?"

Mayor Burke held his hand up. "Allow me to continue. Most people don't know this about Charles but he was—and still is—an incredible talent. He had big dreams of becoming an actor."

O'Malley exploded. "What the fuck does this have to do with anything?"

Mayor Burke continued in a calm voice, "His greatest talent is his impeccable impersonations. He could have made a name for himself, but he couldn't take rejection and turned to drugs. The drugs did him in—they almost killed him. When I re-connected with him many years ago, I didn't recognize him. He told me about the drugs. He'd just gotten through treatment. Knowing he'd had some tough breaks, I offered him a job driving for me. He was my personal driver for over fifteen years before I became Mayor."

O'Malley felt cold, numb—his face drained of color. "I can guess where this is going—he does an impression of you—an impression he used tonight."

"An extraordinary impression," Mayor Burke confirmed. "We recorded ourselves once for the heck of it. Even I couldn't even tell the difference—that's how good he is."

Max looked at the Mayor, a wary look on his face. "That explains who called her but why would he want to pretend to be you? It raises real concern that he'd go to such lengths to talk to her."

"I was in love with Suzette Peterson." Mayor Burke seemed to have aged since he'd greeted them. Deep lines cut around his mouth and eyes. "We met four years ago— just business for several years. I wanted more but she didn't love me. I didn't care about her past and continued to see her once a month—just to spend time with her. Then the incredible happened and she realized she loved me too. She wanted to end the relationship to protect me but I wouldn't hear of it. I did agree to keep it quiet through the upcoming election. She planned to quit the business and concentrate on her acting career once Montana passed the bar. After the election, we were going to marry. Our relationship appalled Charles. He never approved of it."

"When you found out she was missing and you knew your driver was the last person to see her, didn't you talk to him?" O'Malley demanded.

"I didn't know she was missing. Of course I worried when I couldn't reach her—but to keep things quiet, we didn't talk that often anyway, so I thought she was out of town. I knew nothing about her whereabouts until the police found her in that church. Hearing about her death destroyed me. I talked to Charles first. He said he dropped her off at a club in the Meat Packing District. I believed him—I still do."

Joey spoke up. "Why would he drop her off at the meat packing district when she was meeting Montana at a club two blocks from the Coop?"

"I didn't know where they were meeting."

O'Malley was full of bitterness. "You saw how sick with grief Montana was—how desperate she was for answers. Why didn't you tell her this? Montana would have guarded your confidentiality just as Suzette did."

"I didn't say anything because I didn't know what good it would do. How would it bring Suzette back? The city of New York takes precedence over an affair between its Mayor and his girlfriend—who happened to be a call girl. There was no point in making our relationship known. Not even to Montana."

"Let's get back on track here," Max interposed. "Why would Drinkwater pretend to be you and ask her to meet him?"

Mayor Burke sighed again. "When Suzette's relatives showed up, Charles was worried they would find the gifts and love letters I gave her. Suzette had spoken ill of her aunt and uncle so Charles thought they might try to blackmail me. Although I didn't tell him to do it, I am almost certain he broke into Suzette's apartment—I heard about it from Commissioner Durbin tonight. I had a key to her place, which I can no longer find. I planned to ask Charles about that."

O'Malley's brow wrinkled in confusion. "What does that have to do with meeting Montana tonight?" he bellowed.

"My guess is that he wants to know how much she has learned about my relationship with Suzette."

"Neither one of them are answering their phones," Joey muttered.

"It's troubling he's pretending to be you," Max said. "He's gone rogue. I don't like it."

Mayor Burke looked at Max in disbelief. "What are you implying? Perhaps he didn't use the best judgment to lure Ms. Wylde under false pretenses but she's in no danger with Charles. I'm sure he only wants to ensure that my relationship with Suzette remains secret."

"That may be, but we know more about Suzette Peterson's death. We're almost certain the CM did *not* kill her, which means your driver was the last person to see her alive." Max looked him in the eye. "You may not even know what he's capable of—you yourself said that he probably broke into Suzette Peterson's apartment. That's breaking and entering, punishable by years in prison. Now you think he likely impersonated you. I have to say, Mayor, I'm very disappointed in the way you've handled this. Where would he take her?" O'Malley felt like shaking the Mayor.

"I doubt he'd take her to his house because he lives in Brooklyn. All government buildings close down after office hours and Charles doesn't have the security access to get into my office."

O'Malley tried Montana's cellphone again. It now went straight to voicemail. "Think hard. You know your driver better than anyone else does. Where would you go for complete privacy if you were him?"

"I can't think of..." Mayor Burke's head snapped up. "Wait—there is one place. He has access to it because he ran an errand for me earlier in the week. I gave him a key then."

"Where?" a furious O'Malley barked.

"There are some buildings under reconstruction in Lower Manhattan, condemned after Superstorm Sandy wiped them out. Charles has a key to the one closest to completion. He might have taken her there."

"What's the address?" Max pulled a notepad from his pocket.

"There isn't an official address yet but I can show you on a map." He pulled Google Maps up on his computer. He pointed to an intersection close to the South Street Seaport. "That's the place. I've got another key." When he returned, he handed it to Max. "I should come along."

Joey shook his head. "You stay here. Your presence might agitate him. We'll be in touch."

The three detectives piled back into their car. Max called for a backup team to meet quietly at the location the Mayor had given them. Why give Drinkwater any warning they were on their way? If he heard them coming, he might feel like a trapped animal and then there was no telling what he might pull.

Three blocks away they cut their own car's lights and rollers off. As O'Malley always said, surprise is the best weapon.

They were ready to strike.

53

THE GUN was a couple of inches from her head. She was calm and mentally prepared, as her master taekwondo instructor had taught her.

Drinkwater enjoyed exerting his power over her. "You're coming with me," he commanded. "I won't shoot you here. Only a moron would leave so much evidence behind. Besides, it doesn't suit my purpose, which remains protecting our great Mayor from yet another nasty, germ-filled whore."

She waited for just the right opportunity as he continued telling her his plans for her.

"You're going to disappear. I have access to many city vehicles—motorcycles, cars—and a boat." He laughed merrily. "We are taking a short cruise—one-way for you. We needn't go far—just far enough to dump your body. Ankle weights will ensure no one sees you again." Drinkwater did a perfect imitation of Marlon Brando as Don Corleone in the Godfather. "You're gonna swim wit da fishes." He switched back to his normal voice. "An unceremonious death compared to purification—you'll be dumped like the garbage you are."

He began undoing her ankle bindings with one hand while holding the gun in his other. He unlocked the cuff to her left hand. He didn't know that she'd already freed her right. Once the cuff clicked open, blinding rage overcame her.

She could never stop her stepfather's indecent nightly forays into her room. Nor could she free herself from the lunatic on that horrific long-ago outcall. A sharp memory of herself at a younger age sobbing on the shower floor came into furious focus. She'd vowed that *no one would ever hurt her again.*

The fury came rushing back—the years of abuse, holding things deep inside and always taking the meek road. Red-hot rage that had festered inside her since childhood now boiled over. Ten years of taekwondo training kicked in. Her movements were effortless and second nature. She was calm, relaxed, and empowered. She summoned all her strength to make that one perfect move.

It proved to be a good one.

She formed a flawless kick to the left side of Drinkwater's face. He toppled over, disbelief and fury contorting his face. He'd managed to hold onto the gun and quickly recovered from her surprise attack. He raised the gun again but she was ready for it. She kicked it out of his hand. They watched it skitter across the floor.

Now on equal ground, Drinkwater's self-aggrandizing demeanor deflated like a punctured balloon. Still he scrambled for control—scooting on the floor on his belly, desperate to reach the gun.

Montana pounced on him, knocking him down, spinning him around like a rag doll. He didn't have a chance. She straddled him as he stared up at her—the tables now turned. He was again the puny kid of his childhood—the one he'd never stopped being, down deep where it counts.

Her heart hammered with adrenaline as she pinned him to the ground with one leg, reaching for the gun with the other. She caught her breath, giving her time to consider her next move. She didn't have her cellphone. While Drinkwater was driving here, she'd wanted to call O'Malley and had been dismayed when she realized she'd forgotten it.

She heard a commotion in the stairwell. She knocked Drinkwater unconscious with one blow to his neck, got up, and spun around to take on the new intruders. Darkened figures hurried toward her from the back. She lunged at the first one she saw but Max Constantine's training outmatched her own. He grabbed her leg and wrestled her to the ground, holding her down until she recognized him. Finally she did. Max eased his grip.

Then she saw O'Malley, huffing and puffing behind the younger detectives, his own gun drawn. He rushed to help Montana as Joey and Max cuffed the unconscious Drinkwater. O'Malley knelt beside her and removed the tape from her mouth with gentle fingers. She held on to him and sobbed. He didn't leave her side until the backup team and paramedics arrived. They insisted on taking her to the hospital. O'Malley rode along, staying with her throughout the night. In the morning, the doctors released her and O'Malley escorted her home. Before getting out of the taxi, they wrapped each other in a deep embrace.

Some friendships take years to forge while with others, circumstances throw an unlikely duo into a deep friendship in a matter of weeks. O'Malley and Montana were the latter; they would be lifelong friends.

Tonight she'd sleep—and without a Valium.

It was finally over.

Epilogue

Nine Months Later

O'MALLEY PUFFED UP like a proud papa as he watched Montana come into Posta Pinella before she noticed him. He flushed with pleasure when she spotted him and he saw a radiant smile light her face. She made her way to their table through the noon rush. They hugged a good long time.

"Here you go." Montana's eyes sparkled with excitement as she handed him a thin letter.

O'Malley put on his glasses and read the opening statement aloud. "The Board of Law Examiners congratulates Montana Vivien Wylde on passing the New York State bar examination." O'Malley looked at her in surprise. "Hey—I never knew your middle name is Vivien. It suits you—you know—you do look a little like Vivien Leigh. You probably have no idea who she was."

Montana was indignant. "Of course I do. I'm an old movie buff. Vivien Leigh's most famous role was Scarlett O'Hara in *Gone with the Wind*. My mother was a big fan of that movie. Thank God she didn't name me Scarlett."

O'Malley had become her surrogate father, filling a long-standing void. After Montana's nightmare experience with Charles Drinkwater, they had grown even closer. Montana filled the emptiness that had been in his life as well.

He beamed. "I'm proud of you. I knew you would pass that bastard on the first try. From the day we met and you told me you had just finished law school, I knew you had it in you."

She laughed. "I wasn't as certain about you but underneath the Dewar's, your wrinkled suit, and your perennial tardiness, I sensed you were special. I was right." Her mood shifted. "Seriously, I can never thank you enough. You prodded me on when I didn't think I had enough will left to care. You were relentless. No wonder you got all those commendations for your work on the force. No suspect would stand a chance against you."

O'Malley shrugged. "You go with what works. I wasn't about to let you waste your hard work and sit on some pity pot."

Montana's voice grew soft. "I still miss her."

"She lives on, thanks to you—and will for a long time. It sure was great when we found Suzette's will. As her executor, you'll do a great job of putting her money where she'd want it most."

Montana smiled. "I've been working on the foundation already. So many young women will get the help they need to leave the abusive predators who lured them onto the street. And did you hear Mayor Burke agreed to serve on our board? I should have known Suzette would be organized enough to have a will. I thought I knew everything about her yet she had a closetful of secrets."

"Most of us do," O'Malley replied.

The perpetually beaming Sal Pinella came over to the table. He gave O'Malley a hearty slap on the back and leaned down to kiss Montana's cheek. He brought a Dewar's with a beer back for O'Malley and a glass of Pinot Grigio for Montana.

"If it ain't two of my favorite people in this city," Sal proclaimed, a wide grin plastered on this face. "And one of the most gorgeous—and I ain't talking about you old man." He gave O'Malley another happy pat on the shoulder.

"Congratulate the young lady," O'Malley demanded. "She just passed one of the toughest bar exams in this country. We're celebrating."

Sal yelled to the crowd. "Hey all youse—next round is on the house. Give a hand to this lovely woman, whose smarts equal her beauty. She's just passed the bar exam so if any of youse goons need a lawyer, give her a call." He lowered his voice to address O'Malley and Montana. "Dinner is on me." He gave O'Malley's back another smack and kissed Montana's cheek again before leaving them alone.

"I have to commend you on your handling of the Petersons, Montana. You held your temper better than I would have. What a pair of grifters those two turned out to be. I'm glad you derailed their plans to tie up Suzette's estate in a long probate battle."

Montana laughed. "That *was* the best, wasn't it? I will admit that denying those horrid relatives anything from Suzette's estate was satisfying. Suzette left them out on purpose. I thought the Petersons would blow a gasket when they found out that Suzette had named me executor. The court battle could have been nasty and bitter."

O'Malley laughed. "It all came down to your smarts and memory. You remembered the religious quote that came into the Coop's phone line was the same one that Mrs. Peterson spouted off when we were on our way to Suzette's apartment."

"I have to thank Max Constantine for that. The hotel records showed that the call came from the Peterson's room at the Hancock. They were so shocked when Constantine showed them the evidence and told them he was considering charging them with a felony."

"They didn't realize it's illegal to threaten someone like that. It gave you the ammunition you needed. You told them you wouldn't press charges against them if they wouldn't contest Suzette's will."

Montana nodded. "Suzette was smart about how she handled them in the will—leaving them each a single dollar. By doing that, she'd made it clear that she wasn't ignoring them."

"I wish I could have met her." O'Malley grinned. "I have a penchant for smart women—see? I didn't call you a broad, a dame, or a chick."

"You're getting there, O'Malley."

They laughed then Montana turned serious. "Suze almost had that fairy tale ending. Mayor Burke really did love her—I'm convinced of that."

O'Malley nodded. "All those love letters..."

"I still can't understand how Drinkwater could kill Suzette, knowing how much his boss adored her."

"He's sick. He had deep hatred and resentment that he kept hidden for years. It was amazing that Hanky recognized his picture from the video where Drinkwater stood in the background during the press conference when they caught the Church Murderer. He said it had been tickling his brain since the time he saw it."

O'Malley gave a grim nod. "Too bad he didn't remember it sooner. If he had, we might have been able to put it all together before he almost killed you."

New York had charged Charles Drinkwater with first-degree murder, kidnapping, breaking and entering, burglary, and attempted murder, as well as a slew of other, less serious charges. He awaited trial at Rikers without bail. That was a huge relief to Montana.

When the cops raided the basement in Drinkwater's home, they found Mayor Burke's notes, love letters, and gifts he'd given Suzette. Drinkwater had taken them from her apartment. Investigators also found the expensive lingerie set the mayor had sent to Suzette the morning of their final date. Most disturbing was a journal they found—something of a manifesto. It proved that Drinkwater had been obsessed with Suzette since the *Bring on the Cheers* auditions. His admiration and loyalty to Jimmy Burke were also warped. On one page, Drinkwater sang the Mayor's praises with near God-like devotion but on the next, his dismay and rage at the Mayor choosing a whore for a wife was all too clear.

"Drinkwater took down a good man—the one person who had loved and protected him—one who'd given him opportunities when no one else would." Montana shook her head.

"New Yorkers might have forgiven the Mayor's affair with Suzette but all this took the life out of him. Suzette's death wasn't the only thing that destroyed Mayor Burke. Drinkwater's betrayal had to have cut him deep as well. I understand why he resigned."

"Such a shame—so much lost by so many," Montana murmured.

"A murderer has many victims—not just those who are killed. Survivors suffer for years."

Montana mused, "When I was in that building with him, Drinkwater kept referring to the CM as 'The Purifier'—speaking about him as he would a god. I've thought a lot about that night. Despite the many horrors, some good resulted from it."

"That's true. Suzette's foundation will help thousands of young women. You flew over the final hurdle when you passed the bar."

"You've changed too," she replied. "You're a different man from the one I met in April."

He smiled at her, "I was—what do you kids call it—a 'hot mess.'"

Montana snorted. "There was nothing hot about you, O'Malley—believe me."

O'Malley grinned. "You got a point—and you're right. Positive things *did* happen. Speaking of which—how's Rosie?"

Montana smiled. "Rosie—who would have thought I would wind up in an amicable relationship with the woman who used to scream slurs at me? I can't call us friends but we are cordial with each other."

Rosie was the bewigged bag lady who had taunted Montana for years. When O'Malley told Montana that her information helped lead the detectives in the right direction, she had reached out to the strange woman.

She made Rosie a goodwill project. She did the legal work to find her an assisted living apartment and helped her get the social security disability benefits she had coming to her. Montana had also taken her to a clinic, the first she'd seen in years. Montana checked on her once a month or so and brought heaping platters of homemade food. Rosie still eyed her with caution but Montana wanted to repay the funny little woman who had helped save her life. She was still a semi-regular fixture in Lower Manhattan but she no longer screamed obscenities now that someone ensured she took her medications.

"Oh, by the way—I ran into Max Constantine yesterday," O'Malley said casually. "He's your biggest champion."

Montana blushed. "I have a date with him this Friday."

"I know—he said he was going to ask you out. I almost felt like he was coming to me as your papa—you know, asking permission. I didn't mind that he did that."

"I don't mind it a bit."

"So," O'Malley began, "what are your plans now that you're a big shot attorney?"

"Ha—I'm a long way from that. I guess the next thing will be applying for my license to practice but that won't take long. After that, I'm not sure. I thought I'd apply to the DA's office or some private firms but I'm not sure what kind of reception I'll get since everything about my life went public. In a way though, it's a relief. I was sick of living with so many secrets. "

Montana's bravery in stopping a murderer in his tracks had become big news. News agencies wanted interviews, everyone from Oprah on down. They all wanted exclusives. A major publishing house offered her a big advance on a tell-all book. If she wanted to, she could have cashed in on her fifteen minutes of fame but she just wanted life to normalize. The one real positive effect of all the press was how O'Malley's agency had benefited. He was enjoying many more interesting cases than insurance fraud.

"When we get outta here, I want to show you something—see what you think." His eyes twinkled. He was holding onto a delicious secret.

"What is it?"

"Let me show you after lunch? I'd like your opinion."

"Well, okay," she said, now full of curiosity.

Sal arrived with platters of fragrant steaming Italian food, stopping all conversation for several minutes. After they finished their tiramisu, he brought congratulatory glasses of champagne for the house as he toasted Montana's accomplishment. The lunch crowd gave her a standing ovation.

O'Malley and Sal looked like proud papas, each standing beside her. One of the regulars took their picture.

Outside, the air was as crisp as a Granny Smith apple. Montana loved New York's fall best of all.

O'Malley turned to her. "It's a few blocks. You up for a walk?"

Her eyebrows raised in surprise. She stood back and got a good look at him outside. He'd lost a good deal of his beer paunch.

"You're looking great—and it seems you've been doing some walking lately. As for me, I need to walk after all that food—and I'll probably have to hit the trail a few extra times this week."

Five blocks from the restaurant was a renovated building. After taking the elevator to the top floor, O'Malley made Montana close her eyes. He guided her to their destination. When she opened them, she smiled in delight at a new sign reading, *O'Malley Private Investigations*.

Montana gave him a hug and a kiss on the cheek. "This is awesome. Definitely a step up—it seems you're already set up for business."

"So are you." He gave her a mischievous and smug grin as he turned her around to face the adjacent door. "I'm sorry if I overstepped my bounds. It just seemed a perfect place to start."

Montana Wylde
Attorney at Law

Montana gasped in surprise and then smiled, punching his arm in the playful way she often did. She launched into her own Bogie impression: "O'Malley, this could be the start of a beautiful relationship."

Arm in arm, they walked through her new office door. It smelled of fresh paint and hope.

Acknowledgements

I owe a debt of gratitude to so many people. Writing this book was mostly a solitary experience, but many people enhanced it—from good friends to mere acquaintances. These pages serve to thank the many people who helped me make The Purified the best it could be.

I first want to thank my husband, Les Tyler. Not only did he read nearly every version of the book, he also allowed me to bounce ideas off him as he prepared five-star meals while we talked. He is the best editor I could have asked for. Moreover, he is the most wonderful husband that any woman could hope to have. During good times and bad throughout this four-year journey, his support and encouragement were unwavering.

The talented Victoria Thibdeau created the cover for The Purified. I cannot thank her enough for doing such a bang-up job. She gave me just what I was looking for.

Jenn Thorson, whom I came to know on the old Blog Catalog Forum, when I first introduced The Melindaville Blog, answered countless questions about starting my blog and writing in general. Throughout, she offered encouragement and advice with humor and cheer. I could not have had a better mentor for getting this book to press. She is also a wonderful author in her own right. I urge science fiction fans to read her humorous "There Goes the Galaxy" trilogy. She continues to inspire me to keep writing.

Ellen Campbell did a wonderful job proofreading The Purified. She was thorough and quick—not to mention that she has become a valued new friend.

Jeremy Jirik did the preliminary work on my new Melindaville Blog and gave me the concept that inspired the cover.

Ben Zackheim, the talented author of the Shirley Link tween-set detective series, gave generously of his time and energy in offering valuable advice regarding how to display and market this novel.

I could not have persevered without my many friends— my cheerleaders, so to speak. These include my beloved Edward Hemingway, whose artistry and writing brings his characters to life in his wonderful children's literature. Then there is his partner, Geoffrey Bock, who came into Edward's life, and thus into ours: Les and I both love you! Patti Ramelli, whose humor, zest for life, and unflappable optimism in such uncertain times makes me somehow know that things will be okay. Patti's best friend and near sister, Susan Miller echoed Patti's support. I am so glad we have reconnected with one another from our "Wild Women of Borneo" days. Ginger Coyote, Editor in Chief of the Punk Globe, deserves thanks for her love, support, and for naming me Punk of the Month a few years back.

I must also thank the many creative friends whose art, music, or writing has inspired me. These include Lana Gramlich, Jay Winston, Tricia Bolster, Chris Kross, Melladee Lydia Makela, Theresa H. Hall, Geo Epsilantic, Bruce Pollack, Naomi Eisenberg (the great fiddler who was one of Dan Hicks' Hot Licks), and the amazing photographer Robert Altman, who took such artistic photos of me and the troupe during my days with the New Shakespeare Company of San Francisco.

I also want to thank the many old friends that I don't see often enough: Sellier Webster, Sue White, Paul Fleming, Mike Dingle and so many more. If I have forgotten any of you who have supported me through good and bad times, it is not intentional.

Thanks to my many beta readers, who gave me valuable feedback at different times during my many revisions. Their names appear alphabetically below.

Lori Ayers, a longtime friend, read one of the earliest drafts of my book out in her beautiful back garden. She asked hard questions that helped improve several scenes and characters.

Dawn Grosvender, a wonderful friend and mentor, helped with thoughtful editing and suggestions. Her love and caring helped make me a better writer.

Maureen Hebert, a former librarian, spoke frankly about needing to strengthen some characters as well as questioning my judgment with others in an early draft. Her critique helped my characters become stronger and more real.

Karen Anderson Howe, whom I have known since I beat her at tetherball in the 5th grade, caught several errors. She also gave me encouragement on one of the last revisions of the book.

Siobhan "Shamama" Lowe, one of my oldest and dearest friends from my San Francisco punk rocker days (as well as one of the most broadly creative), read one of the first versions of the book. Her praise helped inspire me to persevere until it was ready.

Tiffany Sanders, a wonderful writer in her own right, has encouraged me since I was a newbie with The Melindaville Blog in 2008. She helped me through this labor of love and gave wonderful feedback that I took to heart.

Thank you all from the bottom of my heart.

About the Author

   Melinda Tyler's story is one of triumph over adversity.. A survivor of childhood sexual abuse, after leaving home for the angry punk rock scene, she became involved in the sex industry. She eventually hit a tough bottom, left the sex business, and earned both undergraduate and advanced degrees in Psychology.

   Her unique background gives her a rare perspective on the sex industry and those who fall prey to its allure. Along with her knowledge of what makes us tick, Melinda used that perspective to great advantage in creating The Purified. She sketches very believable portraits of her gutsy female protagonist and a diverse supporting cast.

   Melinda currently divides her time between Boston and San Francisco and is working on The Deceived, the second in the Montana Wylde mystery series.

www.ingramcontent.com/pod-product-compliance
Lightning Source LLC
Chambersburg PA
CBHW061305170626
46817CB00001B/56